The Critics Roar over *The Funeral Makers* by Cathie Pelletier

"This hilarious first novel about the back of beyond is going to put its author out in front of the pack of American humorists. . . . Cathie Pelletier's talent is overwhelming."—*The Washington Post Book World*

"Terribly funny and terribly sad, large and wide and deep and finally reassuring as an order of sorts is restored and the survivors become reconciled to one another and the limits of geography."—*The New York Times Book Review*

"A bitingly funny and highly original novelist."—*Vogue*

"*The Funeral Makers* completely satisfies . . . a clear-eyed yet passionate examination of life in an isolated small town, where the road ends."—*Newsday*

"A morbidly funny tale."—*People*

"As much as *The Funeral Makers* is a comedy of errors, genealogical as well as geographical, it has at its heart the sweet angst of romance gone awry. . . . *The Funeral Makers* sparkles with a comic Gothic veneer, but underneath the extravagant subplots and authorial gestures lies a private garden for each of its central characters."—*The Boston Globe*

"A masterful first novel. Author Cathie Pelletier has woven a tapestry of literary brilliance; each chapter an engaging jewel of sparkling narrative and dialogue."—*West Coast Review of Books*

"A brilliant first novel . . . a seductive book that lures the reader on with a rich mix of comedy, satire, and a gallery of wonderfully drawn characters. . . . Do yourself a favor and read it."—*Bangor Daily News*

"Pelletier spins a lively, fast-paced yarn that will roll you out of your chair in laughter."—Alden Whitman

The
FUNERAL
MAKERS

CATHIE PELLETIER

SCRIBNER PAPERBACK FICTION
Published by Simon & Schuster

SCRIBNER PAPERBACK FICTION
Simon & Schuster Inc.
Rockefeller Center
1230 Avenue of the Americas
New York, NY 10020

First Scribner Paperback Fiction edition 1997
SCRIBNER PAPERBACK FICTION and design are trademarks of
Simon & Schuster Inc.
Manufactured in the United States of America

3 5 7 9 10 8 6 4

The Library of Congress has cataloged the Collier
edition as follows:
Pelletier, Cathie.
The funeral makers.
I. Title.
[PS3566.E42F8   1987]
813'.54   87-13775
ISBN 0-684-82614-3

Grateful acknowledgment is made to Ensign Music Corporation
for permission to use "What Does It Take (To Keep a Woman
Like You Satisfied)?" on pp. 11–12. Copyright © by Jim Glaser.

DEDICATIONS

This book is for JIM GLASER, for all those years of believing, with my greatest respect and affection, and in honor of almost 10 years of laughing and fighting in the cities of the world.

In memory of CHARLOTTE MOIR McKINNON, my great-grandmother, who died in childbirth in 1894, at the age that I am now. And with loving memories of my grandmother AUGUSTA McKINNON O'LEARY, born 1885 at the head of the Allagash Falls, where there are still deep, piney secrets.

But the absolute heart of this book is dedicated to my great-great-great-grand-parents JOHN GARDNER and ANNA DIAMOND who came to Allagash, Maine, in a pirogue in 1835 with my aunts ELIZABETH and SARAH DIAMOND and their husbands. It is to their courage, which pulled them through the hardships of establishing a new home, a new town, a new way of life, that this book is dedicated. I'm sure they would take no exception with the humorous and fictional way I've presented their battle against the obstacles they faced. I know this because they left in their descendants the sense of humor that pervades this entire novel.

ACKNOWLEDGMENTS

A Special Thanks to:

LOUIS and ETHEL PELLETIER (Daddy and Mama) for always being there.

DR. ROLAND BURNS, for his indispensable advice.

My sister JOAN ST. AMANT, who has saved every word I've written since grammar school.

My niece DIANA PELLETIER, a terrible but sincere typist.

PAUL, SUE, and ASHLEY GAUVIN, in memory of Winston the Poodle.

I wrote this book when I was 28 so that I could have a special present to give myself on turning 30. Now I'm 33 and working on another book. It's become a vicious birthday cycle, this.

"Mattagash is an old Indian word all right. When only the Indians was here it used to mean where the river forks. But after the white man come up here and brung his white women it means where the tongues fork."

—OLD-TIMER, Mattagash, 1924

Introduction

"Our ancestors come here after that big potato famine hit Ireland years ago. But I don't think we need to worry about that happening again. The potato farmers is doing real good around here."

—HENRIETTA MCPHERSON, President, Mattagash Historical Society

---

IN 1833 A small band of illogical men and women left New Brunswick, Canada, in a pirogue to battle the upstream waters of the Mattagash River for one hundred and fifty miles until they came to shore at what is now Mattagash, Maine, where the river creates a natural boundary between the United States and Canada. It was the age of wood, wind, and water. England's shipping industry was at its peak, so it was toward Canada that she looked for a means to obtain the white pines that would build the ships' masts. This lust for pine prompted the King of England to offer his colonists grants to the unsettled timberlands of New Brunswick. And it was such a grant that brought the aforementioned settlers to the head of the Mattagash River. The McKinnon brothers, Jasper, Bransford, and William, born of Loyalist stock, had said farewell to hearth and kin to strike out to unknown regions with their wives and enough supplies to battle the elements until permanent dwellings could be raised.

Thinking they were in Canada, and not the area which is now Maine, the McKinnon brothers settled at the head of the Mattagash River. Oral history says they stopped where they did because one of the women needed to pee. In truth, it may have been inaccurate maps. But as a result, even at its inception, Mattagash was a mistake. And if some divine power had had the foresight to look one hundred and twenty-five years into the future to see the genetic entanglement, the implanted hatred, the narrowmindedness that one tiny settlement of Loyalist stock would unwittingly breed, a huge pencil would have descended from the sky and erased the mistake before it had time to take root.

Encouraged that the brothers had a firm footing on Mattagash

1

soil, other families followed, adding a few new surnames to the lot. The town grew only of descendants of those first few families, with cousins marrying cousins, out of necessity if not romance. By the early 1860s, when Union army scouts came that far north into the wilderness looking for fighting men and were told by a settlement of only women and children that they hadn't seen any men in years, it was evident that Mattagash would endure, and so would the ideas and prejudices that were to haunt the next unsuspecting generations.

Its isolation from the rest of the world (thirty miles upriver from Watertown, the nearest settlement), its inaccessibility (no one wanted to paddle thirty miles upriver to watch a few men and women cut down pine trees and feed chickens) kept Mattagash safe from common sense and a spirit of fair play. The McKinnons, already ensconced as the first to put foot upon the soil, became somewhat of an oligarchy and passed their community standing on to their heirs in the same way crowns are passed from kings to their royal offspring. As natural monarchs, the McKinnons believed that no one else was qualified. As natural peasants, the rest of the town believed them.

As the years passed, the log drive became the main source of employment. Each fall the lumbermen left their families behind, left the smoke curling from warm chimneys, and trudged back into the woods to find the best timber. Hired by a large lumber company to cut trees, they worked through the winter, their days spent hard at work with a cross saw, their nights spent at a cribbage board, smoking hand-rolled cigarettes, the northern lights in a brilliant dance over their heads. When spring came they broke up jams in the freezing high water and followed the logs downriver to the ocean. It was a dangerous occupation. Lives were lost beneath the icy waters and many a widow was kept alive by the goodness of her relatives and neighbors. And out of the harshness of life came a bitterness for life, as women rocked on their porches and men gathered around the community stove, and gossip was the only newspaper.

By the time the century turned, the old McKinnon settlers were unknown to the young, except for an occasional excursion into the Protestant graveyard, where the stones of who they were in life, if they could afford stones, crumbled and lay vine-covered.

But no matter how many McKinnon names were carved on granite, there was always a new McKinnon among the living to take over where an old McKinnon had passed on, like a red army, a microcosm of capitalism at work. The McKinnons became the town's selectmen. They made up the school board. They monitored the town's meetings. They ran the church, if it was Protestant, and left the Catholic one to the devil. If they didn't directly control an office, a McKinnon woman always managed to marry someone who did. But if the McKinnons left an elitist heritage to their descendants, other families weren't so lucky.

Within the next group of settlers who arrived a few years after the three brothers was a man named Joshua Gifford, who made the mistake one bright October morning of stealing a bag of oats and an ax from Will McKinnon. No one remembers now *why* Joshua committed thievery. No one wonders if his horse was starving. Or if he had no wood to burn. What everyone does remember, what has been passed down orally for years is that it was Will *McKinnon's* oats and ax.

A McKinnon will carry a grudge with him as faithfully as if it's a family gem brought over from the old country, and Will McKinnon wore his like a medal. Joshua Gifford was never forgiven for the crime, much less exonerated. So after several years of ostracism, he and his sons incorporated and took up thievery full time. Over the years their business grew, with branches reaching outside Mattagash when occasional cross saws and nails were stolen in Watertown. Each family has a sense of pride. A sense of continuity. As soon as the north side of the Catholic graveyard filled up with Giffords whose bodies had broken down with age, who had closed their fingers for the last time around another man's belongings, an initiate from among the living Giffords was sure to take his place.

By the mid-twentieth century there were no male McKinnons left in Mattagash. Some McKinnons who enlisted in the army, and never bothered to come back once they'd seen the world, were probably siring male McKinnons somewhere on the earth. But in Mattagash the name had come to a halt, like an old machine that's finally seen its last production and settles down to rust.

By the time 1960 was threatening to roll around, no one in town could remember who was related to whom, unless it was obvious or within the past few generations, but somewhere back in the dim history of Mattagash's past, the entire town of 456 people was genetically linked, like paper dolls, whether they cared to admit it or not. Most did not.

Marge Succumbs to Beriberi: She's Veri Veri Sick

"If God had meant for me to be religious, he would have alphabetized the books of the Bible. It was just too hard for me to find what I was looking for, especially if I was looking for it through a few glasses of scotch."

—GERT McKINNON, Atheist and Spinster, 1935

THE SUMMER OF 1959 was short and dry. The leaves fell from the trees much earlier than they should have fallen. There was something uncanny about the birds flying south too soon, in the hurried way the squirrels gathered hazelnuts, how the river sucked up its own water for the early dog days. It was all in the signs by the time September arrived and Marge McKinnon became seriously ill. And while the land and the animals had been in a hurry, Marge was not. She held on to her illness as though it were a brooch, a family heirloom, and in a way it was. She was the only person in Mattagash, Maine, suffering from beriberi. It was the town's only attraction and a well-deserved one considering that Marge contracted beriberi because her father, the missionary Reverend Ralph C. McKinnon, died in China of kala-azar.

Someone in Mattagash looked it up in a medical book and discovered that kala-azar is sometimes called dum dum's fever. Many of the townspeople wondered who had had the foresight to call it dum dum's fever without ever having met the Reverend Ralph. His own sister Gert, who had been nipping from the little silver flask in her purse, stood up at Ralph's wake, leaned over the empty coffin, and said, "No wonder they called it dummy's fever. What in hell would make a reverend want to traipse off to China when there's good Christian souls to save right here in his own backyard."

Marge's few relatives could enjoy an unspoken pride in her rare condition. Not to be outdone by even the medical community, the McKinnons had always managed to become afflicted with only the rarest of diseases. Not that Mattagash, for a town of its size, didn't have its share of unusual ailments over the years. A doctor from Watertown, at the nearest hospital, said it was because everyone in Mattagash was descended from a little bunch of people who were foolish enough to leave Canada in a pirogue looking for pine trees. Their descendants were all interrelated, he said. Their genes had gone haywire. Whatever the reason, Mattagash was not unfamiliar with carnival-like maladies. There had been cases of giantism, clubfoot, hunchback, a few untraceable types of cancer, lumpy jaw, brain tumor, two blue babies, and a case of undescended testicles. The latter was the unfortunate Herbie Fennelson, who later went to New York and wrote home that he had caught homosexuality in a movie theater on Forty-second Street. Everyone in Mattagash agreed that it was connected, one way or another, to his early illness. But no one in that town, in the entire country, in this day and age, was ever before or ever again stricken with beriberi because his or her father died in China of kala-azar. When Marge McKinnon went out, she was determined to go out like Halley's comet.

Marge got the news about her father in 1927 from the druggist over in Watertown, who also handled telegrams. The old Reverend was dead. He had been dying for almost two years but had never let on to anyone. Marge, a spinster who had pined for sainthood from an early age, had been saving her dollars to go to China and join her father, to live on polished rice and save unpolished souls. Two weeks after the telegram, she got a long letter from Reverend McKinnon. It had been mailed before he died. He told her all about kala-azar and how a sandfly had bitten him while in the service of God, and that his spleen and liver were swollen from it. He told her not to mourn him, that dum dum's fever assured him a room in the house of God. But Marge wouldn't hear of it. She began wearing only black, and as a sacrifice which the townspeople thought only the hell-bound Catholics capable of, she gave up all food except for polished rice and Chinese tea, saying that if it was good enough for the missionaries of the world, it was good enough for her.

Over the years she lost weight and her legs became heavy and swollen. She was short of breath and had to pay some boy a dime a day to carry her letters in from the mailbox. Finally, her sister Sicily's daughter Amy Joy began sleeping over nights to keep an eye on her. Marge spent her last days writing nasty letters to Sears and Roebuck, insisting they begin a new line of black cotton handkerchiefs for widows, orphans, and people in general mourning around the country. She complained often to her neighbors of what she called "disturbing sensations" in her arms and legs. At last her mind began to go. The doctor said her heart was waterlogged and that she needed to be hospitalized immediately. But there was no convincing her of this. She was a true McKinnon to the end, saying that if kala-azar got the Reverend a room in heaven, then beriberi would get her the one next to it.

Marge never referred to her father's disease as dum dum's fever. She even wrote once to her state senator asking that he petition the AMA to have the derogatory reference removed from medical books, and hinting that her family would be eternally grateful to him and loyal in their votes. She even went so far as to suggest that they consider "McKinnon's Malady" as a proper alternative. Thankfully, she lapsed into a coma before the polite refusal came back. Refusals could really upset her.

Doctor Anderson came over from Watertown complaining of eccentric old women and the hospital being thirty miles away. Sicily spoke up and told him that most folks couldn't always die in the vicinity of a hospital. Sometimes, she said, it caught folks unawares.

The doctor took one look at Marge and gave the signal to summon the family. She was on her last breath. "Any woman who's lived on rice and tea from 1927 until 1959 can't expect much more," he told Sicily and Amy Joy.

"She cheated sometimes," Sicily told him, going on to mention the Drake cupcake wrappers Amy Joy was forever finding in the garbage can.

"The woman needs fresh vegetables. She needs B$_1$. Haven't you ever heard of thiamine?" he asked Sicily.

"Simon?" Sicily looked the doctor in the eye. She wondered why he had not lisped before. "Wasn't he that little MacLean boy who almost died of rat bite?"

"No, Mama, that was *Therman*," Amy Joy said.

After the doctor left, Sicily and Amy Joy sat down at Marge's writing desk, took out her book of family addresses and telephone numbers, and made a list of people to contact.

"We may as well charge this to Marge. It's her ball game," Sicily said, dialing her sister Pearl Ivy, who lived with her husband on the top floor of the Ivy Funeral Home in Portland, Maine. Amy Joy leaned over, chin in hands, to hear the conversation. Her nearness enabled Sicily to inspect her closely.

"Amy Joy, your face is just a smattering of horrible little pimples. Do you have the curse?"

"Nope."

"Are you late, honey? The heat sometimes does that. And all this excitement doesn't help."

"I guess."

"Well, if it isn't the curse, have you been eating Hershey bars with almonds again?"

"Nope."

"Marshmallow cups then?"

"I guess."

"Amy Joy, you're about to come out of your clothes now, and, young lady, if you're left with a single tooth hanging from the roof of your mouth, don't you come squalling . . . Pearl? Pearl, it's Sicily. How's your weather down there?"

A nurse had been hired to attend to Marge's last needs, sponging her forehead and massaging her swollen extremities. Amy Joy stood in the doorway and dangled her pink flip-flop off the tip of one foot. The nurse looked up and smiled.

"A relative?" she asked.

"Yeah," said Amy Joy. "She's my aunt and she gave her life like the great missionaries, to the service of God."

"I thought the doctor said it was beriberi." The nurse glanced nervously at the bed in fear that she'd been sitting with the wrong patient.

"She caught it as a sacrifice," Amy Joy said and blew a pink bubble of gum.

"Oh, I see," said the nurse, and fluffed Marge's pillow.

"She'll have a room in heaven now."

"I'm sure she will, dear." The nurse was sympathetic.

"I'm Amy Joy Lawler. My mom is Aunt Marge's sister. I'm going to be a freshman in high school this fall and travel all the way to Watertown on the bus every day and I can't wait."

"I would have taken you for a much older girl," the nurse said.

"Everybody says I'm pretty completely developed for fourteen."

"Yes, I'd say you are."

"We don't have our own high school yet. We might get one built in 1965 but I'll be graduated by then. At least I hope." She giggled.

"I'm sure you will," the nurse said.

"I got a new boyfriend, too."

"Aren't you too young for that?"

"Mama thinks I am, but she doesn't really know about him. She only suspects."

The nurse put a fresh cloth in a pan of water and wrung it out. She folded it and placed it carefully on Marge's forehead.

"You should listen to your mother, Amy Joy."

"i sure will," said Amy Joy and turned away in her white cotton pants. The nurse thought she heard the seams creak as Amy Joy wiggled down the hallway.

Amy Joy pushed the screen door open and went out to the back porch. She leaned over to see her reflection in the glass pane of the window. She slid a rattail comb up from her hip pocket and teased her brown hair a bit on the top. Her kiss-me-quick curls on each side of her cheeks had dried, so she removed the bobby pins and fluffed them up a bit. She pulled out the tiny sample tube of lipstick that the Fuller Brush man had let her select. It was Shocking Pink, to match her blouse and flip-flops. Amy Joy had flip-flops and lipsticks to match every blouse she had. After a bit of trouble squeezing the tube back into her front pocket, she peered intently at her reflection in the window to see if the results were just right. Inside, Sicily screamed. Something broke into many pieces.

"Good God in heaven above, Amy Joy, is that you out there with your two eyes bugged out like a peeping Tom?" Sicily was on edge. This was really her first funeral. Marge had always taken charge of family functions.

"Mama, can I dye my hair?" Amy Joy asked through the screen of the door.

"Amy Joy, let me recover from one shock before you kill me with another one." Sicily was picking up the shards of a tumbler. Raspberry Kool-Aid was splattered about the kitchen floor.

"The least you could do after scaring the daylights out of me is to help me mop this up."

Amy Joy let the screen door bang on its own accord.

"Amy Joy! Have a little consideration for your dying aunt, and watch out for the ice cubes. They're around here somewhere." Sicily was on her knees, mopping up the mess. Amy Joy perched on a chair and pulled both knees up to her chin.

"I've been thinking of Sensuous Ash," she said.

"What?"

"Sensuous Ash," said Amy Joy. "You know, if I was to dye my hair."

"Watch my mouth as I say this," said Sicily, who felt the situation was important enough to stop mopping. "Now you listen to me. If you so much as alter a single strand of hair on your little head, especially so close to a funeral, if you so much as *buy* a bottle of Sensuous Ash hair dye to even read the instructions, your father will hear of it. And Amy Joy, do I have to tell you what will happen to you if your father hears of it? You wanting to dye your hair with him being principal of the grammar school. What next will you come up with? You know what kind of woman dyes her hair."

"Oh, Mama," said Amy Joy.

"What's wrong with your hair?"

"It's mousy."

"It is not mousy. It's wholesome. Besides that, it's God-given."

"Who is more wholesome than Doris Day or Debbie Reynolds? And they dye theirs."

"Who told you that?" Sicily asked with interest. She found one of the ice cubes. Then the others. She aimed for the sink from her position on the floor and hit the target each time.

"I read it somewhere," said Amy Joy, and went out to swing on the back porch.

"And wipe that pink blob off your two lips!" Sicily shouted after her.

When Sicily went out later to tell Amy Joy that she had called everyone, had checked on Marge, and was now on her way home to cook supper, she found her daughter beaming into the unkempt face of Chester Gifford, who was only inches away from Amy Joy's own plump face. Sicily cleared her throat and Chester jumped as though someone had shot him between the shoulder blades with buckshot.

"Amy Joy, may I speak to you for a moment, dear?" Sicily held the screen door open as an embarrassed Amy Joy stumbled past her, losing a flip-flop as she stepped into the kitchen. When she bent to pick it up, there was a sound of splitting, as wood splits beneath the ax. It was Amy Joy's white cotton slacks finally bowing to the strains of adolescent fat.

"Just leave it there, Miss," said Sicily, and kicked the flip-flop to one side.

"We'll be seeing you, Chester." She let the screen door bang shut and latched it. Then she closed the inside kitchen window and locked it. To help further her point, she closed the two venetian blinds in the back windows and snapped off the porch light.

"We're closed for the night," she said, and turned to Amy Joy, who was studying herself in the mirror of the medicine cabinet on the kitchen wall.

"All right, Amy Joy Lawler. Let's hear it."

"What?"

"You know what, Miss."

"No, I don't."

"Was that Chester Gifford lurking out there like a thief in the night, or was it not?"

"I guess."

"You guess, do you? Well, let me tell you that this will be brought to your father's attention. I'm on my way home now to cook the poor man his supper, and Amy Joy, this is one time *he will be told.*"

"Oh, Mama," said Amy Joy, and squeezed a pimple.

"Don't pick at your complexion," said Sicily. "And you look at me when I'm speaking to you, Miss." Amy Joy turned to look at her mother, a dollop of blood on her chin.

"Now look what you've done to your face," said Sicily, passing her daughter a tissue from her apron pocket.

"It isn't bad enough that you're thirty pounds overweight, you have to go around picking at your face. Amy Joy, what's to become of you? Reading *True Confessions* all day when other little girls your age are reading cookbooks and sewing patterns."

"Who wants to cook and sew anyway," said Amy Joy and turned on the radio Marge had won by punching the lucky name "Perry" on someone's ticket board. " 'Life gets cold and lonely, when your self-respect has died.' " Amy Joy swayed to the music.

" 'What does it take to keep a woman like you satisfied?' " Sicily turned the radio off and grabbed her daughter by the shoulders.

"Now you listen to me, little girl. Have you been seeing Chester Gifford?"

"I guess," said Amy Joy.

"You guess what? What do you guess? Have you or haven't you?"

"Yeah, I suppose."

Sicily sank into the chair behind her and put her head on the kitchen table to sob in the circle of her arms. Amy Joy snapped one last meager bubble, then tossed the dying gum into the trash can at the end of the stove.

"What's wrong with Chester, anyway?"

Waiting for this moment, Sicily lifted her head. She removed more tissue from her pocket and blew her nose. She cleared her throat for the second time that night.

"Amy Joy, you are my only daughter. And you are only fourteen. You're just a baby. I thought God gave you to me as a blessing in my old age, but I swear, Amy Joy, it's getting harder and harder to think of you as a blessing." Sicily looked at the table as she spoke. Finally, she chose a time to look directly at Amy Joy, who was leaning against the refrigerator. A piece of tissue spotted with blood was stuck to the ravaged area of skin.

"For God's sake, take that bloody rag off your face while I'm talking to you."

"It's bleeding, Mama," said Amy Joy, as she retreated to the mirror to dab at the small volcano.

"Well, don't pick it then," said Sicily, raising her voice. This was something she hated to do. Marge was famous for voice-raising and Sicily was determined to pave roads of her own.

"Amy Joy, your friend Chester Gifford is at least thirty years old if he's a day. And not to mention the fact that he's been in trouble with the law a dozen times; you are barely fourteen years old, young lady, and he is a full-grown man with a mustache and everything."

"Oh, Mama," said Amy, inspecting the damage done to the seam in the seat of her pants.

"Oh, Mama what?"

"Haven't you ever been young?" Amy Joy pulled a thread and it snapped.

"Yes, Amy Joy, I have been young, but in my heart of hearts I don't think Chester Gifford ever was. That man was in trouble when he was a baby."

Amy Joy took two slices of Sunbeam bread from the breadbox and popped them into the toaster. She found some homemade rhubarb sauce in the refrigerator and unscrewed the cap. She poured it directly from the jar to her plate, then licked the drippage with her tongue. She waited for the toast.

"I don't believe it," said Sicily, her mouth hanging open. "I don't believe you would resort to that fattening stuff after our mother-daughter talk the other day about diets."

The toast popped. Amy Joy buttered each slice, then spooned rhubarb onto one. She sank her teeth into the combination.

"All right, Amy Joy," said Sicily, putting on her sweater and shouldering the strap of her purse. She pointed to Marge's room.

"I've got a sister in that room dying of beriberi. And I leave you here to see to her last needs, and instead you're gadding about the backyard with Chester Gifford."

Amy Joy finished the first toast and smeared the second with rhubarb.

"Let me tell you how things stand, Amy Joy." Sicily had found her car keys and was twirling them threateningly in her right hand, like they were some obscure, oriental weapon. "If you so much as glance at Chester Gifford again, your father will hear of it. And you know what that means, don't you, Miss?"

"Yeah," said Amy Joy.

Sicily opened the front door. She had the evening paper in her hand to take home and read after a long soak in the tub. Before she closed the door behind her, she looked back at Amy Joy, who had pulled the soggy tissue from her face and was trying to shake it from her fingers and into the trash can.

"If you spoil this funeral for me, Amy Joy, I will no longer be your mother. Do you understand what I'm saying to you?"

"I guess," said Amy Joy.

The Ivy Family
Comes to the Funeral:
The Packard as
a Potential Hearse

"I sincerely believe that the best decision I ever made in my adult life was the day I bought the Packard."
—Junior Ivy to His Father, 1958

At Fifty, Pearl McKinnon Ivy was the middle child of Ralph C. McKinnon's three daughters. She left home at the age of sixteen to attend the Portland School of Hair Styling in Portland, Maine. It was a long way from Mattagash, socially and geographically, and it was there that she met and became engaged to Marvin Ivy, a law student and aspiring politician. Pearl married him, thinking she had bagged a future lawyer, not to mention the possibilities of a governor or, when she dared to think of it, a president of the United States. But Marvin's acumen was not capable of carrying such a strict academic load, and he dropped out in his second year, before he flunked out. They had been married only five months and Pearl was eight weeks pregnant with their first child. She suffered a nervous breakdown the day Marvin came home and threw his expensive law books, one by one, into the incinerator in the basement. Standing on the stairs and watching what she felt was a deranged man and not a future president, Pearl said later that all she remembered was a faint buzzing, as though a swarm of bees had flown through her head. For two full days, she insisted she had gone blind. That she could only see *black*. It was the first nervous breakdown to be recorded in the McKinnon family. At least Pearl *said* it was a nervous breakdown, and never moved from her bed for three months, except to go to the bathroom. The day that the community center burned down, she insisted that Marvin move her to a chair by the window. With her feet on a footstool, she spent the afternoon chain-

14

smoking as she watched the commotion of fire trucks and ambulances. Marvin thought it would jolt her back into the joys of living, but that evening, after the crowd had dispersed and the foundation of the community center was a smoldering pile of water and ashes among the blackened sofas and chairs, Pearl asked to be helped back to her bed. Marvin tried to talk some sense into her. The night he came home with the news that he had finally made up his mind to join his father in the undertaking business, Pearl covered her ears and said, "That's the last straw. There's more bees than ever now. You've driven me crazy. You may as well take me to Bangor right now and lock me up with that Holy Roller we read about in the papers last week, who threw his sweet little baby off the Portland bridge because God told him it could fly."

After weeks of this, Marvin gave up. He had put his best foot forward by going to work for his father, who was the sole owner of Ivy Funeral Home. Certain that the business would one day be his, he soon forgot about law and poured his heart into embalming and burial. Suspecting another woman was the cause of his late nights away from home, Pearl soon abandoned her notions of neurological disorders and concentrated instead on a new nursery. Marvin Ivy, Jr., was born healthy and sound, despite his mother's conviction that the shock of having married an undertaker instead of a president had damaged the unborn baby's nerve endings. He was their only child. The final blow to Pearl's self-esteem came when Marvin Sr. moved his family into the rooms above the funeral home, saying that not only would it save them money, but he would be closer to his work. Pearl would have divorced him then and there had it not been for the baby and the embarrassment of returning to Mattagash with neither a husband nor a hair-styling license. Instead, she gritted her teeth, knowing that if she lavished all her devotion on Marvin Jr. he would one day grow up to take her away from full caskets and sobbing women. But the plans she made during the many nights she sat up smoking Salem after Salem were squelched the day that Junior announced he was engaged to Thelma Parsons and would be the third generation of Ivys to partake in the funeral business. In her middle age Pearl was repaid for those years of motherly love when Junior stopped by to drop off his three undisciplined children for her to babysit. "Those kids could wake the dead," Pearl once said to her husband, whose only reply was, "This would be the place to do it."

When the phone call came from her baby sister Sicily, Pearl was not surprised.

"I could smell death in the air when I got up this morning," she told Sicily.

"It might be coming from downstairs," Sicily said in all innocence. There was not a mean bone in her body. Knowing this, Pearl let it slip by.

"I just hope we get there before she passes on. But even if we don't, we'll at least make the funeral."

"How about the others?" Sicily asked, wondering where in the world she could put up Marvin Jr., his sniveling little wife, and those three brats.

"Marvin Jr. was just talking about a camping trip with the kids last week. He's got himself one of them campers with everything you need that you pull behind the car." Sicily released her breath. She would offer to cook meals for them, but to house the entire group would have been catastrophic.

"And big Marvin and me will get us a nice motel room. At times like this one shouldn't think about money," Pearl said with pride. Despite its being a funeral home, it *was* the only self-owned business in the family.

"That should work out just fine then," said Sicily, relieved. She not only had to worry about getting this funeral off to a good start, she had spent half the night walking the floor over Amy Joy's infatuation with Chester Gifford.

The Ivys made their plans. They would make the trip a family vacation, since they'd probably never have another chance while the children were still small. It would be an opportunity for the grandparents to get to know the children. For the mother-in-law to pass her years of household knowledge on to the daughter-in-law. For the son to talk man-to-man with his father about the Ivy Funeral Home and what kind of future the business could expect.

At nine o'clock the next morning, Marvin Jr. tooted the horn of his new green Packard outside the Ivy Funeral Home. Inside the mobile home, the Ivy children were nestled with a stack of comic books, crayons, paper, and their favorite toys.

"Now don't forget, Cynthia." Thelma was at the door of the

mobile home giving some last-minute instructions to the oldest child, a pudgy girl of ten with two stiff braids sticking out from the sides of her head and tipped with red ribbons. "If you get hungry, just make some marshmallow fluff and peanut butter sandwiches. And there's milk in that little cooler with the ice. Now keep the door locked from the inside so it won't open."

The second-oldest child was a boy of nine, Marvin Randall III, known as Randy to his family and what friends he could find. Randy began to wallop the youngest child on the top of her head with a SORRY! game. This was Regina Beth, seven years old, who lapsed into one of her usual breath-holding sessions. Thelma slapped Randy's hands, took the SORRY! game from him and gave it to Regina Beth, who allowed oxygen to enter her lungs.

"Randy, if you start up on this trip you won't get the new bicycle," Thelma told him. "And Regina Beth, one of these days I'm going to let you hold your breath until your belly button pops open."

"Mama, why can't I ride in the car with the grown-ups?" Cynthia Jane reached beneath her organdy dress and tugged at the crotch of her panties.

"Sissy, are you still chafed?" asked Thelma as she wiped Randy's nose. "Mama will get Daddy to stop for some cornstarch once we're on the road. In the meantime, don't scratch. It'll only get worse."

Thelma gave the children the hand-printed signs she had drawn up the night before to accommodate them on the trip. There were three of them and they said FOOD, BATHROOM, and FIRE.

"Why make a sign that says fire?" Marvin Jr. had asked.

"Mothers like to be safe," Thelma said. "They feel better knowing that they've thought of everything when it comes to their children."

Pearl and Marvin Sr. had two suitcases and an overnight case. Marvin Jr. opened the trunk and made room among his and Thelma's things.

"That's what's so nice about a Packard," he told his father. "All that room."

"Where did you put the children's things?" asked Pearl.

"There wasn't enough room in the Packard, so we put them in the camper," said Thelma.

"There would have been plenty of room if you had just moved

things about a bit," said Marvin Jr., a bit red-faced.

"You're sure we're no bother?" Pearl asked him.

"No bother at all, Mother," said Thelma. Ignoring Thelma, Pearl delivered a small kiss to Marvin Jr.'s face and said, "Thank you, son. You're a good boy."

Thelma was put behind the wheel so that the men could repose in the backseat and discuss business. Pearl sat in front, but could not concentrate on Thelma's talk about the children and whether she and Marvin Jr. should try for another child.

"Don't have another one," said Pearl, thinking *Oh, please, Dear God.* "Three's enough."

Then she turned in her seat to listen to the men. Marvin Sr. had brought along the bottle of scotch his son had given him for Christmas. It was a time to relax, he told Marvin Jr. There was a time for temperance and a time for a drink or two. They drank the scotch from plastic tumblers. Pearl was afraid of her good ones being broken.

"Now as far as the funeral business goes," Marvin Sr. said to Jr. "I think your Grandpa Ivy said it in a nutshell. He said that the funeral business would never die because people can't accept death as the end of human life. They need to believe that we'll all survive it in some form."

"Well, don't we, sir?" Marvin Jr. said to his father. "I mean, that sounds almost as if Grandpa Ivy didn't believe in God. And just knowing how pious Grandma was, well, it's hard to believe she'd allow that sort of thing." Marvin Jr. and his father were silent for a few minutes, both rolling over in their minds the image of old man Ivy, who had died several years before of natural causes, leaving behind instructions for an immediate and simple burial. "I've had my fill of families gathered to see their loved ones off. The fake tears. The fights over the estate. Squabbling over who rides in the car behind the hearse. I want it kept plain. I want it cheap and quick."

His son was named as the only family member to be present, and that was strictly because someone had to take care of the legalities. It was a slap in the face for the family, and especially Marvin, his only son, who really believed that the Ivy Funeral Home, that *any* funeral home, was a public institution and ranked along with churches and schools.

"The old man came over on the boat, son. He was still wet behind the ears. How would you feel if you come straight from Russia to a land of opportunity?"

Marvin Jr. was not capable of even simple juxtaposition, so he said honestly, "I can't imagine." Marvin Sr. patted his leg.

"Of course you can't. You're an American born and bred. So am I. So is Thelma and your mother there in the front seat."

"And a McKinnon, too," said Pearl, opening her side glass for a bit of air.

"The old man got off the boat, took one look around, and said to himself, 'These people don't give a hoot about life, so they're probably scared as hell of death.' He opened himself a funeral business and the rest is history."

"That old man was a Communist," said Pearl. "And an atheist to boot."

"He just didn't believe in the American way of life is all," said Marvin Sr.

"Let's change the subject, dear." Pearl turned to look into her husband's face so that he could see her roll her eyes over at Thelma. It wouldn't be good for Thelma, who had been a chatterbox since the day she was born, to hear this private talk about shady family members. Their secrets would be all over Portland in a week, especially if Thelma should become first lady of the Ivy Funeral Home. Pearl could not visualize it. But that Marvin Jr. and Thelma wanted to inherit the family business was obvious even to a casual observer.

"Dad, what was his *real* name?" asked Thelma, who often feigned interest in family matters in order to be included in the conversation.

"Eye-vee-so-vitch," pronounced Marvin Sr.

"No, it wasn't," said Pearl. "It was something like that, but different."

"Eye-so-vitch?" asked Marvin Sr.

"No, but that's close," said Pearl.

"Doesn't *anyone* know?" asked Junior.

"It's written down on some papers somewhere," Pearl said, pleased that the conversation was finally up to par. But Marvin Sr. was not a drinker and the scotch had loosened his lips for the rest of the trip.

"The old man revolutionized the funeral business, son," he told Marvin Jr., who was taking large sips to catch up to his father. They were a few miles north of Bangor and at the bottom of their third glass.

"It was your grandfather who first realized that you shouldn't bring the mourners in at the foot of the casket, because that way the first thing they see of their loved one is two nostrils. No one wants to remember a loved one that way, son. Don't forget that."

Pearl cringed. As she turned in her seat to lead the conversation off on some other trail, she saw a sign held pell-mell in the window of the camper. It said BATHROOM. Thelma pulled into the next service station and saw to the children's needs.

The car continued on its way. Marvin Sr. began his fourth scotch, which was an unheard-of indulgence for him. The ice cubes that Junior had taken from the cooler at the last stop clinked in his glass. For an hour Marvin Sr. lectured his family in the dos and don'ts of funeralology.

"Son, remember this, if you remember any lesson from life," he said sadly to Junior, who had fallen asleep. "Working in the funeral business leaves you a marked man. People cringe at the sight of you. Jesus Christ, they say, your hands smell."

"Mother?" Thelma took her eyes off the road for a second to see if Pearl was listening. "Mother, I need to ask you this," she said. "What do you say to friends when they make nasty remarks about your husband's occupation?"

"I tell them to mind their damn P's and Q's," Pearl said.

"Women shouldn't discuss a man's business anyway." Marvin Sr. had begun to slur his words. He remembered a business idea Pearl once had after the old man died and Marvin Sr. took over the business. He began to laugh to himself, just thinking of a woman's lack of business sense. The more he thought of it, the funnier it became, until he was laughing uncontrollably. Thelma glanced nervously into the rearview mirror.

"What's so funny?" asked Pearl.

"Remember the time you wanted to . . ." But Marvin Sr. lost control again. He pressed a hand into his stomach to ease the pain of laughing. Tears filled his eyes.

"Well, for heaven's sakes, tell us," said Pearl. "The time I wanted to do what?" Marvin Sr. still couldn't speak. Junior had slowly inched his way over until his head was lying on his father's shoulder. He was snoring now, mouth wide open.

"Are you laughing at Junior?" asked Pearl, who had begun to laugh along without knowing why. Finally, Marvin Sr. said, "The time you wanted to turn the back room of the funeral home into a beauty shop and call the whole thing *The Ivy Funeral Home and Beauty Salon*." Marvin Sr. doubled up with laughter.

"It wasn't that bad of an idea. Women can't always get an appointment right away when someone in the family dies. It would have come in real handy." Pearl was indignant, especially when she saw a trace of a smile on Thelma's face.

"What do you think, Thelma? Men don't understand these things, do they?"

"No, Mother," Thelma said quickly. "They sure don't."

By this time Marvin Sr. had remembered a joke one of his employees had told him and left the image of a huge blinking sign that said *The Ivy Funeral Home and Beauty Salon* behind him. The joke was now all-encompassing to him and very funny. Pearl assumed it was still her beauty salon he found so amusing. After a few more minutes of his snorting and guffawing in the backseat, she turned to tell him that either he stop making fun of her or she would have Thelma drop her off at the very next Greyhound bus station. That's when she saw the sign in the camper window. There was no mistaking it, and her heart pounded in recognition of what it clearly meant: FIRE. Pearl's scream caught Thelma, who was trying to imagine an entire row of women sobbing beneath hair dryers in the back room of the funeral home, totally off guard. The Packard swerved into the gravel at the side of the road as Thelma fought to keep it in control. A pickup truck coming at them in the opposite direction left the road to avoid Thelma's recovery of the car, which sent it wildly into the territory of southbound traffic. The brakes screeched. Pearl looked back, expecting to see flames engulfing the camper at any minute then spreading to the gas tank of the Packard. The entire Ivy family would be wiped out in one fell swoop. "The Lord is my shepherd, I shall not want," she began. Marvin Sr. opened his door, thinking Thelma would soon bring the car to a halt.

"The kids are burning!" screamed Pearl.

Thelma *had* slowed the Packard down and had it almost under control until she heard Pearl say that the babies she had brought into the world, the children she had born to this family of death, were on fire. Thelma put her face in her hands and screamed uncontrollably, leaving the car to steer itself. The Packard took an alarming plunge for the ditch, threatening to tip the camper, which was swaying dangerously by this time. The door Marvin Sr. had opened, in order that he might rescue his grandchildren from a fiery inferno, rocked on its hinges, then closed on his leg, like the huge jaws of a dinosaur.

Pearl had wanted to slap Thelma from the first moment they met, so she let her have one evenly across the side of her head. Then she grabbed the wheel herself, steering the Packard with her left hand, a task Pearl would never have attempted with two hands. She did not drive. But she was a religious woman and, not about to play with fate, she began to pray. "Yea, though I walk through the valley . . ." Unable to open the heavy door, Thelma had rolled down her window and was attempting to climb out. Pearl reached over with her right hand and caught one of Thelma's winglike arms and held on. In the backseat Marvin Sr. was still trying to extricate the portion of leg that his door had closed on.

"This is worse than the war!" he shouted in pain. Then, "Step on the brake, Pearly!"

Pearl struggled to get her left foot past Thelma's and onto the brake. She managed, but not knowing the complexities of the automobile, she pushed the clutch instead. The big green Packard, with Pearl steering by means of her left hand, snaked down the highway. Thelma's crying was out of control when Marvin Jr. woke up with the full effects of the scotch upon him. By this time Pearl had figured out which pedal was the brake and slammed her left foot down on it. The brakes screamed, and the weaving Packard, complete with a camper of innocent children, slowed down.

"A fire in the camper!" Marvin Sr. shouted to his confused son. Marvin Jr. grabbed the tumbler of scotch and melted ice that was still between his legs. He had heard his father in pain, his wife crying uncontrollably, his mother finishing up a hurried rendition of the 23rd Psalm. In an instant Marvin Ivy Jr. knew that he had before him the means to become the hero of his family. He leapt from the Packard with the tumbler of watered-down scotch, shouting "Daddy's coming!" Behind him went the sack of egg-and-tuna sandwiches Thelma had packed for the occasion. Wondering why the earth was moving, Junior bounced along the road. The tumbler followed, leaving a wet, dark trail in the gravel.

"My God, we've lost Junior!" shouted Marvin Sr., who had just managed in his newfound drunkenness to retrieve his leg from the clutches of the door. Pearl, who was on her second recital of the same psalm, looked back in horror, sure her husband meant that the flames had reached the backseat and engulfed her only child. She forgot completely about steering the Packard and let go of both the wheel and Thelma. "He maketh me to lie down in green pastures . . ." Pearl shouted as the bewildered Packard left the road and careened through a field of hay and clover. It came to rest rather abruptly against a huge rockpile, only because it did not have the speed to climb it.

Halfway out her window, Thelma looked up expecting to see her maker, but saw instead a state trooper looking suspiciously down at her, then at the half-killed bottle in the backseat.

Pearl glanced back to see if the camper had been blown to smithereens, leaving behind only bits and pieces of her poor little grandchildren: A ribbon particle. A teddy bear's ear. A shard of tweed skirt. But it was still there. In the window Regina Beth's small hand was holding up the sign: FOOD. Cynthia Jane was standing near the trooper at her mother's window, tugging at her panties.

"Regina Beth can't spell at all, Mama. She held up FIRE instead of FOOD. Are we going to have a picnic right here?"

"Cynthia Jane," said Thelma, trying to recapture some dignity. "Please don't tug at your panties in front of strangers."

"We're hungry, Mama. Can we make a fireplace out of them big rocks and roast hot dogs?"

Pearl was examining the bruise on Marvin Sr.'s leg. "This is some way to go to a funeral," she said to the trooper. "We're lucky it isn't our own."

"Regina Beth is holding her breath again," said Cynthia Jane.

"Good for her," said Pearl.

Marvin Jr. lost both knees of his gray Sunday slacks, including most of the skin beneath. Limping through the field to catch up with his family was a painful endeavor. Each time weight was applied to his left foot, he winced. The ankle, he was sure, must be broken or sprained. There was a great deal of pain in his elbow, which was badly scraped. He stuck his head inside the camper door, expecting to find the charred remnants of his tiny children. Instead he found only Regina Beth, who was sitting on the floor holding her breath and the SORRY! game. Junior scooped the child up into his arms and hobbled painfully around to the Packard. They were all there, including a state trooper who was questioning a tearful Thelma. All except for Marvin Randall Ivy III. When Cynthia Jane saw her father, she ran to him, stepping on his painful left foot.

"Get off!" shouted Junior, putting down Regina Beth, who had begun to breathe again when she saw the policeman.

"Daddy," Cynthia Jane pleaded. "Can we camp out right here? Can we? Please?"

"Where's your brother?" Marvin Jr. asked his oldest child.

"He got off at the last gas station to pee and Mama left him," said Cynthia Jane, still chafed.

"Why in God's name didn't you stop us?" asked Pearl.

"We didn't have a sign that said STOP," said Cynthia Jane, now tugging on her father's sore arm.

"I'll give you a sign," Pearl said, holding up a fist.

Sicily Keeps It Under Control: Mary Magdalene Had a Mom, Too

"If you keep your eyes shut tight and recite the Lord's Prayer, you won't get pregnant. If you swim in the same river with a boy who has just done it with someone, you *can* get pregnant, though."

—AMY JOY to Her Friend, Beneath the Mattagash Bridge, with Sicily's Old Medical Book, 1958

AT BREAKFAST SICILY sat across from her husband. She twirled the lazy Susan that sat between them and watched the bottles go around like glass horses. Edward Lawler sopped up the yellow of his soft-boiled egg with half a muffin and shoved it into his mouth. He slurped up some coffee.

"Ed?" said Sicily, still twirling. "How old should Amy Joy be before she dates?"

"Eighteen," Ed said as he devoured the last of the helpless muffin and reached for another.

"Eighteen?" Sicily gasped. If he had said sixteen she might have conceived a way to keep all of this from him for two more years. But four years was another matter. This nasty thing with Chester Lee was sure to ruin her health.

"But most young girls start dating at sixteen. Some very respectable ones even start at fifteen."

"Well, then, my daughter will be two or three years more respectable than the rest," he said, and pushed back his chair to stand up. The huge belly beneath the striped cotton shirt rolled like a beach ball. Sicily looked at his beginning bald spot and wondered if Ed was too old at forty-nine to be the rational father of a teenaged girl. Especially one as developed as Amy Joy.

"Is that your final word?" She gave the carousel one last spin, and watched the dizzy bottles come to a slow stop.

"It is."

He finished off his coffee and ran water into the cup, then set it in the sink.

25

Sicily was always thankful for these small household acts that Ed performed. Not that they were especially time-saving, but Ed had been born in Massachusetts and spent his formative years there and that showed up in her husband. City-raised children had much more class. Ed never called soda "pop" or dessert "sweets" or anything that wasn't homemade "boughten," like the rest of Mattagash did. Sicily overlooked a lot in her marriage to Ed because of these little extras.

The Lawlers moved to Mattagash when Ed's father was offered a job teaching the fourth grade. It was a long way for him to come, but rumor had it he couldn't get a job teaching anywhere else. There was some hint in his letters of recommendation of irregular extracurricular activity involving some young female student in his Current Events class. In Mattagash, nevertheless, he was offered the principalship at the elementary school. Later, Ed Lawler inherited the job from his father. He had been teaching fifth-grade history at the time and was really the best successor. He had lived with the problems of principalship just by being his father's son. He had been an apprentice for years until he finally sat down in the principal's chair.

"When she graduates from high school," Ed said as he washed his coffee down with a glass of water, "we'll send her off to some professional school that will take her. She might even manage to find a husband who has a job."

"Oh, Ed, I don't know. I mean, Pearl went off with just that in mind. She thought she'd got her hands on a lawyer and ended up with an undertaker instead. You just can't tell what you're marrying nowadays. No, I wouldn't feel right about little Amy Joy gambling like that in a strange town."

"Pearl couldn't tell birdshit from bearshit," Ed muttered.

Sicily silently compared the two substances. Other than the obvious difference in quantity, she herself wondered where the demarcation lay.

Ed went out to mow the lawn. She watched him from the kitchen window lumbering back and forth as though the push mower was a tinker toy in his hands. He stopped to light up a Lucky Strike and wipe the sweat from his forehead. He was looking tired these days. She worried about his health. The fat that had gathered around his middle must surely be taxing his heart.

He smoked two packs of Lucky Strikes a day, and the only exercise he got was an occasional outing with the lawnmower. Sicily had always felt in her heart that Ed Lawler was a victim of his environment. The men in Mattagash made their living in the lumber industry, cutting and stacking it for a living, then selling it to a contractor who sold it to the big paper companies downstate, which in turn sold it to furniture and paper companies in New England. The trees around Mattagash saw a lot more of the world than the people did.

Sicily was sure that if Ed were living in the city with a good office job he would be a different man. He would be around city men who weren't ashamed to wear Bermuda shorts and sunglasses. In the city Ed would have the opportunity to develop as a sportsman, playing tennis and golf each week with other men. In Mattagash, if they even mentioned golf, they called it "gulf," like the gasoline, and all they cared to do was pitch horseshoes in the field above the gas station. The main entertainment occurred each year at the Fourth of July picnic when the festivities included log rolling, log sawing, tree limbing, pulp peeling, and pulp stacking. It amazed Sicily how many means the men in Mattagash had devised to torture a helpless tree.

Now here was Amy Joy, about to become involved with Chester Lee Gifford, who not only was a lumberjack but could barely hold a job lumbering for more than a month without being fired. Chester Lee had gone so far as to buy himself a chain saw on credit and then went off to work for himself as an independent cutter on some wooded acres of Gifford land. He lasted two days. The joke around Mattagash was that he had fired himself. But what really happened was worse. He sold the chain saw after having made only one payment and bought a bus ticket to Bangor so that he could buy Elvis Presley's latest record and get a professional massage.

Sicily envisioned Amy Joy living in the Gifford house that was already bulging with daughters and grandchildren, the latter of which were not all legitimate. Her Amy Joy, helping to bring more little Giffords into a world of petty crimes and occasional arson.

"I should go on 'Queen for a Day' and tell this," thought Sicily. "I'd make that little needle go straight through the floor."

Having Pearl around for a few days would be a consolation.

She needed someone to lean on. A sister was the best answer to problems like these, and Marge wasn't the type to confide in even before her illness. Sicily loved Marge because she had been told it was a sin not to love your family members. She never questioned this. Marge had been something of a tyrant all her life, growing worse as the years went by. Ed used to say all she needed was a bottle of whiskey, a room in the Watertown Hotel, and Paul Bunyan for one night. But it was deeper than that, Sicily sensed. There had been a young man at one time in Marge's life, and then he wasn't there anymore. Sicily, thirteen years younger than Marge, was only seven the summer he stopped coming to court. But she sensed, as a child can, that a change had come over Marge. Something took hold of her and never let her go again. Even now Marge was in its palm.

Sicily had never been told the circumstances of Marge's young man, and she had never asked. Now she was almost sorry for it. Maybe Marge had been angry all these years because no one bothered to talk about the one thing she wanted to talk about. That happened in small towns. Everyone discussed a person's business with everyone but the person.

When Edward Elbert Lawler came into Sicily's life, he seemed to her a godsend. But Marge battled tooth and nail to have him removed from the picture forever. It was the only thing Sicily ever fought Marge about, and she fought her by retreating from her. She stopped speaking, stopped going outside the house, even to get the mail. The day she called Daigle's Hardware Store and ordered a sack of rat poison to be delivered to her door, thirty miles away, Marge sensed a malady too big to handle and relented. Ed Lawler became the brother Sicily always wanted, the father she hardly knew.

The Reverend Ralph C. McKinnon had not been a good father to his daughters because he thought of them as members of his congregation. His religion was a delirium he caught from his own father at the age of seven, and he never shook it until it did him in. Dying of kala-azar in China was the high point of his life. It was the rare bone archeologists spend their lifetimes digging for. The experiment that finally pays off for the scientist. When the Reverend left for China, he left twenty-four-year-old Marge as mistress of the house and she answered the call with vigor. The girls found a peacefulness in their lives after their father disappeared down the road, sitting stiffly in a neighbor's horse and carriage.

Edward Lawler was a good prospect for a young girl. He was a class apart from the brutishness of the men in Mattagash. He once took Sicily to Watertown to see a college play and then to look at a photographic exhibit at the library. It touched her deeply. It brought a world to her doorstep that she had only imagined, and the taste of it was enough to turn her head completely. She was too naive to realize that he knew almost as little of plays and photography as she did, that he borrowed those things to impress her. But impress her he did. Sicily gave in to Ed Lawler on the soft sawdust that had piled up behind the Mattagash Lumber Mill, gave in to talk of the *New York Times* and the Statue of Liberty and Broadway. He promised to marry her and did when she was eighteen, not because he had really meant to, but because she told him she was in the family way. During her regular menstrual period she came up with a story of wicked cramps and a heavy flow, saying, "I must have lost it." But she never doubted that Edward Lawler had guessed the truth. She was almost thirty-three when Amy Joy was born and it was only then that she stopped being afraid. The first time she picked up her baby daughter and held her, she knew that it would be *them* against *him*. And it was. He drifted further into obesity and school board meetings that lasted until one o'clock in the morning.

With Amy Joy for an ally Sicily found it easier to digest Marge's rantings and what the McKinnons considered a lack of culture amid the mosquitoes and horseshoe tournaments in Mattagash. But now she was faced with losing that ally, not because Amy Joy had turned into a woman and was ready—Sicily felt she could handle that. She was losing her because Amy Joy had turned out so badly, because it seemed that there was nothing hopeful to be found anywhere inside her.

"She's becoming a real dipstick," Sicily thought. "But I'll save that child yet, if I have to battle Chester Lee every inch of the way."

Amy Joy called from Marge's to say that the doctor had phoned and would be a little late for his daily visit. There was a childbirth case that needed attending.

"Funny," Sicily told Amy Joy on the phone. "They're dying in one place and being born somewhere else."

"Can I go swimming?" asked Amy Joy.

"Where?"

"By the Mattagash Bridge where everyone goes."

"With who?"

"Kids."

"What kids?"

"Just kids. What are you? A cop?"

"I want to know *what* kids."

"Cindy."

"Cindy who?"

"Oh, Mama."

"Cindy who?"

"Cindy Freeman."

"Be home for supper," said Sicily and hung up. Ed came in, his face puffy and red with exertion. He had taken off his shirt and his undershirt was wet with sweat.

"Christ, it's hot out there for September!"

"You're overworking is all. I'm afraid you might have a stroke someday, Ed, pushing that mower around like you're still twenty years old."

"I've got life insurance." He dropped down into the beige leather armchair in the living room and lit up a Lucky Strike.

"You need to at least sharpen the blades on that thing." Sicily brought him a glass of Kool-Aid.

"You could bury me in the backyard and find a new husband before the sun goes down." Ed was in a good mood after the workout.

"Let me get Marge buried first."

"Maybe you could get a discount from Marvin Ivy by buying two coffins at once."

"Sometimes you joke at the blackest things," Sicily said, thumbing through her *Hersey's 1934 Cookbook*. She needed to plan the menu for when Pearl arrived. There was no restaurant in Mattagash, and rather than see them drive the thirty miles to Watertown, she would take upon herself the responsibility of feeding them.

"Does Exotic Tahitian Pink Salad sound too gay for a time like this?" she asked Ed, who was watching television and didn't answer.

Sicily spent the afternoon baking. The kitchen table held pans of brownies, cupcakes, and cookies. A double-layer chocolate cake sprinkled wih glittering bits sat like a king in the midst of the other baked goods. Ed had gone upstairs to snooze, but at eight o'clock he came into the kitchen and took a beer from the refrigerator. He had showered and was dressed in a clean shirt and suntan slacks. Sicily could smell his after-shave.

"There's a meeting tonight about whether or not to raise the teacher's salaries," he said, and took his car keys from the corner shelf over the kitchen sink and a toothpick from the box sitting on the stove.

"Another meeting?"

"There's nothing I can do about it. It's my job." Ed opened the door and looked back at his wife.

"I suppose I'll just drop by Marge's then and see how she's doing," Sicily said. "I've been by twice today but you can never be too careful. I'll just go by again and see that Amy Joy is tucked in safe and sound."

"I won't be long," Ed said and shut the door. She listened to the car door slam, to the engine starting up, the car backing out of the driveway, and the last sounds until it disappeared down the road.

"Any woman but a McKinnon would follow him," Sicily thought. "Another woman would ask a few questions."

Sicily walked to Marge's. It was only a mile down the road, and a few minutes to clear her head was just what she needed. There was a harvest moon, a huge orange that dominated the night sky. The thought of Marge dying was brought home. It may have been the spectacular moon. It may have been Ed's disappearance on a night when she really needed him home. Whatever it was, there was an aura of death in the air. For the past three weeks, Mattagash itself had been like a huge graveyard. It had emptied the last week of August for the potato harvest, because independent woodcutters could make good money by converting their pulp trucks to potato trucks with grapples to lift the potato barrels. The majority of families piled their belongings each year onto the backs of their trucks and left Mattagash for four weeks to work for the potato farmers in Caribou or Limestone sixty miles away. It was extremely hard work, but even the youngest children could bring in a salary picking potatoes. The Lawlers and Mc-Kinnons were among the very few families who didn't participate in the harvest, and Sicily was saddened each year when school stopped and the children left with their parents. "It's just like that story about the Pied Piper who piped all the little kids away and left the town so sad," she once said to Amy Joy, who had been left behind with a few adults for company.

Sicily was thankful that Marge's lapse hadn't occurred earlier when the harvest was in full swing. She could see the lineup at the coffin: the elderly, one or two cripples, and children too young to walk. But now that the harvest was almost over, most of the families had packed up their potato money and belongings and come home.

Sicily passed the houses of her neighbors, the yellow lights of their windows, the night sounds of their lives. A radio played in one house, a television in another. The supper forks and knives were being put away in one kitchen. Laughter came from a back-yard. The sound of a baby crying came from a screened upstairs window. "These are my neighbors at night," she thought, and she wondered what sounds, what clues to her life might issue from *her* house at night to a passerby.

At Marge's there was no porchlight on. In the yard Sicily picked. up an empty potato-chip bag that had been thrown on the ground. There was no doubt that it was Amy Joy's. The house was quiet. She opened the front door. In Marge's room the nurse was knitting by the bedside. Sicily waved to her from the door.

"Any change?"

The nurse shook her head. The lamp by Marge's bed had a 60-watt bulb. In its light, Marge's features were gray as marble. Sicily felt as though something was about to burst out of the closets or pound on the ceiling. Something that needed to break the awkward silence. After a few seconds her ears became accustomed to sounds she hadn't heard before: the soft clicking of the knitting needles, the curtains moving in a faint breeze, crickets beneath the window. An occasional car passed and disappeared in its own sound around the turn.

"It's very lonely in here tonight," Sicily said, putting a few strands of Marge's hair in place. She was struck with how very white her sister's eyebrows were. "She must have penciled them," Sicily thought.

"It's always lonely when someone is dying," the nurse said.

Amy Joy's room was empty. It was the guest room on the south side of the house. Sicily was shocked at the condition of the room. Dirty panties lay in a pile by the bed. A bra and two belts hung from the door handle. Clothes lay on the bed and covered the wicker chair. Dirty dishes were piled on the nightstand, and by the bed an empty box that had once held a pint of chocolate whirl ice cream sat with a spoon in it. Next to it, an empty Coke bottle holding a deflated straw lay on its side. On the bed a *True Confessions* magazine was opened to a story called "My Husband's Ghost Saved Me From My Neighbor's Lust."

"This is the last straw," said Sicily and kicked a pair of blue flip-flops that had been discarded in the middle of the floor.

In the kitchen she found dishes on the table with food drying on them. But no Amy Joy. Taking a flashlight from Marge's utility drawer, Sicily went out the front door and walked past Marge's dried hollyhocks to the backyard. She listened in the dark for noises. A giggle came from behind the garage. Few people in Mattagash owned garages. The indoor bathroom ranked higher as a necessity than did a warm house for cars and trucks, so if any extra money was found, it went toward indoor plumbing. Cars and trucks had to be plugged into electrical outlets overnight so that they could start up on cold Maine mornings. Or if the block heaters were out of financial range for some people, their cars had to be boosted by kindly neighbors if the blanket left overnight on the hood was not enough. And if a creature as indispensable as a car didn't rate a house in Mattagash, a dog might as well forget it.

Sicily made her way slowly and quietly around to the back of the building. She stood listening. There was a rustling on the ground. She got the flashlight ready, waiting for the cue to action that only a mother knows.

"Amy Joy, loosen up a little," Chester Lee was saying. "Honey, you're too stiff."

"There's a burdock sticking in my butt," said Amy Joy.

"Here, put my John Deere cap under you," Chester Lee said,

in what seemed a wonderful display of gallantry to Amy Joy.

"Ouch! It's still picking me," said a distraught Amy.

Sicily had heard enough. She swung around the corner of the garage and blasted the lovers with a beam of light. Their retinas lit up like tiny comets. Amy Joy's pants and panties were down to her ankles. Her blouse was unbuttoned, bra unsnapped. Chester Lee quickly zipped up his pants and stood up, squinting his eyes in the glare and holding his hands above his head as though Sicily were wielding a rifle instead of a flashlight.

"OK, Miss. Get those clothes on," Sicily said, aiming at the half-naked body of Amy Joy. In her hands the flashlight did, indeed, exert a gunlike power.

Amy Joy stuck one feeble hand up to shield her eyes. Pulling her blouse about her, she burst into loud sobs.

"Caterwaul until you wake up the whole town, Amy Joy. That's all we need," Sicily said.

"Me and Chester Lee is getting married," she told her mother tearfully.

"You get yourself up and into your room. I'll deal with you in there. Chester Lee, just wait right there a minute," Sicily said to a slowly retreating Chester. "We got something to talk about."

Amy Joy, her clothing back in its proper place, broke into a run for the house, shouting behind her, "Don't let her scare you, Chester Lee!"

"She don't scare me none," Chester Lee bellowed. Then he dodged under the lilac bushes and was lost, like a leprechaun, in the black cover of the night. Sicily did not, in fact, scare him. But the thought of Ed Lawler was enough to make him leave his scarcely used green-and-yellow John Deere cap on the damp ground behind him.

In Amy Joy's bedroom there was no sound. Sicily switched on the light. Beneath the blankets and magazines, beneath the discarded clothing and candy-bar wrappers, Amy Joy pretended to be asleep.

"You ain't fooling me one bit, Miss," Sicily said. "A bear in the middle of winter couldn't go to sleep after that mess outside." She poked at the pile on the bed but it didn't move. She stripped back the covers and found Amy Joy cowering there. She had covered her head with her two chubby arms.

"You'd be in good shape if all I did was beat you, Amy Joy. But you're not getting off that easy. The kind of bruises you're gonna get out of this scrape ain't the kind that'll go away in a week or two. You'll carry them inside you for as long as you live."

Amy Joy uncovered her head to let Sicily see the tears in her eyes.

"Me and Chester Lee love each other."

"Is that sordid little scene I was just witness to your idea of love, little girl? That trashy picture I just saw will be burned into my pupils forever. I'll take it with me to my maker. My own daughter in a bed of sin out behind my dying sister's garage."

"It wasn't really a bed, Mama."

"I told Marge not to build that damn garage," said Sicily, sitting on the end of Amy Joy's bed. "She doesn't even own a car. It's a statement of the times, is what it is. Modern living breeds sin."

Amy Joy had never before heard her mother use even the mildest of swear words. She sat up, forgetting her tears, to watch this new development.

"Mama, you just said damn."

"I'm a changed woman," Sicily said as she aimlessly flicked the trigger of her flashlight on and off.

"We *are* getting married," said Amy Joy.

"Amy Joy, you been reading too many of them magazines."

"Are you telling Daddy?"

"What do you think?"

"I guess."

"You guess what?"

"I guess you're telling."

"You just hit the nail on the head."

"I'll kill myself if you tell."

"If I tell, you won't have to kill yourself. Daddy'll be glad to do it for you." Sicily turned to look at the frightened child.

"It wasn't very long ago, Amy Joy, that all you cared about was collecting the material samples out of the Sears and Roebuck. Now look at you."

The two stared at each other. Amy Joy sensed the sadness in her mother, the betrayal she felt by her only child. Sicily saw a confused, scared little girl, the adolescent pimples standing out bigger and redder than ever. They were both tied to a man neither of them could turn to. A man who attended nonexistent meetings on a night when his wife and daughter needed him most.

"It's just the two of us, little Amy Joy," Sicily said softly, knowing, as her child did, that Ed Lawler would not be told about the activities that night.

"I guess."

"Come here, honey," Sicily said and took the tearful Amy Joy into her arms.

The Albert Pinkham
Family Motel Fills Up:
No Room at the Inn

"It used to be that young folks had to drive all the way to Watertown to get themselves a room on their wedding night. Now it's just a skip and a hop over to Albert's place."

—DONNIE HENDERSON, Lumberman

THE ALBERT PINKHAM FAMILY MOTEL was a one-story structure built onto the end of the owner's two-story house. Pinkham had seen progress encroaching on the town line when a six-room hunters' lodge was built in neighboring St. Leonard. So amid his wife's protestations, he went to work on a four-room capacity motel. Albert's architectural design was not the best, drawn out of penury rather than creativity. Each room had a separate entrance, two in front, two in back. A bathroom consisting of a single tub and commode was added to the upper end of the motel so that the tenants had to leave their rooms to reach it. Having an indoor hallway leading to the bath would have been a great convenience to his customers, and would have provided them with privacy as well. But it would also mean added expenses. Nonetheless, not wanting to be outranked by the hunters' lodge, Albert mixed his own cement and ran a three-inch-high walkway around the entire structure. It made a nice porch for his rocking chair. In the evenings he usually sat in front of Room numbers 1 and 2 in the front, if they were empty, and smoked a few cigarettes while watching cars pass.

Hot running water was another matter. No one in Mattagash, not even Marge McKinnon, had pushed that far into the twentieth century. But Albert Pinkham was a man of foresight. Hot water for a quick wash or shave in the mornings was easily available to each tenant by boiling his own on the hot plate in his room. Albert arranged to save a few dollars at the hardware store by buying out the entire stock. Four hot plates made an impressive sale.

37

Sarah Pinkham was furious at what she considered her husband's excesses. The night he came home with the four boxes and stacked them on the table, she broke down and wept. It was not until Albert's plan was laid out before her on paper that the tears in her eyes were replaced with dollar signs. Each hot plate cost, with tax, $9.42. The total purchase of four was $27.68, with ten dollars knocked off for the quantity bought. Albert's idea was to charge each room a quarter a day if they wished to use the hot plate for heating water or cooking purposes. Not only would the hot plates be paid off in no time, but they would continue to make money as time went on. And residents would be supplied with a makeshift kitchen that would save them money at the diners in Watertown.

Sarah was less than pleased to learn how the hot water for bathing in the tub would be made available to boarders. On large index cards left in each room (Albert's nearsighted daughter Belle was given the task of writing them up) appeared the following information:

THE ALBERT PINKHAM FAMILY MOTEL

WELCOME! TOURISTS, HUNTERS, FISHERMEN, AND NEWLYWEDS.
Here is a list of conveniences for you, courtesy of:

ALBERT PINKHAM AND FAMILY

Hot Plate Usage: .... 25¢ per day
(Hot plates can be obtained in the living room from family members only. A day's deposit required. Go around to front door and knock. Dog doesn't bite.)

HOT BATH WATER............................... 50¢ per day
(Hot bath water for the tub must be asked for in advance since it has to be heated on the stove. Plan for your bath ahead of time. That way no one will have to wait. Bath water available between 5:45 P.M. and 8:00 P.M. only. Forty-five minutes of bath time for each room, unless other boarders don't need the tub.)

PLEASE fill out list below:

Room Number _____

_____ YES, I do want to rent a hot plate

_____ YES, I do want to take a bath

I plan to bathe at:

_____ 5:45

_____ 6:30

_____ 7:15

_____ 8:00

First come, first served. Thank you for staying at the all modern:

ALBERT PINKHAM FAMILY MOTEL

"How will I get supper for us and boil water for the boarders at the same time? I only got that one stove," Sarah Pinkham complained to her husband. "Can't we start the bath time later?"

"If we get done at eight o'clock we can watch Milton Berle each week."

"Well, why don't we have the time earlier on Tuesday nights only?" Sarah asked.

"Consistency," Albert Pinkham told his distraught wife. "We gotta be known for our consistency."

"Sounds more like stupidity," Sarah later said to Belle.

"Well, there's no more room on the card anyway," said Belle, who picked a doughboy out of the chicken stew, mistaking it, due to her eye condition, for a potato.

Albert's luck after six months in business ran in spurts. First of all, his best room, number 3, which faced away from the road and had a window opening on Sarah's flower garden, was permanently rented by a young woman who said she was a modern dancer and would be studying Psychology one night a week at the high school in Watertown. The room soon took on the atmosphere of hominess. A window box full of geraniums appeared the second day of her arrival. A small clothes rack sat outside her door on the third day, decorated with delicate female underthings, and was taken in only when the dainty articles were dry. The addition of a braided rug on the cement outside and a bowl in the window with two shimmering goldfish catching the sun convinced Sarah that the attractive young woman really meant to stay for a while. The last thing Sarah wanted encamped beneath their bedroom window was the likes of Violet La Forge. Albert behaved like a silly puppy whenever Violet came into the living room to inquire about certain fixtures in the room and to ask permission to make changes in the decor.

"She's painting the room pink," Albert told his wife after one such visit.

"What's wrong with the beige? I just painted that room." Sarah was testing Albert to see how quickly he sided with the new tenant. Aware of her tactics, Albert said simply, "We'll have to get used to spoiled clients."

Sarah tried another approach, one even dearer to Albert's heart than an attractive young woman.

"It'll cost us money to repaint that room," she said.

"She brought her own paint with her. She said she had it left over after she painted her bed."

"She's got a pink bed?" Sarah asked in disbelief.

"Our bed," Albert said. "She painted our bed pink."

"Well, of all the nerve!" Sarah began listing all the reasons it would be in the best interest of the motel to ask her to leave, but Albert stopped her.

"I won't have you throwing out a paying guest during such a slack time of year. We're lucky to get someone that permanent with the harvest still going. At least she won't be breaking the place up."

With that he went out to talk with some fishermen who had just pulled in for some last-of-the-season fishing. Looking out the window as Violet La Forge unloaded a small orange tree in a wooden bucket from the backseat of her little Volkswagen, Sarah said nothing. "Let him go," she thought. "I'll find out what Miss Modern Dancer is all about. I'll rattle the skeletons in her closet. Oranges this far north."

The fishermen brought their wives with them to stay behind at the room and enjoy a few days of girl talk while the men fished. The two couples rented rooms 1 and 2, facing the road. There was only one room left, number 4, next to Violet La Forge, when the sorrowful Packard limped into the driveway of the Albert Pinkham Family Motel. But it was not a happy family that pulled up to Albert's front door. Drawing from a primitive instinct for survival, Thelma had ridden in the camper for the rest of the trip, where she kept the children in tow. Marvin Sr. drove while a bewailing Junior was hospitalized in the backseat by his doting mother. Pearl saw to it that even old wounds were securely bound and had finally calmed Junior down from the exasperating day. With Thelma riding herd over the children, the rest of the trip had passed uneventfully, which was fine with the disgruntled passengers of the Packard ensemble.

Since there was only room for Marvin and Pearl in the Albert Pinkham Family Motel, and since there was still enough daylight, Junior decided to pitch camp for his family. Pearl called Sicily to announce their arrival and ask about Marge's condition. Hearing that Marge was still on her last breath, they carried their suitcases into Room number 4.

"That's one hell of a long breath," said Marvin Sr. "She's been drawing it since the phone call yesterday afternoon." Pearl flopped down onto the bed.

"A nice hot bath," she told Marvin. "All I want in this earthly life is a nice hot bath."

"You'd better fill this out then," said Marvin, who had been reading Belle's artwork. He passed the index card to Pearl, who read it slowly. She looked at Marvin.

"What in hell does this mean?" she asked.

"This ain't Portland, Pearl. There's no hot water."

"What time is it? Quick!"

Marvin pulled out his pocket watch.

"It's seven-thirty."

"For God's sake, give me a pen," Pearl shouted so loudly that Marvin started.

"We still got time for the eight o'clock water if we hurry."

When Pearl came back to Room 4, Marvin had taken off his shoes and was listening to the radio.

"How'd it go?"

Pearl slumped on the bed and said nothing.

"How'd it go, Pearl? What's wrong?"

"A fisherman's wife in number one just signed up for the last hot water tonight. We can't take a real bath in a tub until five forty-five tomorrow night." Pearl started to cry.

"There now," said Marvin and took her into his arms.

"All day long, ever since the accident, it's all I thought of," Pearl said between sobs. "All that kept me going was the thought of a nice hot bath and a clean bed."

"Don't cry, Pearly," Marvin said soothingly as he rocked Pearl back and forth on the bed. "I'll go get one of his hot plates and we'll freshen up a bit here in the room."

"A French whore's bath!" cried Pearl. "I've driven three hundred seventy miles with birdbrained Thelma and the three little pigs just to take a whore's bath!"

"It's better than nothing, sweetheart," said Marvin Sr., whose usual endearment was simply *Pearly*. He knew *sweetheart* had calming effects on her. *Darling* was downright medicinal. That one he saved for the serious occasions, when he feared another breakdown like the one when they were first married. Today, when Pearl raised her hand to strike Thelma for asking, "Do you still want me to drive?" after the Packard had been retrieved from the clover field, Marvin Sr. almost brought out a *darling*. But the policeman's presence put a damper on Pearl's fiery temper. By the time he left, Thelma had wisely barricaded herself inside the safety of the camper.

True to form, Pearl stopped crying and said, "I suppose it could be worse."

"Of course it could."

"Junior could have been crippled for life."

"Maybe never walk again," said Marvin.

"And there really *could* have been a fire."

"It would have blown us to bits."

"The policeman said if it hadn't been for the rockpile we'd have gone into the river."

"We'd have probably drowned."

"Will you go for the hot plate, then?" Pearl blew her nose.

"Right this minute," said Marvin.

"And put us down for hot water as early tomorrow night as possible?"

"I'll put us down. Where's the card?"

"I gave it to Mr. Pinkham and told him to stick it where the sun don't shine."

"That could be just about anywhere this far north," Marvin said. Pearl's bottom lip began to flutter again.

"I'll get a new one then. You just stay here and rest, sweetheart."

"You're a good husband, Marvin."

"You're a good wife," Marvin told a completely rejuvenated Pearl.

When Marvin Sr. came back, Pearly had undressed and was waiting in her housecoat for the hot plate. Along with the appliance, Marvin Sr. had brought back a small aluminum pan full of water from the bathroom.

"The bathroom's outside at the end of the motel. I'll carry this down for you when it's hot."

"Didn't they give you a bigger pan?"

"Mr. Pinkham said he's trying to discourage people from heating their own bathwater. Seems a couple of hunters were doing that and he had to put a stop to it. He made a joke about it. Said he told the hunters he was losing money down the drain."

"That's not very funny," said Pearl.

"He thought it was."

"Is there a flush in there?" she asked.

"There's a flush."

"Do we have to fill out a card when we want to flush the damn thing?" Pearl almost seemed to blame Marvin Sr. for this predicament.

"Only rooms number one and two can flush it! Get it?" said Marvin, pleased that he had stumbled upon a joke. "Number one and number two. Get it, Pearl?"

"Silly," said Pearl, getting into a better mood.

"Funny thing next door," said Marvin. He slipped off his loafers and socks, then held the socks to his nose to see if they would hold up one more day. He held them up to Pearl for her opinion, but as soon as they dangled within a foot of her nose she made a face and waved them away.

"What about next door?" Pearl stuck her index finger into the pan, waiting for a sign of warmth.

"There's a young woman in leotards doing exercises on the cement outside Room three."

"What?" asked an incredulous Pearl.

"I swear," said Marvin Sr.

Pearl opened the door and put her head out. Violet La Forge was doing sit-ups. Flat on her back, the body suit stretched precariously across her large breasts, which tried to hold her back like boulders when she sat up to touch her toes. After three more sit-ups, Violet saw the disbelieving Pearl in the doorway of number 4.

"Hello, neighbor," she said, stopping the exercise.

"Hello," Pearl said suspiciously.

"I'm Violet La Forge. I'm renting here on a permanent basis."

"You mean you *live* here?"

"Until I decide what I want to do with my career. I might want to become a Psychologist, but right now I'm a modern dancer. I dance in the ballroom of the Watertown Hotel."

"When did they turn that little saloon into a ballroom?" Pearl asked, thinking they must be talking about two different buildings. The downstairs bar at the Watertown Hotel wasn't any bigger than the mourner's room at the Ivy Funeral Home. Violet ignored the slight. Isadora Duncan, she reminded herself, put up with countless insults and innuendoes before being accepted as a true artist.

"If I decide to study Psychology, I'll give up dancing."

"That's real smart of you," said Pearl. "What kind of dancer did you say you were?"

"A modern one," said Violet. "Trained in the school of Modern Dance."

"Well, you'd need a ballroom for that all right," said Pearl.

Violet drew on inner strength to rise above this rude neighbor. Not because there was anything Violet liked in Pearl's demeanor. Violet was a believer of reincarnation. If she accepted Pearl in this life, she would not meet her a second time. And although they'd just met, Violet La Forge didn't want to encounter Pearl again. For karma's sake, she smiled.

"Are you here for just one night?" Her voice was sugary. It was the voice Violet had been trained to bring forth when her male customers wanted to touch beneath the flowing scarves of her dancing costumes. Because Violet had been dealing in Psychology for so long out in the bush, she had decided just weeks before to pursue a degree within the halls of academia. A degree would *prove* that she could read people up one side and down the other.

"My sister is on her last breath. She's a McKinnon from right here in Mattagash. We'll just be here until the funeral."

"Don't be sad about it. Don't think of it as dying. It's only a matter of a free spirit leaving the physical body that is no longer needed. A lot of artists and creative people such as myself believe that we shouldn't fear death."

"Don't tell that to my husband," said Pearl and nodded to Room number 4.

"Sometimes though," Violet went on as she resumed her sit-ups. "Sometimes the spirit isn't ready to depart the body but is pushed out by unhealthy living. Or depression. You know, morbid thoughts that let unfriendly forces rule the body. In that case, one should fight death. There's all kinds of ways to do that if your sister's spirit really isn't ready to leave her earth-body. I've got a lot of written material about this subject if you'd like to read some."

"You don't know Marge," Pearl said. "If her spirit isn't ready to leave her body, believe me, honey, it won't."

"Well, modern medicine will one day regard the psychic healer as a true physician of both the spirit and the body."

Pearl went back into her room. She closed and locked the door. Rather than chance walking past Violet La Forge's room to get to the bathroom she would wait until the morning to freshen up. She crawled into bed beside Marvin. A long piece of twine, which was tied to the little silver chain that pulled the light off and on, was hanging by the bed. Albert had thoughtfully run it across the ceiling from the light bulb and tied it around a nail that he hammered into the ceiling above the head of the bed. The end dangled in easy reach so that the tenant would not have to get up to pull the string. Pearl pulled it and the light went out.

"Is anything wrong, Pearly?" Marvin asked after a few seconds of darkness.

"We're next door to Aimee Semple McPherson," said Pearl.

The Gifford Family:
Chester Lee as a Mythic Hero

"Taking a Gifford to court is like the Japanese bombing Pearl Harbor.
You don't want to wake up any sleeping giants."
—MATTAGASH RESIDENT Who Prefers to Remain Anonymous, 1956

CHESTER LEE GIFFORD was the sixth child in a family of ten. He
was the youngest of the five sons born to Bert Gifford and Ruth
Gifford. Ruth Gifford was a skinny woman with a long, crane-
like neck and small hard eyes. Her children had inherited from
her the dark curly hair and ski-slope nose. She was a vicious
woman, lashing out at her neighbors and daughters as though
they were responsible for the conditions of her life. The Giffords
were poor, living on the support of the town and a monthly
disability check. The latter was in compensation of a mysterious
back ailment that Bert Gifford was suffering from, although no
one in Mattagash had ever seen signs of his ailing back. Bert
supplemented the family's illegal income of reselling stolen goods,
the disability check, and town support by hiring himself out as a
guide in the Mattagash territory and on organized canoe trips
down the Mattagash River. He could easily load a canoe onto the
canoe rack of his fenderless green Ford, unload it, then carry it
on his shoulders several miles over a treacherous course through
the woods to one of the many lakes in the Mattagash territory.
Bert Gifford knew which lake the fish were likely to be biting in,
and when Ruth's tongue proved too much of a whip, he would
retreat, canoe on his shoulders, into the woods to spend the day
fishing. All of Mattagash agreed those were not the symptoms of
a man suffering from disability due to a back injury. But the check
came from Augusta, and in faraway Augusta Bert Gifford was
just another statistic.

Of the five Gifford daughters, Lorraine, Debra, and Rita were
teenagers and still living at home, having mothered four illegitimate children among them. The oldest daughter, Elizabeth, was

married to Ronnie Gifford, a first cousin, and had established herself a hundred yards down the road in a four-room log cabin. At the age of thirty-one she was the mother of five children, as well as a grandmother. Her oldest daughter, Stella, had given birth to a son and moved to St. Leonard, fifteen miles away, with the father of her child, but afraid of losing her welfare eligibility she did not marry him. Elizabeth's four other children were at home sleeping in two sets of bunk beds piled into one bedroom.

The second-oldest of Bert's daughters was Rosie, the only attractive Gifford. Rosie was a quiet girl who was quite intelligent and somewhat embarrassed of her background. When she was an eighth-grader her teacher tried to convince Bert and Ruth to let Rosie move to Watertown and go to high school there. The teacher offered to make room for the girl in her own family and take care of any expenses. But Ruth Gifford stood on the steps of her front porch and ordered the terrified woman never to step foot on Gifford ground again, unless she wished to have both her eyes blackened. The Giffords did not, Ruth told the teacher, accept charity. And in the Gifford mind, they really didn't. They accepted the disability check as something the government owed them, and the town help as something Mattagash owed them, and the goods they stole from lumbermills and contractors as something the rich landowners owed them. It was a philosophy passed down to them by a long line of Giffords, who most likely brought the practice over with them from the old country.

A few weeks after her sixteenth birthday, Rosie Gifford became pregnant. Two months after a hasty wedding, she was killed instantly when logs fell from a loaded truck that she had pulled out to pass on the road to Watertown. It was the first time that the Giffords, in their many years of lawsuits, had a legal right to sue. But they didn't. Mattagash knew why. The owner of the truck was Robert O'Malley, the sheriff from St. Leonard, who bent and twisted the law as he saw fit. There was rumor of a large payoff. Some said O'Malley had collected enough things on Chester Lee over the years that he threatened to put him behind bars if the Giffords pursued the matter. Whatever the reason, the Giffords did not sue. And Rosie, the first genetic combination evolving from generations of mutant Giffords who might have stepped out of the murky slime and onto solid ground, took her place in the Mattagash Catholic graveyard and was soon forgotten.

Chester Lee held the family honor of being the only son not in jail in downstate Thompson Penitentiary. He had learned well from his older brothers who were serving individual sentences for an assortment of crimes. The oldest son, Bert Jr., was convicted of raping a waitress while on a trip to Bangor to take his physical for the armed services. He later bragged that it was one way of staying off Pork Chop Hill. The second-oldest son, Andrew, was sentenced for armed robbery and assault on an aged grocery clerk in Watertown. And the last two sons, twins Ernest and Lawrence, were convicted together of theft. They convinced the salesman at Horner's Car Sales in Watertown to let them test-drive a new 1959 Plymouth. The salesman, who had already heard of the notorious Giffords from Mattagash, was terrified of the two brooding men and handed them the shiny set of keys. Ernest and Larry were apprehended three days later at the Houlton State Fair. The Plymouth, which by this time had a dented rear fender, no radio or hubcaps, and a backseat full of stuffed Teddy bears and beer cans, was returned to Horner's Car Sales. Asked by the judge if they had anything to say for themselves, Ernest Gifford said that the Plymouth was one hell of a car.

One reason that Chester Lee was not incarcerated was because he felt overshadowed by the illegal accomplishments of his older brothers. He became somewhat of a coward, intimidated by those whom he considered the best in their profession. His crimes tended to fall more in the misdemeanor category, and few victims bothered to pursue the issue in lengthy court procedures. Another reason was that Chester Lee confined his actions to Mattagash, where he could operate with a certain amount of safety. The whole town knew him personally, knew the Gifford family's record, understood that prosecuting any of them to the full extent of the law meant that the plaintiff would incur the family wrath from then on. A five-pound bag of sugar would disappear into the gas tank of the plaintiff's car, his tools stolen, his pets shot, his mailbox pilfered, his windows shattered in the night by rocks. Even arson was not unlikely. To rile up the Giffords was not a prosperous move.

Chester Lee did make one ill-planned effort to rank along with his brothers in the annals of Mattagash's best criminal minds. But he ventured only as far as the town line separating Mattagash from St. Leonard. There was a small field at this spot and it was in this small field that Lyman Cole pulled over his traveling grocery truck at twelve o'clock each Tuesday and Friday to eat his lunch. The truck had originally been an old moving van that Lyman converted into a small store and painted an army green. He built shelves inside and stocked them with canned vegetables, sugar, flour, candy, and cigarettes from his store in St. Leonard. As a service to his customers, and knowing that most of the lumberjacks' wives had no means of transportation after their husbands went off to work before sunrise, Lyman discovered it was lucrative to peddle his wares twice a week in his rumbling old truck. Each Tuesday and Friday the housewives posted a child at the window as a sentinel. When Lyman's truck rolled into view, the child ran to the road, arms waving to stop him. Then the woman of the house came out, climbed up the two steps on the back of the truck, and stepped inside to do her shopping.

Lyman was a Christ-like figure to the women in Mattagash as he sputtered down the road in his mobile establishment bringing them packages of yeast. And it *was* a religious service he performed. Through him bread was able to rise like Lazarus from the dead. And if the bread had not come out of the oven there would have been trouble when the men came out of the woods at night for their supper. Lyman was an *institution,* and Chester Lee chose him for his symbolic assault on Mattagash.

Waiting like a snake behind the hazelnut and chokecherry bushes one Tuesday afternoon until Lyman was halfway through his tuna sandwich, Chester burst into the open, riding the Gifford's old white workhorse that had seen its better days yarding logs. With one of his sister's nylon stockings pulled over his face and a shotgun in his hand, Chester Lee Gifford held up the immobile traveling grocery truck. Lyman, who suffered from high blood pressure, nearly collapsed, allowing the scofflaw to escape with a potato sack full of canned goods and Lyman's entire stock of cigarettes. There was no doubt that it was Chester Lee, since the Giffords had the only white workhorse in Mattagash. Bert Gifford told his son later that the nylon stocking should have gone over the *horse's* head, as it was much more recognizable than Chester.

Rather than risk another equestrian assault, Lyman renewed

his prescription for high blood pressure pills, began eating his tuna sandwich in the safety of the grammar school's yard, and left the assailant to answer to God on Judgment Day.

Undoubtedly, the Giffords held Mattagash in the dirty palms of their hands. They were the antithesis of the McKinnons. If the McKinnons stood for etiquette, the Giffords were bad manners. If it could be said that the McKinnons stressed the need for education in Mattagash, then the Giffords stressed the need for truant officers. And Chester Gifford, hovering in the shadows at Marge's house in hopes of procuring Amy Joy as a wife, had in his power the means to bring the House of McKinnons crashing to the ground. Amy Joy, locked in holy union with a Gifford and living in their menagerie, would cause McKinnon ancestors to roll over in graves two hundred years old back in County Cork, Ireland. It simply would not do.

God's in His Heaven:
All's Right With the Ivys

"If you pee on that electric fence, the electricity will come straight back into your body and you can give people shocks for the rest of your life, but only boys can do it because girls can't aim and would be too sissy anyway. There's a man down by Bar Harbour who works in a lighthouse and doesn't even have to turn on the light. That's 'cause he pees on his electric fence every day and gets charged up. Just like a glow-in-the-dark Jesus."

—Randy Ivy to His Sisters, Vacationing in Northern Maine, 1959

Mattagash Was Deluged every summer by hoards of tourists from all over the country who made their way north for some fishing, camping, and canoeing in such an isolated spot. Sometimes as many as thirty in a group, they went through Mattagash with the canoes loaded onto trucks on their way over miles of dirt roads through the woods until they came to the headwaters of the river. Here they put their canoes in the water and, camping at sites along the way, they made the Mattagash River canoe trip that lasted several days until they arrived sunburned and mosquito-bitten to the flat field near the Mattagash Bridge, where the trucks had returned to wait for them. Loading the canoes back onto the trucks, they were happy to leave Mattagash for the safety of the concrete buildings and business suits they knew so well. They had paid their dues. They could sit over martinis and tell anyone who would listen about the wilderness in which they had survived.

Often a tourist unwillingly provided the town with excitement by not wearing a life jacket and ending up another drowned casualty of the fast-moving rapids. To the tourists, the townspeople were strange, narrow-minded bumpkins. To Mattagash, the tourists were greenhorns, city-slickers, sandwich-eaters. Mattagash had nothing to gain from them. There was only one business in town, a gas station, that sold a few items: candy bars, soda pops, fly repellant, so the tourists did not bring much money

into the town coffers each season. In return, the town did nothing
to better the situation. There were no makeshift showers, no cafes.
There were also no outhouses. The tourist went into the privacy
of the woods and braved the situation each in his own individual
way. Those who had the foresight to bring along rolls of tissue
paper braved better than those who didn't.

It was into this world of unwelcomed tourists that Junior brought
his tiny, citified family. Camping out on the Mattagash flat was
not what he had expected. The flat was isolated in the autumn
and it was really too late in the year to be camping out at all. No
facilities took the zest out of it for Thelma, who could not imagine
such a thing. Steering one of her children in among the red and
orange trees to a spot where the poor little waif could squat for
bodily relief was too much to bear. She wished Junior had used
the foresight in buying their camper that he used for the Packard.
They would have a mobile commode with them if he had.

Junior was not an outdoorsman. He had been born and raised
in Portland, in what was considered a city in that part of the state.
Vacations back to his mother's place of birth became more and
more infrequent as he grew older until finally, after his thirteenth
birthday, he quit accompanying his mother, who rarely returned
herself. Family visits usually took place if business called Ed Lawler downstate. He would drop Sicily off at Pearl's and pick her
up again when he was finished. Pearl visited Marge once each
year for a few days. But these visits were short and out of a sense
of duty to the family. To Thelma Parsons Ivy, she was no more
than Jane in the land of Tarzan.

Because of the chilly nights, the children, despite their cries of
disapproval, slept in sleeping bags on the bunks in the camper.
Randy commandeered the top bunk and the two girls shared the
bottom. Outside in the weaving, tilting tent that Junior had erected,
he and Thelma were bundled in long johns and heavy socks as
they burrowed into sleeping bags.

The first morning the situation didn't seem quite so drastic as
Thelma had thought. The children discovered a wild field and
spent the morning picking goldenrod and searching for animal
holes. A game of tag kept them occupied for a while, as did leap-
frog and kick-the-can. Finally, under Thelma's watchful eye, they
skipped rocks into the river, then threw dead leaves into the

steady current where they became boats and were carried off. It was raw nature to Thelma who, despite the lack of facilities, saw it as an initiation for her children.

Loaded down with Audubon Society field guides for trees and birds of North America, the family hiked along the river in the afternoon. Thelma had caught the bird bug and bombarded her family with cries of "There's a Sharp-Tailed Sparrow, Randy!" or "Look, girls, it's a Red-Winged Blackbird. See the colors?" To her husband she said, "Now according to this leaf shape, this should be a Tamarack."

Junior, meanwhile, snapped countless pictures of his family at harmony with nature. In one, Thelma pointed out a deserted field sparrow's nest to the children whose awed faces were frozen on film, caught for posterity, by their father's roving camera. It was a scrapbook day. A collage of memories. Regina pointing out a partridge in the foliage. Click. Cynthia and Thelma inspecting the last withered petals of some shore roses. Click. Click. Junior and Thelma's children munching sandwiches and apples atop a huge rock. Click. Click. Click.

By late afternoon the terror of the day before was almost forgotten. Junior unhooked the camper and made a quick trip to the Albert Pinkham Family Motel to see if there had been any change in Marge. He really expected her to have died by now. Would have almost preferred it so that he could get the funeral over and on with his family vacation. But stalwart Marge, his mother assured him, was the same.

Marge Grows Up:
Coming of Age in Mattagash

"But Jesus called them unto him, and said, suffer little children to come unto me, and forbid them not; for of such is the kingdom of God. Verily I say unto you, whosoever shall not receive the kingdom of God as a little child shall in no wise enter therein."

—LUKE 18:16–17

THERE WAS A time when she could run through the field that edged the forest, scale the steep path through the pine trees, with her endless hair billowing behind her like a veil.

When she was five and an only child, the Reverend Ralph would grasp her small hand in his and walk briskly from house to house preaching the word of Jesus whose blood spewed from his open wounds and gushed down the timbers of the cross for her sins. She understood this at the age of five. That she was a sinner. And often on the black road that wound through Mattagash, the Reverend Ralph practiced his sermon, using her as his tiny audience; and getting caught up in his own fervor, and walking briskly to keep pace with the fire in his words, it seemed he had forsaken her there beside him. Her small legs ached with the adult steps they took to keep up. Sometimes when he shouted outright at the devil, "Get thee behind me, Satan!" his free hand formed a fist that he shook at the invisible man of darkness, and the hand that held her tiny fingers tightened so around them that she thought she heard them crack and snap like kindling. Sometimes it seemed as if the *Reverend* was making her pay for her sins, and not God. But she'd as soon bite the tongue from her mouth and swallow it as let the Reverend know. So they flitted, like an awkward, deformed bird, from house to house to warn the sinners, while the Reverend's Bible pages flapped in the wind like wings.

There were times when she ached to hug him. Only once had she tried, but he pushed her away saying: "Then spake Jesus to the multitude, and to his disciples, saying, call no man your father upon the earth for one is your father, which is in heaven." And he had deposited her upon the cracked leather of the ancient chair in his study with his fat Bible on her lap and had said, "Now you read Chapter twenty-three of Matthew. These words that are typed in red are the words that Jesus spoke." After he had gone, she stayed silent, with the heavy Bible pressing against her thighs, looking down at the words she could not read at five, the red words of Jesus, until they ran into each other like blood and were lost upon the page.

But there were times when the harshness of her father's religion seemed to engulf her, calm her, and she would turn her child's face up to heaven with her thin arms stretched above her head. And thinking of her grandmother, of the sweetness of the old woman's breath, how warm the drooping muscles of her arms were as they encircled the child, and knowing her grandmother was up in the house of the Lord looking down, it was then she would feel the power of the Lord enter into her like a warm, steady stream of water that ran into the top of her head and out her toes.

When she was ten, the visiting missionaries began to come. Four times a year the Reverend invited one to come to Mattagash and tell the stories of the heathen world. The whole house quivered in excitement as lamps were dusted, rugs shook, and the floor of the parlor was clean enough to reflect the very face of God. She was caught up in the expectation. Her whole body breathed and digested it. Standing on a prune box in the kitchen, she helped her mother make cupcakes and fruit pies. The Reverend would unfold his root beer recipe and begin concocting a batch of it, calling it moxie to avoid the word *beer*. And when he talked of the man who was coming, of the tribes he'd saved from hell, the kitchen grew silent as a tomb, and she fell upon each word as if hearing language spoken for the first time. Even the geraniums in the bright windows bent away from the sun to hear, and the rafters of the ceiling pulled close together as the house stopped breathing to listen.

Everyone wondered what he'd look like, this man of God, what stories he'd bring to Mattagash that would leave it buzzing for months after he'd gone.

When a missionary visited in the fall, the Reverend built a fire big as the sun in the parlor which had been filled with neat rows of wooden folding chairs. The children sat on the floor in front and squirmed in excitement, like small mice, waiting for tales of tribes that would terrify them. When the parlor had filled and the lecture hour drew near, a sabbath hush befell the crowd as if they were about to witness the Second Coming itself. And when Reverend Ralph pushed open the heavy oak doors, necks twisted and eyes squinted so that they might catch a glimpse of the mysterious stranger who waited in the dim hallway. And then the Reverend would turn to face his flock and with all the radiance of the forerunners before him would thunder the introduction: "Ladies and gentlemen. Good Christians and neighbors. We have in our midst tonight the noble, the dedicated, the humble Reverend Wallace B. Cody, who has given many years of his life so that he might lead the souls of the heathen Tapiro pygmies from the mountain ranges of New Guinea in the western Pacific Ocean and into the arms of our heavenly father." And the man of God, the man of the world, the man almost as new and strange to Mattagash as he was to the wide-eyed pygmies, strode down the space left him between the chairs, and when the room broke to applause even the orange fire swelled and stretched to welcome the stranger in. When he opened his mouth, red and green and blue words rolled out to tell of the mud huts, of the leg bands and jangling beads. Every word he spoke was Gospel. His stories of poison darts, hanging spears, and woolly heads became as significant to the ears that took them in as the Sermon on the Mount. And when his fragile wife, pale as an angel, unrolled a yellowed map of that pulsing, exotic country and pointed a tired finger at the very spot where she had followed the man she loved, the women looked at her as though she were Mary, mother of God. A gangling daughter with buck teeth passed around crinkled photos of pygmies pasted on cardboard and told how even little pygmy girls of ten had their very own gardens. Having been born in the belly of New Guinea, her debut was an instant success, and mothers strained to touch her braids and pinch her cheek. And when her father ran out of his own stories, he told of other missionaries who were captured by cannibals and eaten, all except the bones. These they used as spears, or little heathen children made them into toys, or women wore them around their necks. One pious missionary is still there, walking from village to village, talking to tribe after tribe, collecting his daughter's bones.

By nine o'clock the other children were as good as drunk with the intoxicating visit. But she would watch her father's face and see it fill to the brim with desire. And she knew that he held nothing so dear to his heart as the spirit of God in the form of a missionary. That he wanted his own stories to pour out to the people like wine. He wanted to glide into parlor after parlor across the country with sagas even the venerable, dedicated Wallace B. Cody would envy. And she was sure that her father would become a great missionary one day. Then the three of them could pack up their belongings and ramble the countryside all their lives, bringing breathtaking tales to warm parlors full of listeners. She could see her mother unrolling the map and pointing out some tiny country in North Africa, while she herself passed around menacing pictures of men with rings in their noses as women kissed her and wished their own daughters were as clever.

Later, when the guests fell upon the food and full mouths repeated the stories they'd heard, popping out bread and cookie crumbs as they spoke, only the Reverend Ralph C. McKinnon pushed the food away and refused to eat. Even as a child she had seen the empty pit inside him that no earthly food could satisfy. For years she had watched this hunger consume him, long after she became too old to pass the pictures around and had given up any hopes of finding a father hidden inside him.

Marge felt the weight of her body pressed back against the bed, as though it were being hurled through space. Drifting into reality and out, consciousness and blackness, the colors of the room came to her, although her eyes were closed. The room was spinning. The curtains that moved in the breeze were not curtains but crouching pygmies poised to throw their poison darts, and the din of crickets outside her window was the war chant of the heathens. She tried to move, to run from that exotic, frightening place, run back to the safety of her house in Mattagash, but the deadness of her swollen limbs nailed her to the bed as though it were a cross and outside the river beat against the rocks like blood coursing through the veins of Christ the Redeemer. She was trapped in her own body, trapped in a small dot on an aging map where no one in Mattagash would think to look for her. Not even the illustrious Reverend Ralph C. McKinnon, who gave his life to do God's work.

Her eyes opened softly and saw only what was in front of her; the flowered pattern on the curtains, small magnolia blossoms that grew into each other. A garbled voice came from the bedside, as twisted and tinny as the Reverend's old gramophone. It was a voice not of this earth and Marge strained to hear, pushed every muscle to turn her head sideways and see who or what owned it. But nothing moved. She had broken down. Fear settled around her like wet leaves in a deep black jungle as the magnolia petals became smooth bones sucked dry by cannibals.

The nurse stopped humming and put down her embroidery work. She had noticed perspiration on her patient's forehead and was afraid that with the cool evenings it would give the old woman a bad cold.

"I don't need you catching pneumonia on me," she said to Marge, who had already drifted back into the dimness of her memory as she carefully, lovingly collected the Reverend's bleached-out bones and clasped them to her bosom.

Funeral Preparations:
Discussions of Death
in the Living Room

"I remember once when I was little and we lived up over the funeral home—I still do, by the way—I went creeping down the stairs one night, and unlocked the door like I was told not to and snuck into the little chapel where the body is kept. It wasn't like I wanted to do disrespect to anyone. It's just I was told *not* to and you know how kids can be. Well, it was an old man and he was all ready for mourners. I have to say that. It wasn't like it was the embalming room and he was all discolored or anything. No, he was all ready to be seen. Like it was Christmas morning. I was scared, I guess. He was my first stiff. And embarrassed. Yes, embarrassed. Like I had no business seeing him. Because he looked so sad, I guess. Because he looked like he should be with some old woman on a porch rocking their lives away. I think that was it. Just that he looked so disgusted with it all. You get over that, though."

—MARVIN IVY, SR. (to a Disinterested Woman in the Hotel Bar), Funeral Directors' Convention, 1956

THE FAMILY GATHERED at Sicily's to begin the painful but necessary funeral preparations. Ed, and even Sicily, felt it was much too soon to delve into such final measures, but Pearl convinced Sicily it was the best thing to do. "You got to get on the wagon as soon as it's about to roll downhill," she said. "And from what the doctor says it sounds like Marge is already picking up speed." It *was* the Ivys' field of expertise, so Sicily invited them over that evening.

Unused to company, Sicily glowed as she hugged Pearl, took everyone's jacket, and served coffee and sandwiches. Thelma, still not convinced that her children were safe around Pearl, sent them briskly out into the backyard to play on Amy Joy's abandoned swing set and to disturb the dust in the empty playhouse that had been deserted when Amy Joy received the impending call to womanhood. Through the living room window, Thelma

59

could keep an eye on them and still partake in the family conference.

Ed and Marvin Sr. shook hands stiffly. As if their arms had no joints. As if they were tin soldiers. Marvin felt quite superior to Ed. After all, Ed was a man with a good deal of education, yet he was destined to exist within a principal's salary and answer to the whims of a semi-literate school board while Marvin, a college dropout, sat at the head of his own business. Ed, on the other hand, felt smug around Marvin, who was after all an undertaker.

Comfortable on sofas and chairs in the living room, the family began with the usual preliminaries.

"Mattagash has changed so much each time I come back," said Pearl, "that one day I won't know the town."

"Old Mrs. Buber finally moved to the Watertown Nursing Home," Sicily told her.

"How's the Packard on gas?" Ed asked Junior.

When Sicily inquired how the drive up from Portland had been, a deadly lull fell over the festal group. Sicily, thinking it was in deference to Marge's condition, said, "Oh, you're right. We really should get on with it. Poor Marge in there wheezing like an old wringer washer and us out here laughing."

The Ivys breathed easier and the preliminaries ended so that the sad details of funeral-making could billow into Mattagash's finest send-off.

"You Ivys are the undertakers. Where do we start?" asked Sicily.

"*Funeral directors*, Sicily. Marvin and Junior are *funeral directors*, not *undertakers*," Pearl said, reminded of one of the many reasons she could never readjust to living in Mattagash. City subtleties were lost on ruralists.

Marvin Sr. was truly on his own ground, for once, in the presence of Pearl's family and he happily opened the ceremony.

"It really helps to have a head start like this," he said. "Most people don't know one of their loved ones has died until the last minute, and by that time they're so shocked that they make all the wrong decisions. But don't you ladies worry yourselves at a time like this with the unpleasant details, such as the coffin and actual burial. Junior and I will handle all that in a jiffy. You just

decide on what she'll wear and the kind of church service you
want."

"I'd like to slap something on her besides black for a change,"
said Pearl. "Something nice and colorful."

"Pearl, I don't really think we should." Sicily spoke as though
Marge had a withered ear to the door, listening for the first signs
of subterfuge. Pearl, enjoying the position of matriarch now that
Marge was indisposed, continued her intimidation of the easily
intimidated Sicily.

"How would she know, anyway? Besides, what would the town
think? She's supposed to be going to Jesus, all decked out and
joyous. Do you want St. Peter to think she's a nun and send her
to hell?"

"Whatever you think is best, Pearl," Sicily said.

"Why don't you stick a sprig of parsley behind her ear?" Ed
had gotten a cold beer from the refrigerator and, as he opened
it, he stretched his legs out until his feet rested on Sicily's inflated
hassock that was clear plastic and had artificial flowers growing
out of fake grass. There had been an argument that morning with
Sicily about just that sort of thing.

"You don't need me there to listen to the death freaks from
Portland lick their lips and plan a funeral as though it was their
dinner. I never liked Marge McKinnon anyway," he had told
Sicily.

"Ed Lawler, I have asked you for few things in my lifetime. I
have demanded precious few minutes of your time. All I ask you
now is to be with me and the family as we make the arrangements
for Marge. And that means taking part and not sitting back with
a beer and your feet perched on my new flower-garden hassock."

"I can't promise you'll be happy with my being there," he had
warned.

"No, I suppose you can't," she had said. Now he was making
sure the victory had not gone to Sicily alone. He would come out
of it a partial winner. He would not acquiesce after these many
years of peaceful marriage. If he did, she would want more. One
night she would want to know just *what* meeting he was going
to and where. Then she'd want to go with him. "The best thing
to do is keep her angry about the wrong thing," he told himself.

Sicily, who was torn between grief and enjoying herself with the new company, looked pleadingly at him as she thrust a bowl of potato chips into his hands.

"OK," said Pearl, who had taken a pad of paper and pen from her purse. "She wears something colorful. Any nays?"

Instead of saying nay, Ed crunched a handful of chips.

Pearl gave Thelma the pad. Thelma, who took it as an act of foregiveness for the Packard incident, scrawled the first decision down quickly and waited for the next.

"I suppose the minister will have to be Elvis," said Sicily. Hearing this, Pearl laughed so hard that she accidentally snorted through her nose. But she was not unnerved by the faux pas. After all, she was in Mattagash, and not one of the better sitting rooms of Portland.

Sicily tried not to laugh, but could not contain herself. Even Ed laughed. And next to number two on Thelma's sheet was written: *Minister, Reverend Benny Macguire,* who was known for his rock-and-roll-like sermons and gyrating hips long before Elvis came bumping and grinding into existence.

Selecting the hymn to be sung caused a bit of disagreement between Sicily and Pearl. Pearl insisted that Thelma, having attended the prestigious Portland School of Voice for several months, was much more suited to sing the last farewell to Marge. Sicily begged to differ with her older sister, but pointed out that surely Amy Joy would be the better choice, having roomed with Marge the past few months.

"They were like two peas in a pod," she told Pearl.

"She should have eaten a few peas in a pod, instead of being one," Ed grumbled. "We wouldn't be doing this silly stuff if she had."

With Amy Joy not there to help further Sicily's cause by at least feigning an interest in singing the hymn, Sicily gave in. It was agreed that Thelma Parsons Ivy, although she had never met Marge, would indeed sing at her funeral. Talent and training would win out over companionship and sincerity. It was a true McKinnon maneuver. Next to number 3 on her list, Thelma briskly wrote: *Mrs. Thelma P. Ivy, Soloist.*

" 'Old Rugged Cross' would be a good one," said Pearl. Thelma, her confidence renewed by the earlier victory, spoke up. " 'My Sheep Know My Voice' is a wonderful solo hymn that would be very appropriate."

"Thelma, you're not Little Bo-Peep," said Pearl, thinking suddenly that Thelma's voice *did* have a bleating quality to it. "I think 'Old Rugged Cross' is right up Marge's alley."

"How about 'Fade Fade Each Earthly Joy'?" asked Sicily, who had been turning hymns over in her mind.

"She may never fade," said Ed.

"Ed, that's my dying sister you're making light of." Sicily went back to the index of hymns in her head. Thelma had taken out her *Songs of Praise* hymn book and was looking at the classified index in the back.

"Now here are some hymns for missionaries that would sure suit Aunt Marge. Here's one called 'To the Regions Beyond,' I know that one and it would be perfect."

"I don't know, Thelma." Sicily was beginning to wish the Ivys weren't so thorough in planning a funeral. "Marge wasn't a *real* missionary, you know. Some people in town might get their noses bent out of shape. They're always watching the McKinnons for a social mistake."

"How about 'Eternal Rest'?" asked Pearl.

"She's having her eternal rest without even dying," said Ed, who was clearly annoyed with the women's lack of organization. His school board meetings ran smoothly, as anything made up of all men will.

"Edward," Sicily said, without looking at him. "I'll ask you again to show some respect for the dying, especially when they're in our family."

"How about 'Look to the Lamb of God'?" Thelma asked. She had moved on from the Second Coming category, feeling they were inappropriate, and settled on Solos and Specials.

"Thelma, would you try to forget about sheep?" Pearl told her daughter-in-law. "This is a funeral, not a state fair."

"Yes, Mother Ivy," said Thelma, red-faced.

"Does that damn book have a funeral category?"

"I think so," said Thelma, suddenly rejuvenated. "Yes, it does. There's six hymns listed under funerals."

"Thank God," said Pearl, and took the battered hymn book.

"All right, now listen to me. I'm going to pick one of these at random and we're going to settle for it. Does anyone want to argue with that?" The room was silent. Pearl touched her index finger to the first title and proceeded down the list.

"Eenie, meenie, minie, moe. Catch a Catholic by the toe. If he hollers let him go. Eenie, meenie, minie, moe. OK now," she said, looking down at the winner, "it's gonna be 'The Last Mile of the Way.' I know you like that one, Sicily, and Thelma, if I remember correctly, there's something about sheep in it. It's settled. We got the hymn. Now let's get on to the next thing."

Marvin, who had been quiet, spoke up since it was clearly time for the male Ivys to show their professional worth.

"As I told you already, Junior and me will take care of the nasty little details of the burial. We'll go by and have a little chat with the local funeral director, just to let him know he's not dealing with amateurs."

"I can just imagine what embalming methods they've got up here in the sticks," Junior said haughtily, his mouth full of chocolate cake. "They probably use a chain saw and a shovel!" Junior had developed this habit even as a child, and it irritated not only strangers, but those people closest to him—he was the author of very tasteless jokes, as well as the only one who laughed at them, unaccompanied by even the more fickle audience. When Junior stopped laughing to select a second piece of cake, Marvin continued.

"In the meantime, while we're all gathered, it would be wise to decide on the memorial now."

"A memorial?" asked Ed. "What has the woman done to deserve a memorial? Memorials are for people who discover countries and penicillin and things like that."

Marvin smiled almost patronizingly, but held back in earlier memories of Ed's temper, especially when sparked by a few beers.

"Ed, you probably call memorials *headstones*, or maybe even *tombstones*."

"A tombstone? Well, that's different," said Ed. "For a minute there I thought you meant a memorial."

Marvin was beginning to sweat a bit. He removed his navy blue suit jacket. The underarms of his white shirt were dark with perspiration, like partial eclipses under his pits. Family after hysterical, mourning, hair-pulling, nail-biting family had come through his parlor doors and not one of them had gotten under his skin. Not even the stingier ones who had sometimes accused him of padding the bill and not the coffin. But Ed Lawler, equipped with a silly college degree, still had the power after all these years to make Marvin lose a bit of his professional sang-froid.

"We've been doing business with the Rockveil Monument Company for years and they've given us no reason to complain." Marvin pulled a booklet from his jacket pocket with a picture of the sphinx on the cover and large letters saying ROCKVEIL MEMORIALS. He passed it to Sicily, who was afraid to touch it.

"It won't bite you, Sicily, for crying out loud," said Pearl. Her family's reaction to Marvin's profession was still a sore spot to her. If she hadn't forgotten her own initial reactions to the Ivy Funeral Home, she might have shown Sicily a bit more empathy. But Pearl had made a habit out of remembering only the things she could use to her own advantage. To tell Sicily she had vomited when Marvin first took her into the casket showroom would be of no advantage to anyone but Sicily. So Pearl kept it buried in her subconscious, under the charred remnants of Marvin's discarded lawbooks, and the heap of other undesirables she had tossed in there to lay moldering and forgotten. She snatched the booklet from Sicily and, opening it to a certain page, turned it around for the rest of the family to see.

"This here is the *Gates Ajar* model. This would be perfect except it's a double monument, or for a family lot. Now this one here's the one we thought would be just right for Marge. It's the *Calvary* model." She turned the book again to the family's view. Thelma and Junior were in agreement with Pearl, while Sicily was still uncomfortable when faced with selecting something that was to actually go in a graveyard. It was clearly not as frivolous as choosing drapes and the notion unnerved her. She would have looked to Ed for support, but he had predicted that morning that the Ivys would drag along the tools of their trade and "peddle their wares," as he had phrased it.

"Now Rockveil will pay the freight charges and even offer an easy payment purchase plan if necessary." Marvin sounded like an insurance salesman. Pearl finished showing the monument to the family and began to read its vital statistics.

" 'Excellent taste is embodied in the selective design of this stately tablet, with the highly polished face and smooth sides. Thirty letters inscribed without additional cost, extra letters and numbers 75¢ each.' Now this is model 285, which weighs 400 pounds and it's only $121.50. Does anyone have another model in mind instead of the Calvary?"

When no one spoke, Pearl zeroed in on the person she had meant all along.

"Sicily, how does the Calvary model 285 suit you?"

"It's all right with me, Pearl," said a pale Sicily.

"It's always been *my* favorite model," said Ed.

"All right now," Pearl went on, "here is a little extra something that I, for one, think is really classy. A couple of Marvin's customers ordered it and one was a doctor. It's a porcelain picture of your loved one on the memorial of your choice. Listen to this: 'Like 17th-century enamel, the picture is heated at 1800 degrees in an electric furnace to ensure everlasting permanency.' "

"Maybe we should just put Marge in an electric furnace and crank it up to 1800 degrees," said Ed, who was on his fourth beer and becoming a bit more rebellious over his captivity.

"My God, Ed," said Sicily, who now wished he hadn't come to the meeting. "That's right on the verge of blasphemy!"

"All I meant was that we should maybe think about cremation," lied Ed.

"Cremation?!" screamed Sicily. "You mean burn Marge? Like she was a pile of dried-up leaves or a stack of old newspapers?"

"I'll go ahead and finish reading this," said Pearl. She had not looked Ed Lawler in the eyes for almost twenty years, and when they were in the same room she pretended he was not there. In a group, no one really noticed this. Especially Sicily. And Pearl did not want Sicily to know. But if Ed Lawler and Pearl McKinnon Ivy were left alone in a room, something Pearl never let happen, she would refuse to speak to him. And then the cat would be out of the bag. Pearl ignored his rudeness, which she felt was aimed at her heart like a poison dart. She knew very well that Ed was aware of how she felt. And hell could freeze over before she would let any barb he threw at her pierce her skin.

" 'Time will destroy valued paper photographs, but a Rockveil porcelain portrait will last forever.' "

"What will they think of next?" asked an incredulous Sicily, who forgot her anger at Ed, as well as her fear of death and the deathly, long enough for a glimpse of the model. It was of a gray-haired motherly woman with a beneficent smile and rosy lips and cheeks, as if even the grim reaper himself could not mar the lifeblood of the departed.

" 'An individual lifelike monument portrait is individual from all other monuments in the cemetery,' " Pearl read.

"Marge would love that," Ed said.

"That would sure stand out in Mattagash," added Sicily.

But Pearl was not done.

" 'Note. For each additional person on same photo add 50% to the price of the original photo.' "

"Additional person?" said Ed, looking for the first time at the model in the booklet. "What are you going to do? Put a picture of Dwight Eisenhower on there with her? Maybe Truman and Roosevelt too, and it'd be just like having Mount Rushmore right here in Mattagash."

Pearl read the fine print carefully, straining to catch each word.

" 'When ordering pictures in natural coloring be sure to state color of eyes, hair, and clothing. Your original photo will be returned.' "

"Marge's eyes are a deep shade of yellow right now." Ed was feeling the anger of years of having been associated with a family he didn't like, because of a marriage he'd been tricked into. And the feeling was like having a horrible umbilical cord twist tighter and tighter around his neck. He really didn't dislike Marge as much as his comments indicated. It was the whole family he was beating his words against. And he was especially hoping that Marvin might come to Marge's defense so that Ed could stick a pin in his sore spot. But Marvin knew better and remained as silent as his pride would allow.

"Maybe we could send her hair coloring in as dark brown, the way it used to be. Or at least the way she'll look in heaven," said Sicily, who had moved next to Pearl and was studying the woman in the picture. "You know who she looks like?" she said, tapping the page. "One of the clerks at Penney's in Watertown."

"OK, Thelma," said Pearl. "Write down *Calvary 285, porcelain picture.* Now does anyone have any idea about the epitaph?"

"How about 'So Long, Marge'?" asked the indestructible Ed.

Pearl thought of all the times she had lain awake at night and cried because of how her family viewed her husband's profession. And yet here was the college man they all fawned over. Mr. School

Principal. "Mr. Alcoholic with a big belly and red nose," she thought. She would tell Sicily later how rude she thought Ed was, would say it as a kind of retaliation for the way Sicily had treated Marvin, always afraid to shake his hand or touch his clothes. And at first she was always saying, "What's that awful smell in here?" every time Marvin came near her. But Pearl bit her tongue. It was best that Sicily found out Ed Lawler was a big failure all on her own. Pearl passed the Rockveil booklet to Thelma, who took it and turned to the list of epitaphs.

" 'Our Little Bird Of Love,' " she read.

"No, that's the epitaphs for kids. Read the grown-up ones." Pearl was irritated that Thelma appeared so scatterbrained in front of Sicily and Ed. While Thelma looked, Pearl took the opportunity to pile a few goodies on a paper plate, which was the only reason she relinquished the booklet in the first place. It was a good weapon to have, that booklet, and she hated to see it go. In her hands it was as good as having something shiny on the end of a string, like hypnotists do, because the whole family kept their eyes on her. Biting into a slice of mincemeat pie, she turned to Sicily and said, "This looks like you been busy in the kitchen."

" 'Death Loves A Shining Mark,' " read Thelma, with enough fervor and interpretation that it could have been the opening line of *Romeo and Juliet*.

"Sounds like a younger person," Sicily said as she passed Pearl another brownie. This part was more literary and she enjoyed it as much as if it were a recital.

" 'A Devoted Mother and Wife'?" Thelma waited for a response.

"Obviously not," said Pearl, mouth full of brownie, and motioned Thelma forward.

" 'Til Morning Breaks And Shadows Flee.' "

"I don't understand that one," Sicily said and Thelma took it as a sign to go on.

" 'The World Is A Better Place For Her Having Lived,' " Thelma soliloquized. There was a tremendous silence in the room. Not even Ed attacked that one and Thelma, finally taking the hint, moved on to the next.

" 'Asleep In Jesus'?" she asked.

"That's enough for me," said Ed, and with difficulty stood up. "I can't listen to any more of this. She's not asleep in Jesus, for

Christ's sake, she's asleep in her bedroom and I'm done planning a funeral for someone who is still alive." Taking a jacket from the rack behind the kitchen door and a beer from the refrigerator, he went out in the night.

Left behind, like a lamb to the wolves, Sicily finally spoke up. "A lot of pressure at school," she told the Ivys.

After a bit more discussion, the family voted unanimously for " 'Not Our Will, But Thine Be Done.' " And the meeting was over. Marvin got a ride back to the motel with Junior. Pearl wanted to visit Marge. She had stopped in briefly that morning, but now, with Sicily, would take the time to pay what last respects she had to her older sister. When she went to use the bathroom, Sicily glanced at the Rockveil Memorial booklet that was left lying face down on the coffee table. She picked it up and read the back cover. DON'T PLAY WITH FATE, it warned in heavy black letters that hung on the page like rain clouds. HAVE YOU NOTICED THAT THE THINGS WE THROW AWAY ARE THE THINGS WE NEED SOON AFTER, AND THE THINGS WE KEEP ARE NOT NEEDED FOR MANY YEARS TO COME? KEEP THIS CATALOGUE. SHOW IT TO YOUR FRIENDS.

Sicily was still looking at the warning issued by the Rockveil Monument Co. when Pearl finished in the bathroom and came down the hall toward her. Listening to her footfalls come closer, Sicily tried to visualize Pearl as she was years ago. The memory of her, suitcase packed and waiting for her ride to Watertown to catch the Greyhound to Portland, came to Sicily in a flash. The Reverend Ralph McKinnon was already in China saving souls the day Pearl left. Sicily, who had only been twelve years old at the time, was busy looking for her calico cat along the river. She had run past the front porch where Pearl waited for old man Gardner to take her in his pickup to Watertown for a dollar. That afternoon forced itself on Sicily's mind. She almost remembered that Pearl was crying. But all her mind could pull back about that ancient day was that Frisk the cat was missing somewhere in the wild roses along the shore and she was afraid he'd drown.

"I can still see you sitting on our front porch with that dollar in your hand the day you left, Pearl," she said. Pearl sat on the sofa beside her and patted her hand.

"I saved that money to get me to Portland and into school by picking berries and canning them and selling them to anyone who'd buy them. Remember how stained my fingers always were? I used to visit other girls in their rooms at school when we were up late talking and I'd keep my fingers curled in like a fist so no one would see how discolored they were."

"Frisk has been dead so long I hardly remember him," Sicily thought, then said, "I should have hugged you, Pearly, the day you left for Portland. *Someone* should have hugged you." The tears that had built up to a dangerous, thundering roar inside her loosed themselves as Pearl put her arm around her and held her tightly.

"Poor baby," she said. "Poor little Sissy. I was always afraid that never being held and never being loved would hurt you the most someday."

"Pearl, my life is such a mess. My family is in a shambles." Sicily tried to blow her nose on a Kleenex from her pocket, but after exhaling through her nose once the fragile pink tissue tore as easily as a flower's petal. Sicily gave up and sniffed instead.

"We'll have some coffee and you'll tell me all about it. There's been too many years of hitting back for me. And it never should've been you I struck back at anyway, Sissy." Sicily nodded, but knew she would never be able to open up more of her private life to Pearl. It just wasn't done that way.

When Pearl went out to the kitchen to make coffee, Sicily picked up the Rockveil Memorial booklet. DON'T PLAY WITH FATE, she read again. KEEP THIS CATALOGUE. Before Pearl returned to the living room, Sicily had already tucked the booklet safely under the cushion of the sofa.

Dressing as an Art Form:
Amy Joy as a Waddler

"On Lammas eve at night shall she be fourteen
'Tis since the earthquake now eleven years
for then she could stand alone, nay, by the rood
she could have run and waddled all about."
—Nurse (About Juliet), Act I, Scene III, *Romeo and Juliet*

In Her Bra and panties with the silk heart that said TUESDAY, Amy Joy twisted on her vanity chair. She studied each angle of her face, sucked in her pudgy cheeks to produce cheekbones, and cocked her head provocatively to one side. This, she decided, was indeed her best stance. Her Fuller Brush lipstick samples were in a colorful disarray before her and she studied them as though they were tasty candies. After profound, almost mystical deliberation, she settled upon Pink and Pouty and buried her lips beneath it.

Dressing was Amy Joy's favorite ritual. At fourteen, the adolescent's limbo, it was her only ritual and she threw herself into it with the same fervor as a dying nun about to encounter the beatific vision. Amy Joy worshiped dressing. Once Pink and Pouty had been established as the color of the day, it set the tone for the rest of the outfit. Out of the closet came a white cotton blouse with a large pink carnation sitting above a gold stem with two gold leaves. The slacks were her straight-legged cotton ones, a shocking pink. Her flip-flops were a mediocre pink compared to the rest of the uniform. Amy Joy had cleverly added a dash of white to accentuate the white of her blouse by attaching a tiny cloth daisy to the strap of each flip-flop.

Her hair, being thick and frizzy by nature rather than answering fashion's cry for smooth and curly, disappeared into the folds of the familiar French bun. The hairdo was further decorated with a cluster of tiny plastic daisies she had found at J.C. Penney's dime sale. They were glued to a bobby pin that was painted a bright gold. From months of training, the two pin curls on each

71

cheek fell quickly into place, as though they had sprouted out of skin and bone. A wave of perfume added the final panache, and she stood back to examine the whole. This was Amy Joy Mc-Kinnon's finest hour.

Opening the door to her bedroom a crack, Amy Joy peered out to see if the intruders in the living room were still making the funeral arrangements. Lumbering down the hallway as quietly as her plump thighs would allow her, considering the principle of friction, Amy Joy heard her mother's voice and Aunt Pearl's, but no others. Thankful that she would not have to slip past her father's barricade, which was virtually foolproof, Amy Joy made her way out the back door and disappeared on the path that led to the old American Legion Hall.

Why the subject of death seemed more appetizing to her parents than the love she felt for Chester Lee was not clear to her. Not that she didn't feel remorse about Marge's dying. She did. But the hours away from Chester Lee were like years, and each opportunity lost was gone for good. As Marge drew her last breaths, Amy Joy was immersed in loving for the first time, in being caressed and whispered to by a man who reeked of the wonders of the world.

There *had* been good moments. Evenings together on the porch, while Marge was still strong enough to shell the peas from Sicily's garden, the two watched those last evenings creep over Mattagash like a shadow, memorized every song the crickets knew, and if Marge fell asleep on the swing, it was Amy Joy's warm young touch that led her to her bed and sleep. If the promise of Marge's imminent death was lost on Amy Joy, it was because the fat promise of life had caught her up in its frenzy.

But there were times, in the stillness of night, devoid of her cacophony of colors, that she'd come awake, drenched in her little-girl flannel gown, and the first sound she listened for was the clock's ticking in the hallway, as though it were Marge's weary heart pumping its final blood on earth. And in the deep of night, when Chester Lee's man-smell was no longer with her, when the burn of his whiskers had healed on her face, and the blood to her excited nipples had receded, it was then that she listened for the steady ticking, and only when she heard it could she curl back into sleep, like an embryo feeling the sure thump of its mother's heartbeat.

Amy Joy Loves Chester Lee:
The American Legion as a
Hollywood Set

"I saw *The Birdman of Alcatraz* three times at the Watertown drive-in. And I got tears running down my face each time. You tell anyone I said that and I'll black both your eyes."
—CHESTER LEE (Exhaling Smoke) to Amy Joy (After the Act), 1959

IN THE FIELD above the Lawler house and nearly hidden in trees sat the defunct American Legion Hall, a large square building with white paint peeling from its boards. The door was fastened to the jamb by only the top hinge. There was a hole where the doorknob had been. Inside, the tables and chairs were still arranged for the Saturday nights of the past. Some empty liquor bottles sat on the shelves behind the bar. The small stage built to accommodate the musicians was piled high with boxes of odds and ends. A microphone stand grew out of the heap like a leafless tree. The windows had been broken, some still holding shards of glass. The guilty rocks were scattered about on the floor. A bartender's manual lay unopened on the bar. The floor, made of wide pine boards that had been varnished by the women's auxiliary, had begun to sag. A swallow's nest clung to one corner of the high-ceilinged room. Beneath it, a pile of dried droppings on the floor and a few feathers were the only reminders of the family that had been raised there.

Amy Joy put her fingers through the hole where the knob had been and opened the door carefully. The last hinge squeaked and threatened to let go. Inside, she let her eyes adjust to the light, then tested the floor in front of her with her right foot. When it convinced her it would carry her weight, she crossed between the tables and chairs to the bar. The only sound in the empty hall was that of her jaws as they thoroughly chomped and kneaded the pink glob of bubble gum she had bought from the traveling grocery truck that morning.

Nightfall was not far away and the room was dim.

"Chester Lee?" Amy Joy asked the empty room. There was the sound of an occasional car passing on the road outside. She had taken extra precaution in not being seen, as Chester had instructed her. She had come through the field behind the building and only when no cars were heard approaching did she run to the front and slip inside. Now, alone, the emptiness engulfed her. What if a crazy man wanted for murder had hitchhiked up from downstate and was watching her now from behind the boxes on the stage, running his finger up and down the sharp blade of a knife.

"Chester Lee, are you trying to scare me?" Amy Joy said this as loudly as she could without shouting, and tears filled her eyes. She had spent all afternoon in her room with her lipsticks and makeup laboring to achieve just the right effect. She had come to the Legion Hall of her own free will, against her parents' wishes, against the very Bible. She had done this because of the raging love she felt for a man, and to give that man her innocence. For the latter, at least, she had certainly expected him to be waiting there to scoop her up into his arms. The filmstrip she had been running all day in her mind of how the events would go was not what she was seeing now. The stab of loneliness, the sharp twinge in her stomach was, she felt sure, a sign of womanhood, of adult love.

The door squeaked as someone opened it and Amy Joy thought again of killers from downstate. Maybe even *out of state*, where mutilations and weird sex crimes were committed. Her hand flew to her mouth, but she was careful not to smear her lipstick. Only if death was imminent could Amy Joy be that careless with lipstick. She squatted down behind the bar, as much as her tight pants would allow her, and waited. Steps came toward the bar and stopped.

"Amy Joy?" It was Chester Lee.

"You scared me half to death, Chester Lee Gifford," Amy Joy said, her face blushed from the strenuous exercise of squatting. "And where were you? You said to be here at six o'clock and you'd be waiting for me."

"This is why," Chester said and held up a bottle full of a thick, dark liquid. He was very pleased with himself. Amy Joy soon forgot she was miffed.

"What is it?" she giggled and reached out to touch the bottle.

"Only about the best damn wine you can get this side of Bangor," Chester bragged.

"That ain't no wine bottle," said a suspicious Amy Joy. "That there's a mason jar."

"Amy Joy, how old are you? Any fool knows that wine don't *have* to come in a bottle. This is some of Old Ned's blackberry wine and it's laced with a little bit of whiskey."

"That could kill us," said Amy Joy.

"Amy Joy, Old Ned has sold this stuff to people as far away as Bangor. People who know a lot more about wine than me or you. And there's a hunter from Portland who heads straight for Old Ned's every blessed time he comes up for hunting season. Says he couldn't hit an elephant at two feet without it."

"It stinks."

"Do you wanna sound fourteen all your life? That just means that it's aged. Don't you know wine has to get old and smelly to be good? Now come downstairs and stop being so damn spoiled."

Amy Joy followed him down the narrow stairs to the basement. Chester lit one wooden match off another until he found the kerosene lamp. The contents of one corner of the building came into focus. A twin bed with a thin mattress was carefully made up. A woolen coat had been folded to make a pillow. A huge poster of a Harley-Davidson was tacked to the wall above the bed. A potato barrel turned upside down made a table that held a black comb with several teeth missing and the rearview mirror of a car. Along the wall were cans of soup and vegetables and several bottles of homemade moxie. On an apple crate next to the bed, Chester had placed a Pepsi bottle full of goldenrod. The dim light of the lamp hid the dust balls and mice droppings in the corners where Chester had swept them that morning.

"God, it's beautiful," breathed Amy Joy.

"I figured you'd like it." Chester pulled two Dixie cups out of the sack he had carried the wine in and filled them up. Amy Joy's first sip went down with difficulty. She was not used to drinking any liquor, and Old Ned's homemade concoction was a challenge for even hardened guzzlers.

"You might've brung tin cups instead. The wine might eat up these paper ones," said Amy Joy, who had noticed a slight fizzing in her cup.

"Will you just drink it and shut up?"

They lay back on the cot, Chester's head on the pillow-coat, Amy Joy's head on Chester's arm.

"I sure miss the old Saturday nights upstairs, when the Legion was going full blast."

"Tell me what them days was like." Amy Joy looked up at Chester in adoration of the grown man that he was. She watched the ends of his mustache twitch in the lamplight like the tiny arms of a conductor, getting the best out of his words. She was very taken with the mustache.

"There'll never be anything like 'em again. Not in our time," Chester said and poured himself more wine. Amy Joy snuggled closer.

"People would start getting here about seven or eight. Hardly anybody wore their work clothes. The women usually had gone to Watertown and got their hair done up at that hair place. Had it all curled and sprayed. And if there'd been any good sales that day, them that could afford it had on new clothes. Bonnie played here then with his band. Now he's working in Connecticut in a factory that makes a little part to go on airplanes."

"There's a lot of Mattagash people working in Connecticut," said Amy Joy, and sipped on her wine. "Daddy says it's 'cause the lumbering business is so slack." Chester Lee didn't want to discuss the economy.

"Bonnie played the guitar, and his baby brother, Alton, played the drums. He had a guy named Boss Robbins singing and playing bass. Lord, that man sounded just like Ernest Tubb. If you shut your eyes when he sang 'Walking the Floor,' the hair would raise up on your neck, that's how much he sounded like Ernest Tubb. They say he got the music somewhere back on his Momma's side. Boss Robbins was from over by Caribou. He's probably gonna be a big star someday if he ain't already."

"I don't think I ever heard him on the radio," said Amy Joy. Chester's fingers went quickly to the buttons on Amy Joy's blouse and undid them.

"You could get a shot for twenty cents in them days. The war was over. Folks had their spirits up. I was fifteen when the war ended and real disappointed I wasn't old enough to have killed a German or two. Maybe drove one of them big tanks."

A mouse scurried across the top floor and Amy Joy shuddered. Chester held her tighter.

"You'd have loved it, Amy Joy. The dancing and joking. And every Saturday night there was a fight or two. You could bet on it. The Swedes from New Sweden would drive up and stand around the bar looking at our women, who were all dumb enough to look back. They thought potato farmers like the Swedes was more civilized than lumberjacks. They was all big men, too, and real towheaded. We used to call 'em buttercup heads and a fight was bound to start. The girls would scream and run for cover. I'll never forget the night one of the Swedes told Willie O'Brian to take the door. Willie just said, 'OK,' walked over to the door, took it off its hinges, put it in his car, and beat it for home. Jesus, we laughed over that. The Legion commander made him bring it back the next day. You don't remember Willie O'Brian. He was poling his canoe upriver not long after that to do some fishing and the lightning hit him."

There was a silence between them in memory of Willie O'Brian. Then Chester told Amy Joy about Willie's wife, Margaret. The whole town knew how Willie beat her severely during his drunken brawls. A month after his death, she hanged herself at the age of twenty-nine.

"Used to a beating and no one to give it to her," Chester said to Amy Joy. "At least that's what Margaret's mother said at her funeral." Chester had the enthralled Amy Joy out of her blouse and was fumbling with the buttons on her pants.

"On special occasions, the women's auxiliary would put up real pretty decorations. And have box lunches. And door prizes. It was just like the movies in them days, Amy Joy. Now look at it up there. All going to hell and to the mice and swallows. And a man's got to drive thirty miles to Watertown to sit on a barstool and drink."

"I wish I'd have been growed up then," said Amy Joy, a bit maudlin with the wine. "It must've been just like *Gone with the Wind.*"

"It was a lot like that, all right," said Chester.

"Chester Lee, I'm scared. Are you sure we're doing the right thing?"

"Honey Bun, of course I'm sure. This is as right as it was between Adam and Eve."

"But they got throwed out of the Garden of Eden."

"Amy Joy, Mattagash, Maine, is a long, long way from the

Garden of Eden. I could tell you things about Mattagash that'd make your hair turn gray. Believe me, this is the best place in the world to get throwed out of."

"I guess," said Amy Joy, and let Chester take the Dixie cup from her hand. He put it next to his on the apple crate.

"There's just one thing, Amy Joy. I never ever want to have to go up against your daddy about this. It ain't that I'm afraid of him. It's just that never having been to school much myself, I got a lot of respect for a principal. So don't you dare tell a soul. This'll be our little secret."

"I won't tell anybody, Chester. Especially Daddy. He's just about the meanest, fattest man that ever drew a breath."

Chester kissed Amy Joy's neck and ran his hand along her chubby thigh.

"Why did you fall for me?" he asked, still struggling with the complicated network of buttons on Amy Joy's pants.

"I don't know. I guess it's because you look so much like Eddie Fisher," Amy Joy said and deposited her gum on the headboard of the bed. She had to assist Chester Lee as he peeled the tight pants from her hips, knocking off the flip-flops as they came completely off.

"Eddie Fisher? Really? Because of my hair or my face?"

"Both, I guess."

"Eddie Fisher don't have no mustache."

"You're still the spittin' image of him."

"No kiddin'?" said Chester. As he eased himself onto his plump devotee, Amy Joy closed her eyes tightly, feeling a stronger kinship to Debbie Reynolds than she had ever felt before.

Ships That Clash in the Night:
Ducks and Drakes in the Dark

"If Isadora Duncan was living in Mattagash today she'd be up against this same shit."

—VIOLET LA FORGE, Painting Her Toenails, 1959

VIOLET LA FORGE opened the door of her room a crack when she heard the familiar rapping. It was hard for her eyes to adjust to the silhouette outside because she always kept the room in darkness on nights when she expected Ed. That way the Pinkhams would not see who was coming or going from Room 3. Seeing it was indeed Ed, Violet quickly pirouetted and dropped to one knee, extending an arm out in welcome. She had practiced this all evening, in the event that Ed managed to get away.

"I didn't think you were coming tonight," she said after she had planted a small wet kiss on his lips.

Ed gathered her up as close to him as he could, allowing for the immensity of his stomach, and held her without speaking.

"Come," said Violet taking his hand, "come sit here on the bed and let Violet give you a nice back rub. She's got you all upset again and your muscles are crying for love."

"They've *all* got me upset," said Ed. "The whole damn family. Sicily's oldest sister is in a coma and the other one is up from Portland with her family of skulls and crossbones. They're all in comas too, but they're still walking around. They're staying here in the motel."

"My God, that must be them right next door. That must be her I talked to last night."

"You'd know if it was Pearl. She isn't easy to meet and forget."

"This woman was real pushy."

"That's her."

Ed took his shoes off and sighed heavily.

"Eddie, if you don't transform that negative energy that they create inside you into positive energy, you'll only meet them again

79

in your next life and the cycle will start all over again." Violet was rubbing like a sculptress.

"Yeah, well remind me to take a shotgun with me when I leave this life," said Ed. "That way I'll be ready for them."

"Oh, Edward, you don't mean that." Violet was always thrilled to hear Sicily or her family get trampled into the ground beneath Ed's feet. It was not easy for an artiste to double as a mistress.

"I'll have to be careful when I leave," Ed told her.

"You will be. I'll see to it. I'll put you inside my purse and carry you out."

"I can't stay long."

"That's nothing new. You never can."

"Oh, Violet, for Christ's sake. *You're* not going to start, are you? Don't tell me I've jumped out of the frying pan into the fire." Ed flopped onto the bed and flipped a cigarette out of his pack. Before he could light it, Violet, biting her lip, took the book of matches from him and struck one up. In the orange glow she saw the sad lines around his eyes and on his forehead that seemed deeper than the last time she had noticed them there. Suddenly the rage of the woman scorned lifted from her, and she bent to circle his temples lightly with her fingers.

"Last night I left the house to come here and suddenly I couldn't. Do you know what I did, Violet?"

Not caring that she shook her head in the darkness, Ed went on.

"I went down to the river and skipped rock after rock across the water. I couldn't even see if they were skipping or not. I just threw them like we did as kids in the millpond behind our house."

"In Massachusetts?" Violet leaned over and lit a candle protruding from a wine bottle that was a colorful mountain of dribbled wax.

"In Massachusetts," said Ed. "If anyone had told me back then, when I was a kid, that I'd end up going to the ends of the earth to live, end up living with a woman I pity but don't love, with a daughter who can't stand to look me in the eye, I'd have jumped into that pond and so help me, if I had to hang on to rocks on the bottom, I wouldn't have come back up for anything."

"You poor baby," Violet said as she kissed the tip of his nose. "You're feeling so lonely tonight."

"I'm always lonely, Violet. Don't you know that? Doesn't anyone in this goddamned town ever see inside people?"

Violet reached into the sack Ed had brought under his arm. It said BLANCHE'S MARKET and held two six-packs of cold beer.

"Violet, look at my hands," he said and held one out to her. "Look at the skin. What do you see?"

Violet brought the candle in for a close inspection, then, kissing the hand in question, said, "I see a very long life line."

"Shit. You don't understand." Ed drank the first bottle out of the sack and reached for a second. The earlier beer he had consumed, as well as several shots of bourbon from the bottle hidden in his study, was beginning to take its toll.

"What don't I understand?"

"That I didn't come to you for any answers. When *I* look at this hand I see crepe paper. Now I don't really care what *you* see. *I* see crepe paper. And my whole damn life is crepe paper. Hell, you can sit back in a town like this and just about plan your life. Lay it all out like a big ugly blueprint. A vacation every year if you can afford it. A kid here. Then a grandkid there. The mortgage paid and then you wait to die. That's where that word comes from. Mortgage. From death. Then there's the waiting and rocking on the front porch, like dogs watching cars go by until the kidneys go, or the heart, or bladder, or one morning you just don't get up because you're sick of looking into the mirror at age spots and sunken cheeks. You get tired of taking your teeth out of the goddamn glass by the bedside. And then there's the funeral. Do you know what the best excitement is around here? It's when someone dies who isn't supposed to. Dies before his time. When that ambulance goes by, shit, women would throw their babies to the wolves just to find out who it's come for. It seems to brighten their day, unless it's one of their own. It keeps them feeling alive. It keeps them happy that it isn't them who's taking that ride to the cemetery in the back of some hearse."

"Ed, I don't know what to make of all this," Violet said honestly, afraid to say the wrong thing.

"And Sicily," Ed went on as though Violet hadn't spoken, as though she weren't in the room with him, "you can't blame the poor woman. I've heard that that old son-of-a-bitch Reverend was the hardest, coldest bastard that ever walked when it came to his own children. I feel sorry for Sicily, yet what would she do if I left her? Take night classes, learn accounting or real estate? Maybe join those stupid groups that women form like a pack of geese, and all they talk about is how to spend the alimony their husbands pay through the nose while they tell each other they're independent. They don't need anyone. They did it all on their own. But if that alimony check doesn't come in the mail, shit hits the fan. They got a group going in Watertown now called Women for Better Prisons. Can you believe that? Most of them don't know where their kids are or if they've eaten that day, and they're out trying to help murderers and robbers while their kids are left alone at home learning how to become just that. Do you know why? They're all afraid of sex. Men behind bars don't scare them like free men can. They talk, talk, talk about issues and everything you can imagine just to keep their little minds off sex and the fact that they hate it. That they're afraid of it. Christ, I get sick just thinking of the pack of them."

"Edward Lawler, are you going to spoil our evening together? We don't have that many, you know, hon, and I had something special planned." As Violet spoke she pulled several flimsy scarves of various colors from her dresser drawer and began to lay them on the bed. "In the three weeks we've been seeing each other, I've never danced for you in person. So, because you're so special to me, I'm gonna give you a command performance."

Ed lay a few minutes looking at the candle's tongue flicking, as though trying to catch flies for food, manna from heaven that had fallen through the very roof of Violet La Forge's room in the Albert Pinkham Family Motel. He wished he was smoking a cigarette but didn't want to expend the energy it took to light one up.

"Well?" asked Violet.

"Sure." He decided the cigarette was worth the bother after all. And there was beer. It could be worse than this. Much worse. He could be ensconced in the middle of his own living room, inhaling the horrible breath of the Ivys that filled the air like embalming fluid. Still on his back, Ed looked over the mountain of his stomach at Violet, who was busy entwining the scarves around her body in what seemed to be an ordered sequence, at least in the ballroom of Violet's mind. He thought how the candlelight was kind to Violet, how the soft flickers washed away the lines not even a thick layer of makeup could cover. "This is my own dance. I put it all together myself. It's about Isadora Duncan's life. Each movement comes from individual feelings, just like she said it should. It's in three parts."

Ed slid up on the bed and into a sitting position. It was hard for him to concentrate on Violet's words. The pain inside him was worse, probably brought on by the entire army of Sicily's family. Sometimes he thought of the pain as a kind of tumor that grew and sprawled inside his gut, pushing his stomach out so that it hung like bread dough over his belt. It was not beer nor food that had created the monstrosity of his body. It was pain.

"The first part is about her life in France and first performance in the United States."

Inside his body of fat was a college athlete who had worked hard to see his muscles strong and his body toned. For years he swore he would one day go on an all-out plan to lose the weight, would take up some sport again. Maybe basketball. Maybe just a hobby that called for a lot of physical workout. Probably coach a team of kids in football. No one played football in Mattagash. No one played basketball. There was no gymnasium. No one did anything but work hard long hours in the woods and drink hard and long on Saturday nights.

"The second part represents the anguish she felt when her two sweet little children were killed in a car wreck."

There were times, getting out of a chair or a bed, that the slender young man inside could barely lift the heavy body. Then the heart pumped more than it should. The lungs hurt from nicotine. The liver swelled with alcohol. And the truth about himself settled down like lead with such a thud that he hurried to the whiskey bottle in his study, and only with two straight shots tossed quickly down his throat could he quell the demons of regret and free his hands from shaking. It was then that the calm settled in, and the warmth in his stomach allowed him to turn to old yearbook pictures and look down at the confident face of the young Ed Lawler, study the muscled body lines, and think about dusting off his old football the next day and rallying the boys into a game.

"The third part is very sad and is done with this long black scarf. I call it the 'Scarf of Death' and it's about how her scarf got caught in that car and choked her."

Violet launched into her dance, hands and arms flailing like

cobras, scarves aflutter, and when it was over, Ed was only relieved. The first part was almost indiscernible from the last. Only
to Violet was there symbolism and interpretation.

"It was lovely," he told her and she gushed, looking girlish in
the candlelight, gyrating her hips for him as she said, "Thanks."
The dance had stripped her of all the scarves, as though she really
hadn't stripped but simply followed the dance routine. It made
her less ridiculous to him. She was naked before him and he
looked at her. Her body was holding up well. The exercise it got,
in spite of the quality of the dancing, was enough to keep the
lines well defined. She sipped only an occasional glass of wine,
ate only fruit and vegetables. At forty-six she looked years younger.
And that's what brought him to her. She had served her body,
not abused it. That was the power she unknowingly wielded as
she did her countless sit-ups and stretching exercises. And when
he came to lay his head against her bosom, he ignored the fact
that modern dancer or not, she was a stripper in Watertown.
Because after the ridiculous scarves had been cast aside the first
night he watched her dance, he had seen the body beneath and
the respect she paid it, even if it was out of fear of aging, or fear
of being too old to make a living. And he came to her on nights
when his own terror became too great and it seemed his angry
heart was refusing the heavy workload. He came to her and held
onto her firm thighs, pressed his heavy belly against her solid
one, thinking he was safe. Certain she could save him.

Violet came to sit on the edge of the bed near him, fanning the
cigarette smoke away from her face.

"You hate breathing smoke into your lungs, don't you?" he
asked her.

"It's worth it if it's your smoke."

"I should quit."

"You would if you were happy, and what you need to make
you happy is the perfect woman for you."

"I don't think there is one for me," Ed said as he stubbed out
his cigarette. "Not unless it's Aphrodite rising up from her clamshell."

"Aphrodite? She danced at the Purple Tortoise just before I did
down in Boston."

"I don't think it's the same one, Violet."

"Well, that's funny because when I was dancing that circuit I ran into this weird dancer who had an act just like that. Had this record player with her that played only sounds of ocean and waves. I would have sworn that she called herself Aphrodite. She had this big old clamshell made out of plaster of paris and one night she goes to step out of it, all covered in green stringy stuff to look like seaweed, and the whole side of that big ugly thing broke and crumbled."

"Aphrodite broke her clamshell?"

"She cut her foot real bad and tried to sue Dewey. He owned the Purple Tortoise. Dewey said she had a reputation for causing trouble. How did you ever meet her?"

"Trust me, Violet, it's not the same girl."

Ed rolled his modern dancer over on her back and pushed between her thighs. Beads of sweat popped out on his forehead. With the excess weight he carried, everything was becoming a chore, even making love to Violet. He was always afraid that he might be too heavy for her, that he might relax the weight he balanced over her and come crashing down like a house. Touching the firmness of her legs, he felt a sorrowful wave come washing up inside him and before he could stop it, it burst out and the tears he hadn't shed since childhood threatened to drown him.

A shocked Violet clasped his head to her chest and held him, rocking him, saying, "There, there," and wiping tears that ran into the lines of his face away, until he fell asleep feeling the warmth of her body flowing into his, rejuvenating him.

Only Violet was awake to hear Marvin Sr. unlock the door to number 4. She listened two hours later as Pearl came in and heard their soft voices through the wall as they said goodnight. With Ed's large body asleep in her arms, she watched the candle burn slowly down until it flickered and went out, saw traces of dawn come to the window, and wanting to hold the man she loved in her bed forever, she lay as still as she could, not even moving to cover herself with a warm blanket when cold crept up her arms. But regardless of how still Violet lay, an instinct born from years of marriage, of being bound to the clock, stirred inside Sicily's sleeping husband, and he came wide awake, saying, "Christ Almighty, it's daylight!" and reached for his shoes.

Sicily Suffers the Slings and Arrows: Pains in the Rib Cage

"And the Lord God caused a deep sleep to fall upon Adam, and he slept; and he took one of his ribs, and closed up the flesh instead thereof; And the rib which the Lord God had taken from man, made he a woman, and brought her unto the man."

—Genesis 2:21–22

ALL NIGHT SHE lay in bed and listened to the crickets, listened to each car that passed on the dark road outside, longing to hear one turn into the yard, to hear Ed slam the door, and then his footsteps downstairs. But each car went on its way, lost in red taillights around the turn. Looking out at the moon, Sicily noticed streaks on the window and scolded herself for not having them spotless while the Ivys were in town. The next day, she promised herself, she would wash them until they shone. The moon floated higher over Mattagash like a slow-moving balloon broken from its string. The river was quieter than usual, being low for September. A good rain would make it sing again. Frogs were awake in the marsh across the field and Sicily listened to their conversations.

"I suppose they got family problems, too. Just like us," she thought. The house was so silent that she was almost certain she could hear her heart pumping sadly in her chest. She looked at the clock on the nightstand. Ed had never before stayed out until two-thirty. Had something happened to him? He could have gone off the road somewhere between Mattagash and Watertown and no one would find him until morning. There were places along the road where there were no guard rails to protect anyone from dangerous banks that dropped down to the river. The state should really do something about it. Two young boys from Watertown had driven off the bank by Labbe's potato house and into the river. No one found them until the next day when their frantic families went looking for them.

86

They had taken their girlfriends home from the drive-in movie. So the sheriff started at the girls' homes in St. Ignace and drove slowly back toward Watertown. That's when the policeman riding with the sheriff spotted a flash of red in the bushes along the river. It was at that terrible turn in the road that had no guard rails and a fifty-foot drop. It was something red he saw, and it was the car. The two boys were inside. One had died instantly, the driver hours later. He'd been pinned behind the wheel and couldn't move. Sicily thought of his poor mother, living with the knowledge of her son being only a few miles away and trapped, waiting for someone to find him, or waiting for death, whichever came first. They said that boy's mother woke up at exactly the same time the coroner said he died and she woke her husband and said, "I dreamed of raspberries. Bright red raspberries by the river. We need to go pick them." And then she turned over and went back to sleep. Two teenage boys taking their dates home. Dead. The state should've put up guard rails after that. It was three o'clock and Sicily's eyes were beginning to feel the lack of sleep. She rubbed them, thinking, "I've got to stay awake." She crawled out of bed and reached for the extra blanket that lay at the foot. The autumn chill moved to her arms and she felt goose-bumps spring up.

"Someone's thinking of me," she said. Wrapped in the blanket, she pulled her little wicker chair up to the windowsill and looked out again at the night and the narrow road that curved past the Lawler house. At four o'clock she was still waiting, still listening to the night sounds, still hoping one car would shift gears and make the turn into her driveway. But none did.

When the Reverend Ralph C. McKinnon took two suits of clothing and a box of Bibles and went off to save the lost souls of China, she had just turned nine years old. She used to think of China as the place where her mother was waiting for her. Once a little girl at school, trying to wrest a doll from Sicily's hands, had lost. So she pointed a small finger at Sicily and shouted, "You killed your mama." Later, she had asked Marge what that meant and Marge, only in her twenties but with the burden of a family, had run into her bedroom and wept for hours. It was after supper that same evening when Marge told Sicily that their mother never recovered from giving her birth and had gone to God when Sicily was only three weeks old. But the Reverend had talked so of

China all those years before he finally packed up and went, that China loomed in her child's mind as a magical place, a place God had moved to in masses, in the forms of sacrificing missionaries. "God is working in China these days," the Reverend would tell his flock. "God is alive in the rice paddies of China. Our Savior is moving among the heathens of China's vast lands." It was obvious to Sicily as a child that God was indeed in China. And that meant her mother was in China, too, since everyone, even the Reverend Ralph, had said that she was with God.

After Reverend Ralph gave his three girls a stiff, uncomfortable hug and climbed into the carriage, he never turned once to look back. Marge had taken her old Brownie camera out and snapped a picture of the carriage as it pulled out of the drive and onto the main road. They stood on the front porch and watched him go, the horse's hoofbeats getting fainter, the Reverend's black hat becoming smaller and smaller until it was the size of a period at the end of a bumpy sentence. Only Sicily waved, waved the entire time, her small arm aching, so sure she was that he'd turn in the carriage and wave one last goodbye. But the small period finally disappeared around the turn and the last picture his daughters took of Reverend Ralph was of his back.

For three years Sicily had watched down the road, expecting him at any moment. She refused to believe the few letters he sent home saying his life was in China and that he would never see his homeland again. There was no love in his letters. Each began with "Dear Daughters" and ended with "Hoping God Keeps You Safe In His Bosom." Sicily often wondered if he'd forgotten their names. Each Sunday Marge gathered them together in the parlor and they wrote him letters. Sicily mentioned each of their names as often as she could, to help him remember. But his letters never referred to his daughters individually. And every day she would find herself staring down the bleak road, expecting to see the Reverend round the bend driving six white horses, her mother sitting like Lazarus beside him, finally rescued from faraway China and brought home to the living and into her daughters' empty arms.

At three-thirty Sicily thought of phoning the sheriff. All that stopped her was the thought of the gossip that would spread across Mattagash if Ed's car was discovered behind the Watertown Hotel or some other motel, and if he himself was found, not dead in the river, but in some woman's arms, very much alive. Sicily didn't allow herself to think about the other women, although she was certain they existed. Ed had not touched her in years, which relieved her. But she was sure he would take his actions far enough away from Mattagash that she and Amy Joy would be safe from the tongues. Ed would look out for his family. He was a decent man in that respect. She was certain of it. At four-fifteen, she was no longer certain of anything. Downstairs in the kitchen she made coffee and tried to work on a crossword puzzle from the *Bangor Daily Times*. She gave up on the second clue and read the front page instead. But the black words ran into each other. The obituary page held no entertainment for her. She was too frightened to look at the names, afraid one might be Edward Lawler, as if the world, or God, were playing a nasty joke on her, having taken Ed away without telling her. "The wife is always the last to know," she remembered Lucy Matlock saying about a woman in Mattagash whose husband had been sneaking into the new schoolteacher's house after dark.

At five o'clock she stretched out on the sofa in the living room, her sweater spread over her arms, and lay there waiting. Her physical body was giving out, her eyes hurt, a small sharp pain had begun at the base of her neck. She fought off sleep as long as she could, but finally the eyelids dropped like shades and images old and new bumped together and took their places in the subconscious. There was a bright red car shining from the bushes along the river and she walked forever, then ran as hard as she could to get to it, but it kept moving from her. When she finally grasped the door handle in her hand and opened the door, expecting to see the crushed bodies of two young boys, she found instead the Reverend Ralph behind the wheel and Ed in the passenger seat, both alive, both laughing.

"We're driving to China," Ed told her and her hand let go as the car drove out onto the water, as weightless as Jesus, and floated down the river until it was out of sight.

She was left behind shouting, "Come back! Come back!"

When Ed turned the doorknob softly and put one foot inside the house, Sicily heard it in her sleep and dreamed it was the Reverend Ralph come home with her mother. She sat up on the sofa, the warm autumn sun already established throughout the house. She sat up and said, "Mama?"

Survival of the Fittest:
The Ivy Genes Get Tested

"I figured that marriage wouldn't last when the little man and woman on the top of their wedding cake got into a fight."

—MARGE McKINNON, About Newlyweds, 1955

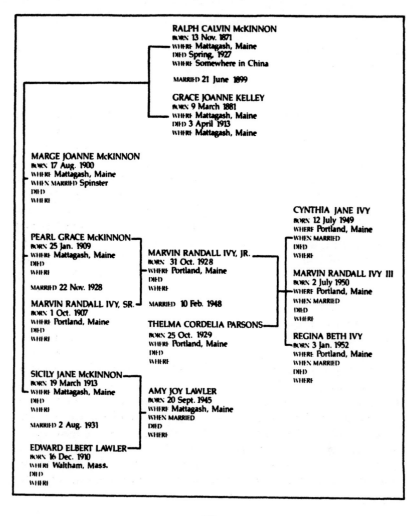

RALPH CALVIN McKINNON
BORN 13 Nov. 1871
WHERE Mattagash, Maine
DIED Spring, 1927
WHERE Somewhere in China

MARRIED 21 June 1899

GRACE JOANNE KELLEY
BORN 9 March 1881
WHERE Mattagash, Maine
DIED 3 April 1913
WHERE Mattagash, Maine

MARGE JOANNE McKINNON
BORN 17 Aug. 1900
WHERE Mattagash, Maine
WHEN MARRIED Spinster
DIED
WHERE

PEARL GRACE McKINNON
BORN 25 Jan. 1909
WHERE Mattagash, Maine
DIED
WHERE

MARRIED 22 Nov. 1928

MARVIN RANDALL IVY, SR.
BORN 1 Oct. 1907
WHERE Portland, Maine
DIED
WHERE

SICILY JANE McKINNON
BORN 19 March 1913
WHERE Mattagash, Maine
DIED
WHERE

MARRIED 2 Aug. 1931

EDWARD ELBERT LAWLER
BORN 16 Dec. 1910
WHERE Waltham, Mass.
DIED
WHERE

MARVIN RANDALL IVY, JR.
BORN 31 Oct. 1928
WHERE Portland, Maine
DIED
WHERE

MARRIED 10 Feb. 1948

THELMA CORDELIA PARSONS
BORN 25 Oct. 1929
WHERE Portland, Maine
DIED
WHERE

AMY JOY LAWLER
BORN 20 Sept. 1945
WHERE Mattagash, Maine
WHEN MARRIED
DIED
WHERE

CYNTHIA JANE IVY
BORN 12 July 1949
WHERE Portland, Maine
WHEN MARRIED
DIED
WHERE

MARVIN RANDALL IVY III
BORN 2 July 1950
WHERE Portland, Maine
WHEN MARRIED
DIED
WHERE

REGINA BETH IVY
BORN 3 Jan. 1952
WHERE Portland, Maine
WHEN MARRIED
DIED
WHERE

90

FROM HIS PERCH atop the steep, tree-lined ridge that followed the river, Marvin Randall "Randy" Ivy III lay flat on his stomach and peered down on his sister Cynthia, who was comfortably sprawled on a blanket beside the camper. In her hands she held her doll Ginger, whose hair had just been brushed vigorously one hundred times and who was being changed from pajamas to swimsuit to evening gown by a dissatisfied Cynthia. Thankfully, Ginger's body was plastic; the excessive wardrobe changes would have worn skin to the bone. But Cynthia was a fussy mother, already having inherited the role from Thelma, who in turn had come from a long line of nitpickers. Randy sucked in his breath and, silent as a snake, slid along on his belly until he was directly behind his unsuspecting sister. Still concealed by the bushes along the shore, he lay in wait, patient as a General safely positioned at head-quarters.

"If you don't learn to hang up your clothes, young lady, you just won't get any new ones." Cynthia was warning the indifferent Ginger, whose stiff legs, movable at the crotch, were being made to walk across the blanket to an imaginary bedroom.

"Now you just stay there in your room, without any supper, until you've learned a lesson." Cynthia shook a younger version of Thelma's bony finger at the doll, who stared, unblinking, up into the blue sky that covered Mattagash. Cynthia jumped to her feet and went off into the camper to search for the miniature makeup kit that Ginger would need when the punishment had ended.

Seeing the path cleared for an attack, Randy stuck an arm above his head and with one finger straight out fired several shots.

"Bang! Bang! Bang!" he shouted and swooped down on the vulnerable Ginger. Scooping her up by her well-brushed hair, he swung her around above his head as though she were a lasso. The startled Cynthia stepped down from the camper with Ginger's makeup kit just in time to see the body of her favorite doll-child flung far out into the Mattagash River. Her cries of agony paralleled those of her mother just two days before when Thelma thought her babies were on fire. Cynthia jumped up and down several times, braids flapping from the sides of her head like wings, and her tears seemed endless. Thelma rushed from the camper and Junior, who had been napping in the tent, crawled out rubbing his eyes.

"What in hell was that?" he asked Thelma.

"Sissy! Sissy!" Thelma shook her oldest child. "Tell Mama what it is! Did you see something?"

Cynthia, who was unable in her agony to speak, simply nodded, mouth wide open, face twisted with grief. She pointed to the river.

"You saw something in the river?" asked her father, who suddenly noticed Randy for the first time at the end of the camper, where he stood kicking ground with his new PF Fliers.

"What did she see, Randy?" he asked.

"I dunno. A sea monster, I suppose." The PF Fliers went back to work.

"A sea monster? Are you crazy? Listen, baby," Junior said, trying to take the girl into his arms.

"It must've been a log. There's no such thing as a sea monster."

But Cynthia, who had just been witness to murder, fought him off, kicking and stomping the ground until her frustrated parents gave up and waited for her to come around enough to tell her story.

"She gets that from your mother," Thelma whispered. "Gets into such a tizzy that she's all nerves and can't talk."

When the pain of loss subsided enough to make speech possible, Cynthia wiped the discharge from her red nose on the sleeve of her sweater, and with the mien of a star witness on the stand said, "Randy drowned Ginger."

"Oh, my God!" shouted Junior. "Who's Ginger?!"

"It's her favorite baby doll," said Thelma, whereupon Cynthia lapsed back into the rhythms of sobbing. Despite all the television commercials about the Mercury-like ability of the PF Fliers, Junior caught Randy, who had broken into a getaway run, fifty yards from the camper, caught him up by the neck of his shirt. Dragging him back to camp like a POW, Junior stood him up to face the indomitable Cynthia who, fueled by Thelma's coddling, had broken into the dramatics of a wronged Southern belle.

"My baby, my only baby," she wept on her mother's breast.

Marvin Randall "Randy" Ivy III, unable to be sent to his bed until the camper was prepared for bedtime, was sent to the Packard where he was to stay, forever if necessary, until he apologized to his sister and promised to buy her another doll out of his own allowance, which had already been crippled by the promise to purchase a set of toy tableware for Regina Beth, Randy having nailed all twenty-four pieces of the latter to the telephone pole by the bridge. His hammer set had been locked in the trunk of the Packard to further the punishment, and now Randy himself was confined to the isolated cell of the Packard's backseat.

"I don't know what's in that child to make him do what he does," Thelma said, trying to mop the perpetual flow of Cynthia's nose. "There's no dispositions like that on my side of the family."

"Will you quit trying to blame someone else because you should have beat his brains out years ago and didn't. You always pampered that kid, Thelma." Junior had not yet vented his anger about the Packard incident, and if Thelma pushed him any more, by God, he would.

"You always told me *not* to spank him because he was a boy, and boys shouldn't be spanked. He was your little man, you said. Gonna follow his daddy's footsteps straight into the Ivy Funeral Home."

Junior's eyes narrowed slightly and Thelma noticed the change. When his eyes narrowed, it was time to retreat.

"Is the doll gone for good?" she asked her husband, who looked down the fast-moving Mattagash River and said, "I suppose."

This sparked Cynthia again, and only with the solemn promise that they would drive to Watertown the next day and procure a replacement for Ginger could Thelma soothe the little girl.

Junior went back to his nap and dreams of large-breasted choir girls on the calendar in the MALE EMPLOYEES ONLY restroom of the Ivy Funeral Home. Half into sleep, the blast of the Packard's horn assaulted him like the mating call of a frenzied moose and broke through to his reflexes. He bounded from the tent, stepping forgetfully on his still sore ankle, just in time to see his prized Packard, with a vengeful Randy at the helm, coast slowly down the incline and into the Mattagash River. The front fender, slamming into a large rock ten feet offshore, stopped the Packard as water swirled up above the tires.

Randy, who had already decided that they could have the rest of his measly allowance to buy the family a new Packard, let up on the horn. As silence crept in over the front seat, he settled down, his father's son, and waited for the enemy on shore to make the next move.

Sarah Pinkham Keeps Watch:
Big Brother with Binoculars

"Nobody's got that much attention since Grammie caught her tit in the wringer."

—WINNIE CRAFT, About Violet La Forge, Sarah's Party, 1959

IN ALL HER years in Mattagash Sarah Pinkham had never personally known a loose woman. There had been gossip. There had been brown-eyed children born to many blue-eyed couples over the years, and more than once a woman whose husband was out of town would send her children to their grandmother's for the night and close the venetian blinds. But gossip and whispers were one thing. Doing exercises in skimpy leotards and hanging underthings out where the world could glimpse them was suggestive of something deeper.

Violet La Forge was the first loose woman Mattagash had ever encountered in the flesh. And the vigilance committee Sarah Pinkham had managed to organize over coffee and doughnuts meant business. That their husbands lingered too long in Albert's dooryard whenever Violet was outside exercising was evident even to the fishermen's wives in rooms 1 and 2. That the men from Mattagash told jokes back and forth about the dances Violet did in her scarves at the Watertown Hotel was evident to everyone but Violet. It was all too much to ask of any decent homemaking woman in Mattagash to have trash like that flaunted beneath their noses, and if flaunting it beneath their noses wasn't bad enough, Sarah Pinkham had it flaunted beneath her own bedroom window.

When Albert sweated and tossed in his sleep, Sarah lay awake and wondered if Violet was exercising in his dreams, the thin material stretched across her large breasts. And the indefinable fear that swelled up inside her, the knowledge that she could watch Albert closely all day but could not follow him inside his head at night, was almost too much for her to bear.

At night Albert Pinkham went inside his mind and closed the door. There was no way for her to jiggle the lock and make him come back out. No key to have duplicated so that she might check for herself in the morning, sorting over disconnected images and parts of dreams that had piled up during the night, and rifling through the countless players who acted in Albert's nighttime dramas. But if she could, and found Violet La Forge's smiling face there amid the pictures, she would tear it into a thousand shards, scatter it about in Albert's brain until it was lost.

It was only Albert's subconscious, his private place to go to in sleep and release the daily tension. But to Sarah it was a bachelor pad. One night she deliberately coughed loudly when a dream seemed to hold Albert longer than usual. He sat up saying, "What? What?" Hearing Sarah say, "It was the dog barking at a car," he went back to sleep.

Sarah realized that her husband needed a good night's rest, and that she must stop kicking him in the shins, as if by accident, when she had overused the coughing method. But even the fresh smell of lilacs drifting up to the windows at night now pained her, as though it were the perfumed breath of Violet La Forge, taunting her as it slipped into her snoring husband's nostrils and betwitched him. Something had to be done before Albert Pinkham went the way of all flesh.

"Has she done anything outright?" Martha Fogarty asked, hoping that Sarah knew firsthand of several things.

"She exercises in them leotards in broad daylight. That's enough, don't you think?" Sarah asked Winnie Craft.

"Lord, you wouldn't catch me in them little tight things," said Winnie. "I been too embarrassed to even wear a pair of pants since way back when Lennie was a baby."

"That ain't the point. Even if you could, you wouldn't wear 'em. No decent woman, not even one that looks like her, would flaunt herself like that."

When Sarah reminded them that decency was involved, they soon lost track of that glimmer of objectivity that hit Mattagash minds at intervals but invariably flickered out, leaving behind a trail of smoke that impaired the sight more than ever.

"The woman has got a flower's name," said Sarah.

"She does wiggle more than her share," said Winnie.

"Them things fit her like Scotch tape," said Martha.

"And the men hang around here like old dogs frothing at the mouth whenever she's outside." Sarah let this drop like a dainty bomb.

"Does Freddie?" asked Winnie.

"Does Bert?" asked Martha.

"Sometimes," said Sarah.

The vigilante committee decided upon a letter, not wanting to address the modern dancer directly. They gathered after supper to compose it. Several other women, tired of children that looked too much like their husband's family, or wishing for a wet drop of excitement to fall into the dry days and nights, came along to hear the outcome. Sarah's parlor filled up quickly. Sandwiches had been made and salads had been brought. Coffee brewed. Among the gathered literati, Martha Fogarty was chosen to take charge of the composition, hers being the best handwriting.

"Do we start with 'Dear Violet'?" asked Winnie.

"That sounds too friendly," said one of the group.

"How about 'To Miss La Forge'?" asked Martha.

"What is this pink stuff? It's good," said Winnie, who was bulging like a barrel from years of overeating.

"It's called Hawaiian Delight," said Flora Gardner. "I got it out of the *Bangor Daily News*. A woman from Portland sent it in. She got it from her sister in Boston. It was a chain-letter recipe. If you broke the chain all your baking for one full year would turn out bad."

"It's real good," said another woman, and the whole room silently conceded that, at least at this gathering, Flora had taken the prize for a recipe that was most uncommon.

"It takes a whole can of Eagle Brand milk," Flora offered, then said no more, merely adding to the mystery of the recipe.

"Why isn't Sicily here?" asked Winnie.

"I didn't think she'd want to leave Marge. And Pearl is back in town," Sarah told her, concealing the real reason—that she suspected Edward Lawler had been a frequent guest of Violet's when the moon was full and most eyes were closed. All eyes except Sarah's, who watched the comings and goings of life at the motel the way a serious birdwatcher keeps up a vigil for rare and exciting birds. When this nasty little episode with Violet was over, she would let the cat out of the bag about Ed Lawler. She never liked Ed. He always thought his education placed him a head and shoulders above the other men in town. Her Albert might have only gone to the fifth grade, but he did own his own business. And Sarah really did like Sicily. She wasn't like the other McKinnons, who thought they could walk on water. Especially Pearl. She wouldn't enjoy telling on Ed for Sicily's sake. But it was a small town and she was obligated to tattle. It was her neighborly duty.

"Did you see Eva McPherson's mother's ring the kids all got together and bought her?" Winnie asked the group as a single entity.

"It's the prettiest thing," she went on, not waiting to hear if anyone had. "The oldest and the youngest was both born in January. The second-oldest and the second-youngest was both born in August. Then Perry was born in June and Penny in October, so she's got a red stone on each end, two light greens next to each red one, then that little opal and that pearl right fair in the middle. It's the prettiest mother's ring I ever saw. Just like you went down to the jewelry store and asked the man to do it like that on purpose."

"If my youngest, my little April May, hadn't been born in March I'd have had a nice setting," said Grace Henderson. "That March stone clashes with the others. She was supposed to be born the last of April or the first of May, but being premature God gave her to us in March. We kinda got used to the name we'd picked out by then. But April would've been a good stone. It's a diamond and that goes with everything. If it had been a boy we were going to name him Ralph after Roy's grandfather. But that March stone ruined my ring."

"How about 'To Miss La Forge'?" Martha, pen still poised over paper, patiently asked again.

"I doubt if she *is* a 'Miss.' She's probably got a dozen husbands and kids somewhere," said Sarah. "Just put 'To Violet La Forge' and let it go at that."

TO VIOLET LA FORGE:
  IT HAS COME TO OUR ATTENTION THAT YOU EXERCISE IN PUBLIC A LOT WEARING VERY LITTLE. ALSO YOU ARE A DANCER AND STRIPPER OVER IN WATERTOWN. AS

MOTHERS OF CHILDREN WE DON'T WANT THEM TO GROW UP AND BECOME LIKE YOU. WE THINK YOU SHOULD LEAVE TOWN AND GO SOMEWHERE ELSE TO LIVE, AS YOU ARE NOTHING BUT THE CENTER OF GOSSIP HERE AND DON'T FIT IN.
—CONCERNED CITIZENS
P.S. WE STILL HOPE GOD WILL FORGIVE YOU AND SAVE YOUR SOUL.

Violet La Forge, not knowing she was the uninvited guest of honor at Mattagash's first autumn social event, donned her leotards and began a series of vigorous exercises on the pavement outside her room.

"Well, as I live and breathe, speak of the devil," said Sarah and guided the committee to the window, where each glared incredulously through Sarah's small binoculars at Violet, who always began her exercises with a few minutes of yoga. She was in the lotus position. Only twenty feet away and magnified in the binoculars, as well as in the committee's mind, her breasts took on proportions no mortal woman was capable of bearing. Those committee members who were only along for curiosity and a cup of coffee soon became embroiled and the binoculars became as popular as one pair of opera glasses at the opening of *Madame Butterfly*.

"Boy, don't she think she's the best thing since sliced bread," said Martha, aiming the binoculars just as Violet thrust her legs into a bicycle exercise.

"Let her," said Sarah. "When we're done with her there'll be only bread crumbs left."

The Gifford Outhouse:
A Home Away from Home

"Once when we was little and the only bathroom at the school was still the old outhouse, I dropped my little butterfly barrette down one of the holes by accident. And I asked Chester Lee Gifford to get it out for me. He said, 'I don't dig around in shit.' I said, 'Well, you live in it, Chester, what's the difference?' And he grabbed me and drug me inside the outhouse and stuffed my head down one of the holes and kept me there until I almost passed out. Mr. Fortin was on duty that day on the playground and he saw the commotion around the outhouse and came and got me out of there. That's the kind of insane boy Chester Lee was."

—PATSY KELLEY, Schoolmate to Chester Lee, Later a Housewife, 1960

CHESTER LEE GIFFORD, named for his uncle Lee, lay sprawled on his bed in a stream of warm September sun that struggled through the unwashed windows of the Gifford house. He twirled one panel of the plastic curtains into a tight roll, imagining that the ugly parrots that covered it were having their necks wrung. He wore no shirt and dots of sweat formed among the curly hairs on his chest. His green work pants smelled at the crotch of urine, and he tugged at them to ease the itching around his genitals. Two days' growth of beard spread across his face and neck. He slipped his tongue across the buildup on his front teeth. His head felt like a run-over pumpkin, the combination of wine-liquor having taken its toll. It was on mornings like this that Chester Lee appreciated the no-work lifestyle set for him by his ancestors.

Snapping the curtain in midair, he let it fly in a swish that resembled the flapping of wings, and the tortured parrots were free to escape. Chester lit up a cigarette and threw the match onto the bare wooden boards of the floor. Downstairs, the kitchen had linoleum on the floor, an imitation of red brick, that Bert Gifford had discovered in a logging camp owned by one of the large landowners and toted home to Ruth. It was a true Gifford reaction, their own "Finders-Takers" philosophy. But the linoleum was the only modern convenience the house could boast of.

An outhouse sat out back, swathed in a shroud of houseflies and odors. This structure was still functioning even among a few of the better citizenry of Mattagash, but those who had them were forced to have them, and each fall the money from the potato harvest was made in hopes of using it for the purchase of a commode. The bathtub would be added the following harvest, or whenever the money might be raised. In the meantime, the outside toilet was a source of embarrassment to the owner, with folks from Watertown driving by on Sundays with relatives from out of state who didn't believe that outhouses were still in existence, and laughing behind the locked doors of their cars as they drove through Mattagash counting the eyesores so that they might take the statistics back to Boston, where even Watertown was laughable.

Those unfortunates who were still destined to relieve themselves in bathrooms not connected to their homes tried to beautify the situation. The women painted them bright colors and planted flowers about the door, laid bricks in the earth path for a cobblestone effect, or painted two discarded car tires white and sank them in the ground where they became a gateway for the outhouse path. The seat, usually a two-holer, was scoured twice a week with a scrub brush and lye soap, and air fresheners bought from the Fuller Brush man hung promisingly from the inside ceiling. The men moved them often to newly dug holes, covering up the old ones, so that the refuge would not pile up enough to be unbearable to sight as well as smell.

Only the Giffords took a natural pride in their outhouse, never lifting a finger to improve upon what they considered a functional machine. It remained unpainted, the rough boards turning gray in the weather, and the smell permeating the area enough that the two skinny dogs, Chainsaw and Dusty, chose to sleep on a neighbor's porch in order that their dreams be unbroken by such an assault on the nose. The man-hours and work involved in moving the building to a new site was not the problem for the Giffords that it was for others in Mattagash. When the pile of feces began to scale the top of one hole, all bodily activity was simply transferred to the remaining hole. Even when that one was no longer usable, the family was not panic-stricken. Small mounds appeared behind the outhouse and along its sides, while crumpled catalogue pages of bicycles or of kitchenware were left outside to blow with the wind onto the main road until the town issued an ordinance that the family move the outhouse and clean up around it. But issuing an ordinance to a Gifford was like tacking a notice up on some tree in the woods asking the animals to stop defecating in the forest. The law simply didn't apply to them, they felt, and it went unnoticed. The sheriff-delivered letter did have enough of an impact that Chester Lee would disappear into the bowels of the American Legion Hall and Bert would take to his bed complaining of his back, and citing as proof the monthly ADC check from Augusta. There was nothing the town could do but undertake the unpleasant chore themselves, hiring a highly paid demolitionlike crew, complete with gas masks and gloves, to go in and set things in order.

When the cold nights struck in December and January, it always pleased Bert Gifford immensely to hear that someone's inside bathroom had frozen pipes and was unusable.

"Good enough for 'em," he would tell his family. "People got no business shittin' in their house."

There were no doors in the Gifford house, no privacy to be found among so many occupants, half of whom were old enough to be arguing, the other half young enough to be squawling. Many times Chester Lee retreated to the Gifford outhouse even when his body had no need for it. He looked upon it as a kind of office, a haven where he could go and think out some of his most pressing problems while thumbing through the catalogue pages of women in bras and cotton panties.

He slid his legs over the side of the bed and let his head adjust to the new vertical position. Downstairs, his mother Ruth was scrambling a package of powdered eggs that were part of the relief supplies the Giffords were entitled to: two packages per person in the family per month.

Because the Gifford daughters Debra, Rita, and Lorraine were still under Bert's roof with their four illegitimate children, the family consisted of ten people, the current boyfriends of the daughters not being eligible even though they were frequently there. This brought the relief count to twenty packages of scrambled eggs, three pounds of lard, five pounds of margarine, two boxes of cheese, one large bag of flour, ten cans of potted meat, five bags of rice, five bags of beans, two sacks of cornmeal, two sacks of sugar, and five sacks of powdered milk. This was enough to sustain the Gifford brood for a month. Ruth added extras with the ADC check and town support, but any cash in the house was rare and usually went to the purchase of beer and hard liquor. As most of the family had grown to detest the bland taste of the powdered eggs, the burden of eating them fell upon the four children and two dogs, which accounted for the ribwork that showed through the animal's hides, and the whiny dispositions of the children. Ruth had biscuits made and Chester Lee grabbed a handful from the baking sheet, not stopping for margarine or any extras, and headed for the back door.

"Anyone in the toilet?" he asked and kicked open the screen door, letting in some noisy flies that had had their way with the outhouse and were anxious for the biscuits. Chester Lee ate a biscuit as he staggered toward his office, still feeling the dizziness of drink. Behind him Ruth's shrill voice peaked as she shouted a warning to a child, then a brisk sound of hand against skin and a second of silence until a child's uncontrollable sobs dominated the other house noises. A radio was playing in one of the bedrooms upstairs, the one that Debbie slept in with her little boy. In the yard outside, Chester Lee spotted Boyd Henderson's shiny new pickup parked brazenly close to the back step. The two dogs were engrossed in sniffing the urine they had newly deposited upon the tires. Boyd was Debbie's latest boyfriend and that explained the music coming from her bedroom.

Chester Lee felt that wild thump in his gut that arose whenever he saw a new automobile. Or even a slightly used one. He felt an intense jealousy of Boyd. It didn't matter that the bank was in the process of chasing Boyd down to reclaim it; it was in his possession now. And there was nothing that Chester Lee wanted more than a car. A Plymouth with fins had been his dream, but even a pickup could make his heart race, and when he sat inside an automobile and closed his eyes he could smell the thick odor of vinyl, the intoxicating aroma of gasoline and grease, and as he caressed the metal coolness of the keys in his fingers, nothing, not even a beautiful woman in cotton panties, could equal the stirring sensations in his groin, the ache of desire that filled his being. Chester ate one of the biscuits as he took in the shape of the pickup, the curve of the hood, the sleekness of the paint job, then went off to the outhouse. Inside he turned the piece of wood that had been nailed to the inside wall from twelve o'clock around to three o'clock so that half of it protruded a few inches onto the door. Since the door opened inward, the wood served as a convenient brace, affording privacy and costing only the price of one nail.

Chester Lee laid his biscuits on the floor, dropped his pants, and situated himself over one hole until his buttocks were evenly distributed and he was comfortable. Turning to the ladies' lingerie section of the catalogue, he found the brunette that had captured his attention from the day the new catalogue arrived, her rear snug in tight panties and just a shadow of breast above the bra's extra support cups.

But no amount of concentration could bring the usual wave of sexual excitement, no amount of self-stimulation could carry him off into the page where he could firmly glue his lips to one of the brunette's pert breasts. Reaching for one of the biscuits on the outhouse floor, Chester Lee admitted out loud what he knew silently. His words pushed around the mouthful of biscuit and he let one fist fall against the knotty boards to reinforce the urgency.

"I got to get me some wheels!" he lamented.

Beyond Courtly Love:
A Slow Pirogue to China

"Do you wanna know why the McKinnons think they're the crust on the loaf of the bread? It seems this Prince named Charlie went up to Scotland a couple hundred years ago to get back his ancestors' home. But no way in hell did he finagle that. There was this McKinnon with him—McKinnons always turn up for a throne-grabbin'—and anyway, Prince Charlie gives this particular McKinnon a secret recipe he had for a hell-raisin' little quaff. And that there secret recipe has stayed with the McKinnon family ever since. If you was to ask *me*, Charlie should've given away his recipe *before* the battle. It might've made all the difference, 'cause when men get to drinkin' in battle, and considerin' them little skirts they wore, well, I imagine that they were trippin' all over the place. But if you care to gaze upon the McKinnon coat of arms, you just go down to the Watertown Liquor Store and turn over a Drambuie bottle. The McKinnon coat of arms ain't on display in Mattagash, it being a dry town."

—GERT McKINNON, Historian and Drambuie Drinker, 1937

HE HAD ARRIVED with holes in his shirt and a battered Bible he said had belonged to his grandfather. He was only twenty-eight but already a missionary full of the zeal all of Mattagash hungered to see. He thrilled Reverend Ralph's parlor group with his escapades in Africa, sang them African songs which he pounded out on a set of drums a chieftain had given him. Marge was twenty-three the day he rapped on the screen door and asked to see her father. He had curly dark hair and such black eyes, and a full, brooding mouth. She felt a small stirring in the pit of her stomach, almost the same as if she were going to be sick. It was autumn when she answered the door, and all around her the world was red and orange and yellow, and when he asked, "Is the Reverend Ralph McKinnon at home?" it seemed all the colors of Mattagash began to swirl about her like crayons melting in the sun, and it occurred to her that she might faint. Might faint there in the doorway, only to wake and find him gone. She didn't want that to happen, because she knew as easily as she'd know the devil by his tail and trident, she knew this man would be her lover. That those hands inside those worn pockets would hold her. Those lips would press against hers. She knew this. As a woman knows. So she held on, putting one hand against the doorjamb to steady herself and tried to focus on his eyes, listen to his words.

"Are you all right?" he had asked.

"Yes. It's just the weather. No, I must've gotten up too fast from sitting."

"Is the Reverend at home?"

"Yes, come inside," she told him and opened the door wider for him, stepping back so he could pass. As easily as that she let Marcus Doyle into her life.

The Reverend was impressed with him. The town was impressed. He was by far the most interesting of the visiting missionaries, with the flair of a Hollywood actor. He motioned with swooping gestures as if to catch and hold the very words he spoke. And after each funny story he told, after each tearful one, Marge's was the first face he looked to for approval, which she always gave by blushing quickly or nervously fingering the handkerchief on her lap. He knew how he captivated her. Understood that just short of signing autographs and being rich he was as good as Valentino to her. To Mattagash. When he let drop the statement that he was looking for a church where he could preach, a community he might settle in and call home, the Reverend quickly asked him to linger there awhile, to share the church duties with him for his room and board. It was only a matter of months, he told Marcus Doyle, before he would be embarking for China. What a perfect way to train some promising young preacher to take Reverend Ralph's place. The congregation responded warmly, all echoing the sentiment and praising Reverend Ralph for his foresight.

Marge went to bed that night and was unable to sleep, knowing Marcus Doyle slept on a cot in the summer kitchen, directly beneath her bedroom window. In the dark she kissed the back of her palm, pretending it was Marcus's warm lips that she kissed and all night she heard noises in the house she had not heard before, or at least had not *cared* to hear, or *listened* to hear, and she thought of them as the deep soft breaths coming from his mouth as he slept. Only when the sky turned gray with dawn did she finally let go of the excitement enough to sleep.

From that day on her life, which she once thought was over at twenty-three or at least doomed to spinsterhood, became new. She was born again in the spirit, and as she went about her daily chores of housecleaning, she told herself it was *their* house she was taking care of, hers and Marcus's. The evening meal became to her an adventure in itself. She tried new recipes, most receiving her father's disapproval as being too frivolous, but he saw what might happen between the two young people and the prospect of a spinster daughter was more untasty to him than jalapeño cornbread.

She redid the summer kitchen so Marcus would feel more at home, dragging in and cleaning pieces of furniture that had been stored in the shed, covering his cot with her best quilt, leaving fresh goldenrod in a tall glass by his bedside, sorry that the river roses had passed their peak and were gone.

After supper each evening they would sit on the front steps of the sagging old porch and talk about Africa, the church, about God and the words of the Bible. Knowing that Henry Taylor drove home from his job in Watertown every Saturday night, they would walk a mile down the dirt road every Saturday evening, just to stare breathlessly at his new model-T automobile and run their fingers carefully over its surface, like petting the skin of a rare animal. And on the walk home their hands would accidentally touch and he would gather hers up and hold it carefully in his, delicately, her pulse throbbing as if he held her beating heart. The road would waver beneath her as she grew giddy from his touch, and she knew how drunkards felt trying to make their way home after a long night in the taverns, and she understood why they drank.

He began his seduction of her slowly, making her comfortable in his room by bringing her there often to show her relics and pictures from his suitcase until eventually she came and went in his private room as though it were her own, with only a soft quick knock to let him know it was her.

He let her catch him barechested one day, his shirt slung over a chair, and at first she was quite taken aback to see him like that before her, but before she could say so, or react, he quickly said, "Look, here's a picture of my mother. See? I told you how much you look like her."

And as she leaned forward and said, "Silly. There's no resemblance at all," she noticed a few beads of perspiration scattered among the fine hairs of his chest, and she smelled the aroma of his man's scent that clung to her hair and clothes even after she'd left the room. Closing his door behind her, she leaned her back against it, that same upheaval in her stomach as the first time she saw him. She stayed with her back pressed to his bedroom door, feeling like lead drawn to a magnet. Tears suddenly appeared in her eyes when she realized a woman in her wanted to open the door and run back, wanted to trace the lines of his chest and press her face against it.

In the darkness of her bed that night she curled deep into the softness of the blankets and relived every second of the incident, how he looked at her, the words they shared, the warm redness of her blush. But it was his smell she remembered most vividly, and twisting her hair around her finger she could breathe it again, as if it had embedded itself in her hair, in her skin, burned itself forever into her woman's mind.

Downstairs on his cot in the summer kitchen, Marcus Doyle lay staring up at the ceiling, imagining Margie's young body above him wrapped in a soft nightgown that would evaporate at the touch of his hands. Remembering her blush from that afternoon, how it inched its way across the whiteness of her face like a sunrise, made him want her all the more.

For a few days she avoided his room, but soon she found herself knocking to tell him his supper was on the table and waiting. Then she began to enter it only when he was away, telling herself it was just to tidy it up. One day, coming back with a water pail from the spring, she noticed some particularly fluffy goldenrod waving at her from the edge of the field. She picked some and left them by his bed in the same tall glass. Two days later, she came to his room after supper and knocked. When he said, "Come in," she did, and sat on the foot of his bed for the first time, showing him what she held in her hands and saying, "It was my mother's father. I didn't know him but I think you look a lot like him."

In the weeks that followed he spoke to her often of his love, and although he never mentioned marriage to her, she was sure it was marriage he had in mind. She set about fixing up her trousseau, sewing handkerchiefs and crocheting doilies, packing each item carefully into the trunk and thinking of the day when they would happily be unpacked. But it was not a trunk of knick-knacks and linens that Marcus Doyle was anxious to open.

After two months, when he had tired of church and community life, he told Marge he would be leaving Mattagash, perhaps to go back to the dust and tents of Africa, or elsewhere in the world, blazing trails where no missionary had gone before. Because he did not mention taking her with him, she wept in her room for hours. The night sounds of the house mocked her now. The ticking clock, the attic creaks, the deep sounds of breathing were all like tongues whispering and hissing, "Spinster! Spinster!"

She slipped from her bed and reached for her robe. The floor-boards were cold. She shivered in November's night. From her window she looked out at the field that lay north of the house. There was a frost that night that covered the dead stubble of hay. The round white moon was shining down on it and the sparkles on its crust danced like little ghosts. The river was white as bone in the moonlight. A little wind was about and she saw the bare branches of the birch trees along the bank swaying slightly. What would Christmas be without him? Could she ever bear to look out that window again, to spy upon the night beauty of the world, if he were not in the same house with her? If he were not hers? Could she stand to string one strand of popcorn, wrap one gift in soft paper, knowing he was off, lost somewhere in the world? Could she ever again bear to hear the sound of laughter, or even worse, would she ever hear her own again if Marcus was not there to hear it too?

She shivered as she left her room and crept softly down the stairs. Little goosebumps spread over her arms as quietly as petals opening. It was, she told herself, the chill of the night that caused the strange tingling that engulfed her. Outside his door she could smell the wonderful smell that was Marcus Doyle, a mixture of cologne and tobacco, could hear his breath coming and going as he slept. The doorknob was alive in her hands, turning itself, a will of its own. Even if she had vowed not to turn it, even if she had changed her mind, saying, "This is wrong," it would have turned, as it did, and opened the way for her into Marcus's room. There was moonlight on the bed and she sat where it shone, smoothed her hair back, wet her lips. She wanted him to wake and see her drenched in moonlight. She wet her lips again and said, "Marcus?" laying her cold hand on his bare shoulder. His skin was so warm it almost burned her. She nearly pulled her hand back expecting to see it seared, nearly ran from his room. But in an instant he had come awake, took her in his arms, and kissed her face.

"I knew you loved me," he told her. "I knew you loved me this much." And as easily as that, he pulled her down beside him and took her robe. She kept her eyes closed, tears behind the lids. She was twenty-three years old. The oldest unmarried girl in Mattagash. She could not be sure if her eternal damnation in hell would be half so bad as eternal damnation in Mattagash. At least in hell she would see the familiar faces of her neighbors. In spinsterhood, there would be just her, giving way to wrinkles and unusual habits. Maybe gathering a houseful of cats or collecting buttons from the neighbors. Painting everything in the house a hideous color. A pink stove. Pink table. Pink floors. Those were the odd things that spinsters did. Anything to clutter the mind. To occupy it with things. The way one fills a trunk. Or a bookshelf.

In the days that followed, there was no mention of marriage between them. And there was less and less talk of love from Marcus, unless she asked, "Do you love me?" Then he would say, "Of course I do," and go on to another subject. This worried her greatly. But no longer did he mention leaving Mattagash, so she settled for that small favor.

On days when the Reverend was out among his congregation and the girls were off somewhere involved in their own lives, he would slip quietly up behind her, kissing her neck and whispering, "Tonight. Be sure now. When they're asleep." Or he would slide a note under her bedroom door showing only a small heart pierced by an arrow and the initials *M.D.* It pleased her when he did such things. No other man in Mattagash had such flair, for the notes that Marcus Doyle hastily scrawled and pushed beneath her door became sonnets to Marge. They were to be treasured and admired, to be kept locked in her mother's jewelry box, to be kissed and lovingly reread.

It was on a Thursday evening after supper. Marge had taken her embroidery into the parlor. It was a doily that she worked on. One that would soon take its place among the anxious contents of her hope chest. The supper dishes had been washed and put away. She had spent the afternoon planning and preparing the meal and it had gone well, with an abundance of compliments from Marcus and the girls, and no complaints from the Reverend.

The girls, Pearl and Sicily, had been agreeable at the table, sitting up straight, chewing their food properly. Fighting between the two was never a problem when their father was about, but at other times they tried Marge's patience. She warned them to act like young ladies, telling herself that after her marriage to Marcus he would surely let her take her sisters, who were really more like daughters to her. That evening the girls were models of good manners and Marge showed them her approval as often as she could, catching their eyes as she passed them mashed potatoes or offered them a slice of homemade bread. There was an electricity in the air, an expectancy. The whole house groaned and swelled with it, as it had when Marge was a little girl and the first of the missionaries began to come. The huge plates of food hummed as they were passed around the table. The forks and knives all clinked in harmony like parts of a wind chime. The meringue on the lemon pie stood up like a wave of foam and the coffee, poured steaming from the pot, created tiny curls at Marge's temples. Seeing them in the mirror over the kitchen sink as she later did the dishes, she found them feminine, almost beautiful, then blushed at her own vanity.

Marcus retired to the summer kitchen and his cot, saying his reading had suffered lately and so he would make amends. There had been no note that day, no whispers or kisses on her neck, but she reminded herself he'd been busy lately. And surely the wonderful tone set at supper was an indication of how things stood between them. He had caught her eye several times and she had seen a moistness in them, as if they had suddenly teared, and she believed the sentimentality of the moment had captured him.

She had sent the girls out to play, allowing them to escape the chore of washing dishes. This she wanted to do herself, afraid someone else might wash her lover's plate and saucer, might trifle with the fork that had been in his mouth. It was her duty as a woman, as a wife-to-be, to take care of her man's needs.

It was Thursday, November 3, 1923, when she went into the parlor to finish her embroidery in front of the warm fire, and to bask in the warmth she felt within. The Reverend had removed his shoes and was wearing his ancient slippers, ones he'd owned even before his marriage. The family dog, a yellow animal of mixed descent, came to the Reverend's chair and stood quietly, waiting, watching him closely with its sad black eyes. Still unnoticed after a few minutes, the dog moved closer and put its nose against the Reverend's hand, its tail in a halfhearted wag.

"Get you!" the Reverend shouted and, with newspaper folded, swatted the poor creature on the head until it retreated, yelping, back to its mat by the kitchen door.

"Poor thing," Marge had thought. "Still trying to be his friend after all those slaps on the head. Just like all of us who know him are still trying."

And she had risen with her embroidery, thinking how unpleasant the room had suddenly become. That's when the Reverend, without looking up from his paper, cleared his throat and said, "Marcus Doyle has left us." She stopped where she was, at the entrance to the parlor, and put one hand out to steady herself, just as she had done the first day she met Marcus Doyle, and said softly, "What? What did you say?" The sensation in her stomach was not the same as that first day. That first day her stomach had squirmed as if full of something, as if she were pregnant, like a morning sickness. Now it was lead inside her. Something dead. About to be stillborn. She kept her back to him, not wanting to see the pleasure she knew must be in his eyes.

"Left why? Gone where?"

"Gone back to his wife and children, I hope. After supper this evening, I told him to leave."

"He isn't married!" She had never shouted at him before. Had never shouted at anyone.

"A young woman from Portland. Anna Doyle. Has two sons."

"But how? Who told you this? It's a lie someone in Mattagash has started out of jealousy. It's a lie!" she cried at him, trying to think who it could be that would slander her Marcus so, and leave her looking like such a fool.

"I wrote letters to the men that he mentioned having worked with side by side. I thought it my duty to check on him. Those men had never heard of him. One had even died ten years ago and so certainly never had the pleasure of meeting Mr. Doyle. Then the police helped. They have his record. He's a bit of a con man. The last gimmick he came up with was as a geography teacher down on the southern tip of the state. Any place where he can get a good meal and some diversion until he's tired of it and ready to move on."

"Africa?" She had turned to him now.

"Lucky if he's been out of Maine. I suppose his stint teaching geography helped with his tales of Africa. He was more than happy to get the chance to leave without being reported. But we were lucky too. The scandal would have ruined us all. Tomorrow I'll say that he went back to Africa, and your reputation will be safe. You should be thankful no one else discovered this first."

"I'm glad Mama died," she whispered. "I'm glad she didn't have to live a whole lifetime with you," and she ran from the room without ever knowing if he had heard, flinging her apron aside and pushing through the screen door, ran with tears that wouldn't fall down the dirt road to Henry Taylor's. Ida Taylor was cutting dead flower stalks from around her front steps when the shaken Marge reached her.

"Good Lord, child, have you just talked to the devil?" Ida said, straightening herself and pushing a hand against her sore back.

"Did Marcus walk by? Did you see Marcus?"

"He went by a good two hours ago. Henry wasn't home to drive him to Watertown so he went on to Ned's to catch a ride there."

"How did he look? What did he say?" Marge's hair had come loose and fell about her face in wet curls. She reminded Ida of a painting she'd once seen of Joan of Arc with fire all around her.

"He didn't say nothin'. Just walked down the road like he owned it."

"Did he look back, Ida? Did he turn around and look back?"

Years later Marge would wonder why she had asked that question. Ida never told anyone what she knew about the day Marcus Doyle left Mattagash, that Marge McKinnon had come tearing down the road asking about him. At least it never came back to her as gossip, and in Mattagash it would have to surface, like oil to water. In 1937 Ida Taylor died of cancer, taking with her Marge's secret. Up until the last day Marge cooked her soups, sat up with her during the painfully long nights when Ida wished for death like some people wish for money, read her passages from the Bible. It was the least she could do. And for all her life she would remember crying out that day to Ida, "Did he turn and look back?" And for all those autumn evenings that would follow her down the years, when the deer would come to the edge of the road to eat, and the leaves raged red and orange as fire, and she would bring her handiwork to the front porch until the light failed her, and before she lifted herself from the steps and up to bed, she would remember Ida Taylor, bless her soul, saying, "No, Margie. He was just whistlin' and kickin' at pebbles. His hat tipped back on his head. He just went walkin' down that road like he built it."

Now that Marge seemed restful again, the nurse came to the kitchen for a cup of coffee. Sicily poured one for her, then one for herself.

"Just black," the nurse said.

"You're lucky not to use sugar. It's so fattening."

The nurse moved to the back window that looked out on the river. The far mountain was caught up in the reds and yellows, and under the warm sun it looked ablaze with the foliage, a mass of soft pastels melting in the long afternoon.

"You're so lucky to live in such a pretty place," she told Sicily.

"Yes, I guess we are. It can get lonely, though."

"I suppose. But I grew up in Philadelphia and I think I'd be less lonely here."

"It does depend a lot on where you was born and raised. Do you want a doughnut with that?"

"Oh, no, thank you." The nurse turned away from the window and, finishing her coffee, rinsed the cup and set it in the sink.

"I'd better get back to her," she said. "She's been having a hard time resting."

"Is she better now?" Sicily selected a chocolate doughnut from the plate.

"A bit. She's been mumbling a lot. Almost as if she's trying to say something."

"Poor soul," said Sicily. "There should be a better way for us to go out of this world."

"By the way," the nurse turned at the kitchen door. "Who is Marcus?"

Foreclosure on Room 3:
Violet Takes It All Off

If no one ever marries me,
And I don't see why they
    should,
For nurse says I'm not pretty
And I'm seldom very good.
If no one ever marries me
I shan't mind very much.
I shall buy a squirrel in a cage
And a little rabbit hutch.
And when I'm getting really old,
At twenty-eight or -nine,
I shall buy a little orphan girl
And bring her up as mine.

—LAURENCE ALMA-TADEMA

NEVER A LATE sleeper, Violet arose at eight o'clock. She had been restless the night before, waking several times with the alarming thought that she had forgotten something important, like a candle left burning. Or a pot smoking on the stove. Each time, she looked at the little clock by her bedside and saw that the hands had crept only a short distance since the last time she'd awakened. She sensed a fear that she hadn't felt in years. The room she had so lovingly made a home seemed ready to attack her. The chair sat menacingly, its open back a large mouth that would snap at her legs if she walked too near. The items on her dresser were alive, the brush standing on its countless legs, the comb a row of razor-sharp teeth. Even the stuffed Raggedy Ann that had been hers since childhood was ready to leap from the corner the minute Violet's back was turned and strangle her from behind.

When daylight finally came, with the truth about the objects in her room, Violet felt at ease, the long terrifying night quickly lost, except for a vague feeling of doom that wouldn't shake itself from her.

"Exercise," she thought. "A good workout will take it away." She pulled on her leotards and did a few minutes of warmups before stepping out onto the pavement. But outside there was a thin, stringy rain falling. It was then she saw the note attached by tape to her door, and her heart beat wildly. In her hands the envelope was damp.

"It must have been here all night," she thought. Inside her room she laid it gently on the bed and sat and looked at it, touching a tip of one finger to it. She was afraid to open it, afraid that if she tore back the flap something she had never seen before would jump out like a jack-in-the-box and frighten her. She didn't doubt that it was from Ed Lawler, but what it might say she could not decide. When he had left her room the previous morning in the full light of Mattagash, there was no doubt in her mind that he would not be returning to her arms, to her bed again. There was a finality in each of his movements, in the tone of his words. He had left her, shirt slung over his shoulder, saying, "Be good to yourself. Take it on the chin," and when she had tried to ask him, "When will you be back? When can I see you again? *Will* you be back? Oh, please don't say you won't be back." When she had tried to let all these words flow from her mouth, he had merely put one finger lightly to her lips, and then he kissed her and was gone.

For all her seeming citified ways, for all her unorthodox philosophies, Violet was a small-town girl. As a professional dancer she was Violet La Forge from Boston. But in truth, and according to the birth certificate she kept carefully hidden under the secret flap in her purse, she was Elizabeth "Beth" Thatcher from Kingsman, Maine, down on the New Hampshire border, population 729. And as ten-year-old Bethie Thatcher, she had watched the circus set up their tents each year in the field behind her house. The tents were full of unusual animals and flouncing performers and sounds never heard naturally in New Hampshire. The Ferris wheel reached above the treetops in the Thatcher yard and from her bedroom window Beth could see the excited faces of the riders, a strange combination of enjoyment mingled with fear. She would lift her window to let the noises in, the metallic whirring of the rides, the screams, the jaunty music. For one week each year, the world lay in her yard. She would run between the tents, taking in all she could, but stretching her allowance to last the whole week. At eight o'clock she was back in her room for bedtime but much too excited to sleep. As her mother switched off the light she would warn her, "Now don't you be at that window watching the circus." And Beth would lie in bed as the flickering lights performed for her on the ceiling, waiting for her mother to be busy downstairs, and then she would slip from bed and run to lift the window, and gaze out at the gay lights and colors etched against the darkening sky. It might have been Piccadilly Circus, because from her perch above the glitter she saw all the world pass by. In the morning they would be only huge rusting machines, asleep in the field, but at night the monsters reared their heads and stretched their arms and beckoned to Beth to come and ride them forever.

When the last Sunday night came and went in a blur of cotton candy and laughing crowds, she would try not to look, on Monday morning on her way to school, at the silent machines, the tents being dismantled, the animals loaded onto trucks. On her way home from school, it would all be gone. Like it was never there. Like she had only imagined it. As if the earth had opened and swallowed it whole. And later, when the closest she could get to those lights and that glitter were the spangles she wore on her costumes, and whatever spotlights the joints she danced in had packed away in the basement, she came to see it all as a circus. It was all a Fourth of July blaze that could only get so big and so good and so spectacular before it got smaller and smaller until it wasn't there anymore. Until the morning you finally woke up and realized you could no longer tell the reality from the dream, and that it no longer mattered if you could or not. She had read once about a man who fell asleep in a garden and dreamed he was a beautiful butterfly, fluttering about among the luscious flowers until he awoke. And when he did, the dream about the butterfly was so vivid that he couldn't be sure if he was a man who had been dreaming he was a butterfly, or if he was now a butterfly dreaming he was a man. Violet had copied this from the book she found it in, and still carried it folded in her wallet because something about its simplicity led her to believe that it had value to her, that it was about people like her. She no longer knew if she was Violet La Forge dreaming she had been Bethie Thatcher or if she was still Bethie Thatcher, asleep with her Raggedy Ann in the swing on her mother's long winding porch while the image of Violet La Forge danced beneath her twitching eyelids.

But no longer did she deceive herself about the men who paraded themselves through her life. They were ringmasters, all of them. They came with shouted promises of what was waiting inside if you paid the price of a ticket. Touters. Nothing more.

When Ed Lawler left her room that morning she knew what it meant. That the merry-go-round had stopped, that the horses were tired of spinning endlessly and getting nowhere. It meant the circus was leaving town. And she was left again to kick her toe about in the colored remnants, to stand alone on the spot where the Big Top had been and wonder what exotic place the circus was headed without her.

Now here was a note taped to her door. Did it mean that Ed, being an educated man, felt he must put goodbye in writing, must shape the letters with ink on a paper to hold the thought from escaping, to chain it down to earth so that she could read and reread the painful words forever? But what if? She was afraid her heart might fail her if she dared to think the alternative. What if it said: "I love you. I can't live without you. I'll leave the circus. There'll be no more shows." What if it said that? After all these years of looking for a man who would love her for what she perceived in life, who would respect her for carrying the story of a man dreaming he was a butterfly into shabby nightclubs and bleak strip joints, had one really come along this late in her life?

"I'll just make a cup of tea before I read it," she thought and turned on a burner on the hot plate. She poured water from a thermos into a small pan and waited, teabag in cup, for the water to boil. The cup shook in her hand.

"Silly," she thought. "You've coped all these years. Don't break now. It can only be the best news you've ever had, or the kind you've grown accustomed to. What've you got to lose?"

The water boiled and she filled her cup with it. She brought the letter over to the chair and, taking a deep breath, finally tore it open.

"TO VIOLET LA FORGE. IT HAS COME TO OUR ATTENTION."

Violet read the letter carefully, read each word as though such painstaking perusal would change them into words of love from Ed. She had never been a crier before, had always turned to quiet meditation rather than to opening a floodgate of tears.

But this time her eyes filled with them. She read the last line a second time, "P.S. WE STILL HOPE GOD WILL FORGIVE YOU AND SAVE YOUR SOUL. PLEASE BE GONE BY THREE O'CLOCK TOMORROW." Sarah had added the last line herself before taping the letter to Violet's door.

"What have I ever done to God?" Violet thought. "What have I ever done to these women?" And she crumpled the letter within her fist, the tears now coming so quickly that one rolled into another until a tiny stream burst down each cheek. She went to the bed and lay on it, clutching a pillow to her chest, something to cling to until she could manage the pain. How nice it would have been to have Ed there, to hear him lambaste the lot of those women, calling them hypocrites and liars, and telling her to ignore them, that they were only jealous, to "take it on the chin, kid."

It was late afternoon before Violet moved from her bed. After so many hours of tears, her eyes were swollen and she rinsed them with some water from her thermos. She had spent the afternoon tearing apart each fragile lie that she had spun around herself like an ugly cobweb, growing larger each day, catching up only the undesirable, creeping, crawling things that life shoved laughingly at her. There had been the numerous club owners who took a romantic interest in her, promising her endless love as well as her overdue paycheck until the audience had learned all the secrets of her body and were no longer surprised when her breasts came bouncing out. Onto the street she would go, brokenhearted over another man's lies, and short of a month's pay. Another costly ticket paid to ride on the merry-go-round.

And there were faces in the crowd who pursued her with drinks and hints of a family life and security, who no longer watched her dance once they'd taken her upstairs to a room, rented for twenty-four hours, and spent thirty minutes with her. A room rented for twenty-four hours and used for thirty minutes had always seemed such a waste. After the man had gone, she would run a bath and soak for as long as she could stand it, then crawl into bed and sleep the night through, alone, some man's smell still lingering between her thighs and among the sheets. She would use up as much of the twenty-four hours as she could. It had been another ticket bought, and it was another lonely ride.

In Room 3 of the Albert Pinkham Family Motel, Violet La Forge sobbed for hours before she admitted that she was not a modern dancer but a second-rate stripper. That at the age of forty-six the last shabby circus had dragged its tattered tents, its sick and dying animals through her life and had passed her by forever.

Sicily as Instructress:
Chester Lee
Gets a Little Manna

"Hell, it ain't like I got a bushel to pick from. If you was to put on a beauty contest here in Mattagash, you'd have to ship in contestants from other towns."

—CHESTER GIFFORD, of His Preoccupation with Amy Joy, 1959

IN THE CANDLELIGHT Chester Lee Gifford studied the lineup of new Plymouths on the advertisement page that Horner's Car Sales had placed in the *Watertown Weekly*. The 1960 models were already on sale and looked as shiny and delicious as forbidden fruit. Chester Lee traced the shape of one with his index finger. He could almost feel the smooth body come through the newspaper. There was something about the warmth of a car after it had been sitting all day in the sun, a heat that went through his hand and up his arm until he felt he was part of the car, like an extra aerial, or a curb feeler. Even a woman sunbathing all day in cotton panties could not give off that kind of heat. And a car was so indifferent. So cool. Like a cat. Cars weren't stupid. They were very, very smart. Women you could push forever. All except Margaret O'Brian, who had hung herself after Willie, were hit by lightning. "Used to a beating and no one to give it to her," Chester Lee mumbled. What a stupid thing to do. A car would never do that. Cars just didn't care.

There was no doubt about it, he *understood* cars, and yet it seemed that he was doomed to be a pedestrian for the rest of his life, watching all the world cruise by. He felt a warm tingle in his genitals and touched them. Just the thought of owning a car could do that to him quicker than any woman could. Chester Lee closed his eyes and imagined his hands on the wheel of one of Horner's new 1960 Plymouths. The dark blue one. With a handmade mat in the back window of pink carnations made from bathroom tissue. The kind the women's auxiliary made for Legion members.

Some yellow flames down each door. A big set of foam rubber dice dangling from the rearview mirror. A fancy broad from Watertown, with big breasts crammed into a tight pink sweater, sitting next to him in the front seat. You could take your pick of any broad when you had a hot car. And the backseat, all soft and cushiony. There was no better place on earth to screw a woman.

Chester heard faint footfalls on the floor overhead. No one but Amy Joy knew about his hideout in the basement. He zipped his pants up and crept softly to the bottom of the stairs and listened. It wasn't a man. The steps were too light and springy. It must be Amy Joy. He had told her never to come there without his permission, but she had come at a good time. He could always take her on the cot and pretend that beneath them was the warm vinyl of the Plymouth's backseat. It was better than being alone.

"Amy Joy, I'm down here," he shouted up the stairs and then went back to his cot. The footfalls inched their way slowly down the creaking steps and stopped at the bottom. Chester Lee had gone back to the advertisement page. He quickly forgot about the dark blue Plymouth when he heard Sicily say, "Chester Lee, it's time we had a little talk." He bolted upright on the bed and flung the papers fluttering to the floor.

"You sound like a turkey trying to get off the ground," said Sicily, "but this is one time you ain't getting away from me."

"How did you find me?" he asked, unable to look at her. Giffords rarely looked the rest of mankind in the eye.

"I heard you whispering about it to Amy Joy the other night."

"I'll have to move," he told himself, wishing there were some underground caverns he could swim to, like Jesse James had done. He was just starting to feel at home in the basement of the old building. He especially liked the quiet, as compared to the Gifford outhouse. And since no sheriff had come poking around after the traveling grocery truck robbery, he felt quite sure it was law-proof.

"I don't want any bad words or anything like that," Sicily assured him. "I hope we can work this out like two decent people." She realized this might prove difficult, since in most eyes Chester Lee was anything but a decent person.

"Work what out?" he asked her.

"You know very well what. I want you to leave little Amy Joy alone. She's only a child. Stick to women your own age."

"Women your own age," he thought. How old could Sicily be? Forty-something. He was thirty-two. That was pretty near his own age. He looked at Amy Joy's mother closely, with new interest. It was one of two things: She would either be easier to get than her daughter or harder. It was always one extreme or the other.

"I don't want Amy Joy, although she's a very nice little girl."

"You seem to."

Chester Lee poured himself some of his wine-whiskey and pointed to the extra tin cup that sat next to the bottle.

"Want some?"

"I didn't come to drink with you, Chester Lee," said Sicily. Her nerves were on edge. She had had very little sleep for the past two nights, one waiting up for Ed to come home, the other worrying over where he'd been the night before. Her marriage was stretched to the limit. She felt something was about to happen, but divorce wasn't the answer. That would scandalize the family. Mattagash could accept a marriage that didn't work out as long as nothing was done about it. But *change* seemed to be the one thing that no one in town could tolerate. Yet the McKinnons had always been the style setters, the fashion makers. Sicily knew that if she got a divorce almost every other woman in Mattagash would want one too. She didn't relish that kind of social pressure resting heavily on her shoulders.

"Look, could I talk to you?" Chester asked her, head down, staring sadly into his glass of fizzing wine.

"About?"

"Something that really hurts me. Something I never told no one before."

"I don't know if I want to hear it." Sicily leaned against the wall, feeling a bit perplexed. She had never thought much about the human side of Chester Lee. Now, in the dim light of his candles, he looked almost boyish.

"Is it still daylight upstairs?" he asked her.

"Of course. It's only suppertime. But it's raining."

"I never know down here. Sometimes I think there's been a bomb dropped and everything and everyone is gone. Blown to smithereens, and I go up and stick my head out the door just to see if it's all there. I never know down here. I just light the candles and I lay on my bed and think, and I never know."

"Why don't you go up where there's light and get a job like everyone else? You're no better than a mole down here." As Sicily moved away from the wall, she noticed a small black spider inching its way down a strand hanging above her head.

"You don't like me because I'm a Gifford. I can't get a good job because I'm a Gifford. Everyone says I'll just up and quit. That gets to preying on your mind when you're trying to put in a good day's work. Finally, you just throw it in. Why disappoint a whole town? And I don't want to cut pulp like everyone else does, anyway. I want to be different. Be something special."

"Well, you're different, all right."

Chester Lee put his head in his hands and held it, like it wasn't his head but a ball someone had thrown him and he was forced to catch it. By instinct. He waved one hand to Sicily, a signal that it was simply too painful to go on. She came to the cot and sat on it, brushing what looked like half a moldy biscuit to the floor. The right words were hard to find. She really had judged Chester Lee for his family name. Had she been blind?

"I've got no one to talk to," Chester Lee said and picked up his wine. "Will you hold this for a second?" he asked her, and Sicily took the cup from his hand so that he could blow his nose. He stuffed the hankie back in his pocket, a custom of all the men in Mattagash and one that she hated. Seeing it done had always made her weak in the knees. Once Farley Baker had taken his hankie from his pocket at Blanche's grocery, right near Sicily's face. Before she could turn away, he had blocked off one nostril with his index finger to build up pressure in the nasal passage and then fairly hooted as he snorted like an old bull into his handkerchief. It was so obscene that Sicily found it necessary to drop down on one of Blanche's fifty-pound sacks of Robin Hood flour to let the nausea pass. Some men working in the woods, or simply caught without the accouterment, did the same as Farley, except without the handkerchief, aiming for the ground then snapping away any residue with thumb and finger. Other men raised it to the level of high art, jerking their heads, one foot placed firmly ahead of the other.

"What's botherin' you?" she asked, trying to let her maternal

Christian feelings override the knowledge that Chester Lee was sitting beside her with a pocket full of snot. He did look upset, and she could see that, in truth, Chester Lee Gifford was an attractive man. "He looks a little like Eddie Fisher with a mustache," she thought.

"It's kind of a love story," he said and poured wine in the other cup.

"This is your wine here."

"A love story about someone you know very well. Someone who is doomed because of his love," he said and drank some wine from the second cup.

"Who?" Sicily was interested. She took a sip of wine. Chester Lee almost smiled. He knew the best way to get a Christian woman was to let her think there was a real-life parable floating around that she hadn't heard.

"This is awful stuff," she said.

"Someone who lives in Mattagash. Always has."

Sicily drank a bit more wine, her face puckering from the taste.

"What makes me so sad. What makes me not keep a job is that I've loved someone all my life and she married another man." The candles flickered. The room hushed. The mice were asleep. It was only Sicily and Chester Lee and a gallon of wine-whiskey imported from the vineyards of northern Maine. He could feel the electricity about to snap in the air around them.

"And I know her?" Sicily finally asked. The wine didn't taste all that bad. She'd just finish off that one cup. A glass of wine or beer now and then was good for the soul.

"She's a few years older than me. I used to watch her when I was a little boy, and I'd tell myself that when I grew up we'd get married. But by the time I got old enough she'd already married someone else."

"How sad," said Sicily. "How very, very sad."

"You're the only living soul who knows, so don't tell."

"I promise," she said, "but who is she?"

Chester Lee waited a minute. He didn't want to feed her so much birdseed that she'd fly the coop on him.

"You know how I been over talking to Amy Joy and you been real mad about it?"

"Mad ain't the word."

"Well, I just go over and talk to Amy Joy cause I want to be near the woman I've always loved."

Sicily thought about this for a second. She drank the rest of her cup of wine. Marge? Surely not. An affair with Marge would be as stupid as booking a return ticket on the *Titanic*.

"I've loved you all my life," he said, realizing she had missed his point. "Watched you. I think you're real beautiful."

"That's enough," said Sicily and stood up. "I'm a decent married woman and I'll thank you to watch what you say around me."

"You used to wear a blue dress that swished when you walked by, your little nose up in the air. I used to think you was just like a real princess."

Sicily put her empty wine cup on the barrel. She felt a bit giddy. She must have stood up too quickly. She put a hand against the wall as she cautiously climbed the stairs.

Chester heard her feet walking across the upstairs floor. He didn't mind giving a woman the right to be insulted, or the time it took to clear the air as to who was a whore and who wasn't. He would know in a matter of minutes if he had succeeded. He picked up the page of Plymouths again and waited. He heard the same small footfalls cross the floor above his head. Soft as petals dropping. Soft as Jesus walking on water. They paused at the head of the stairs. Chester pushed his paper under the cot and quickly filled both cups with wine.

"A Plymouth wouldn't be that stupid," he thought.

Sicily came unsteadily down the stairs. At the bottom she stopped.

"I didn't come back because of what you said. I came to tell you to let Amy Joy be."

"You don't have to worry none about that. It was only to see you anyway."

"I'm years older than you. I would've thought I was already married when you was barely born."

Sicily had tried, upstairs, to calculate the date of when she was married against how old Chester Lee must be, to see if there was any truth in what he said. But she had been so distraught lately with Ed and Amy Joy and Marge, and now this. And mathematics had never been her long suit. The numbers had tumbled over each other and were lost. Only the poetry, ageless, classless, had remained.

"Did it have a little narrow white belt?" she asked him.

"Did what?"

"That blue dress. Did it have a little white belt and two pleats down the sides?"

"Your waist looked as tiny as that," said Chester Lee and made an O with his thumb and forefinger.

"I bought that on sale at Penney's. I'd almost forgotten it," said Sicily and sat on the cot.

"There was a lot of nice memories in the old days," she said. She was relieved to talk to someone, especially a man. Men were strong and had heavy arms that could wrap around you until you felt safe. Sicily hadn't felt safe in years and every autumn brought more uncertainty. Some nights she would wake up from a troubled dream and run to the closet to see if Ed's clothing was still there, his suitcase still under the bed. The past few weeks had convinced her he was planning to leave. She'd heard of husbands running off to foreign countries like that and never coming back. It was like a big map of all those exotic places had folded up and swallowed them. They were somewhere in the world and the world was too big to go hunting for them. The thought of Ed abandoning her to the gossips of Mattagash was a chilling prospect.

"I don't think you're happy," Chester Lee said.

"You can tell?"

"Sometimes I think I know how you feel every minute of the day."

"You do?"

"Because I love you."

"Do you think I'm still pretty?"

"Beautiful. Like a picture. Prettier than the girls in the catalogue."

"Sears and Roebuck or Spiegel?" asked Sicily.

"Both," said Chester Lee.

Sicily sipped on her wine. Why couldn't these words have ever come from Ed's lips? If they had, maybe she would have been more like the woman he wanted. Maybe she would have been more like the women he went to when the screen door slammed behind him all those nights and she listened to his car drive away. Women who had no names, no faces, no addresses, but she knew they were there, could even tell when he'd tired of one and went on to another. Women who hovered about her marriage like ghosts she would never see.

Sicily began to cry. She was feeling quite maudlin. Chester put his arm around her shoulder. She leaned against him. He took the cup from her hand, just as he had Amy Joy's, and put it aside. He kissed her forehead, squeezed her hand. Sicily tried to remember why this was wrong. It was something worse than a McKinnon woman alone with a Gifford man. It had something to do with Reverend Ralph, with the Bible, with God.

"You're so soft," he told her. Her mind was swimming with thoughts that kept moving, that didn't stay long enough to present themselves to her, to advise her what to do.

"You smell so nice." He stroked her hair gently. If this had been Amy Joy, he told himself, he could have had her naked and hanging by one leg from the ceiling.

"The older ones take more pruning," he reminded himself.

Each flat button of her blouse felt like coins in his hands as they slipped easily out of the holes and were free. He pushed the blouse off her shoulders. Sicily did not help him by lifting her arms. Chester lifted one limp arm and pulled it through the sleeve. Then the other. Sicily sat on the cot in the dark basement of the American Legion Hall. A room full of dustballs and mice droppings. Mildewed boxes of newspapers and pamphlets that had melded together gave off the aroma of basement living. Some old army uniforms, used mostly in parades, cascaded out of a trunk in the far corner. A pants leg hung here, a collar stuck out there, an empty sleeve dangled, its buttons catching the candlelight. It reminded Sicily of a trunkload of soldiers fighting to get out. Like the picture she saw at the movies in Watertown of all those American troops storming off the boats at Normandy. It became almost funny to her, the sleeves reaching out like drowning men. "We're *all* trying to get out of this town," she thought. "The living *and* the dead."

Chester Lee unhooked her bra, clumsily, finally grabbing it up in two hands and almost hurting her. He slowed his efforts once the two hooks came undone. He reminded himself this was not Amy Joy and that at any moment his subject might spring from the bed and dart home, dragging her clothes behind her.

"I don't want her shifting gears on me," he thought.

Upstairs the wind had caught an open shutter and banged it shut. Two barn swallows that had flown inside to shake the rain from their feathers flew around the big upstairs, frantic until they found a window free of glass and escaped back into the drizzle. The old building held noises and sounds that Sicily did not care to hear. She let Chester Lee push her cautiously back against his cot and slide her skirt and half-slip up around her waist. When he stood up to undress, Sicily thought of the first time she had given in to Edward Elbert Lawler, on the scratchy sawdust behind the lumber mill. He, too, had pushed her skirt up about her waist and had pulled her panties down until they circled only her right ankle. "He should have taken them all the way off. Should have taken off my skirt. It should have been on clean, white sheets."

Sicily unzipped her skirt and took it off. She slipped off her panties and folded them, as she did on laundry days. Ever since that first night with Ed, when he never completely undressed her, but left her like an unopened package, the bright paper torn back to expose the contents. Ever since then, she had felt violated. Like a Crackerjack box left behind on the ground after some greedy kid has run off with the prize. To Sicily, the irony was that Chester Lee thought that the prize was still there, at least that there was something to be won if he seduced Sicily McKinnon. And his eagerness for her made her feel that she was all wrapped up again. That she had the opportunity to redo an old mistake. She'd undo *herself* this time, rather than let another man leave her half-undressed, half-naked. It wasn't Chester Lee's fault. She guessed that all the men in Mattagash made love to their wives in that manner, pushing flannel nightgowns up on cold winter nights, trying to arouse women whose feet were wrapped in warm woolen socks. Hair trussed up in pink foam-rubber curlers. Women groggy in their sleep. How many men in Mattagash turned their wives over in the night and, reaching a hand inside the crotch opening of their longjohns, made love to them quietly, quickly. Because the alarm clock would ring rudely at five-thirty. Because undressing was too much bother. How many women sleepily patted their husbands' shoulder, whispered good night, and then turned away to sleep, thankful it was finally over.

Surprised at Sicily's boldness, Chester Lee followed suit and stripped himself of all clothing. He hadn't counted on this. It was

difficult to believe that Sicily was going to be almost as easy as
Amy Joy. Easier, really, since he didn't have to court her. He had
lost his favorite John Deere cap the night Sicily found him behind
the garage with Amy Joy. That had been costly. And trying to
peel off Amy Joy's tight pants was a part-time job in itself. He
had even, once, painfully broken a fingernail. All the mother was
going to cost him was a couple cups of wine-whiskey. And he
would have to concentrate on not looking at Sicily's red hair. He
always hated red hair. The stripper staying at Albert Pinkham's
had red hair. But it was dyed. You could tell. It was brassy. He
didn't mind it on her so much because she had a nice body. Real
firm. Sicily's body didn't look that bad in the candlelight, but she
was twenty, maybe twenty-five pounds overweight. She had
wrinkled some around her mouth. He'd try not to look at those
wrinkles and the red hair. He would think of the brunette on
page 437 of the Fall-Winter issue of the 1960 Sears and Roebuck
catalogue. He pushed one slightly dirty finger into Sicily and the
unclipped fingernail caused her to wince.

"I'm going to make the best of this," she thought. She pulled
his hands away and playing with the hairs on his chest said softly,
in a voice young enough to be Amy Joy's, "Kiss me first. Let's
don't rush."

Chester Lee was always a man who understood that a little
knowledge was a wonderful thing if you didn't have to go to
school to get it. The girls from Watertown who occasionally let
him lead them up the backstairs of the Watertown Hotel were too
drunk to care. One had even fallen asleep, which was much to
the advantage of the forever experimenting Chester Lee Gifford.
She awoke the next morning with a hangover and complaints that
she was "sore everywhere." To Chester Lee it was simple: What
she didn't know had hurt her.

As for the other women in his life, the prostitutes in Bangor
just did what a man told them he wanted done. Amy Joy had
squeezed her eyes shut, and scrunched up her face. Looking
down at her, she looked like Shirley Temple getting a polio shot.
But it didn't particularly matter to Chester Lee. If you separated
the women from the girls, they all had the same thing between
their legs. But here was a woman wanting him to change his style,
to do things her way. And he was smart enough to let her. He
could only learn something more to add to the exhaustive library

of feminine knowledge he had accumulated over the years. "If you milk the cow right the first time, it'll stand still for you the second time," he thought and kissed Sicily's neck and lips. Outside the rain was falling, a trickle coming through a leak in the roof and pattering, a drop at a time, onto the bar upstairs. The swallows had returned and perched atop the door leading into a small cubicle that had been the toilet and still held parts of the procelain tank and commode. They tilted their heads, eavesdropping on the words between Sicily and Chester Lee, ready to fly if the lovemaking seemed a danger to them.

Darkness fell over Mattagash with the rain that had dropped steadily all day. Plates were being laid out on tables inside all the warm houses that lined each side of the narrow twisting road that followed the river. Forks and knives were clinking. Women dished up bowls of cabbage and ham. Took biscuits from the oven. Slapped the hands of children that reached for them too soon, saying, "Don't spoil your supper now." Sweaty men who could not wash the spruce gum stains from their hands sat at the heads of tables all over Mattagash and said, "Dear Lord, We thank you for this food. Amen." When Sicily kissed Chester Lee back, as though his mouth was something good to eat, all of Mattagash was eating, seated at different tables up and down the road, inside warm houses that had blinked on yellow lights in the gathering dusk. Like different pictures of the Last Supper.

"I wonder what Ed will do for supper," she thought, but felt no guilt. "Let him have what I'm having. Like he has for years. He's grown fat as a pig on these kinds of suppers."

It occurred to Chester Lee how unfortunate it was that Marge was in a coma. It would have been quite an accomplishment to hang on his belt: the youngest McKinnon, the middle-aged McKinnon, and the old McKinnon. "Just like the Three Bears," he thought.

Sicily closed her eyes. "I'd like to live in a town where the road is straight," she said to Chester Lee. "Where it don't follow no river. Just goes where you can look straight ahead of you and see what's there."

When she felt Chester enter her, she smiled and thought, "Every woman in Mattagash has owned a blue dress at one time in her life or another."

Rain in the Night:
The Ark
Leaves the Campground

"That was the fall Pearl McKinnon's son and his family camped out on the flat by the bridge. I remember that puny little wife of his going around with a book with bird pictures in it. I could've told her in a flash which bird was which, but she kept looking through that book. Did I know, she asked, that the wrens had gone south for the winter all the way to the Gulf of Mexico? I said to her, 'Ma'am,' I said, 'I lived up here all my life. When the birds go south I'm satisfied they winter somewhere down around Bangor.' I don't like the way some city folks carry on. I don't like it. And what's more the birds don't like it."

—OLD MAN GARDNER, Pseudo-Taxi Driver, 1961

By EARLY EVENING the rain was still falling, covering the valley in a fine mist with fog filling each dip in the road and settling beneath the trees along the river. The yellow headlights of passing cars were swallowed up by it, indiscernible from a short distance. The autumn leaves that had earlier caught the sun so spectacularly sagged under the weight of the raindrops, their colors lost in the moist film. By nightfall, the drizzle was still coming down with no promise of stopping. Water gathered in a large puddle in the middle of the dirt road that crossed the field by the bridge. It built up into a small reservoir that burst at 3 A.M. and cascaded down the hill in a muddy inch-wide stream. Finding the indented path made by campers on their way to the river, it changed its course to the pathway and followed it down into the tent of Junior and Thelma.

Regina, afraid to repose in the camper because of Randy and the dark, in that order, snuggled in sleep between them, mouth open and Teddy bear in her arms. The water pushed beneath the tent's flap and quickly saturated the blankets. Within minutes the entire sleeping equipment of the Ivys, including Junior's new sleeping bag, were sopping with cold September rain. Junior twitched in his sleep, telling himself to wake up, that the Packard's radiator had sprung a leak. Thelma dreamed of her new Kenmore Wringer Washer flooding over and drenching her basement floor. She squirmed, trying to rescue her cardboard boxes of Christmas decorations that she had always meant to put up on a high shelf, in case the Kenmore ever did spill its guts. Regina dreamed she had peed in bed.

Hearing the faint gurgle, Thelma was the first to face the truth, coming suddenly awake and shouting to her husband, "Oh, my God! There's a flood! The river has flooded!"

Junior Ivy was granted, for the second time in two days, an opportunity to save his entire family. He struggled to abandon the sleeping bag, managing to get one leg out, but catching the other pants leg in the sharp teeth of the zipper. Trying to leave the tent by means of one leg in a sleeping bag proved more difficult than vaulting drunkenly from the backseat of the Packard.

Thelma continued to scream, accompanied by Regina, who was now convinced that she had indeed peed in her pants and was confused over what she considered her mother's overreaction.

"We'll drown!" Thelma prophesied. Regina covered her eyes and wept in embarrassment. She knew she had a bed-wetting problem, but had never thought of it as a danger to her family.

Junior stood up, hoping it would enable him to free his leg. At that moment Thelma, in an extreme case of hydrophobia, lurched for the flap opening and knocked her husband to the ground.

Junior pitched forward, pulling up the pegs of the tent and taking the unlucky structure with him into the blackness until he felt the ground stop him. Pain flickered in his right wrist, which had positioned itself in an unnatural angle in hopes of releasing the pants leg from the zipper and was not prepared for breaking a fall. The wrist snapped. Junior heard it. Knew what it meant. A broken right wrist to accompany his sprained left ankle. He held the right arm across his stomach to protect it as he worked clumsily with the left arm to free himself of the tent. Everyone was wide awake now and dealing with the situation with honesty.

Regina, who had checked her panties and found them to be reasonably dry, felt an apology was in order. She skulked off to the camper, where Randy and Cynthia stood sleepy but round-eyed in the door.

Because her husband had uprooted the tent, Thelma found herself on the open ground. The bedding was now being bombarded by rain, as well as the water running down the pathway. But there was no flood. She was quite sure of that now. She heard Junior moaning. The pole light the town had erected near the campsite provided little light in the downpour. Thelma could see what looked like a living mountain of canvas swaying to and fro in the wet night.

"Junior? Are you under there, honey?"

"Oh, my wrist," moaned the hulk of canvas.

"God! You look so funny!" Thelma burst out, when her eyes finally adjusted to the contours and discovered what must be Junior's form beneath. She was seized with laughter, uncommon in Thelma, who perceived excessive gaiety as unladylike.

A crude syllogism surfaced in Junior's mind. *Major premise:* He had broken his wrist when Thelma had stupidly shoved him in the dark and sent him sprawling with the tent. *Minor premise:* He went sprawling because of his imbalance created by one pants leg being caught in the zipper, which happened because Thelma had shouted, "Flood!" *Conclusion:* Kill Thelma.

Junior dove, tent and all, in the direction of Thelma's laughter, which had moved nearer to him. Thelma, who could see, stepped aside and let the bulky form hurl past her. She stopped laughing.

"What are you trying to do?" she asked her husband. "Don't you want me to help you?"

"I'm trying to kill you, Thelma," Junior shouted. "You can help if you want to."

Hearing a savage, entirely primitive noise coming from the throat of the man she had married, Thelma ran for the camper, shoving the children back inside and locking the door. Junior shed the tent and ran after her, forgetting about the symbiotic sleeping bag that still clung to him. He fell face first into the remains of what had been, before the rain, a pleasant morning campfire. Now it was wet ashes and charred remnants of wood. By instinct he had thrust both hands to break his fall, forgetting one hand had a broken wrist. Messages of pain were quickly sent to his brain, along with flashes of Thelma in her wedding gown, Thelma with their firstborn, Thelma decorating their Christmas tree. These images were sent by the civilized part of Junior's psyche, which was trying to tell the primitive part not to murder his wife and the Christmas-loving mother of his children. They were not received.

"I'm going to kill that woman," he said, wiping the rain from his eyes with his good hand and leaving his face smeared with black soot. There was soot about his neck, a smell of it in his nose, a taste of it in his mouth. He quickly realized that the only way to discard the sleeping bag was to take off his pants. He unzipped them and slipped out of them. The ashes had blackened his coffee-colored shirt, a father's day present from Thelma and the children. But Junior had forgotten anything Thelma had given him except a sprained ankle and a broken wrist. He tore the shirt off, popping the buttons, and mopped his dripping face with it, better circulating the soot.

In his white T-shirt, blue boxer shorts, and Thelma's red woolen knee socks he had donned to ward off a chilly night, Marvin Randall Ivy, Jr., wearing the colors of the American flag, lunged for the camper, that tin lunch pail which held something delicious to gobble up.

Thelma saw the flag approaching, but it was difficult to see its face under the dim light.

"Give me the flashlight, Randy! Quick!"

Cynthia had thrown herself on the bunk that was hers and wept loudly as Atlanta burned all around her. Regina was holding her breath. Randy handed his mother the flashlight.

"Do you think he'll really kill you?" He was excited. This vacation was turning into more than he'd expected. Better than "Flash Gordon." Thelma shined the light out the door's window in time to illuminate what looked like a deranged member of a minstrel show.

"Open this door, Thelma!" the man in blackface shouted and rattled the knob. Thelma was reminded of what Junior had told her about his mother's breakdown. She decided that he had gone crazy. She always thought he took after Pearl.

"Junior, for God's sake. It's me!"

"I know it's you!" He rattled the knob again and this time pounded on the door. Cynthia howled. Randy squealed and clapped his hands.

"Do you want your little children to be scarred for life?" Thelma cried.

"I want *you* to be scarred for life," Junior said and went around to the same window that had held Regina's sign declaring fire. He tried in vain to open it, but Thelma had had the foresight to lock it.

"Do you think he'll drown you or beat you with a stick?" Randy asked his mother. Thelma shined the light out the window and into Junior's eyes again, hoping the brightness of it would bring him back to his senses.

"Are we all going to die?!" Cynthia wailed and clutched to her chest the new Ginger, who was not as pretty as her predecessor, but was the best that Watertown's J. C. Penney could offer.

"No, just Mama," Randy reassured her and received a slap on the head from Thelma.

"Stop scaring your sisters, Randy. You're as bad as your father." She kept the light in Junior's eyes. He was still trying to open the window.

"Maybe he'll strangle you," said Randy, putting his two hands around his own neck and squeezing. "Like thith," he lisped, tongue hanging out. Thelma grabbed him by the neck of his shirt, and checking to make sure Junior was still at the other window, she unlocked the door and pushed her only son out into the night.

Junior rushed around to the door, expecting to find it open. He found Marvin Randall Ivy III sitting on the steps.

"How are you going to kill her?" he asked his father, and spit theatrically onto the ground. "Are you going to put her feet in cement and sink her?" Randy gestured with his head toward the river. This was even better than "The Untouchables."

Lights stronger than a flashlight flooded the camper and campground. It was a car.

"What's going on?" Pearl shouted, sticking her head out the car window.

"Daddy's going to kill Mama!" Randy shouted back to her.

"Be careful," Pearl said to Marvin Sr. as they opened their doors and got out of the car. "There's a colored man with little Randy. He must be a burglar."

"There's no coloreds in Mattagash, is there?" whispered Marvin Sr.

"You can never be too sure," said Pearl as they inched their way cautiously toward the camper.

When Pearl realized that the man in blackface was her own

Junior, she ran to him and put her plump, motherly arms around him. Thelma's flashlight hit her squarely in the face. Squinting to see who was behind the beam of light, Pearl kicked the door and said, "Turn that off, you nitwit."

"He's trying to kill me," Thelma shouted.

"I'm not a bit surprised," Pearl told her only daughter-in-law. Junior, finally realizing what he had tried to do, began to sob on Pearl's shoulder.

"There, there," soothed Pearl. "What did she do to you?" Hearing this prejudiced lullaby, Thelma burst into tears herself. Marvin Sr. knocked on the camper door.

"Who is it?!" screamed Cynthia.

"Come in," said Regina.

Thelma unlocked the door and let her father-in-law inside.

"What happened?" he asked her. She fell into his arms and he patted her back. He *almost* liked Thelma. Or at least didn't *dislike* Thelma.

"He just went crazy," she told him.

"Well, it's OK now. We'll go get dry at the motel. Get the kids ready. I'll drive you and the children over in the Packard. We'll have to pick up the camper tomorrow."

Thelma selected some dry clothing for herself and the children. "Let Pearl get Junior's clothes," she thought.

Outside, Pearl was questioning Junior.

"I figured you'd get rained out. Marvin borrowed Pinkham's car so we could come check up on you. We figured you'd get rained out, all right, but we never figured on this mess."

"Mama, I wanted to kill her," Junior sobbed.

"I can understand that all right," Pearl said, remembering the trip up to Mattagash in the Packard. She led her son over to Albert Pinkham's blue Ford.

"We'll cramp up for the night in our motel room," Pearl said.

"I could only see red."

"Me and Thelma and Regina will sleep in the bed."

"I could hear the kids crying and I still wanted to kill her."

"The rest of you will have to sleep on the floor around the bed, but at least you'll be dry."

"I wonder if I'd have really done it if you hadn't come when you did," Junior sobbed.

"Tomorrow we'll get Sicily to put us up between her place and

Marge's. Don't think about it anymore, darling. Tomorrow's a new day." Junior allowed his mother to settle him in the driver's seat of the car, her coat around him.

"I'll be right back, honey. You just stay right there."

"I just heard this awful roar inside my head. This real strange noise," Junior said as Pearl closed the car door. Pearl opened the door again.

"Did it sound like a swarm of bees?" she asked her son.

The Ivys as Nomads:
Nuclear Family About to Blow Up

"All happy families are like one another; each unhappy family is unhappy in its own way."

—Leo Tolstoy, *Anna Karenina*

PEARL WAS AWAKE first, or at least opened her eyes first. Everyone but the children had slept fitfully. Regina kept a foot pressed to Pearl's stomach throughout the night and, no matter how many times Pearl shoved it away, it came back in a matter of minutes. Thelma cowered on her side of the bed, not sure whether she was more afraid of an outburst from Junior or her mother-in-law. On the floor by Pearl's side were Junior and Cynthia. Randy and Marvin Sr. shared the floor near Thelma. Pearl had managed to persuade Sarah Pinkham, who was a bit ruffled at being awakened past three in the morning, to let them have extra blankets and pillows, but the room was not a large one, and the cluttered bodies lay upon the bed and floor like the sad remnants of a refugee camp.

"We're stuffed in here like sardines," Pearl thought at 5 A.M., when Regina's small hoof kicked her again. "This is as bad as them German camps."

At six-thirty, Cynthia sat up and rubbed her eyes. She remembered being brought to her grandparents' room in the middle of the night. It had been raining. But why they had left the campground was a bit vague. She remembered shouting and crying and threats of violence. There had been a fight between her father and mother, she suddenly remembered, and looked to see if they were still alive. Since they were, the night before was immediately filed in the back of her mind where its information might or might not be used someday. Like a television commercial. She started humming "Pop Goes the Weasel" and twiddling her fingers, sometimes snapping them loudly in hopes that the others would wake up. So much for Thelma's prophecy the night before that the children would be scarred for life.

Randy heard his sister and sang along with her, his fingers giving in to occasional snapping themselves.

"It's time for cartoons," said Regina and sat up.

"Stupid, there's no TV up here in the sticks," said Randy.

"Aunt Sicily's got TV, stupid yourself," Cynthia said.

"Shut up," said Pearl. "We need some more sleep. If you want to talk, go outside."

"Children, hush now," said Thelma, terrified to excite Pearl again.

"It's raining out," said Cynthia, who had lunged over her father, stepping on his sore wrist, to get to the window.

"Oh, Jesus Christ," said Junior. Swearing was not one of his usual methods of expression, so Thelma feared he had been riled up again. She got up quickly, realizing the children were up for good, and tried to collect them into an orderly group. Pearl put both feet on the floor and clutched her housecoat about her. Marvin Sr., who had slept in his pants, splashed some water on his face, then got out of the others' way. The rest of the group dressed arduously, bumping into each other, passing items back and forth, requesting that backs be turned, or eyes covered when strategic parts of the body were exposed. Junior and Thelma did not speak. Thelma and Pearl did not speak. Pearl was angry at the children. This unhappy family was definitely unhappy in its own way.

It was decided that Pearl and Marvin Sr. would drive the injured Junior to the Watertown hospital, where his wrist could be X-rayed and treated.

"It's broken all right," Junior whined to Pearl. "I heard it snap."

"What snapped was his mind," thought Thelma, then felt a wifely instinct to pamper Junior, but Pearl had the position secured. Junior was her baby again. It felt good to be needed as a mother once more.

While the others were in Watertown, Thelma was to unpack the cooler and feed the children their breakfast. Some cereal and doughnuts and milk would be enough until they returned and plans could be made to distribute Junior and his family between Sicily's and Marge's. From the window, Thelma watched the Packard pull away from Pinkham's yard. The children were fussing more than usual. Randy managed, by eight o'clock, to slap each of his sisters twice.

The fishermen in the opposite room, who were unable to fish because of bad weather, pounded on the wall each time one of the girls wailed. When Randy pulled Cynthia's freshly made braid hard enough that the ribbon came off in his hands, the sound that left her vocal box could have shattered crystal. Thelma kept her hand pressed to the child's mouth until she was quieted. But she could not muffle the sobs of a crying child and Randy at the same time. He had seized the tin pan provided by the Albert Pinkham Family Motel for heating water and beat the wall with it, pretending he was sending a drum signal to the fishermen. They signaled back loudly. Randy answered. Violet La Forge beat out a coded message on her own wall as well. Even the advanced stages of meditation could not raise her above such incarnations as the little Ivys. Caught up in the thunderous pounding that now surrounded him on two sides, Randy ran to the wall that had let Violet's message through. Thinking of her as another, distinct tribe in his Western drama, he pounded out a response: *Bang. Bang Bang Bang Bang. Bang Bang.*

Thelma was a frail, easily frightened woman, who usually came within a hair of passing out cold in the dentist's chair. When visiting her doctor's office for a checkup, she always took a Mason jar that she had cleverly painted dark blue and covered with little blobs of yellow paint for flowers. When a nurse knocked on the bathroom door to collect the usual plastic container with Thelma's urine sample, the dark blue Mason jar would emerge in Thelma's shaking hand. She simply could not bear to have her personal body fluid exhibited in front of everyone, sloshing about like rainwater in a tin pail. Thelma did not deal well with cogs in the machine, and Marvin Randall Ivy III was the biggest cog Thelma had ever encountered. For nine years old he was large, having the genetic structure of the Ivys and the McKinnons. Beating out at Thelma with his fists and leaving her in tears was not uncommon. But he had learned to control as much of his negative personality as possible when his father was around, letting only a vestige of his true nature through. If Thelma complained to Junior in the evenings that Randy had thrown another wicked tantrum, hitting and kicking herself and the girls, Junior merely continued to look at his newspaper.

"Randy, you mind your mother and leave your sisters alone"

was the best support Thelma could get out of him. So she had long ago thrown her hands up in despair. She was an abused mother. And her daughters were the unlucky victims of brotherly rage. Still pent up with tears from the way the vacation was turning out, Thelma saw white, the way Pearl had seen black during her breakdown. The way Junior had seen red the night before. They were a family of colors, a family of sad crayons scraping against each other in the box.

She caught Randy by the arm, leaving Cynthia free to loose her anguish. In the struggle between mother and son, a quart bottle of milk crashed to the floor and splattered the tile and wall.

"Look now what you've done, you little monster!" Thelma screamed. Suddenly, she hated Junior. Hated him because Randy looked so much like him, because the seed that had sprung from Junior's body into hers had created him. It was all right for Junior to spoil the children and he did in the short time he spent with them in the evenings before bed. But she was left with the aftermath of his fatherly affections, left with criticism from Junior and Pearl concerning their behavior.

Randy chose this moment to kick Thelma in the kneecap and sling his arms so that the box of doughnuts flew through the air and scattered like small tires about the floor. Cynthia and Regina stepped on two as they ran for the safety of the bed, mashing them well.

The fishermen had stopped their war drums and retaliated by going for the head chief himself, Albert Pinkham.

Violet came out onto the patio and peered through the window, unable to see the bedlam because of the curtains Sarah Pinkham had gotten on sale at J. C. Penney's in Watertown. They were white with a bevy of pink swans floating about on them. As Violet turned to look in the direction of Albert's house, the swans parted to let through a Mickey Mouse cereal bowl that broke the window and shattered on the pavement outside.

"My God, I could've been killed," Violet whispered and put a shaking hand to her mouth. Corn flakes clung to her hair like crisp, brown snowflakes. Violet stepped back from the window just as another missile came whizzing out. It was a coconut-coated chocolate doughnut followed by Regina's corrective shoe. There was a mixture of noises coming from inside Room number 4, as if a chicken coop had been placed next to a cage of foxes.

"I'm sorry you was ever born," Thelma was heard to say. "I should have left you right there in the hospital. I should have taken another baby. Even that colored woman's baby. Anything would've been better than you."

Violet prayed that Albert would hurry. "That poor little boy," she thought. "And they wouldn't let me adopt because I'm single and a dancer."

Cynthia popped her head through the broken window and stared with big eyes at Violet La Forge. Behind her, Regina was still in tears over an incident concerning Randy, herself, and her one remaining corrective shoe. Thelma was shouting threats of leaving Randy in a straitjacket on a colored man's doorstep and taking home a small dark child instead. Randy romped around the room waving Thelma's bra over his head. Pretending it was a slingshot, he loaded it with a glazed doughnut and threw the entire apparatus in Thelma's face.

"Are you the loose woman?" Cynthia was a paragon of the old saying about little pitchers having big ears and filled hers often at the streams of adult gossip.

"Go away, you awful little girl," Violet said. She had still not recuperated from the cruel words she had found taped to her door.

"Are you the woman who exercises with big titties?"

Hearing Albert Pinkham's voice followed by Sarah's unmistakable squawking, Violet retreated into her room and locked the door. She did not want to see Sarah Pinkham until she was ready for her.

When Pearl and the male Ivys returned at ten-thirty from the Watertown hospital, they were in a cheerful mood. The huge breakfast at Belle's Diner and Takeout had been a pleasant one. The bone in Junior's wrist was cracked, but not broken, and it was now securely wrapped in a bandage. They were all willing to forgive and forget. To prop the train back on the track. To pull together as a family. But the first thing they saw when the Packard turned into Albert's drive was Thelma and the children straddling Pearl's and Marvin's suitcases. All four were huddled beneath a colorful red-and-white umbrella that one of the fishermen's wives, out of pity, had brought out to protect the outcasts from the rain still falling. The ground around them looked as if the birds had been having a messy breakfast and had dropped doughnuts and cereal from the sky. Thelma sat with her face in one hand, the other holding the umbrella. Regina had picked the gravel from one chocolate doughnut that still held remnants of coconut, and her cheeks now bulged with it. Cynthia was trying to dry off Ginger, who had been dunked in a glass of milk during the fracus.

Randy ran to the Packard, shouting, "Daddy! Daddy! Mama threw my Mickey Mouse bowl out the window and broke it."

The Ivys in the Packard stared in amazement. This was not a train back on the track. This was three cars and a caboose that had definitely been derailed.

"My God, what do you suppose happened?" Junior asked.

"She's taken to throwing the children's things," Pearl said.

Dividing the Ivys:
One More Story in the Naked City

"The bride wore a floor-length gown of organdy trimmed with small cloth daisies about the waist and hemline. She carried a daisy bouquet and was given away by her father, Theodore Parsons of Portland. The mother of the groom wore black."

—THE PORTLAND *MESSENGER* (of Thelma Ivy's Wedding), 1949

―――――――――

DIVIDING THE IVYS up between Marge's house and Sicily's proved more difficult than would be expected. Space was not so much the issue as personality differences. At first Ed told Sicily it was the Ivys' own fault that they were asked to leave Albert Pinkham's premises. They should have had Junior sterilized when he was a baby. Then he went beyond that, saying that if Pearl had been stupid enough to marry an undertaker in the first place, she should have had the foresight to put their firstborn in a sack, take it down to the river, and drown it, like they do to unwanted kittens in Mattagash. Finally, he said it was the entire Ivy family's fault it was raining. In the end, Sicily persuaded him to let Pearl and the two girls stay with them. They would share Amy Joy's bedroom.

"As long as there's no male Ivys in this house overnight," he insisted. "They're just a long line of undertakers. That little boy is gonna be an undertaker too, unless someone from outside the family takes him to the vet and has him put to sleep first."

When Sicily drove to Marge's with the news, she saw the camper parked in the yard. Randy's sad face was pressed against the window, looking out at the rain.

"He reminds me of the doggie in the window that Patti Page sung about," Sicily thought. "Poor little boy. He can't be that bad. After all, he's got Junior and Thelma for parents."

Inside, she found Marvin and Junior watching Marge's big television set. In the kitchen Pearl had made coffee and was having a cup. Cynthia sat on the floor near the table and brushed Ginger's hair.

145

"Where's Thelma and the other little girl?" Sicily asked.

"In the room Amy Joy's been sleeping in." Pearl poured Sicily a cup of coffee. "It doesn't look as though this rain is ever going to let up," she said, looking out the window over the sink.

"Autumn rain," said Sicily. "Poor farmers. I hope they can get their potatoes out all right. I'm sure they must be almost finished by now."

"I suppose folk'll all be getting back from the harvest soon," Pearl said.

"A lot of families already are. The Farleys finished for that farmer over in Limestone that they go for each year. And Ronald's family is back. I saw the truck loaded down with their stuff yesterday. They do good each year. All of them little kids, and they got a hundred, all of them earn enough money for their school clothes. Winnie told me that even the little ones in the early grades earn enough."

"That helps a family out," said Pearl, who no longer wanted to hear about potatoes and farmers and child labor. She had left that gladly behind her years ago and was not anxious to have it forced back upon her memory. Sicily had no choice but to level with Pearl about the predicament as to who stayed at her house and who didn't. Pearl didn't mind who stayed where as long as she and Thelma did not bed down under the same roof.

"She's in the bedroom now and it's all I can do to stand it. Even though I can't see her I can feel her near and it's driving me crazy."

"Who is?" asked Cynthia, who rarely missed out on the spoken word.

"Spelling don't help none," Pearl warned Sicily. "She knows how." Pearl and Sicily went out to swing on the back porch.

"Who's driving you crazy?" asked Cynthia, who had thrown down Ginger to follow them.

"Stay here!" Pearl ordered, and Cynthia's bottom lip dropped as she tried to muster up some tears. But she couldn't. The incident at the motel that morning had simply drained her. So she turned and went off somewhere in the house.

"That kid's the spittin' image of her mother," Pearl told Sicily. "They even dress alike. Thelma had a whole wardrobe of identical outfits sewn up. They look just like twins born twenty years apart."

Pearl and the two girls made plans to stay at Sicily's. The others would stay at Marge's. Marvin Sr. and Randy could sleep on Marge's sofa that made up into a bed. Junior and Thelma would take the room that Amy Joy slept in. And Amy Joy would have to return to Sicily's and bed down on the couch.

Pearl took what things she'd need and put them into Sicily's car. If there was a choice between Ed Lawler and Thelma, she would choose Ed. That's how strongly she felt.

"You're lucky you don't have no daughter-in-law," she told Sicily on the ride over.

Cynthia and Regina were in the backseat, a paper bag between them that Thelma had filled with pajamas, toys, and a fresh change of clothes for the next day.

"Lucky you don't have no what?" asked Cynthia.

At Marge's Thelma drew herself a hot bath. She needed one desperately after two horrible days of roughing it in the wilds. She and Junior had not spoken a word since the angry ones they had shouted at each other the night before. This was one time she was not going to bend. If *he* wanted a reconciliation, he would have to come to *her*. She was tired of being his slave. She felt like one of those women in John Wayne movies, except without the romance at the end. And as for her mother-in-law, Thelma would see to it that all of Portland heard how shabbily Pearl had treated her. And she would let them know how shabbily Pearl had been raised, in a town of rusting chain saws, pulp hooks, and a family of nitwits. Not to mention the alcoholic. "If only I'd been born with a higher pain threshold," she thought.

At five o'clock she fried some hamburger patties, mashed potatoes, opened two cans of peas and put bread and pickles on the table. There was a cake on the counter that Sicily had brought, so she arranged several slices on a plate. She laid out plates, forks, and knives for three. She put margarine on the table, then went to the living room door, where Marvin Sr. and Junior were watching a Western.

"Dad, it's ready," she said to her father-in-law. "The milk is in the Frigidaire. Someone has to go unlock Randy." Then she went back to Amy Joy's bedroom and closed the door. Let them fend for themselves. They were grown men. If they needed anything else, they could surely get it on their own. Even Randy. She was not yet ready to welcome the prodigal son home. Junior had taken the camper's key and locked him in when the truth about the events that morning were unfolded by Cynthia and Regina. Randy's character had not emerged well and he was sent to the camper for the afternoon.

"What if I need to pee?" he had asked his father.

"You should have thought of that this morning," Junior said and locked the door.

The three male Ivys ate in silence, except to ask each other to pass the salt or a slice of bread. They ate Thelma's supper and then went back to the living room, to the newspaper and television. Later, when Thelma left the sanctity of her new bedroom for a sandwich, she found the dishes just where she'd left them, covered with cake crumbs and scraps of food. Rings of dried milk decorated each glass. Food particles were melded to the silverware. If it had been her house, she would have left them there. But it was not her house, and she was just introspective enough to realize that it was too late to start sporting a new personality. Besides, Junior wouldn't approve of her being an outspoken woman. "He's seen enough of that in this mother," Thelma thought and went about cleaning the kitchen. She fixed herself a cold plate supper and took it back to her room. As she passed the living room door, she saw the back of Junior's head as it rested in the recliner. He had dozed off watching television. A wifely ache raced through her. "He looks so cute," she thought. "Like a little boy."

Marvin Sr. had undone the sofa and created a bed. He had already made it up with sheets and blankets from Marge's linen closet. It was not a tidy job but Randy had thrown himself upon the result and was fast asleep. Sleeping did him justice. Thelma walked past her husband and bent over to brush Randy's forehead with her lips.

"Did he spit out his gum?" she asked Marvin Sr.

"It's on the coffee table," he said and pointed to a teepee of pink gum.

Thelma tousled Randy's hair and covered his shoulders with the blanket.

"The trip's been hard on him," she said to Marvin Sr.

"It's been hard on us all," he answered.

Junior had come awake in the chair. "Did the sheriff get killed?" he asked his father, who shook his head.

"Poor Junior," thought Thelma. "He still thinks Matt Dillon is gonna get killed."

"Good night," Thelma said.

"Good night," said Marvin Sr.

Walking past Junior's chair, Thelma didn't say a word. She wanted to, but didn't. There was something very sad in the way he was scrunched down in the chair, in the angle of his shoulders, the droop of his head. He looked defeated. A few minutes later, Thelma heard a slight, almost inaudible rap on her bedroom door. She pulled on her housecoat and opened the door a crack. It was Junior, looking sheepish and kicking the toe of one shoe against the door casement.

"I guess I'll sleep in the trailer tonight," he said.

"Whatever," said Thelma.

"I guess it'd be better till things calm down."

"Whatever you think."

"I'll see you in the morning, I guess." He was hoping she would fling the door open and sweep him into her bedroom as though she were a spider who hadn't seen a fly in a long time. But Thelma whispered a throaty "good night" and softly closed the door. Tears immediately filled her eyes and she made small fists out of her hands. It was the first time she had not reached her hand in and helped pull her husband up out of an embarrassing situation. He could not say the words "I'm sorry." She knew that. Before, she quickly accepted his apology in whatever form he might offer it: movie, flowers, dinner, or sometimes just his hurt, boyish attitude. He had chosen the latter tonight because there were no movies, florists, or restaurants in Mattagash. It was his only alternative. After his outburst last night, he ordinarily would have tried all four. By instinct. Like a general uniting all his forces for the final *coup de grace*. Outside the closed door, he hung his head, wondering how in the world other men in Mattagash apologized. If they did, they had to rely on cunning, with no delicacies of the modern world to aid them. Like the early pioneers. A box of chocolates, Junior supposed, could have gone a long way crossing the prairie.

For a few seconds Thelma almost threw open the door and ran after him. It may have been physical exhaustion which prevented her. After fights between them, Junior liked to make up with a bout of lovemaking, but after two harrowing days of vacation,

Thelma did not feel like making love. So she let him go. She heard him outside in the camper as he slammed the door with a force that seemed excessive.

"He just wants me to feel sorry for him because he's sleeping out there," she told herself as she crawled into bed and snapped the bedside light off. The frogs and crickets were noisy. She snuggled down beneath the blankets. It felt wonderful to be in a bed again with clean fresh sheets and plenty of room to stretch. A car passed on the road outside. The beam from the headlights raced across the ceiling and wall, then disappeared back into the blackness, and the sounds belonged to the river again, and the night creatures, and the steady rain that was still falling over Mattagash.

Before Thelma fell asleep, she put her arms around the spare pillow and held it as though it were alive. For eleven years she had shared her bed, as well as her life, with a man. Her husband. For better or worse. Now here she was at the end of the road, at the end of the earth. Alone. "This is definitely for worse," she thought, and drifted off to sleep, thinking of her mother, who had died several years before, and wishing there were some way she could talk to her, directly, instead of telling God, who was just another man, to pass it on. Some things only women understood.

At nine-thirty Amy Joy tromped through Sicily's kitchen, grabbed a doughnut, and headed for her bedroom.

"Where have you been, Amy Joy?" Sicily, who was having a snack at the table with Pearl, asked her daughter.

"Out."

"Out where?"

"Just out."

"With who?"

"No one."

"Where?"

"Oh, Mama." Amy Joy turned back for a handful of chocolate mints that lay defenseless in a candy dish on the table.

"Watch your complexion now," said Sicily, squeezing Amy Joy's plump hand until she released a few of the mints.

"I swear, Amy Joy, when the doctor slapped your bottom you didn't cry. You reached for food."

"I'll see you tomorrow," she told her mother.

"Just where do you think you're going?"

"To Aunt Marge's to go to bed. I'm real tired," Amy Joy said.

"You're staying here tonight," her mother said.

"What?" asked Amy Joy incredulously, forgetting about food for the time being.

"Junior and Thelma are sleeping in your room at Marge's and you're staying here."

"But I can't!" Amy Joy was panicky.

"Well, you have to. It's already set." Sicily kicked Pearl under the table and winked. She had just been telling her how close Amy Joy was to Marge, how protective she felt.

"I gotta stay at Aunt Marge's!" Amy Joy wailed.

"Well, you can't. I'm trying to tell you that Junior and Thelma are probably already asleep in your bed."

"They *do* go to sleep early," Pearl said, to help Sicily's cause.

"I don't care how early they go to bed, they ain't staying in my room." Amy Joy was on the verge of a tantrum for the first time since she was ten years old and wanted Ed to take her to the girlie show at the Watertown Fair. When he refused she had thrown her plumpness upon the ground in front of the show tent, screaming and kicking, until Ed bodily dragged her back to the car, threw her into the backseat, and flew for home with her. Sicily wanted to take her to the Watertown hospital and get a shot of something to calm her down.

"I'll stop at Mickey's Tavern and get us all a shot," Ed had said but didn't stop the car until he was outside his own door.

Amy Joy was frantic again. As frantic as that day at the fair.

"I just have to stay at Aunt Marge's!"

"Amy Joy, have you gone completely crazy? It ain't gonna kill you to sleep over here for a few nights."

"Yes it will! Yes it will! It will!" She was all but jumping up and down.

"What's this racket down here?" Ed had left the room upstairs that he'd converted into a study when the reverberations of Amy Joy's protests bounced up the stairs and intruded on his thoughts.

"What in hell are you bawling about?" he asked his daughter. Amy Joy fell to pouting and was silent. It was her usual stance against Ed, even when things were running smoothly.

"She wants to sleep at Marge's, though I've tried to tell her that Junior and Thelma are using her bed," said Sicily.

"Do you want to sleep with Junior and Thelma? Is that what you want?" Ed always used this approach on Amy Joy. Asking her if she wanted the ridiculous and forcing her to answer.

"Well, do you? Is that what you want? To snuggle up between Junior and Thelma?"

There was a pause, but Ed was patient. He would wait it out. Finally, tears filling her eyes, Amy Joy said, "No, sir."

"Well, then. That's more like it. Your mother's made up the sofa for you. Now get in there and go to bed. You should have been in this house over an hour ago. Your mother lets you run wild."

Amy Joy went slowly, begrudgingly, into the living room. Sicily had left a clean nightgown for her on the sofa and she took it and went off into the bathroom to change.

Back in the kitchen, Ed said to Sicily, "You spoil her. She minds me because I don't let her get away with all that shit." Then he turned and went back up to his study.

"Poor kid," thought Pearl.

"Poor little Amy Joy," thought Sicily and went in to kiss her daughter good night.

Braille as Sexual Expression: Chester Lee Discovers the Holy Grill

> O what can ail thee, Knight at arms,
>   So haggard and so woebegone?
> The squirrel's granary is full
>   And the harvest's done . . .
>
> —JOHN KEATS, "La Belle Dame Sans Merci"

RUTH GIFFORD WAS mixing scrambled eggs in a plastic bowl. Her granddaughter, Summer Daye, sat near her on the floor with a jar of marshmallow fluff and a spoon. The sticky mixture covered the child's face and her hair was matted with it. The dog, Chainsaw, sat waiting for the occasional opportunity to move in, lick the spoon quickly, then retreat before being kicked by Ruth or slapped on the nose with a sticky spoon.

"You already gobbled down half a jar of that stuff. Now put it away or you'll git sick," Ruth told the little girl, who ignored the advice and continued to spoon out globs of marshmallow.

"Chainsaw got as much as she did," said Chester Lee, who'd been watching the diners with amusement.

"Get away, Chainsaw!" Ruth shouted as the dog dived in for a lick when the little girl glanced over at Chester. Chainsaw got one last taste before Ruth caught him up by the skin of his neck and heaved him, fleas and all, out through the screen door. He whined several times through the mesh, his nose pressed against it, then went off to lie on the front porch and lick the last of the fluff from around his mouth.

"Doggie! Doggie!" squealed the little girl, her fat arms above her head. The spoon fell to the floor. Ruth took the jar away, helped Summer Daye to her feet, and pushed her off into the living room, where her mother was sleeping on the couch.

"Summer Daye's gettin' so big. Look at her waddle!" said Ruth.

"What a stupid name," said Chester.

"What's wrong with it? Debbie saw it in a magazine a long time ago and remembered it."

"It's pretty stupid to call a kid that when we only got three months of summer and the rest of the time we're up to our asses in snow," said Chester Lee.

"It's to *remind* us of summer, dummy. Can't you ever think poems?"

"I'll tell you what I think," said Chester Lee. "Debbie better quit spending her winter nights in bed with Boyd or we're gonna have so many *summer days* around here we'll think we're in Florida."

"You just mind your own business," said Debbie, who came into the kitchen to get a bottle of beer from the refrigerator. "Ask Chester Lee where he's been hitchin' his horse lately, Mama," she said to Ruth and winked.

"There's usually a herd of horses at your hitchin' post," Chester Lee said as he ate the plate of eggs Ruth put in front of him.

"I know where he's been," said Ruth. "Them McKinnons has had their noses up in the air for so many years their kids is born looking like little pigs." Ruth Gifford was one of the first to make a connection between personality and genetics.

"Amy Joy is fat enough to be a little pig," said Debbie. "Does she oink, Chester Lee? Or does she squeal?"

Ruth Gifford laughed with her daughter. Despite the teasing, there was an unspoken pride in the Gifford household that one of their own had scaled McKinnon walls and Chester Lee basked in the warmth of his social triumphs.

"Oink! Oink! Oink!" said Debbie as Chester Lee heaved a biscuit across the room. It hit her on the shoulder, then rolled off under the table where Chainsaw would be happily surprised to find it at breakfast.

"What are you gonna do if you get that little girl up the stump? That ain't no laughing matter." Ruth's "facts-of-life" talks with her children had always been helpfully instructive, ranging from religion to politics and the legal processes.

"You get that little girl in the family way, Chester Lee, and Ed Lawler'll bury you so deep in jail all we'll ever see of you again is your cowlick."

"I ain't afraid of Ed Lawler," Chester Lee lied.

"Ed Lawler catches you somewhere where it's dark, he'll hit you on the head so hard you'll have to unlace your shoes to blow your nose."

"Don't you worry none about me. I got it all under control."

"Chester Lee, you need more trouble right now about as much as Noah needed more rain," said Ruth.

"I ain't gonna be in no trouble."

"Then keep your pants up," said his mother.

"Or keep Amy Joy's up," said Debbie and ran from the kitchen when Chester Lee pushed back his chair as if to chase her.

"OINK! OINK! OINK!"she shouted again from the living room, before taking Summer Daye up to bed.

"I'll see you tomorrow," Chester Lee told his mother and went out into the rainy night.

Leaning on Marge's garage and finishing off his Lucky Strike, Chester Lee cupped the cigarette in his hands as he smoked, hiding the telltale orange glow from detection. He mashed the stub beneath the heel of his boot and flicked it into the lilac bushes. He wanted as little evidence as possible left behind, and a Lucky Strike stub could be incriminating. Even on mere social visits Chester Lee rarely touched the objects in the room around him, and left few fingerprints. He never knew when the urge to take something would come upon him. The drizzle was still coming down, and he was anxious to get inside and into a warm, dry bed. He spit on the ground and wiped his mouth on the sleeve of his jacket. He could have easily settled for claiming Amy Joy on his cot in the basement of the Legion Hall, but something about crawling between the whiteness of McKinnon sheets in a McKinnon house was a challenge any true Gifford would take up. It would bring McKinnon noses down that had been up for generations.

But that was not the principal reason Chester Lee was anxious to visit with Amy Joy in her bedroom. She had promised she'd take the roll of money Ed kept hidden in his desk when Chester Lee hinted to her that money was all that kept them from a hasty wedding downstate. Away from Mattagash no one in their right minds would believe that Amy Joy was only fourteen. She would pack her suitcase and they'd go off together. That's what he'd told Amy Joy, and if he had allowed her to come to the Legion

Hall he'd have been bound to take her with him. Telling her he wanted to make love to her in a real house, in a real bed, like they were married, had made her romantic heart flutter and she'd agreed quickly. Now he could take her body one more time, take something a McKinnon *owed* a Gifford. It would be his last laugh. Then he could take the money, leaving behind a promise to wait down the road a bit in Boyd's pickup truck. Alone, he would be free to get to Watertown the best way he could to catch a Greyhound bus downstate. What would Ed Lawler tell the police? That Chester Lee had crawled through his willing daughter's open window, made love to her, took money she had eagerly stolen for him from her father, and then ran off? Chester Lee knew Ed Lawler would consider it worth the money to have him out of town and out of Amy Joy's life forever. It was a job, really, and Chester Lee would be well paid. It warmed his heart to know that a man like himself, with no major education to speak of, could outsmart a college man who was a principal. He knew he was paving inroads for the Gifford clan.

The window to Amy Joy's bedroom was waiting for him. A spool of thread had been placed to wedge it open, so that the dirt-ridden hands of Chester Lee Gifford could slither inside and push it up to the hilt. Amy Joy had done this early in the evening so that she wouldn't forget. It was a sentimental gesture, one of love, and Chester Lee was almost touched by it.

The window lifted easily, noiselessly. Chester Lee was surprised that Amy Joy was not waiting for him with a blush on her cheeks at the window. When he heard the soft breathing that meant sleep coming from the bed, his ego was a bit bruised. That Amy Joy could fall asleep when she expected him had never occurred to him. Was he losing his charm? Had she come to her senses and decided not to rob her father after all?

He carefully eased the window down behind him, resting it again on the helpful wooden spool. He gave his eyes several seconds to adjust to the objects of the room. The bed was against the opposite wall and he inched his way toward it, one hand in front of him to avoid a collision. He could hear the sounds a woman makes in sleep, the short half-snores, the smooth breathing. He wondered if Amy Joy might be pretending to be asleep. Or if she was all naked and waiting for him. Waiting to say *Boo!*

when he reached for her. He groped around in the darkness for the sleeping form. Finding her face, he bent down and kissed it. He felt for her breasts and, touching the prominent ribs on Thelma's skinny body, Chester knew immediately it was not the body of one whose main diet was ice cream and Hershey bars. It was not the fatted Amy Joy Lawler.

"You could scrub socks on these ribs," thought Chester, realizing that this was the skinny little woman married to Amy Joy's cousin. Chester Lee had spied on the Ivys one evening while he waited for Amy Joy behind the hazelnut bushes that grew along the road across from Ed Lawler's house. That was the evening the Ivys had come to Sicily's to discuss the funeral preparations, and Chester Lee had given each one a close scrutiny. Thelma Ivy was not enticing to him but, after all, it *was* dark in the room. *Any port in a storm* was navigational advice any true Gifford would be happy to heed. And she *was* a city woman, born and bred away from Mattagash. The curiosity of making love to a real city woman who was related to the McKinnons was enough to put flesh back onto Thelma's empty bones.

She moaned softly at the touch of hands on her small breasts. Junior had never been quite so forceful a lover. He had always been rather subdued. Almost indifferent. Once, during lovemaking, he had looked down at her and asked if she'd remembered to make the monthly payment on the Packard. Now he was feeling her body as though he were touching it for the first time, yet with authority. Like John Wayne touched the women in his movies. Brutish, but boyish.

Thelma's sex drive, which had always been asleep, awakened, and she wrapped her arms around the male body that hovered above her. In her half-sleep she murmured "Junie, that feels good." Chester Lee had already unzipped his pants and pushed the crotch of Thelma's panties aside. He kissed Thelma's tiny mouth. It was hard to believe the good luck he'd been stepping in lately.

After she began to menstruate at the age of fourteen, Thelma had thought often in her life about rape. An issue of the *Reader's Digest* warned women about the wiles of men in parking lots or behind bushes. Men who stood on the street outside a lonely woman's house, smoking a cigarette down to the butt while star-

ing up at the bedroom window, waiting for the light inside to
unsuspectingly go out.

Nights when Junior worked late at the funeral home, she kept
the doors and windows securely locked, her heart hammering if
an oak branch should scrape a window in the wind. In the parking
lot of Cain's Grocery, she scanned all directions before finally
unlocking the car door and throwing bags of groceries onto the
front seat, sometimes breaking eggs and mashing bread. In the
event that an assault *should* take place, Thelma had asked God to
let her pass out. That way, she could come to blinking her eyes
in the warm sunlight, surrounded by scattered cans of vegetables
and cornflakes to find the mysterious rapist gone, the act com-
pleted, and dinner waiting to be prepared for her family. She
would never tell a soul. Not even Junior. And if a child should
come of it, no one would be the wiser, unless, knock on wood,
the rapist was a colored man. That could really let the cat out of
the bag. There *were* a few colored in Portland, but Thelma was
reasonably sure her assailant would have the decency to be white.

So having armed herself with the *Reader's Digest*'s helpful hints
on what to kick and where, and having made her pact with God,
Thelma faced each day with the conviction that she was more
prepared for rape than the average woman. But when the coarse
mustache of Chester Lee Gifford pressed down upon her thin
lips, the *Reader's Digest* article vanished as though the words had
been written with invisible ink. Strangely, she suddenly remembered a little pink comb set that she had gotten on her seventh
birthday. The brush had been too bristly and hurt her head whenever her mother brushed her hair. When Thelma felt the stiff hair
touch against her mouth she wondered, "Whatever happened to
that little pink brush?" Then she tried to remember why Junior
would be wearing a mustache.

When Thelma Parsons Ivy realized she was being made love
to by an unknown man with a mustache, that the pet fear of her
life was becoming a reality, a terror gripped her that could not
parallel the Packard incident or a husband threatening murder.
This was something much more personal. And if God promised
her she would pass out, He lied. The screams that came from her
throat reminded Chester Lee of a cross saw cutting tin. Or a stuck
pig. She beat her frail arms against his head, forgetting the vital

areas suggested by *Reader's Digest*. Chester Lee, really not a rapist at heart, lifted himself from off his supposed victim and staggered for the window.

"Rape!" Thelma shouted, her life having become a series of brief one-word ejaculations. The *Digest* article had suggested women should yell "Fire!" for it would take the rapist by surprise and bring others to her defense much quicker. But Thelma had heard "Fire" yelled enough on the hazardous trip up from Portland. If Pearl had yelled "Rape!" instead of fire, it might have made a world of difference.

But yelling "Rape!" was surprise enough for Chester Lee. And it was an insult. He had been accused of many things, but raping Thelma was not one that he felt presented him in his best light. One leg out the window, he stopped and shouted, "I'd rape a chicken first!"

The events of the past few days caught Thelma up in their frenzy and she wailed now in the enormity of the past grief she had borne because of them. "Rape! Rape! Rape!" she chanted, drawing from the experience of her past cheerleading days at South Portland High, where she had rattled pompoms and shouted, "Go! Go! Go!" or "Fight! Fight! Fight!" until her school-spirited throat became hoarse. She locked into the same rhythm now, using the word as a mantra, blocking out the real, physical world, as a kind of hysteric meditation settled over her.

Chester Lee decided he would let her think what she pleased and proceeded out the window, letting it drop behind him with a thud. He did not, he conceded, understand city women. One minute they wanted it. The next minute they cried rape. From beneath the lilac bushes in Marge's backyard, he could hear the frantic cheers of Thelma Ivy still coming from the house. He heard Junior Ivy burst from the camper parked in Marge's driveway. Marge's porch light flicked on.

Not one to linger needlessly at the scene of the crime, especially if it was raining, Chester Lee left the sanctity of the lilac bushes. Where could Amy Joy have gone? He almost expected to trip over her plumpness out there somewhere in the dark, her fat little fists full of money. But she was nowhere in the darkness of Marge's yard. Fearing the incident inside might get out of hand if Junior Ivy decided to come outside with a gun in search of a rapist,

Chester Lee abandoned the dream of money and escape from Mattagash. He would retreat to his hideout until things cooled down and he might poke his head up out of the earth to see whether he could see his shadow or not. It was when he turned in the direction of the Legion Hall that he saw her, sitting all sleek and silent in the yard, her silver grill glistening and wet under the porch light, flashing at him that sexy, Packard smile.

Wailers and Demons:
Thelma Makes Use
of Her Voice Training

But oh! that deep romantic chasm which slanted
Down the green hill athwart a cedarn cover!
A savage place! as holy and enchanted
As e'er beneath a waning moon was haunted
By woman wailing for her demon-lover!

—SAMUEL COLERIDGE, "Kubla Khan"

THELMA HAD WRAPPED her arms around her pillow and was standing up on the bed when Junior burst into the bedroom and felt for the light switch by the door. He had come as fast as a cracked wrist could open doors and a sprained ankle could cross floors.

"Rape! Rape! Rape!" Thelma hollered, as though an imaginary crowd of basketball enthusiasts were behind her in the bleachers stomping their feet in unison. Junior grabbed her hands and tried to calm her but it was impossible. He did manage to pull her down from the bed and take the crumpled pillow from her, but to soothe her damaged psyche was not possible, at least not in a matter of minutes. She could no longer speak in sentences. Junior collected words from her and puzzled them together, working with *mustache*, *window*, and *man*, until he felt he had decoded the events of the evening.

At the window he found the empty spool of thread, saw one curtain hanging outside in the rain like a dead appendage. This was not one of Thelma's flukes. This time, he decided, she was onto something.

"I'll be right back, honey. You stay here," he said to his quivering, quaking leaf of a wife.

Thelma launched into "No! No! No!"

"I just wanna take a look outside."

"No! No! No!" Thelma clenched the pillow again and held it

161

to her chest like a doll, rocking it, lulling herself.

"What's going on in here?"asked the nurse, who stood in the doorway in a pink terrycloth housecoat, her hair mashed beneath a net.

"Stay with Thelma," Junior said and rushed past the startled woman. Outside on the front porch, Junior saw the red taillights of the Packard as it left Marge's yard, being driven by a stranger, being touched by a stranger, being handled by a stranger. A jealousy arose in him that had not surfaced when he discovered his *wife* had been handled by a stranger. When his father came up behind him and said, "What in hell's been going on?" Junior slammed his fist against the porch railing and said, "Somebody stole the Packard!"

"What's Thelma crying about now? This whole damn family's turning crazy."

"Thelma!" thought Junior, and raced back into the bedroom to comfort a wife who had just been test-driven by the elusive Chester Lee Gifford. Marvin Sr. stood in the doorway and surveyed the goings on in Thelma's room. The nurse, in her fuzzy pink robe and hairnet, looked like a giant cone of cotton candy. Thelma rocked a pillow and mumbled words to herself. Junior was trying to comfort her and asking, "What did he look like?"

"Ma-us-sta-ash," was the only identifying clue that came from Thelma.

Randy stood by the foot of the bed, watching his parents as he picked his nose, the product of which was slyly deposited upon a bedpost or the leg of his pajamas.

"A man came in the window and did something to her," Junior told his father and pointed to the spool of thread. Marvin Sr. inspected it carefully and lifted the window to look out into the black, wet night that engulfed Mattagash.

"When?" asked the nurse and gathered the pink fuzz about her neck, thankful she still was, after a lifetime of professional nursing and celibacy, intact.

"What did he do, Daddy? Mama, what man? What did the man do with the spool of thread?" Randy, now drilling for facts, had forgotten the natural resources in his nose.

"Go back to bed, Randy!" said Junior, who had not known his son was present.

"But I ain't sleepy no more. What man was it, Daddy?" said

Randy, who felt a genuine television script was being unrolled just for him. It had been a wonderful vacation, all excitement and danger, and now here was more of the stuff Hollywood was made of.

"Did he have a fly's head and hand?" asked Randy as Marvin Sr. took him firmly by the shoulders and scooted him out the door.

"We need to call the police," said Junior.

"Do you think you want this kind of thing spread around?" Marvin Sr. asked, knowing full well what Pearl's attitude about the issue would be. A McKinnon's daughter-in-law assaulted in a McKinnon bed. In Mattagash. In the heart of McKinnonland.

"Well, we've got to report the Packard," said Junior.

"The Watertown police, if you can get them up at this hour," said Marvin Sr., looking to see that it was 1:10 A.M., "are thirty miles away."

"Whoever stole the Packard is the same man who came in the window, and where could he go but toward Watertown? Toward downstate? He sure as hell ain't going far the other way. What would anybody do with a Packard on a dirt road in the woods in Canada?" Junior was rambling, trying desperately not to give in to the tears that pushed behind his eyelids. The Packard was the one thing, other than his family, that he valued. All the years in grade school when he had walked home past the other kids, overweight from Pearl's constant supply of candy and pastry, when he had heard the cruel taunts about the Ivy Funeral Home, the nicknames associated with death they had attached to him, he had set his sights on something special, something none of those other boys could have, the way a crow yearns for something shiny. That aura of being above the rest was realized when he bought the magical Packard. He purposely pulled into the service station where Ron Blackburn, the football captain in high school, was working as a mechanic.

"Can you check her over, Ron?" he'd say. "There's a little slackness in the brakes." Then he'd stand back to watch the grease-laden fingernails and desperate shoulder droop in what had been Portland High's resident celebrity. Seeing Ron, who used to refer to Junior as "Formaldehyde Thumbs," with such greasy hands always amused Junior.

"I bet Connie Woods wouldn't let one of them fingers into her now," Junior would tell himself, remembering how Connie, the captain of the cheerleaders, the Connie he'd been so enamored of, had clung to Ronnie Blackburn their entire senior year. It was Ron Blackburn and Connie Woods, the captain. And it was Junior Ivy and Thelma Parsons, one of the second-string cheerleaders that Connie only allowed on the floor during a game in which Portland High was more than twenty-five points behind and all the first stringers were too embarrassed to bound back onto the floor.

"A real beauty of a car," Ron would tell Junior.

"Anyone hear from Connie?" Junior would invariably get around to asking before he drove the shiny vehicle out of the garage and spun off down the street. It was always the same response. A simple "Nope," and that would end it. Connie Woods Blackburn, who took their two children and ran off out of state with a man who was still married and played in a band called The Four Travellers that appeared nightly at the Red Lion Lounge on West Salmon Street. Junior Ivy felt a smugness each time he drove by the Red Lion and saw the new sign the management had put up to replace the old one: THE THREE TRAVELLERS, TUESDAY THROUGH SATURDAY. The Three Travellers have been at the Red Lion a long, long time.

"I want that Packard back," Junior told his father.

Marvin Sr. went to the telephone and dialed the operator.

"They should at least have a sheriff in this goddamned town," he muttered into the receiver. When the operator connected him with the police department in Watertown, Marvin Sr. had difficulty convincing the janitor, who came in nights to clean up, that it was, indeed, an emergency.

"The chief's over at Rock's Diner," the janitor told Marvin Sr.

"Would you go get him for me?" Marvin Sr. couldn't believe the inadequate police system in northern Maine. He was relieved to be a southerner.

"Is it for a felony?" asked the janitor, "or a misdemeanor?"

"Will you go get the goddamned Chief of Police!" Marvin Sr. thundered into the phone.

"All right," said the janitor. "But he ain't gonna like it if it's only a misdemeanor."

Back in the bedroom, under Junior's constant interrogation,

Thelma had begun to wail again. The nurse had found a sedative among her professional paraphernalia and, with Junior's help, they forced it down Thelma's throat and waited for it to take effect. A restless Randy came back into the room wearing his Batman costume and mask. Junior pointed one finger at the door and, understanding the tacit order, Randy pivoted on his heel and went back out as quickly as he had entered. It was difficult to enjoy himself when it seemed all the excitement lay with the adults in the bedroom drama from which he had been banned.

"The police have the Packard's description," Marvin Sr. told his son. "They'll be on the lookout for it. If he does head south, they'll get him for sure."

"Who would head north?" asked Junior. "Who in their right mind would drive a Packard into the wilderness? This damn town is as far as you can drive a Packard to. He'll have to go south. Anybody in their right mind would drive a Packard south." Junior was beside himself. The nurse eyed him with a sleek, professional scrutiny. She wondered if a pill should be forced down his throat as well. After all, she had plenty. And he *was* rambling.

Thelma had calmed a bit, her own pill beginning to take effect. The nurse's gentle hands sponging Thelma's forehead reminded her of her mother, Madeleine Parsons. Maddy. Thelma began to relax. Those wonderful motherly hands. The kind that had spent a lifetime giving. Not like the hands that had just touched her body. Those were molded by a lifetime of taking.

"Mama. Mama. Mama," Thelma was saying softly now.

Junior laid her back against the pillow.

"Darling, I'm right here," he told her. "I'll stay right here until you fall asleep."

The nurse smoothed back Thelma's hair.

"Poor little thing," she whispered to Marvin Sr. "Who in the world do you suppose it was?"

"He had a mustache," said Junior.

"Captain Kangaroo has a mustache," Marvin Sr. said, as something crashed to the floor in Marge's bedroom.

"That sounded like a bedpan," said the nurse, who recognized the music of her profession the way some people recognize songs.

Junior and Marvin Sr. bounded into the room in time to find Randy, still in his Batman costume and mask, standing on the end of Marge's bed, the bedpan before him on the floor.

"I didn't do it," he said, stepping back to avoid his father's one good hand, as it grabbed for him. Randy stepped on Marge's foot, then her hand, as he dived for the head of the bed to give Junior the slip.

"Get that child off my patient!" the nurse shouted. She was so accustomed to talking in soft tones from years of administering to the dying that she was surprised at the punch in her words. Like they were made of metal and being tumbled about in a glass.

The house had been quiet since the day Marge had slipped out of the reality of Mattagash and into the pleasant tones of nontime. The years were hers to play with. A day in 1947. One in 1930. Time had no name, no dimensions, but existed to her now in pictures and images that paraded themselves before her like an endless 3–D movie. Montages: the calendar from Blanche's grocery in 1948 that had as its picture a basket of puppy dogs with red ribbons around their throats. The Reverend's Bible flapped its pages in one memory. In another, her mother's face, sickly and forlorn, came and went. The laughter of Sicily and Pearl she had heard a thousand times as they dressed and undressed their dolls on the front porch. But the one image that she tried so desperately to hold a bit longer, just to study it once again, as one would study a rare painting in a museum, knowing it's yours only to look at quickly, was the angelic, satanic, marvelous face of Marcus Doyle. The mansmell that was locked in her memory suddenly flooded her nostrils. But the face lost its delineations, became a blur, then again came quickly into focus, then was lost again. As though her mind were a pair of binoculars she was having trouble adjusting. Or that Marcus Doyle lay so distant in the past that precise focus was no longer possible. Memories pushed themselves against each other. Marge squirmed inside the prison of her body. She strugged to free herself of its weight. She had carried it through life like a knapsack full of rusted relics. Unfinished dreams. Like a bag of drowned kittens, heavy, and beginning to rot.

There were sounds now to go with the disjointed images, external sounds, noises of the outer world. The face of Marcus Doyle came to her once again, a wisp of a smile about his mouth, then gone. For the first time since she'd lost consciousness a week earlier, Marge struggled to come to the noises outside, to follow the blurred face of Marcus Doyle toward the light, like the surface ring of water to the diver, to grab him up again to her bosom and take him back with her into the wet darkness, into the summer kitchen of 1923, onto the soft cot that November night when her woman's soul had fluttered high above Mattagash to meet his. She opened her eyes to see Marcus Doyle and focused on a miniature Batman hovering above her head, one bat foot on her pillow, the other kicking at someone.

"Am I dead?" she wondered. Thinking surely that a McKinnon would be met at the Pearly Gates by St. Peter and not Batman, Marge lay in a state of confusion. The figures moved in, one on each side of her bed. It was Marvin Sr. and Junior Ivy, both with arms outstretched.

"We're gonna get you," Junior said to Randy.

Marge, quite cognizant now of her circumstances, recognized the two faces that lunged toward her, heard the deathly, occupational threat, and knew that she was very much alive.

"Sweet Jesus, the undertakers have come for me," she thought, and in a split second decided that Pearl McKinnon Ivy had something to do with it.

"I'm alive," she whispered, too inaudible for the room to catch and then she was lost again down the black tunnel as the room and its careless, trifling people spun away from her, like a little universe of its own, detached, while her own world burned softly down and threatened to flicker out.

East of Mattagash:
James Dean Meets Lucky Lindy

I know that it is quite all right,
There are no tigers here at night
And if there were they wouldn't bite
But somewhere lurking out of sight
There may be tigers and they might.

—From "Faites Vos Jeux," by Herbert J. Warren,
Maine Poet Whose Heart Blew Up One Day,
Alone, in His Cabin

In Mattagash the road stops. Dead ends. A dirt road takes you farther into the wilderness of northern Maine and Canada. There is no passing through Mattagash. A strange car with an unusual license plate that drives through town will eventually turn around, usually just past the Mattagash Bridge where the tarred road stops. And it will come back giving all of Mattagash a second chance to see if the plates are Rhode Island or Connecticut. In Mattagash your back is up against those trees like they form a wall. To get out of Mattagash you must first go farther back into Mattagash territory, following the river northeast until it turns and dips south, like a drunken dancer. To get out of Mattagash, you must first trick her, let her think you're heading north. Then at Watertown you drive directly south, down a twisting road, but always south, as fast as you can drive, never looking back for fear the brittle hand of every McKinnon before you, of every Gifford, of every dead ancestor who went into the earth there will reach out, catch you by the coattails saying, "I saw my only days on this earth right here and so will you," and pulling you back into town where you will stay until you die. To escape Mattagash, you must be very cunning.

Chester Lee turned the Packard into the forgotten driveway of the American Legion Hall, mowing down the goldenrod and mustard that had established themselves there over the years of nonuse. He turned the engine off but sat inside the car, listening to the rain against the roof and remembering the summer he was nine years old. Bert Gifford had taken him along with a party of canoers he'd been hired to guide down the tricky Mattagash River. After driving miles up into the Mattagash territory they had waited in buses, old converted school buses, for the rain to let up so they could put their canoes in the water and begin the three-day journey back to Mattagash. But the rain had gone on and on, coming down in torrents that set old-timers to speculating as to when it had ever rained so hard and so long before.

Chester Lee and Bert Gifford had been given bunks on the bus since a few were vacant, and sleeping in the old Ford was unnecessary. On the bunk above his father, Chester Lee had lain close to the ceiling as the tin fists of the rain hammered all night, all day, all night again, ringing in his ears until it massaged him, kneaded him, like tiny hands pressing over his body. That was the summer he was away from Mattagash for the first time. Away from the people he had grown up with. And he had discovered a new sensation that summer in the company of men from out of state who did not look upon him as a Gifford, but just another person from Mattagash. Back in Mattagash he was born no good. Born to steal and cheat and spend his days escaping jail.

For the two days of rain while the party waited on the bus and for the three days it took to complete the canoe trip, Chester Lee felt like a weight had been lifted from him, as if the stones of his ancestors' faults had been rolled away and he was resurrected to be the person he chose to become. He walked straight and stopped hanging his head. He tried hard to please. Once, when a man named Bob passed him an orange crush, Chester Lee said "thank you," then turned crimson at the sound of his words, at "you're welcome" coming back to him, the brief interaction one he had never shared before with another human being, and it both embarrassed and pleased him. He felt an affiliation with the rest of mankind, a sense of belonging to the whole, of being one of the many creatures responsible for the working of the planet. He went back to Mattagash with his newly found individuality, but on his first day at school was made to empty his pockets before the fourth-grade class because twenty-five cents of lunch money was missing from the teacher's desk. He could still feel the lint inside one pocket as the tip of his finger touched it before pulling the pocket inside out for the spectators, and fear build up inside him that perhaps a quarter *had* been hidden all this time beneath the lint and it would not be the same quarter but they would say it was. The teacher would say, "There now. We knew, didn't we?" turning it in her fingers before the class like a prize. Back in his seat Chester Lee felt the expressionless mask return to his face, a mask Giffords are all born with, a sneer of contempt to hide behind. The teacher had instructed the class to search their desks for the quarter in case "someone might have hidden it there." Chester Lee did not lift his desktop, did not move, but pressed the lint firmly between his thumb and forefinger as desks slammed all around him like trumpets on Judgment Day and papers rustled in his ears like angel wings. It was then she said, "Never mind, class. Here it is. I must have slipped it into my lesson plan and forgot about it." And then the class filed out, each child caught up in the incidents of his own life, eager to be out of school, the case of the missing quarter already a memory to them. Chester Lee had stayed in his seat until the last lunch pail disappeared through the classroom door, giving her the opportunity, expecting something *back* for what she had *taken*. But when she glanced up and saw him frozen in his seat, she quickly said, "I found it, Chester Lee. You can go now."

Without a word he left the room, left her rifling through the papers on her desk. Mrs. Florence Carpenter, who died ten years later when a load of pulp she met in front of Albert Pinkham's house broke the stakes and cascaded down upon her car like Tinker Toys.

That was the same day he unwrapped the sheet of the *Watertown Weekly* that held his molasses sandwich and saw that the black ink had embedded itself on the bread, little backwards letters on the bread, and the girls saw it before he could wrap it up again. From then on, when she thought of it, Patsy Kelley circled around him at recess saying, "Let us read your sandwiches, Chester Lee. Tell us what the news is before you eat it."

He wanted to tell those girls that to Bob and the other men from out of state all of Mattagash was poor. That Patsy's dress wasn't the city dress she thought it was. That her tuna fish sandwich was nothing compared to what some kids must have in the city. But instead he said nothing. For years. And if a quarter was missing, by God chances were it *was* in his pocket, if they found it at all before he got away and spent it, or hid it in the tree behind the Gifford outhouse. And when the eighth grade finally came and went, Chester Lee took his books and went down to Mrs. Carpenter's room and threw them on her floor, then stalked out past his classmates whose arms were loaded with pine boughs to decorate the new gymnasium for commencement, and whose talk was about diplomas and gowns and futures. He knew then that futures were inherited, that chances were passed down from father to child, and that Bert Gifford had left no will for his sons, that Ruth Gifford had no trousseau to give to her daughters. That's when Chester Lee decided that the world owed him something and that he should set about collecting it. He was no different from the man from the bank who came after cars and houses and chain saws when someone couldn't pay the bill. If the town had taken it upon themselves to make him a Gifford, they would pay a fee for his being one. It was a contract, and the same that his ancestor, Joshua Gifford, had signed the day he stole the ax and oats.

At the American Legion Hall, Chester Lee found Amy Joy's letter wrapped in Saran Wrap and pinned to the door. She would be waiting for him by Sicily's lilac bushes. The envelope was damp but the note inside and the money were safe. Chester Lee quickly thumbed through the stack of twenties. Two hundred and sixty dollars. The letter didn't interest him but he read it quickly to see if there were any new developments he could make use of. There were none, so he crumpled it up and tossed it over his shoulder. He threw everything that caught his eye into the pillow case he had taken off his pillow. It had yellow flowers and had been sneaked out of Sicily's linen closet by Amy Joy, who wanted to better her lover's boudoir. In went a pair of pants, two shirts, socks, his gum rubbers, the alarm clock, mirror, comb, a few cans from the larder of the grocery truck robbery, as well as two pairs of monkey-faced gloves that had once dangled happily from a dusty corner of Lyman's truck.

Out at the car Chester Lee opened the back door and threw his makeshift suitcase into the backseat. The rain was heavier, with fog thick as soup, and the damp chill of autumn had crept into the air. The Packard purred quietly when Chester Lee turned the key in the ignition, but before driving her he sat behind the wheel and took a deep breath. If only there was a good enough road to get him into Canada through the woods, he could be sure of not being caught. But only tractors could survive the dirt roads, and potholes, and fallen trees. That meant trying to get past Watertown. It was such a trap. All of Mattagash was a big mousetrap where someone had taken the cheese years ago. Just an empty trap waiting to spring its rusty mouth shut.

His only chance was getting past Watertown. He could spend the night in Houlton, pick up a few cans of spray paint and paint the car a different color. Blue would look nice. The Packard climbed onto the road leaving the American Legion Hall behind and sped toward Watertown, its red taillights barely noticeable in the fog.

In an instant, Chester Lee realized he was leaving Mattagash forever. He thought of Ruth and Bert Gifford. Would they look for him in the morning? And when the sheriff finally followed his scent to their door, telling them their son had escaped in a stolen Packard, would they miss him? He knew the answer. Bert Gifford would slap his knee and say, "Son of a bitch! A Packard!" and Ruth would mix less eggs for breakfast and at bedtime Debbie would move her two little girls off the couch downstairs and put them in Chester Lee's bed. In a few days, after the excitement of what he'd done had died down, there would be little talk of him. Family life would go on as it had before, and Bert Gifford would curse the mail for being so slow in bringing his disability check and Ruth would continue to curse her neighbors from behind the fly-covered screen door of the Gifford house and soon Chester Lee would be a dim memory. They would forget him, he was sure, the way dogs forget the puppies taken from them.

In the Packard he felt lonely. The night was black around him and the winding road seemed to trick him at places where he thought, after years of driving over it, there were no tricks left to play. The Packard had a radio but in Mattagash the reception allowed for only static with an occasional line of song here and there coming out of a dip in the road. He was sadly alone and was reminded of the movie he'd seen at the Watertown Theater about Charles Lindbergh crossing the Atlantic.

"This must be how he felt," thought Chester Lee and fumbled in his shirt pocket for a Lucky Strike.

Two deer that had come to the edge of the road to lick the salt raised their heads out of the fog and stared blindly into the Packard's lights. Chester Lee slammed the brakes on, afraid they would cross the road in front of him, but they both jumped over the ditch behind them and, white tails flashing in surrender, disappeared beneath the trees as the Packard roared by.

At the LEAVING MATTAGASH, COME AGAIN sign that the women's auxiliary had one of the high school students paint, Chester Lee tipped his greasy hat with the advertisement IRVINE BROTHERS LUMBERING, INC. and said, "No, thanks," to the extended invitation. "This here's a one-way ticket," he said and smoked his Lucky Strike in quick, short draws to calm his rattled nerves. This was not galloping out of the trees on a workhorse with a gun and scaring the daylights out of poor old nervous Lyman who had a weak heart anyway. This was the big time. This wasn't homemade. It was store-bought. And if only his gamble paid off. If only he could get past Watertown. But maybe he was worrying for nothing. Maybe no one even knew the Packard was gone. Maybe that skinny little woman was screaming and yelling so loud no one heard him drive off into the rain. He touched his genitals. She was crazy to cry rape. He didn't even get the chance to finish. Had to pull out and get out of her damn bedroom before she had J. Edgar himself in there to investigate. He hated not finishing. It was like sowing the kernels, then not bothering to pick the corn. If he had only known the Packard was there *before* he climbed into the window. He had seen it at a distance at Marge's, and on the flat by the river, and he had admired it. Wanted it badly. But stealing it outright had not been something he planned. To get the money from Amy Joy and then the Greyhound out of Watertown were his only intentions. But when he saw the sleek car there in the driveway, so close he could almost hear it breathing, he had to get inside it, to get away from the woman, from the frustration of uncompleted sex, to satisfy the adrenaline pumping over screams in the dark and the touch of a new woman. Before he analyzed the situation, before he reckoned with the reality that stealing the Packard would almost certainly assure him a cell next to his brothers' in Thompson Penitentiary, it was too late. He had the Packard now. Should he abandon it? He could stop right there, just a few miles south of the town line, and run it into the trees by the river, then get to Watertown the best way he could. What could they prove? Maybe he *should* just run it into those hazelnut bushes above Lyman's store. Then there would be no cops to worry about. But the smooth Packard beneath his hands was a sensation no Gifford had ever known before. The Packard had needed no salesman singing its praises as to how it held the road, how plush the seats felt. It sold itself and Chester Lee could no more ditch it than he could abandon the girl in the lingerie section of the Fall-Winter issue of the Sears and Roebuck catalogue if she suddenly materialized all warm and naked before him. The Packard was his dream come true. His tuna fish sandwich inside a shiny lunch pail. It was his pockets bulging with his own silver quarters, like a pocketful of trout he himself had caught. It was the five-day feeling of self-respect he had found the summer he was nine. And now, twenty-three long years later, it had come back to him like a boomerang, like words he had shouted down the Gifford well that had been in echo all those years and just now managed to break through the dark water and come back to him. Words like *thank you* and *you're welcome* and *please*. Words that almost hurt his mouth to form, so foreign they seemed to him. Like Italian. Or French. That's what the Packard did for him. And that's why he drove her on through the rainy night, over the twisting, foggy road to Watertown.

When Chester Lee saw the young doe in the road, saw it jerk its head, frantic for a direction to run in, it flooded his memory in a flash, the boiled white skull that had hung on his bedroom wall. It was the first deer he had ever shot. He was thirteen and downed it with four badly placed bullets until it could no longer run but crawled under the boughs of a young cedar that were still wet with dew. He had broken the boughs away, exposing the injured animal, whose blood lay like rose petals on that thin layer of snow that hunters love and bleeding deer dread. It's a white sheet of paper spread out over the woods to collect the dots of blood that drop, so that the hunter, using his gun like a pencil, slowly, easily connects the dots.

Chester Lee had stared down at the animal and felt remorse at what he'd done. As Cain must have felt looking down on the lifeless Abel. He could not bring himself to unsheath his knife until he heard his father and brothers catching up to him, and before they could see what would be a weakness to any man in

Mattagash, Chester Lee had pulled out his knife and slit the creature's soft throat, shouting back at the men behind him, "The little bitch put up a good fight!"

Later, as they dragged the dead deer away, he saw the cedar boughs scattered about on the snow and knew that in Mattagash, as it was in nature, everything you put up to protect yourself, to shelter yourself, would be broken away by somebody, sooner or later, and your very hide would be stripped from your bones, leaving you naked and shaken beside the red drops on Mattagash's white snow.

And later, when his brothers showed him how to push a wire up into the cranium and pull the brains out so that the skull could be boiled, then varnished and hung as a trophy on the wall, he had felt the same remorse return. Digging out the animal's brain was like stealing its secrets, its memories of the fresh deep woods and the soft fur of its mother. Simply because it had been born a deer.

Because it was his first deer, and although he couldn't give words to his emotions, he felt they were kindred spirits. That Mattagash had robbed him of his past simply because he had been born a Gifford. And many times over the years when night had settled about the house and darkness rolled in around his bed, he would come awake in a sweat and see the gleaming skull, the eyeless sockets, the horns like a crown of thorns on its head, and he would think of Jesus and the blood that spilled from the cross and he was afraid of hell then, afraid of his sinfulness, and of the skull that hung like crossbones on his wall.

He could not stop the Packard in time. The deer didn't run, but stood, stunned by the invention of headlights, stood looking into them like mirrors, until its bones met the metal of the machine and crumbled inside its skin like pieces of chalk as the body slid gracefully across the hood and crashed through the windshield, leaving it in tiny bits of glass, like blue fragile tears.

The sensation of being inside an automobile as it left the firm earth and became airborne for two seconds was, to Chester Lee, one of amusement mixed with fear. As though he were in a chair on the Ferris wheel that had broken free and was falling, and he almost giggled, almost cried, in the seconds he had left. And then the sound of metal against hardwood, against birch and pine, as if a lumberman's ax was busy at work, the same noisy sound his ancestors had brought years ago to that quiet place, was the last thing Chester Lee Gifford heard as the steering wheel lurched at his chest, as glass flew at his flesh, as blood rushed to the gaping spaces where teeth had been and then burst up, bright red, from inside him, as though he were a thermometer on a hot day, and filling his mouth with sticky blood. His hands unclenched the wheel and flew like Raggedy Andy's against the door and dashboard. As his broken chest settled back against the plush seat in the now motionless car, he felt almost embarrassed to be caught so helpless, to be stumbled upon in the morning looking so grotesque, and he knew, as he said goodbye to Mattagash, that the Packard, the one thing in the world he felt he could trust, had turned against him.

The Bird of Time Gets Shot Down:
Marge Poles Down the Milky Way

"Marge McKinnon is so sorry a human bean that she just went ahead and shriveled up way before her time. It's that damn McKinnon blood. They get a notion into their heads and there's no turning them around. She's so stubborn she's even *more* stubborn than a McKinnon. There must of been some of that French Canadian blood mixed in with the McKinnons over the years that no one wants to own up to. Them frogs is as stubborn as anybody."

—GLADYS O'ROURKE, Childhood Friend of Marge McKinnon, 1957

SICILY HAD BEEN asleep for only two hours when the phone rang at seven o'clock. She was hoping Ed might get up and answer it, knowing what kind of night she'd had, but on the fourth ring she realized he must have had more than the usual to drink and didn't hear it. She stumbled, half asleep, down the hallway, holding one railing of the stairway as she made her way down to the phone. It would probably stop ringing just as she reached it. Bert Fogarty and his wife had an extension in their bedroom. If Ed wasn't so obstinate, they could afford the few extra dollars each month. He spent tons more on the booze he put away.

"What Pearl must think each time she comes home. She must feel just like that Margaret Mead when she stepped off the boat into that litter of natives," thought Sicily, and answered the phone. She yawned as she said hello. It had been an incredible night. Marvin Sr. had called after one o'clock to tell them that Marge was sinking fast. The nurse said her blood pressure was dangerously high and she feared the worst. Sicily had phoned for an ambulance, then she and Pearl had gone out into the rain to see their oldest sister leave the house she had always said she'd never leave except to go to China, wrapped in blankets on a stretcher and whisked to Watertown as fast as slick roads would allow. Arriving in Watertown twenty minutes after the ambulance, the sisters and Marvin Ivy waited for word. But Dr. Sullivan sent them home to get what sleep they could for when they'd really need it. It was too soon to tell.

Back at Marge's, they made coffee and crossed their fingers, listening in the meantime to the bizarre tale that unfolded about rape and car theft and answering all the phone calls of curious neighbors who had seen an ambulance speed by, its blue light flashing in the black night and, knowing Marge was the only one sick in Mattagash, had called to hear the details. It didn't matter that it was almost four o'clock in the morning.

Between phone calls and listening to Junior lament his loss, Pearl kept saying, "*Thelma?* Are you sure he wanted *Thelma?* Could he have meant it for the nurse?"

Finally, after calling the hospital once more to be told that Marge was the same, they'd gone on to Sicily's and left the Ivys still in a tizzy.

Sicily and Pearl had finally turned out the lights a few minutes before five o'clock. Now it was seven and she heard Dr. Sullivan say, "She's gone. I'm sorry. We did all we could."

After Sicily put the receiver back on the hook, she stood for a while looking out across the river at the fire of the trees, and wondered if Marge's soul was walking just then, among the leaves, a wisp of a girl again, dancing between the magnificent white birches, her hair thick and auburn the way Sicily could almost remember it, the way a man or woman can almost recall their mother's face when they were little and she bent down to pick them up, and tears rolled down Sicily's pale face, tears of sadness and guilt because she had not come to love her sister in spite of the faults. Because she had forgotten until then what Marge's young face looked like in the lamplight as she leaned down to kiss Sicily good night.

"I hope her soul stays along the river," Sicily said and went to Amy Joy's bedroom. Cynthia and Regina were sleeping soundly on the two cots Sicily had brought up from the basement and unfolded. She sat on the bed and waited a few seconds before she put a hand on Pearl's shoulder and shook her gently.

"What?" said Pearl. "What?" Then, when she saw Sicily, "What time is it? Have I been sleeping that long?"

"She's gone, Pearly," said Sicily, her lips quivering at having spoken the words, having now made Marge's death official.

"Oh, no," said Pearl softly. Knowing that something bad was going to happen was not at all like having it happen.

"Marge is gone," Sicily said again, and Pearl pushed back the

covers to slide her legs over the side of the bed. The two sisters
sat quietly, side by side, until Sicily reached for Pearl's hand, took
it in her own, and held it.

"Knowing her," said Sicily, "I always thought she'd beat it.
That one day she'd just up and outta that bed and be well again."

"I guess I knew she couldn't. I see more of death than you do.
Even the young and rich, Sissy." Pearl felt tears come to her eyes.
"Beneath all that tough stuff she was only a mortal human. We're
all only human. We'll all go too."

They said nothing for several minutes, both watching a beam
of sun that came through the parted curtains, past the geraniums
in the window, and landed squarely on the seat of a chair, as
though it had come in just to sit down.

Then Pearl said, "She must've felt this way when Mama died.
Only worse. She was all alone with no husband or family."

"She was like a mother to us," Sicily agreed sadly. "It must
have been hard on her back then, a young girl with two children
to raise."

"And that old devil to live with," said Pearl, and Sicily was not
even shocked at the anathema. It was the same word she had
often conjured up in her own mind to define their father, Reverend Ralph, but she had always kept it to herself.

"Well, at least the rain's done," said Pearl, still looking at the
yellow stream of sunlight. "A funeral's bad enough but rain makes
it so much sadder. Everyone huddled beneath black umbrellas
and chilled to the bone and so much water you can't tell anymore
who's really crying and who isn't. I've seen a hundred of them
in the rain. At least the rain's done."

"I'll get us some breakfast," Sicily said and left Pearl sitting on
the bed.

"I suppose there's no need to hurry now," Pearl thought and
began to straighten the bed. Her granddaughters were still asleep
and she looked upon them fondly for a few minutes. They were
enough to drive her to an early grave at times, but watching them
sleep and thinking of Marge with no one to carry her blood mixed
with theirs down through the years, Pearl was thankful for Junior's children.

"Maybe they'll outgrow it," she thought and took a dress from
her suitcase.

When Sicily opened the front door to bring in the two quarts of Maine dairy milk, she saw Amy Joy asleep in a yellow raincoat under the lilac bushes, her head resting against the little vinyl case Sicily had gotten her with Green Stamps as a Christmas present.

"What in the name of God?" said Sicily. She'd been so accustomed to Amy Joy spending the night at Marge's that she had not missed her on the sofa when the frantic call from Marvin had come, nor when she answered the phone at seven.

"I've had so much on my mind with Marge that God only knows what that child's been up to," Sicily said, and slippers on, padded out through the damp grass to retrieve the water-logged Amy Joy.

At the sound of her mother's voice, Amy Joy sat up and sneezed. The clothing she wore beneath the raincoat had remained relatively dry, but the lower legs of her pink stretch pants and her bobby socks were soaking wet and the little girl was shivering.

"I can't wait to hear the story behind *this* stunt," Sicily said, pulling Amy Joy up by the neck of the shiny raincoat.

"You look just like a big fat dandelion laying out here in the yard for all the neighbors to drive by and see. Oh, when is this ever gonna end? Will I ever see you grown up and married with a family of your own, knock on wood their last names won't be Gifford."

"I was waiting for the milkman," said Amy Joy, her sneakers squishing water as Sicily marched her to the house. "I wanted him to leave a quart of chocolate milk."

"Well, you're a hell of a watchdog, Amy Joy. He tramped right by your head and left my milk and I suppose he ain't gonna blab this up and down the road today on his stops. I suppose he ain't gonna say to every woman who buys a quart of buttermilk from him, 'You'll never guess what I saw rooted under Sicily Lawler's lilac bushes?' "

When they were both on the front porch Sicily said, "Oh, my God," and put a hand to her mouth, remembering what was more important that autumn morning than the milkman's gossip.

In the kitchen she helped Amy Joy out of the wet clothing and wrapped her in a blanket. She fixed her a cup of hot cocoa and dropped two slices of bread into the toaster. There would be time to diet after the funeral. Amy Joy sat expressionless at the table and sneezed occasionally.

"Take four of these Johnson and Johnson baby tablets," said Sicily, holding the little pink pills out in the palm of her hand. "I can always tell how big you're getting by how many baby tablets I give you. It used to be you were just a baby and could only take a fourth of one mashed up in some milk. I suppose now you're really more than old enough to take aspirin or Anacin. It's just trying to keep you little, I guess, that makes me get out the Johnson and Johnson baby tablets."

"I'll probably be taking fifty some day," said Amy Joy. "A whole bottle at a time."

Sicily laughed at this but she knew she had to tell her daughter about Marge. It was just that Amy Joy already seemed so consumed with sadness that she hated to add to her adolescent troubles. But after Amy Joy had sipped some of the cocoa, she put her arms around the woolly bundle and said, "Honey, Aunt Marge is gone. She passed away this morning."

Amy Joy looked at her mother and said nothing. She tried to cry but was too exhausted. What she did feel was a sharp stab of guilt that she had rarely looked into Marge's room these past few days, rarely let Marge or her illness enter her mind, so cluttered it was with visions of lassoing the elusive Chester Lee.

"I'll miss her," she said to Sicily, who had started to cry softly but stopped long enough to say, "We all will, honey. All of us."

Pearl came into the kitchen red-eyed, followed by her granddaughters. The girls were still sleepy and unusually quiet. They could sense, as children do—even Junior and Thelma's children—that grief had struck the adult world a heavy blow.

"I'll go wake Ed," said Sicily just as he walked, hair tousled, into the kitchen and poured himself some coffee.

"Marge passed away," Sicily told him, not knowing what his response might be.

"When?" he asked, with a man's instinct for detail, and stopped pouring.

"At a quarter to seven this morning. They took her to Watertown last night. You were asleep and I didn't want to wake you," Sicily lied, not wanting to say that Ed was dead drunk. She took tomato juice from the refrigerator and poured him a glass, then coaxed three aspirins from their bottle and placed them beside the glass of juice.

"She's done that so many mornings she's forgotten what it's

really for," thought Pearl and buttered the toast that had popped.

"I'm sorry, Sicily," Ed said. "I'm really very sorry."

Surprised at his reaction, Sicily burst into tears and Ed came to her and put his big arms around her.

"She's better off," he said. "She was unhappy for so long."

"I suppose," said Sicily. "But I can almost remember her when she *was* happy, and, oh, I miss *that* Marge so much." Sicily pulled a battered tissue from her apron pocket.

"She was the only mother you knew," he said softly.

"Yes, she was."

"And the only father."

"I know it."

"Amen to that," said Pearl. "She was both mother and father," and put cereal and toast before the two little girls.

"I want some orange juice," said Cynthia.

"Me too," said Regina.

"Monkey see, monkey do," said Cynthia to her sister.

"I am not a monkey!" said Regina, her mouth full of toast.

"Are too."

"Am not! Am not! I'm a girl! Grammie, am I a girl?"

Pearl almost couldn't answer positively, but under the sober circumstances put an end to the argument by saying, "Yes, you're a girl. Now leave her alone, Cynthia, and eat your breakfast."

When Pearl's two granddaughters finished eating, she sent them outside to play in Amy Joy's empty play house. Then she helped herself to a bowl of fruit cocktail, a boiled egg, and toast. Ed had passed on breakfast, as was usual, and sat at the head of the table drinking black coffee. Sicily tried to eat one slice of toast, just to put something in her empty stomach to give her strength to go through what lay ahead that day, but she gave up, unable to swallow the bread, and sipped her coffee.

"Amy Joy, stop making those noises," Ed said, breaking the silence that had settled in the room.

"What noises?"

"You know what noises. You sound like three baby pigs at a trough big enough for two."

Eating fruit cocktail for Amy Joy was a ritual involving a process of elimination. The pineapple chunks, which she disliked, were eaten first, but the cherry, a fruit she prized, was saved for last, and all other pieces around it were eaten first. Then the syrupy liquid it lay floating in would be sucked up until the cherry lay helpless and exposed on her spoon. It would take Darwin only a few breakfasts with Amy Joy to conclude that eventually all fruit cocktail fruit would evolve to look like cherries in some distant millennium.

"It's only fruit cocktail," said Amy Joy as the cherry met its fate and disappeared in her mouth like a tiny red bird into a dark cage.

"Well, let it *sound* like fruit cocktail, and not swill." Ed stood up, rinsed his cup in the sink, and said to Sicily, "I'll be upstairs if you need me."

After he'd gone, Amy Joy looked at her mother.

"Who put a cold turd on *his* cereal?" she asked.

"Amy Joy, do you make up those things all by yourself?"

"Sometimes," said Amy Joy, and hoisting her blanket up so as not to trip, she left the two sisters sitting alone in the kitchen.

"I think she hears a lot of that at school," Sicily said to Pearl.

"I'm sure she does, Sissy," said Pearl reassuringly.

No Hope for the Hope Chest:
The Legion Hall as a Cenotaph

"I got to get those big boys out of prison so they can get us some offspring that we know about and are legal. If I don't, and with Chester Lee dead, the Gifford name's gonna die out. Just like the McKinnons."

—Bert Gifford, at Chester Lee's Funeral, September 1959

THE ORIGINAL McKINNON homestead had stood on the same site as Marge's house. The summer kitchen, shingled inside and out and attached to the back of the house, was closed off during the winter months. It was the only remaining part of the original house. Marge had been hesitant to see the last vestige of the old homestead disappear. But instead of completely remodeling the structure, she maintained it by replacing an occasional floorboard or shingle or pane of glass. Sicily once told her that if she went around with a piece of chalk and marked each shingle or board or nail that was new, she would find that nothing was actually left of the old materials. That it was *all* new. That the old kitchen was indeed gone. But Marge insisted that the spirit of it was still intact. That tearing it down all at once would allow its memories to escape like butterflies into the open air.

"The summer kitchen is all that's left of Mama," she would say, tack in mouth, as she steadied a new shingle to be nailed onto the gray spot where the old one had crumbled. And each year she sealed it off to save heating it during Maine's long winter months. When spring finally came back she opened the windows, gave the floor a good scrubbing, put up clean curtains, and pretended the old kitchen, once used for canning and pickling, and keeping the cooking heat out of the main house in the summer months, was still a functional part of her world.

The house itself had been rebuilt. Marge had stayed on in it, unmarried, while her sisters were safely installed in houses of their own. But it was still this house that represented home to Pearl and Sicily. The same river flowed behind it, the same hayfields surrounded it, the same forest edged the fields, and except for a few deaths and a few births the same neighbors remained a respectable distance up and down the road from the McKinnon house.

There had been the usual land changes. In the spring of 1947, when a particularly heavy buildup of large ice chunks in the Mattagash River thawed and came tearing along its banks, young trees were uprooted, bushes destroyed, even parts of the road washed out. The shoreline was greatly altered. And some of the older trees on the mountain or along the fields had given in to budworm or old age.

One favorite landmark of their past had been a huge pine tree near the side of the main road that they had always simply called *the old pine.* Many summer evenings someone would say, "Look at the sun in the old pine," and everyone knew where to look, and when they did they found a red ball of sun caught in the pine's needles until it dropped off beyond the horizon.

When the main road was tarred in 1955, the highway department cut the pine down. They said it had only a few years left. That it was dying. That it had never recovered from the lightning bolt that split its trunk years before.

Sicily had been to Watertown that day for her groceries and to take her green stamps to the redemption center and pick up the canister set she'd been saving for. On the bumpy ride back to Mattagash she was thinking of how wonderful the new road would be when they finished with it. She had driven on tarred road the few trips they'd made downstate to visit Pearl, but until that year the tarred road had only come as far north as Watertown and it stopped. As if no one lived beyond it. Or as if no one *mattered* who lived beyond it.

She stopped at Marge's to drop off her medicine and when she looked up the road and saw the sun going down in plain view, with nothing to hide it, nothing to filter its reds and pinks, she went inside and said to Marge, "I've been looking up the road as if I'm trying to remember something. There's something different."

"You're trying to remember the old pine," said Marge. "They cut it down." And together they stood looking up the road at the pile of sawed blocks that had once been a landmark to their youth.

"They just wanted something to cut down," said Marge. "It was fifteen feet from the road." Sicily had brought them each a cup of tea and they sat in rocking chairs and sipped the tea and watched the men loading up their equipment for the night onto the backs of pickup trucks. When the last of the trucks had disappeared around the turn and the land was quiet again, without the noise of machinery and voices, a small breeze came up and sifted through the branches of the trees that still had branches, and Sicily wondered if the old pine still felt it had limbs, like the stories you hear of people having arms or legs amputated and still feeling pain where they once were. Like they were ghost arms and legs. And she wondered if the old pine felt its branches were still moving with the wind and aching with age from having borne all those cones and held all those nests and children who had climbed up into her just to look down. And she had felt the sadness in Marge, who rarely showed her sadness to the rest of the world.

"Men around here are like that," Marge said finally, as dusk came up to the porch and listened. "They get those damn chain saws out and crank them up and feel them shaking and buzzing and before you know it they gotta cut something down. They said the old pine never recovered but men don't give things a chance to recover. They don't have the patience a woman has." And she had gone on that evening to tell Sicily for the first time how a doctor from Watertown had insisted that their mother had not recovered from the complications in birthing Sicily. He had kept her confined to bed for days on end, against her wishes, until finally, with nothing else to do, she died, too weak to hear Reverend Ralph's anxious prayers by her bedside asking God to save her sinful soul.

"They just want something to cut down," Marge had said again before Sicily went on out to her car and Marge went inside her house, flicked the porch light on, and rolled down the venetian blinds.

In Marge's driveway Sicily and Pearl sent the two girls inside to Thelma while they stayed outside, walking around the backyard, remembering the old house as it had been. The morning sun was brilliant and after the long rain the mountains glittered beneath it.

"Someone ought to come get these hollyhock seeds. They'll go to waste," said Pearl, crushing a dried husk of seeds in her hand, then throwing them into the grass by the garage.

"Those'll come up next year," said Sicily. "Hollyhocks spread fast."

"God, how Marge loved these hollyhocks," said Pearl. "Remember how we used to squeeze the flower to trap a bumble bee inside, then slip a jar over the flower and let go?"

"It worked every time," said Sicily.

"Bert Fogarty used to get a full jar of bumble bees. Twenty or thirty in a big jar, then fill it up with water."

"The boys were always cruel to animals and insects here in town. Most of them, anyway." Sicily put a piece of hay in her mouth and bit on it.

"Now they're cruel men," said Pearl.

"Not all of them are, Pearly. Hunting deer and bear always bothered you to hear about or see, but it's just that their daddies did it at times when food was scarce, and now, for the ones who really don't need it, it's just a habit to them."

"I've seen them shoot sparrows off the barn roof and beat workhorses half to death in the woods."

"Out-of-state hunters come up and kill the deer and animals, too. It ain't just men here."

"I suppose," said Pearl. "But it's still a hunger for blood I never could stomach."

"Marge always had hollyhocks of every color up and down both sides of the house. You should have seen them earlier this summer, Pearly. They were just as pretty as when we were kids."

"Remember how we used to gather up the seeds in a big bag and give them to anyone who wanted them?" asked Pearl. "Where did Marge ever get those seeds to begin with?"

"I don't know," said Sicily. "From a seed catalogue, I suppose. She used to tell me that the first hollyhock flower started out in China."

"Imagine that," said Pearl. "Starting out in China and ending up here in Mattagash."

"I suppose that's just like Daddy starting out in Mattagash and ending up way over in China."

"I suppose," said Pearl. "Except it's bumble bees biting them and not whatever it was bit him."

"A sandfly," said Sicily. "And the bumble bees don't bite the flowers. They steal their honey."

"Whatever," said Pearl and opened the back door to the old summer kitchen. Inside were shelves of empty Mason jars, covered with a fine dust. A rocking chair sat motionless, a hand-crocheted cushion on its seat that said, "The Lord Is My Shepherd." There were packed boxes of old clothes in one corner. The stove had a poker still sticking up from one burner, and some sticks of hardwood were still in the woodbox by the door.

"Looks almost as if somebody's gettin' ready to cook," said Pearl and ran one finger over the oilcloth on the table.

"There's been a lot of dust gathered since spring. Marge got me and Amy Joy to clean it up in May. I don't know why she never tore this down and saved us all a lot of work. Look at those Mason jars just pickin' up dust. She hasn't canned a thing in years."

Pearl opened the cedar chest that sat near the boxes of clothing. Marge's hope chest. It was full of papers, old bank statements, business and personal letters, some war ration stamps, an empty lard can of buttons, and other items that may have had value once, to someone, but were now motheaten and smelly from years in a closed trunk.

"We'll have to go through that someday and throw out what's no good," Sicily said.

"It's probably all no good to us," Pearl said. "But to her it must've meant something."

"Too bad she never had a family of her own," said Sicily. "It seems like only your own kids should go through your belongings after you die."

"I can see Thelma going through mine now."

"It would've been so different if she'd only gotten married," said Sicily and jumped as a spider fled from under a letter and burrowed deeper under the items in the trunk.

"She almost did," said Pearl.

"What?" said Sicily. "When?"

"You've forgotten all about Marcus Doyle. You were real young.
I was about thirteen back then."

"I remember him a little, but not that much," said Sicily. "I got
a bad memory even as a grown woman."

"He stayed with us two months or more and he and Margie
loved each other. I used to spy on them. See them kissing and
holding hands," said Pearl, picking up a stack of handmade doilies that had become gray and fragile with age.

"What happened?" Sicily asked.

"I never really knew. I think Daddy might have done something
to split them up."

"That sounds like him."

"Now why in the world didn't she ever use these? They just
went to waste out here. And that's some fine handiwork in them
too." Pearl threw the doilies back into the chest. "Marcus Doyle
used to sleep out here."

"Out here?" asked Sicily. "In the summer kitchen?"

"On a cot right over there." Pearl pointed.

"No wonder she didn't want to tear this old building down,"
said Sicily, and her eyes filled a second time with tears for the
older sister she had never come to know. "She's like the old pine.
She just never recovered."

Pearl put her arm around Sicily and said, "Don't cry, Sissy.
Whatever it was happened in Marge's life to make it so awful,
it's over now. And so is Mama's. And even Daddy's. And soon
ours'll be too."

"That ain't cheering me up none." Sicily blew her nose on the
tissue she had in perpetuity in her pocket.

"No, but it's true. At least Marge has got someone crying for
her. I don't remember anyone crying when we heard about Daddy.
We just stood around for a few minutes, shuffling our feet until
it sunk in, then we went on about our day and that was it. The
only difference was that Marge didn't make us write those god-
awful letters to China every Sunday."

"Why did Margie want to go with Daddy so bad? Especially if
he stopped her from marrying a man she loved?" asked Sicily.

"It was her only way to get out of Mattagash. I don't think she
wanted to get old in Mattagash alone. With no husband or children. Even dirty old China, full of short little heathens, sounded

better to her than that. Or maybe she wanted to go off looking for Marcus Doyle somewhere in the world. He was a missionary, you know."

Pearl pushed at the trunk with one finger to avoid dirtying her hand, and the cover of the hope chest fell with a thud, scattering bits of dust about that caught the sun before settling again. Leaving the precious letters stacked neatly, lovingly, at the bottom. Overlooking the moldy hearts with the hastily scribbled *M.D.* in each center, and the piercing hand-drawn arrows. Abandoning it all to the darkness and the weather and time.

"If you're a homely girl and you happen to be Catholic, you're all set," Pearl continued in one of the socioreligious treatises she was well known for. "Have you ever seen a pretty nun? And it wasn't even that Marge was unattractive. There wasn't any men her age around here. She always used to say that she was the only baby born in Mattagash for seven years. A Protestant girl bound for spinsterhood is in big trouble. We got no convents to hide in."

"Pearly, can we live in such a little town and still keep secrets from each other?" Sicily asked. "Can we live in the same family, in the same house, and still hide our pain from each other?"

"Some of us can," said Pearl. "And there's some that can't hide anything about themselves in a small town no matter how hard they try. It's just a knack, I guess. Some have it. Some don't."

There was an awkward moment between them, each wondering into which category the other fell.

"I don't know if it's a talent worth having or not," said Sicily. "Sometimes it seems that keeping it all in turns it into cancer in your stomach. Marge wouldn't have turned out the way she did if she'd just talked to someone."

"The river sounds like a downpour of rain," said Pearl.

"We never hear it, we're so used to it." Sicily took the poker from its niche in the burner and hung it from a nail behind the stove.

"I didn't ever hear it when I lived here," said Pearl. "Listen! Someone's yelling to us."

It was Thelma. There was a phone call for Sicily. Pearl closed the door to the summer kitchen. The one leading into the main house had been locked from inside, so the two went around to the back porch and through Marge's back door.

"I heard the news," Winnie Craft told Sicily. "We're all real sorry for you and yours."

Sicily thanked her and told her those details of the previous night that did not need to be censored. There was a knock on the front door, and Pearl went to answer it. Sicily tried to say goodbye to Winnie, who was not ready to hang up without a complete rundown. It was the sheriff at the door asking for Marvin Ivy, Jr. That much Sicily could hear.

"I suppose you heard the other bad news last night?" asked Winnie, savoring the words.

"No," said Sicily. "No. What news?"

"Well, Sicily Lawler, where do you live? In New York? Almost everyone knows by now. Sarah Pinkham just happened to pick up her phone to call Martha Fogarty and she heard the sheriff calling for an ambulance. The wreck was just above Lyman's store so the sheriff was calling from there. Lyman and Sarah is on the same line."

"What wreck?" asked Sicily.

"The sheriff told them don't hurry. He was good as dead. Had been for a while. Ain't that just typical of him, though? A stolen car?"

"Who, Winnie, for God's sake? Don't drag this out any more! Who!"

It was representative of the way Mattagash women delivered bad news, turning the words in their mouths like morsels of food, savoring them, for fear it might be the last food in their lifetimes.

"Chester Lee Gifford. Dead as a doornail in a stolen car. The sheriff didn't say whose. Sarah's trying to get Lyman on the phone now to find out. But ain't that just the kind of mess you could expect to find one of the Giffords in?"

Sicily heard another receiver being lifted on her party line. "Phones must be going up all over town," she thought.

"Someone's rubberin', Winnie," she said. "I'll talk to you later," and she put the receiver back on its hook.

The sheriff was telling Junior, who was white-faced with fury, that his Packard had been demolished and was at that moment being towed to Watertown by Bob's Wrecker Service and Car Wash.

"Chester Lee Gifford dead," Sicily said softly. She felt an instant flash of relief. There would be no gossip about her now. And

Amy Joy could grow up safely and slowly. Then guilt washed over her. "My God, that poor man is dead," she thought.

Reaching for her coat, she came to the living room door. All the Ivys had gathered there to listen to what details the sheriff had to offer them.

"They'll be planning a funeral for the Packard this afternoon," thought Sicily and, catching Pearl's eye, she motioned with a finger for her sister to come closer.

"I'm just going back home for a minute."

"It was Chester Lee Gifford," said Pearl. "He's dead. The sheriff said he found forty dollars in cash in his pocket and that he was all packed and heading south when it happened."

"I'll be back before too long," said Sicily and left the excited Ivys in a noisy huddle in the living room.

Amy Joy had just taken a hot bath and was still wrapped in a large blue bath towel and sitting on the end of her bed clipping her toenails when Sicily told her. Told her as gently as she could. As gently as one *can* be told, even one so young as Amy Joy, that your lover, the man you wanted, *planned*, to spend the rest of your days with, was no longer among the living. Had disappeared. Like the white, feathery bristles of a dandelion, had drifted off, had gone back to take root in the earth, to become the earth, so that every stroll taken by a widow through wild hay leaves her feeling as though the man she loved is reaching out with a thousand fingers to stroke her thighs as she walks. Or he's watching her from among the pine boughs in the forest with eyes that belong to the forest as stars to the universe. And the wind is his warm breath and he's alive somewhere, waiting, for old age, or scarlet fever, or a slippery stone along the riverbank, to reunite him with his female soul so that they can run the endless moors together, wild and free. The living, who don't know what answers the dead have learned, are forced to ask the questions over and over: Can he hear me? Is that light blinking in the attic a sign from him? Is hearing this old song a clue? Can he watch me undress? Does he know how quickly my memory of him grows vague?

Amy Joy began to weep. The towel undid itself and fell open, exposing the little girl's fat breast. There was a purple mark on it the size of a quarter, like a bruise, or a grape, or a little violet flower. Sicily knew it was from Chester Lee and that it was probably all he had left behind him. Like a dusty canvas, the artist long dead in his bones. And when it disappeared, there would be nothing left to show he'd been alive. Except for some papers, maybe, with his name on them, like the ones in Marge's trunk. Or a few pictures that would lie around in boxes until the owners died their own deaths and their souvenirs were thrown away in the rubbish.

Amy Joy had quickly covered herself with the towel, but something about the mark left behind by Chester Lee, above her daughter's beating heart, above the life in Amy Joy's body, as if he would be part of her until it gradually dissolved and he was free to go, left Sicily shaken. She felt tremendous grief for Chester Lee, and her daughter's warm body reminded her that his must be cold as ice, without sound or heat, like the vacant houses in Mattagash during the harvest. And she wished that they could keep the mark where Chester's lips had blossomed alive, nourishing it daily, like a tiny secret garden of their own. But she knew they couldn't. She knew it would slowly fade. Like the river roses, in a few days, a week, it would be past its peak and gone.

The Disciples Arm Themselves:
Shootout at the OK Motel

"We used to see her go by every day on her way to Watertown to strip. She had her head so high up in the air you'd have swore she was on her way to church. She had that little car loaded down with books, all strewed about the back window. Donnie Henderson saw her go by one day, books flapping in the back of that little red Volkswagen buggy, and he says look, boys, there goes the *hook-mobile*. He's always quick like that, Donnie is. But I tell you what. If I could have got a little of that action myself and come out clean back at the house, I'd have jumped onto her as quick as a horsefly on a mare with no tail."

—BERT FOGARTY, Lumberman, and Martha's Husband, 1964

SARAH PINKHAM GATHERED her committee about her on Winnie's front lawn and gave them some last-minute instructions.

"Don't hold up your signs until I tell you," she said. "Cora, did you get Becky's megaphone?"

"I got it," said a woman from among the group, "but she wants it back by five o'clock. She's practicing her cheers for when school starts."

Sarah counted heads. Twelve. Girdy Monihan wasn't there, but Sarah was relieved. Thirteen might bring bad luck. Her mother always used to say, "If your husband has twelve mistresses, he might still come back home. But if he has thirteen, start forwarding his mail. Even decent men have a breaking point."

"All right now," she said to the mini-mob. "We'll go in my car, in Winnie's, and in Martha's. That'll be four to a car and enough room for our signs. Drive right in my dooryard behind me and get out. Don't be afraid. She can't hurt you."

"Are you sure?" asked Emily Hart.

"What if she has a gun?" asked someone else.

"Honey, she's got a gun all right," Sarah said. "Only she don't fire bullets with it."

"What if she won't come out?" another voice in the crowd asked.

"She'll come out," said Sarah, reaching for the megaphone that had been passed forward to her, "or we'll smoke her out."

"What do we do with her then?" asked Winnie.

"We pack her stuff and load it into that little Communist car of hers and wave goodbye to her," said Sarah.

The three-car posse rolled quietly through Mattagash toward the Albert Pinkham Family Motel, like the funeral procession of an unpopular relative, and pulled into the driveway. Sarah got out first and motioned for the others to get out. She had planned the day well. Albert had left that morning to drive to Watertown and would not be back until after supper. This was the day when the newly formed Mattagash Historical Society had chosen to meet for the past two months. They had gathered in Winnie's living room to sort over old photos and deeds, drinking coffee and censoring out the past people and actions that they felt presented Mattagash in a less than radiant light. What posterity didn't know wouldn't hurt them.

Car doors opened and closed, hats were straightened, dresses smoothed, throats cleared. Sarah moved to the front of the Mattagash Historical Society and held one hand up to speak. At this mistaken clue, signs were hoisted into the air, some spray-painted, others done with nail polish, or lipstick, or crayons. Wilma Fennelson, who had no children, therefore no crayons, who wore no makeup, therefore no lipstick or nail polish, was nevertheless a good cook, as was any woman worth her salt in Mattagash. Her sign had been done with food coloring and she held it up proudly, a watercolorist at her first exhibit. VIOLET, GO HOME it said in red letters that were done with such a sweet, artistic hand that they might as easily have read HAPPY BIRTHDAY, VIOLET.

Winnie Craft, the most literary of the group, had written a poem: "MATTAGASH DON'T NEED THIS TRASH."

Martha, usually the group clown, held a gold spray-painted sign that said NO STRIPTEASE, PLEASE.

"No! No! Not yet," said Sarah, motioning for the signs to go back down. After a rustling among the biblically strong who were picketing the meek there was a reasonable silence. Sarah cleared her throat. Her idol had always been, would always be, Eleanor Roosevelt. Once, when someone told her there was a great resemblance between herself and the former First Lady, especially around the mouth, Sarah stopped dreading her plainness and vowed to do justice to a woman she resembled, not only in physicalities, but in spirit.

"What we are doing today is historical," she told the women. "We are cleansing our town for our children and their children. Just like Jesus cleared the temple." Sarah looked at Winnie and nodded. Winnie took her camera out of her purse and snapped Sarah's picture.

"Hold 'em up NOW!" Sarah said, and signs flew like balloons into the air, some white, some brown, some yellow, integrated signs of all colors and shapes living and waving in harmony. Pat Sturgeon's was on gray cardboard that had been the inside of a Tide box. The opposite side read FOR A CLEANER WASH.

Winnie snapped some candid shots of the protestors, then put her camera away.

"We'll go around to her room in single file," Sarah told her followers. "Then we'll form into three rows of four each, to look like we're more than we are." She thought suddenly of Jesus dividing the loaves of bread and the fishes to feed the multitude. "Maybe he just lined them up right," she thought.

Off they went, like a line of chickens behind Sarah Pinkham, around the corner of the Albert Pinkham Family Motel and stood in front of the door to Room number 3. The women held their breath. This was it. The time had finally come. It was no longer just idle talk, their mouths full of sandwiches and cake. It was no longer just a few basic tactics jotted down on paper. This was the real McCoy. The first recorded, documented confrontation of good versus evil in the history of Mattagash. Who knew what this might lead to? What domino effect could follow their actions that day? Today it was Violet La Forge. Tomorrow it could be the Giffords!

Sarah lifted her sign that said KEEP MATTAGASH CLEAN!—a leftover from the Fourth of July cleanup campaign that had taken place in 1955, its target being the Gifford outhouse. Little Belle had done such a painstaking job in forming each letter and had spent so many hours on the border alone that Sarah always suspected that was when her eye trouble began. What do doctors know? She had kept the artistic sign in case a cleaning campaign should ever arise again. And now one had. She had given Violet

La Forge every opportunity to spare herself this kind of disgrace. Violet La Forge had had ample time to throw her things into that hideous little German car and drive off. But what had she done? Had she appreciated the committee's kind gesture? No. She had come to Sarah's door early that morning, clad in her body-hugging leotards and said, "You won't get rid of me that easily. I'll see you at three o'clock." Sarah had had to sit down for a few minutes before her breathing became regular again, that's how shocked she was at Violet's insolence. She very nearly began to hyperventilate, which had only occurred once before when she read a magazine article about FDR that said he had a mistress who was with him when he died. She'd been sitting under the hair dryer at Chez Francoise Hairstyles in Watertown when it happened, and Francoise, who was from Quebec, Canada, and spoke little English, had pulled Sarah out from under the dryer and helped her over to the sofa where she collapsed. All Sarah could think of was poor Eleanor. When you wash and iron a man's shirt, you like to think you're the only one who's going to unbutton it. It was all so nasty to her. Him a cripple and still chasing women. If he had been Sarah's husband, by God, she'd have locked the little wheels on that chair of his in a second, President or not. It was nothing more than a little whorehouse on wheels. But Lucy Mercer and Violet La Forge were the only two women unscrupulous enough to cause Sarah Pinkham to hyperventilate.

Violet had until three o'clock to clear out. When Sarah left at noon to go to Winnie's, there was still no evidence of packing. The eviction signs were ready. The historical society was waiting. At two-thirty Sarah and Winnie cruised slowly by the motel and saw Violet's car still sitting in the driveway, no suitcases inside, no dresses hanging in the backseat.

"So she's gonna beat it into the ground, is she? She's gonna take it down to the wire," Sarah said to Winnie. "Well, she's holding a pot full of you-know-what and we're gonna make it stink."

Now they were huddled strategically before the door that held the little plastic number 3. No one spoke. Finally, Sarah moved forward and, casting one eye back for assurance, knocked loudly.

"Who is it?" asked a teasing voice from inside. "Is this a knock-knock joke?"

Sarah rapped louder, incensed at Violet's flippancy. She felt a bit of difficulty in breathing and asked God to let her hyperventilate later in the privacy of her own home and not during her confrontation with Delilah. Suddenly the door was opened a crack and Sarah looked into one of Violet's eyes. It was a lovely shade of blue, almost violet. Just like the magazines said Elizabeth Taylor's were like. Sarah was taken back at this. She had never known anything personal about Violet the woman before, and now she was looking into the beautiful, almost sad color of her eye, like it was one of the violets that grew on the hillside, knowing it had to be picked sooner or later, and Sarah felt suddenly as if she knew Violet La Forge. Or at least knew that Violet was real, no longer the unseen presence at all the recent gatherings whose purpose was to decide how to oust her. Sarah felt almost embarrassed. Violet might have been any woman standing there. Someone's daughter, sister, mother. Sarah was unable to speak. Her mouth opened and nothing came out. "I have seen the enemy and it is I," she thought.

"Look, Mrs. Pinkham," Violet said, so softly that Sarah almost had to lean forward to catch the words. "Look, I've got a goodbye present for you," and she opened the door for Sarah, who gasped to find Violet naked. Behind her, scrambling for his boots, with a blanket wrapped about his waist, was Albert Pinkham, Proprietor. Sarah covered her mouth. She felt the crowd surge forward, pushing for a better look. Rather than let them see this, rather than feel the shame of a woman with a faithless husband, Sarah Pinkham stepped into the den of iniquity and closed the door behind her.

"She tricked me," Albert said. "I swear to God, Sarrie, this was the only time in all these years. I lost my head. She wrote me a note to come visit her before she left."

"Seems like everyone's gettin' notes these days," said Violet, sitting cross-legged in her little rocker and stroking her Raggedy Ann's head.

"She said she was leaving today and I knew you had your meeting at Winnie's. She even said to leave my pickup in Dewey's gravel pit and she'd pick me up in her Volkswagen. She hid my pants. Where are my pants, you bitch?"

Albert could not stop talking for fear Sarah would start. Violet reached inside a packed suitcase and tossed Albert his pants. Sarah was white enough to pass out but, not one to miss anything, she clung to consciousness by a mere thread.

"I'm sorry, Albert, that it had to be you. But just once in my life I had to fight back," Violet said.

Sarah finally spoke, not looking at either Albert or Violet. She was looking at the big Raggedy Ann and thinking about poor little Belle. "The sins of their fathers," she said.

"Sarrie, as God is my witness."

"You leave God out of this," Sarah told her husband. "God had nothing to do with this mess."

"Do you want to let the committee in?" Violet asked, hand on the doorknob.

"No," said Sarah.

"It could have been any one of them out there. Any one of their husbands. It was yours because this was your party."

"Will you leave now?" Sarah said and pushed Albert's hand away. Albert, now dressed, sat helplessly on Violet's pink bed and flicked his nail clipper up and down.

"As soon as I can get everything into the car. Take the women away so that Albert can leave."

Sarah nodded and heard Albert begin to weep. She almost went to him, but knew she couldn't. Knew she would never go to him again. In sickness or in health. For richer or poorer. Until death did them part, Albert Pinkham would simply be the man in her wedding picture.

"She's leaving. She just wants a few more minutes," Sarah told the group outside.

"We made these signs for nothing?" asked Martha.

"I got this megaphone for nothing?" asked Becky's mother. The group, like bored Romans, had gotten a taste of blood, had built up a curiosity about the lions.

"I guess so," said Sarah, as the Mattagash Historical Society followed her back to their cars.

On the ride back to Winnie's the women were quiet, sensing a new development in the Violet La Forge scandal. Wilma Fennelson and Martha Fogarty distinctly heard *a man's* voice. Wilma Fennelson distinctly heard *Albert Pinkham's* voice. Sarah realized that the women knew already that Albert was inside Violet's room,

or they would figure it out. Life in Mattagash had gone, in ten
minutes' time, from being enjoyable to being unlivable. That's
how things stood in a small town. There were no slopes. Just
sudden sharp drops. No gray areas. Everything was an extreme.
Changes were drastic and occurred quickly.

Sarah turned her car in Winnie's driveway and waited for her
passengers to unboard.

"We'll call you later," one said to her. "See you soon," said
another, all of them saying something to her with their oily tongues
and in the same tone Sarah had used so often to outcasts that she
recognized it for what it really meant: *Leave so we can talk about
you.*

On the drive back to the Albert Pinkham Family Motel, Sarah
wanted to laugh out loud at the irony of it all. But instead, she
let tears slide down her face.

"There's no starting over in Mattagash," she thought, "and
they never let your children forget, or your grandchildren. You
don't get a second chance here." And she wondered why they
had even bothered to form a historical society when the minds
in Mattagash were all bulging museums open to the public year
round, and inherited by those not even born yet.

Sarah pulled the car off the side road that fishermen used to
drive down to the river. The goldenrod was still yellow along the
road but the berries were dead on the bushes and some of the
leaves after hanging on so long had finally let go.

"The leaves will soon be gone," thought Sarah. "I wonder if
the trees start worrying at this time of year? The way a man
worries about getting old and losing his hair?"

It had been a busy day. She had hardly given much thought
to the fact that the sign reading WELCOME TO MATTAGASH, POP.
456 was no longer true. Marge McKinnon was dead. So was Chester Lee Gifford. But the sign was already wrong. Martha's grand-
son had been born in August. And Tim Morse and the wife he
met in the Army had just had their first baby. That meant the
sign was right again. Two born. Two died. "Poor Marge Mc-
Kinnon. What a long lonely life. And Chester Lee. What a short
miserable one," thought Sarah, realizing now that Chester Lee
had suffered all his life, just as she was suffering now. By the
isolation. The refusal to acknowledge you as a person. As if you

were a member of a wonderful club for years and then, one day, you get a notice in the mail that your membership has been cancelled.

Sarah cried in her car by the road that led to the river, by the dead berries and falling yellow leaves, cried for every soul who had come and gone through life, through Mattagash unhappy. Finally, her eyes swollen from the effort, she started the engine and drove slowly home. Violet's car was gone. On the front step Sarah found the key to Room number 3 wrapped inside the note that the committee had written, asking Violet La Forge to leave. "They may as well have written one for me that same night," Sarah thought.

Inside, she put some water on to boil. A nice cup of tea would help calm her a bit as she tried to sort the day's mess out in her mind, as one sorts dirty laundry.

Sipping on her tea in the comfortable old chair that sat by the oil heater, Sarah thought of Eleanor Roosevelt and how lucky she had been that Lucy Mercer was a shy woman

Marge's Will Be Done:
The Phoenix Rises from the Ashes

"Met Marcus Doyle today and I felt like my heart would sprout wings and leave me, like my soul leaving my body. Like an angel fluttering up to heaven."

—MARGE McKINNON'S DIARY, 1923

THE SUBJECT OF the will began as an accident. Sicily and Pearl were having coffee in Marge's kitchen. It had been decided that Pearl and the girls would move over to Marge's with Thelma and the menfolk. Pearl could keep an eye on things until the funeral was over and a decision could be made about closing up the old homestead.

Marvin and Junior had driven to Watertown to check out the local undertaker, size up his wares, see if he was capable of embalming with the big boys. Sicily and Pearl were deciding whether to wake Marge at her own house or at Sicily's. Pearl was telling Sicily how people in Portland would think it a really barbaric and strange custom to wake a loved one at home.

"Well, I can't imagine anyone in Mattagash doing any different even if we did have a funeral home. I know if it was me that had departed I wouldn't want my body to be traipsing around among strangers," said Sicily. "A loved one should be in their own home, among family and friends, even if they didn't get along real good before."

"It'll change up here too," said Pearl. "You have to give in to change when it comes."

"I don't think that'll happen in Mattagash. Look at old Mrs. Bell. She died from a ruptured appendix because she wouldn't let the doctor lift up her dress and examine her. Said God and her husband were the only two men who belonged under there. Do you think for one minute she'd let the undertakers strip her?"

"*Funeral directors,*" said Pearl, and put a hand to her forehead. There was a headache coming on, she could tell.

202

"I'm sorry," said Sicily. "But even being of a younger generation I couldn't tolerate sleeping in a strange funeral home, with
men I don't even know."

"Sicily, do you think funeral directors are rakes or something?
Do you think they get dead women down in the basement to take
advantage of them, for God's sake?"

Sicily knew she had pushed it too far. She kept forgetting that
Pearl was associated with that profession by marriage. When Marvin Sr. and Junior had left the house, taking their funerary smell
with them, she thought of Pearl as just another housewife.

"Do you remember," Sicily said, laughing, hoping to iron out
the waves she had created by mentioning undertakers, "do you
remember when old Rosie McMahon waked her husband Ben?"

"God, yes!" said Pearl. "I'd forgotten that altogether."

"We were just little kids. Remember how Daddy dragged us
along? And remember how dark it was that night? And we went
running on down the road ahead of Daddy?"

"Oh, yes," said Pearl. "And Rosie had Ben propped up in his
casket right in the window for everybody to see?"

"Just like the coffin was a flowerbox or something!"

"And she had a gas lamp flickering at each end of the coffin!
He was all lit up from head to foot. Palmer Mack called him the
Titanic. Do you remember old Palmer with only one leg? He used
to tell people he lost it in 'The Big One' so they'd buy him free
drinks, but a tree fell on it and smashed it." Pearl was glad to
remember some things about Mattagash with humor. It had taken
years to let go of the feeling she had in regards to her old home
town, a feeling of anger and resentment.

"He never did say what war," Pearl went on. "Someone would
say, 'Palmer, what war did you lose that leg of yours in?' and
Palmer would lean back and spit out some tobacco juice wherever
he could get away with it and he'd look real sad and say 'The Big
One, boys, I lost it in the Big One.' "

Pearl was full of the past now. The days before adolescence
came and brought the message that something was terribly wrong.
The days when playing in the fields or along the river was enough
for any child and at night, if you walked to the store on an errand,
you could listen for a minute or two to the men who had gathered
around the big Warm Morning stove to spit and talk and you took

all the time you could filling the grocery list. You would have taken forever if you could. Would have stayed with your back to that stove, over in the corner by the shelf that held the spools of thread and buttons, as the back of your legs grew warm, and the men were so near you could smell the sweat of their day's work, and outside the snow coming down in thick white gusts that threatened to bury you there, inside that store, with those shelves and shelves of lovely things you might buy someday if you saved your money. And then those men told the stories of horses pulling logs in the moonlight and whose team was best, and who cut the most logs and who drowned in 1873 on a log drive and who could stop blood and who crossed the river once while the ice was breakin' up and the warmth moved up your legs and spread over your arms until you were drowned in it and you wanted to shout "Yes!" to the snow coming down. "Yes! Yes! Bury me here. Let me stay in this minute forever!"

If you were a *girl*, you picked out your items quickly and went home. It wouldn't look good any other way. Even if you were only ten or eleven. If you were a *good* girl you took your things and went on home, maybe once or twice looking back in envy to catch the face of some boy in your class sitting by the stove, listening with rapture, knowing he'd grow up some day and be a part of it all, would inherit the old stories, then become a story himself. So you left them there, gathered around the heat, their red and black jackets hanging from nails along the wall and mittens thrown down to dry. You left them sitting beneath the mushroom cloud of smoke from their pipes and rolled cigarettes. Like it was an umbrella. Like no rain would ever fall on them. Because they were men. If you were a girl, you went home.

"There were some good times," Pearl said softly. "Some good memories of the old days."

"That was the only dead person I ever saw," said Sicily, now no longer enjoying the merriment. "I just stay out in the kitchen where the food is. I never go in where the body is being waked. I don't think I ever got over seeing Ben McMahon like that. I don't think I'll even be able to go in and see Marge when they bring her home."

"That's OK, Sissy," said Pearl. "Just remember her the way she was in life."

Amy Joy came into the kitchen and took some things from the refrigerator to make a sandwich. She'd been crying all afternoon over Chester Gifford. For once, Sicily was glad to see her interested in food again. Before long Chester Lee would be just a childhood memory, lost among the birthdays and Christmases and puppy loves that were still to come.

"I suppose we should wake her here in her own house. I think that's what she'd want," said Sicily.

Amy Joy piled a slice of bread on top of a trapped tomato, piece of ham, and some cheese and slapped the sandwich twice to make it hold together.

"I thought Aunt Marge didn't want to be waked," she said and took a bite of the sandwich.

"For heaven's sake, child. Where did you get an idea like that?" Sicily was being very careful how she handled Amy Joy. There had been a slight confrontation between them as to whether or not Amy Joy could go to Chester Lee's funeral. It wouldn't help any at all, Sicily told her. If she kept away, the gossip would eventually die down and things could get back to normal. Besides, her father would never hear of it. But if Amy Joy wanted to ask him herself, she could certainly do so. This had put a damper on Amy Joy's funeral plans.

"Where did you hear that?" Sicily asked her again, noticing that Amy Joy's eyes were puffy. And they were pink as a rabbit's.

"That's what she put in her will," said Amy Joy and left the kitchen with what remained of the helpless sandwich. Sicily and Pearl looked at each other.

"Amy Joy!" Sicily shouted toward the living room. "Get back in here!"

Standing at the kitchen door, Amy Joy wiped a ring of milk from her mouth.

"What will?" asked Sicily.

"The one the lawyer wrote for her," said Amy Joy.

"What lawyer?" asked Pearl, sensing trouble.

"Aunt Marge's lawyer."

"Marge had a lawyer?" Pearl asked Sicily.

"I never heard of one," said Sicily. "Amy Joy, is this another one of your *True Confessions* stories?"

"He came to Aunt Marge's one day last year and they did her

will. I came in from school and asked her what they was doing and she said they was drawing up her will and not to tell anyone and she would leave me her television set."

"I don't believe it," said Sicily. "A will! What's this world coming to? The living dividing up their treasures for when they're dead!"

"It's true. When I left I heard her telling him I could have her television set and to be sure and write it down. Do we have any doughnuts?"

"Do you know the lawyer's name?" asked Sicily.

"He's that same man from Watertown that Daddy talks to about school stuff."

"That's a Mr. Levine. He just moved to Watertown about five years ago. From Portland, I think, Pearl. Or somewhere down in your neck of the woods," said Sicily.

"Good God! Can you just imagine what Marge and a Jew lawyer from the city must have cooked up?" said Pearl.

"Why wasn't I told about this?" Sicily asked, more of Marge's ghost than of those still among the living.

"There's a letter all written to the family members in the bottom drawer of her dresser telling all about her lawyer and all," said Amy Joy and poked the last bit of crust inside her mouth.

"Well, how was we supposed to know that?" asked Sicily. "Why didn't she just tell us about it? Does she think we can read minds?"

"Oh, Sicily, come on," said Pearl. "I know Marge McKinnon well enough to know she'd expect the whole damn world to go to hell in a basket before she'd really believe she was going to die. Sacrificing for the missionary cause, my foot. Marge always did what she could to get attention. Like a cat walking on your newspaper while you're reading it. She just carried this little charade too far. Yes, sir, this is just one little stunt that backfired on her."

"I'll call up that lawyer right now," said Sicily, picking up the phone book on Marge's little rosewood desk. "Amy Joy, go get that letter. Why do you suppose she never let no one know about it?" Sicily asked Pearl.

"She said the first place Aunt Pearl would look the minute she was dead would be among her personal papers," said Amy Joy, thinking that Marge was referring to Pearl's business qualities and not her weaknesses.

"Oh, ain't that just like her vicious tongue!" said Pearl. "She hasn't changed one bit. Even in death it's still wagging."

"Now, Pearly, she liked picking at you more because you were like her oldest daughter. It's 433-2769," said Sicily and began to dial.

"What about me?" asked Amy Joy. "I'm your oldest daughter and we get along OK."

"Amy Joy, wake up and dream something else," said Sicily who hung up the receiver. "It's busy," she said.

"A Jew's phone is always busy," said Pearl.

"Imagine that. A will," said Sicily.

"I got a good mind to go right down to the morgue and let her have one or two good slaps on the mouth," said Pearl, red-faced and puffed up.

"Pearl McKinnon Ivy, don't you dare talk about your deceased sister that way. You ask God to forgive you tonight when you say your prayers and don't you forget," said Sicily.

"I'll ask him to take the arrow that's pointing toward the Pearly Gates and point it the other way when he sees Marge coming," Pearl said and took a sip of coffee she was simply too numbfounded to taste.

Sicily's eyes filled with tears. Blasphemy was not her long suit.

"I can't stand to hear things like that said. We wasn't raised like that. I feel scared to death to hear it. What are we? Animals?"

"I'm sorry," said Pearl and patted Sicily's arm. "I won't say no more. And I'll talk to God tonight."

"Thanks, Pearl," Sicily said and took the letter from Amy Joy. She opened it carefully, as if it were an ancient manuscript that might crumble when exposed to air, and read it silently.

"Well, that old bat," she said and handed the letter to Pearl.

"Uh-huh, uh-huh, uh-huh," said Pearl, going down the letter. "Boy, don't this sound like Marge drawing water from a Jew's well? Listen to this, 'Funerals are too expensive and a waste of money. There will be none. Instead of flowers, mourners are asked to contribute to the Widows of Missionary Brothers fund.' Mourners all right. She'll be lucky if one little measly bunch of dandelions shows up. What in hell is the Widows of Missionary Brothers fund?" she asked Sicily.

"Marge probably meant to form it before she died," said Sicily.

"That's what WOMB is," said Amy Joy.

"WOMB?" said Sicily, twisting Amy Joy's plump wrist until she dropped her handful of mints from the candy tray.

"I heard her talking a lot of times to someone on the phone about WOMB. That must be it, see? Widows of Missionary Brothers. WOMB."

"God, that's sick," said Pearl. "You tell me if that's not a perfect example of unsound mind. Who in their sound mind would want to give money to something called WOMB? She'll be leaving the house to Madalyn O'Hair next."

"Was she in *Gone with the Wind*?" asked Amy Joy.

"It says here," Pearl went on, "that WOMB has five members and is headquartered in Bangor. Now don't that sound like a good place for it? This address is probably at the mental institute."

"Bangor?" asked Sicily. "Who does Marge know in Bangor? Are you sure it's Bangor?"

"Number 287 Pine Street," said Pearl, handing her sister the letter. "Right in the heart of crazytown."

"I just don't understand," Sicily said, running a finger up and down the letter as though it were a map.

"Why would anyone even *want* to die if they ain't going to have a funeral?"

"She just did this to upset us. Trust me, Sicily," said Pearl. "Have you ever known me to be wrong?" Sicily stopped reading and looked at Pearl.

"Didn't you want to turn the spare room of the funeral home into a snack bar or something?" she asked her sister.

"A *beauty salon*, Sicily," said Pearl through clenched teeth. "I wanted to open a *beauty salon*."

The Last Stone Unturned:
Another Poet Bites the Dust

The last of the red-hot lovers
is leaving town today.
The girls who adored his running board
all cry as he pulls away.

The first of the next generation,
a sweet little bundle of shame,
comes squalling in with the April wind,
but without a father's name.

The last of the old Old-Timers
is tarrying near the door, ·
but I'll make a bet he'll never forget
who is and who isn't a whore.

—ED LAWLER, Submitted to *The Maze*,
College Magazine. Rejected, 1932.

THERE WAS A deadness about the land at that season of the year. It wasn't just the idea of autumn being a time of death so that spring could come with her rebirth. That was just the typical literary theme he had learned in college, soft words on paper, a kind of pseudophilosophy that pimpled students stayed up all night memorizing, sure they understood its meaning. In Mattagash autumn came like a knife, slicing leaves off the trees, embedding itself in Ed's fat gut with a thrust that left more fear than pain.

When the trucks loaded down with family belongings began to leave town for the harvest, it was a very real kind of death. Left behind were the old, the very young, one or two crippled or feebleminded, Sicily, Amy Joy, and Ed Lawler. Some mornings he would drive over to the school and sit alone in his office, and the empty halls of the little schoolhouse were silent as a tomb. No erasers being hit together. No bells ringing. No voices from the playground. He felt the way the sheriff of a ghost town feels.

It was all a ridiculous ritual. You had children in school for three weeks, had them settled finally into the routine of a school year that lay ahead, had the teachers settled in, the schedules memorized, and then came the potato harvest and four weeks' vacation so that the children could join their parents in picking potatoes and bringing in a sizable paycheck each week. When they returned to school the process had to begin all over again of settling into the school year. What a waste of time. Why not start school after the harvest, he'd ask the school board, and extend school for three weeks in the summer? But that would entail change and Mattagash was not eager to change. The school board couldn't be blamed. They were all victims of their own circumstances. One member signed his name by rote, another with an "x." One member, new to the school board, voted for a prospective teacher with a bachelor's degree over one who had done work toward his master's, saying, "This out-of-the-way place is better for a bachelor. They resettle quicker than the married ones."

This was what Ed Lawler was up against when he tried to bring innovative ideas to minds that had not progressed since their forefathers constructed the very first outhouse and set about life concerned more with the bodily functions than those of the mind. Eating, working, and making love. Those were the three "R's" in Mattagash and nothing anyone could do would change that. At least Ed saw no change approaching in his lifetime. And if the burden of social and academic advancement was to be placed in the hands of Amy Joy and her peers, it was likely that the machine set in motion would come to a grinding halt and sit rusting until someone in the next wide-eyed generation strayed far enough from the norm to at least wipe a little rust away. "They'd tear down the schoolhouse to put up another outhouse," he thought.

This was the year Ed Lawler gave up, stopped beating his head against the stone minds of Mattagash, threw the gauntlet back down into the heap of rubbish, and turned his back to it.

"Some of us go to our graves with our dreams," he thought, unable even to remember what his had been. Was it a boy's camp? Was it a school for gifted children? A community center that offered courses in art and photography and dance? Were these all just random thoughts he had had over the years or were they his lifetime goals? He could no longer remember if they had been very important once or if all he had really expected from life, wanted from life, was to not be *unhappy.*

Ed walked to the window of his study and looked out at his view of Mattagash. The neighbors were not close. Houses were scattered up and down on either side of the road that followed the river. Most of the houses had small grassy fields or trees as natural boundaries between them. From Ed's window, Bert and Martha Fogarty's house sat on the same side of the road as the river. Beyond that, an eighth of a mile farther up the road was Tom and Wilma Fennelson. Beyond them, and out of sight of the Lawler house, sat the abandoned American Legion Hall. A half-mile more was the congested part of town, twenty houses or so whose yards were joined, the school, grocery store, Albert Pinkham's Family Motel, and then back to scattered homes here and there, some close to the road, some farther back. It was a town he had hated all his life, and the more he lived in it, the more he lost sight of who he really was, where he was really from, and what he was really capable of achieving.

He looked out his window at the leaves that had dried after the rain and were sparkling with color again. He had seen them turn from green on the tree to brown on the earth for so many years that he was sick of them. Tired of hearing every woman in Mattagash who stopped by the school or met him at the store say, "I think the leaves are prettier this year than they've ever been." Year after year he had heard this until he wanted to say, "Isn't there a limit? Can't the goddamned leaves just get so pretty and then they can't get any goddamned prettier?" It was this blind sense of optimism floating vaguely over Mattagash that he disliked the most. He could take a good old pessimist any day as long as he was in touch with reality.

When winter came with six feet of snow and temperatures that fell to 30 and 40 degrees below zero and stayed there for days at a time, it was all he could do to bear it. The liquor helped some, but couldn't keep him numb forever. Spring was easier, even if it arrived late, bringing slush and muddy roads that never seemed to dry. It was usually around late June and July that a peacefulness would settle in and he felt he could survive another year in Mattagash, maybe the rest of his life. He would go off with a fishing rod, a can of earthworms, and a cooler full of beer long before the sun was up. And in a boat on Falls Lake he could almost believe that life was not as bad as he thought. A sharp tug on the line, the sound of birds in the trees, the warm sun on his back, a wild deer standing on shore gazing out at him were all signs that he was alive. That his heart, buried beneath all those layers of fat, was still beating. That things would surely get better.

What are the last actions a man takes when he knows he can no longer function with the living? Do those actions become overly important to him? Does the pencil he touches to write goodbye with become like a gem to him because it's the last one he'll ever touch? Does the envelope against his tongue taste like honey? Is the ringing telephone he dares not answer a symphony?

Ed took the gun from his drawer, from behind the paperbacks that hid it from view, and laid it on the desk in front of him. He used to say that a gun was the pen used by the men in Mattagash, the only pen they knew, the only method they had to communicate. During hunting season he had seen their moist eyes as they looked upon the dead deer tied to the tops of their cars or sprawled in the backs of their pickup trucks. It was the closest they could come to expressing themselves; what they felt looking upon the animal they had killed, he knew for a fact, was an appreciation of beauty, a pride in a hunt well done, and a sadness for death. The way a woman looks at a beautiful vase she has bought on sale, just as it slips from her hands and scatters broken on the floor.

Ed had always been afraid of guns. He purchased this one on a spur of the moment, when Amy Joy was just a few years old. He and Charlie Ryan had gone into the hardware store in Watertown looking for some chairs for the teachers' lounge at school. (Charlie was janitor there before he died of pneumonia and old age combined.) Together they had loaded six, maybe seven chairs, he couldn't remember, onto the back of a borrowed pickup truck and when Ed went back inside for his receipt, the clerk pulled out a box and said, "This little beauty just came in this morning," and Ed, for no reason, bought it, hid it from the janitor, from Sicily, from himself for years. Tried to forget he had it. Tried not to ask himself why he bought it. Until finally it was not so loathsome to him. Until he saw it for what it really was. Admitted he had bought it the way some people buy a bus ticket.

The first time—drunk and feeling a bit maudlin—that he realized the gun was an expedient, he became so frightened of it when he woke up the next morning, sober, that he wrapped it, hands shaking, in an old T-shirt, drove up to the American Legion Hall, and threw it down over the bank and into the bushes along the river. But that night, calmer and looking to the future with a steady eye, he went back and found it there, in the dusk, felt for it like an unmarried mother, repentant and looking for the newborn child she has left in a basket on someone's back step. He carried it back to his study and hid it behind the paperback copies of *Walden Pond* and *Leaves of Grass* and some Hemingway novels. Books that Amy Joy and Sicily would rather die than read, so it would be safe there.

When he placed the gun on the desk, the metallic sound made him jump, as if it had prematurely discharged. When his hands were steady again, he took paper and a pen and wrote a letter to Sicily and then one to Amy Joy. He didn't believe one word he wrote, but didn't care. He would let the living have their peace. It would be his legacy to them. Something Sicily could arm herself with to face her neighbors. Something Amy Joy could give her children one day, crumbling and yellow, and say, "This was your grandfather." How could he tell them the truth? How could he say to Sicily Jane McKinnon: "I never wanted to marry you. I looked at you on our wedding day and knew I'd never love you. I've felt trapped all my life. I used to wake up in the mornings and see your red hair against the pillow and think of blood and that I wanted to be anywhere but in bed with you." How could he say to Amy Joy, "I never hated you, but I never loved you. I hadn't learned to love *myself* before your mother was legally attached to me, like finding out one day you are really a Siamese twin and this other person shows up and hooks their life to yours and you drag them around until you're just too exhausted to do it anymore."

He told Sicily he loved her. That the fault was not hers, but his. It was his own failure. His inability to survive the onslaught of old age without realizing his early ambitions. The usual reason men give for suicide at that age. He told Amy Joy she would always be his little girl and to study hard and be a big success someday and help her mother all she could and he loved her dearly. It was a letter written countless times before by many shaking hands. Ed wondered now how many of them had been truthful. How many of them had been nothing more than his was, a formal kind of apology for no longer being the head of the household, for preferring death to the daily sight of red hair, the daily sound of adolescent prattle? "They probably all lied, poor bastards," he thought and left the two envelopes on his desk. Putting the gun inside his jacket pocket, he turned the desk light off and left the study, closing the door behind him. He listened to the sound of his own footfalls coming down the stairs, the last time he would descend those steps. He almost stopped at the refrigerator for something to eat, then laughed at the useless notion.

"It'll make the coroner's job a little less unpleasant," he said to the empty house.

The screen door slamming behind him was as loud as a gunshot, the sound of the car door closing enough to give him goose bumps. The whole night was pulsing and swelling with sounds and noises, and the air was heavy, so difficult to inhale that he became aware of the very act of breathing. It was almost dusk when he backed out of his driveway. For a few minutes he sat there in his car, out on the main road, looking at the yellow lights of his home, studying each shingle on the roof, the brown shutters, the shrubs in the yard. It all seemed like a dream to him now, like it was someone else's home and he had only been renting it until the owners returned. A car came up the road, slowed to go around Ed's, and he saw Bert Fogarty and his son Ernie, who was in the seventh grade, looking curiously into Ed's eyes, wondering what he was doing sitting in his car in the middle of the road in front of his own house. Ed waved, and they waved back and went off until they disappeared around the turn near the American Legion Hall. Ed knew he had made them a part of Mattagash history, that the next day Ernie could excitedly tell the story of seeing the principal in his car, embellishing it for effect, and Bert could tell a thousand times how he and Ernie were the last ones to see Ed Lawler alive and how strange he had been acting, just sitting in his car in the middle of the road. And it would be passed on to their descendants how their grandfather, then great-grandfather, then great-great-grandfather had come upon the principal of Mattagash Grammar School just before he shot himself: "They'll have me dancing on the hood of the car wearing nothing but a lamp-shade before the week is up," Ed thought, and drove on down the snaking road, along the Mattagash River, to the black building of the school. No one would be surprised to see his car in the yard. Many nights he worked there late, or simply sat in his office and drank whiskey, preferring the empty, quiet school to a house inhabited by Sicily and Amy Joy.

The office door opened with its usual squeak. He snapped on the desk light, although it was not yet dark outside. Papers were strewn about his desk, folders piled up. A cup half full of cold coffee and layered with mildew sat where it had been placed on the last day of school. A wooden plaque saying IF YOU DON'T WANT ANYONE TO FIND IT, PUT IT ON MY DESK was sitting on his dictionary. It had been given to him by the teachers and his sec-retary for his birthday several years before. He liked the plaque. It showed a spark of humor among his colleagues that was rare.

Ed sat in his swivel chair and placed the gun on the desk. This time, deadened by the stack of papers, it made no noise. Sicily couldn't get into his office at school to clean his desk as she did at home, putting things in places where he couldn't find them.

He drank directly from the bottle of whiskey he kept hidden in the top drawer of his filing cabinet. His secretary knew it was there but said nothing. After all, she was his secretary. What could she say? She'd been with him since the first day of his princi-palship at Mattagash Grammar School, had even been with his father, and where Ed was concerned she looked at him sadly, as a pious mother does her drunkard son. Wringing her hands be-neath her desk where he couldn't see them, she asked God every working school day to make the demon of alcohol leave him forever, but said nothing to the earthlings around her. Especially the curious ones who asked her about the principal's drinking habits.

Ed thought of his father, a man with quiet intelligence who headed the school when it was a two-room wooden building and inaugurated the new brick building in 1940, coughing with tu-berculosis but too stubborn to die until he saw the work done and his son safely enthroned as principal. It was a phenomenal feat, his managing to raise the money and the town's conscious-ness high enough over the years to do what was thought to be nearly impossible. Even Watertown, with all its 8,000 people, had only acquired a brick building in 1938. But once a consciousness in Mattagash was raised it was likely to fall with a thud. After they proudly finished a school they hadn't even *wanted* until Lester Lawler came to town, they soon went back to their rackety gossip about him.

Ed had none of the old man's tenacity. He wasn't as driven. He often wondered if the incident that brought Lester Lawler to grief had been the thorn in his side that kept him fidgety, kept him on his toes, an achiever. Ed himself knew little of what had happened. Sicily had asked him once, shortly after they were married, what his father had done to that young girl in his Current Events class that had made it impossible for him to continue as a teacher in Massachusetts. It was the first time Ed had ever heard of it. Sicily had heard it from old Mrs. Feeny, Sarah's mother, who said teaching Current Events in school instead of the Bible was the cause of such goings on. It never came up again until Amy Joy came crying into his office one day because Raymond Caulder, who wanted the very swing on the playground that Amy Joy had gotten to first, had said to her, "Your grampie was a no-good womanizer," and had sent the little girl to her father's office in tears. Ed could do nothing. For another child, he would have brought the slanderer into his office and demanded an apology for the injured party. But he realized that for him, as principal, to insist on an apology to his daughter would only perpetuate the gossip concerning his father. He could see Raymond's mother, Beatrice Caulder, a god-awful woman with a tongue that could level cities, banging on his door the very next morning, her ironing board beside her as a battering ram.

If he had reacted with typical Mattagash strategy, he would have said to Amy Joy, "You go out there and tell him that his mother goes to the Watertown Hotel on Saturday nights and begs men to dance with her." But he refused to become a part of their microcosm of social warfare. Instead, Amy Joy was told to turn the other cheek, to ignore nasty people, and was sent unappeased back to the playground, that land mine of past and present bombs that could explode at any moment, little Molotov cocktails made at home by their mothers and fathers, but mostly mothers, and given to their children each morning as they left the house, like goodies in a lunch pail.

Amy Joy was born several years after her grandfather died. She had never met him, yet she was being taunted about an incident that happened in another state. In the 1920s. By a boy in Mattagash who was also born several years after Lester Lawler died. It was a strange inheritance. "No matter that Lester Lawler had built them a school, turning up early every morning, hacking and wheezing," thought Ed. "No matter he watched every brick that went into the building to ensure their children a decent place to receive an education. The education they got at home, the oral histories and biographies, was more important."

Before Ed found the courage to ask his father about the incident, Lester Lawler went to his grave with the truth about the girl student. The truth may die, but the myth lives on, an evil vine sprawling and spreading, growing larger and longer. Ed surmised the truth couldn't have been too serious, or there would have been legal consequences. An infatuation, he thought. Maybe some stolen kisses after school. What more could it have been? He felt a kinship to his father, realizing that he had very nearly followed in his footsteps. He understood what being trapped in a marriage for life before you were old enough to avoid it could do to a man. Ed was young during those years in Massachusetts, too young to remember the trouble. Or it had been cleverly hidden from him. He wondered if his father felt the same apathy toward him that he felt toward Amy Joy. Ed's mother had grown old young, tight-mouthed with anger, her hands wrinkling before their time because of the fists she made. Even listening to a humorous program on the radio, and while he and his father were doubled up with laughter, she would clench her fists and hold them on her lap like something she had knit. Only after she died did she allow herself to relax. Ed and his father had become bachelors again, but they kept a clean house and learned to cook for themselves. His father never remarried and it was difficult for Ed, after his marriage to Sicily, to readjust to a woman bustling about the house. A woman's things were breakable and fragile, and he had come to think the same of Sicily. But he wouldn't be responsible anymore if she broke, with him not there in the house. He had broken himself and he hadn't asked anyone to pick up the pieces. It wouldn't be so hard on Sicily. Not as hard as a divorce would be. Any woman in Mattagash would prefer the suicide of her husband to divorce. Divorce might mean another woman.

In his last moments, with only so many thoughts left inside his head before they ran out, Ed didn't want to waste them on Mattagash. He wanted to think of other things, of other people, people who had given him strength over the years, given him faith that all mankind was not a huge, haphazard, biological mistake, that some lives had been worth the living, had given the world *back* something before they went out. So he thought of the poets, of Chaucer, and Shakespeare and Pound. Of the artists, Michelangelo, Raphael, Goya. Of Cézanne, bloated with wine and leaving his masterpieces to rot in the fields where he created them. And he thought of the composers who had given the world music, of Beethoven, Chopin, and Bach. Of Plato and Socrates and Aristotle. Of explorers, the discoverers of serums, planets, and dinosaur bones.

For an hour he sat at his desk. Finally, he tore a sheet of paper from the scratch pad on his desk, wrote "I was here" on it, and tossed it among the clutter. It was what Amy Joy had written on the school building once when she was seven and was waiting outside for Ed to finish his work and take her home. His first reaction was to punish her. To take the chalk from her and demand she erase it. That she never write on the school again. But instead, he had simply taken her by the hand and led her home. "We're not drawing pictures of bisons in dark caves anymore," he had thought. "We're out in the sun now and trying again."

The gun in his hands, he suddenly remembered vividly the man from Watertown who had sold it to him, saw each button on his shirt, the day-old growth of beard, the color of his eyes, saw him as plainly as preachers swear one sees his Maker just before death.

As he held the gun to his head, he foolishly wondered if Kennedy would win the election, then hated himself for wasting a precious thought. Instead, he thought of ducks and drakes on the millpond behind the big old house in Massachusetts, before the elusive girl in the Current Events class, who would be an old woman now if still living, before his mother's hands took up their angry statements, like the hands of a tongueless woman engaged in sign language. He thought instead of the pebble, smooth and cool in his hand, thought of the action needed to skip it just so, the pressure of the thumb and index finger, the exact angle of the wrist, the quick release that sent it skipping, spinning soundlessly across the black water until it was gone.

Sea Changes:
The Siren Quits Singing

And they are gone: aye, ages long ago
These lovers fled away into the storm.
—John Keats, "The Eve of St. Agnes"

The Greyhound Bus left Watertown at 9:15 each morning heading downstate, stopping in one forlorn, out-of-the-way place after the other, its final destination Portland. At 8:45, when the driver finished his coffee at LaBelle's Drugstore and came outside to unlock his bus, Violet was standing there, the first to buy a ticket. She bought one to Bangor and then helped the driver lift her two suitcases and cardboard box of costumes and knickknacks into the belly of the bus. He kept his eyes on Violet's breasts as much as he dared, letting her catch him once, just in case she was interested in a little frolic further down the line.

Violet's lips tightened as she pushed the box closer to her suitcases for protection. She worried about her Raggedy Ann on buses like these. Once, when she was scheduled to dance at a club in Paris, Maine, the box had been smashed by all the other luggage and the first thing she'd seen at the unloading was the doll's arm hanging painfully from the side of the box, like the arm of a drowning child. That same night she dreamed of baby-sitting children, strange children she had never seen before, and that she began to dance and while she was dancing all of the children swallowed nickels or safety pins. Violet was worried by what their parents might say and she woke up afraid and held Raggedy Ann and fell asleep holding her.

"Will you not pile any suitcases on that box?" Violet asked the driver, catching his stare this time.

"Whatever the lady desires," he said, flirting, sizing her up. She'd seen this routine a thousand times from clerks, gas attendants, bag boys, policemen, doctors. She had come to the conclusion years ago that she looked the part. The showy red hair, the loud clothes, the absence of a wedding ring. She had considered buying a wedding ring just to see if it might discourage these advances, but soon changed her mind. A friend who was married, another dancer, told her it was only worse. It was a safety device to men already married, and most of them were. A single girl sometimes frightened a married man. Before he knew it she was in love and wanting him to divorce his wife and marry her. Have their own family. They gave men a real hard time around Christmas and Thanksgiving. But a married girl was a different story. She had as much at stake, as much reason to keep things under the table. No, a wedding band would only make it worse.

"Would you like a cup of coffee?" the bus driver asked her.

"No thanks," said Violet. "Can I board now? I'd like to get a back seat before they're all gone."

"I can bring it out to you," he said, opening the door of the bus for her. "I'm Larry Beecham. They got paper cups for carrying out."

"No thank you, Larry," Violet said as, with her shoulder purse and the *Watertown Weekly* under her arm, she made her way to the last seat on the bus and dropped wearily into it.

It had been a long night. After leaving the Albert Pinkham Family Motel, she had driven to Watertown to quit her job and pick up her last paycheck. Then she got herself a room upstairs, and the bartender, Jimmy, who had always been nice to her for no ulterior reason, helped her carry her suitcases and cardboard box up the long stairs.

From there she went to Al Hersey's car lot. Al had been over to the Watertown Hotel often to see her dance. He reminded her of a stuffed toy, the way his stubby arms and legs jutted rigidly from his short, fat body, as though bending them in the act of drinking a beer or smoking a cigarette might cause them to burst and spew batting about the room.

After her show was over and she walked past his table, he was forever pulling her down close to his round face and wheezing into her ear, "You need a car? You come see Al." She had driven from the Watertown Hotel to Al's lot and waited in the parking lot for him to finish with a customer. He beamed when he saw her, all of his teeth suddenly appearing beneath his thick lip like Chiclets. As if some higher power had summoned them all to show themselves.

"I need to sell the Volkswagen, Al," she told him. He put one arm on the car and leaned down to her. For one second, Violet thought the action might tip the car, and smiled at the thought. She looked up at him and listened to what he was saying, but she was struck by how many tiny hairs were growing inside his enormous nose, as though it were a terrarium. There were white ones and black ones, long and short, some reaching out, others turning inward. "Probably all cars he's sold," she thought.

When Al was done telling her what the book price was on a 1955 Volkswagen in perfect condition, she said, "How much can I get, Al?"

He stepped back and gave the car a long look. One of those understanding looks that car dealers give cars, as if to say "Come on, you can tell *me*. What's the state of things?" and then listens as the car sobs, "I got higher mileage than my gauge reads. I stall and my brakes are about to go. It's been hell. They've really abused me."

Al walked slowly around the Volkswagen. Finally, he came back to her window, leaned down, and said "We're talking one hundred bucks." Violet looked calmly at the Chiclets.

"You've got to be kidding," she said.

The Chiclets came closer.

"If you've got an hour to spare we're talking a hundred and fifty. A few little extras and you might even get old Al to say two hundred."

Violet stared straight ahead, her knuckles on the steering wheel about to burst. She would not say anything. She would leave this town and go somewhere to start over. And to leave town she had no choice but to take Al up on the offer. She needed the money.

"It's yours for a hundred bucks," she said and got out slamming the door.

"I always took you to be a good business woman. Knew a good deal when you heard of one," Al joked nervously. He felt pressured. He had always assumed—hoped—he'd get Violet into bed some day. It was his only chance of an affair, even for one night. Watertown had no other women as morally loose as Violet La Forge. At least none that still looked as good as she did. With his physical deficits, sex wasn't something he could wallow in. Violet went inside his office and he followed her. Sitting behind a desk was a small woman with clipped gray hair layered like feathers.

"Mother, write the lady a check for a hundred dollars," Al said. "Violet La Forge."

"Your *mother*, Al?" asked Violet, her voice rising like Jeanette MacDonald's. "How very very nice to meet you, Mrs. Hersey," she said, shaking the old lady's wrinkled hand until the ancient arm threatened to leave its socket and come away in Violet's hand. "But, Al, you did say that for those *little extras* the car had, it was worth at least two hundred, didn't you?" There was just a moment that lapsed before the Chiclets disappeared for good. Went back into the wet cave that had borne them, as realization settled down upon Al Hersey.

Outside, Violet gave Al the title and gathered her personal belongings from the car, a comb, a mirror, some letters, chewing gum.

"I'm cashing the check when the bank opens in the morning, Al. If it's been stopped, I'm taking your mother to lunch."

"You whore," Al said. "What difference does it make to you how you get the two hundred bucks? How can you be so uppity? I know where most of your money comes from. Everyone knows." Violet was several feet away. She stopped and turned around. She looked at Al slowly from head to foot, letting him know what she thought of his appearance.

"Al," said Violet softly, "I don't charge. I may have lost a million bucks, but I don't charge. Besides, you got what you wanted. You wanted to get screwed and in the office a minute ago I screwed you." She waved the check at him and crossed the street to the drugstore to ask about the bus schedule. Al went back into his office and watched her go.

"Who was that loud woman?" asked Mrs. Hersey, licking a stamp for an envelope.

Violet boarded the bus and settled down in the backseat as Watertown came to life around her. A few passengers got on. At 9:15 the vehicle was almost full and the driver had taken his seat. Violet caught his eye in the mirror. "A bus length away, over all these heads, and he still manages it," she thought.

A young soldier took the seat in front of hers and kept his nose pressed against the window like a sad puppy dog. Violet looked out her own window to see what interested him so, and saw a young girl standing by the drugstore, holding a baby in her arms. Violet noticed the round swell of her stomach.

The bus pulled out and Violet opened the *Watertown Weekly*. The editorial page was written by a young assistant editor who had no journalistic training. He had become popular among all the subscribers simply because of his nonsensical articles and among the more literary because of his nonsensical articles *and* his flagrant misuse of the English language. An unintelligent scribe, he had managed to do what Shakespeare had accomplished: He united the classes in a common bond, for they *all* thought the assistant editor ridiculous. Violet turned to the commentary. It dealt with the open moose season that the state had granted to Maine hunters. The goal was to kill 700 moose and bring the population down to a respectable number. "That's all those maniacs need," thought Violet, "a reason to kill." The commentary, however, only touched upon the population problem. The assistant editor was very angry because of a letter he had received signed ANGRY AT PAPER. An angry man was questioning why the assistant editor had not printed the picture he had sent in. The angry editor retaliated by writing: "I could not print the picture of he and his moose because I had already printed three pictures of people with moose." The moose was the only one not angry. "These people are really serious," thought Violet, and wondered why she had lingered so long in this land of pulp and guns. But she knew why. It was getting harder and harder to find a job. She had dropped her agent, who was booking her at bottom-of-the-barrel places and his young strippers at upscale ones. Now she was trying to phone club owners herself and the phone bill was topping her agent's 10 percent cut.

But the real reason she had spent more than a month in Watertown was Edward Lawler, and the glimmer of hope that he might be the end of a long bumpy ride. She had dreamed of Ed the night before, of the last time she saw him. She dreamed she was stepping out of a huge clamshell, like the dancer named Aphrodite had done, and Ed stood up in the crowd with his arms outstretched and she went to him. But his flesh was cold as ice and the men in the club began to jeer and taunt her. She woke up, said "Ed?" softly, as though the name was a tiny pain wrapped up in one syllable, a little sad song, and then she went back to sleep.

Violet threw the newspaper aside, unable to concentrate on the schoolboy rhetoric, and eased her head back on the seat. The bus stopped in several little towns. An hour away from Bangor, Violet thought about what she would do. She would get a room in Bangor. Dye her hair as close to its natural color as possible until it grew back to dark brown. She would buy a couple of nice dresses. A cotton one, maybe. Or even a nice skirt and sweater. Then she would call her mother over in Kingsman, Maine, on the New Hampshire border. Her father had died five years before. Violet found out on Christmas day of 1956, when in a moment of holiday loneliness she broke her vow never to call again and dialed the familiar old number. Her brother, who must have been up from Portland for the holidays, answered. When Violet said "Bobby? It's Beth. I called to wish Mama and Daddy a Merry Christmas," he had screamed at her into the phone. Had called her names. "Bitch!" he had shouted. "The old man's been dead for two years. Don't you ever call here again!" She heard her mother crying in the background, asking for the phone. Her mother loved her, she was sure, in spite of it all. It had been the old man, a self-styled Calvinist, who had banned her from the house when Bobby told them what Violet's real profession was. He had turned up one night at a club where she was dancing and was as embarrassed for her to see him there as he was at seeing her dance. "Poor Bobby," thought Violet. "The first time he told on me I was four and I'd pulled up Mama's tulips. Then he told on me for skipping school and going to the circus when I was ten. For smoking when I was thirteen. For dating Freddy Walstrop when I was sixteen. I guess he was just in the habit of telling on me. On seeing Daddy whip me. You can get used to things like that. That's how Hitler got all those Germans to keep on doing what they did. One day it just becomes a habit." Her mother loved her. Now maybe they could start over. "With Daddy gone, we'll be good for each other. We'll get a big tree at Christmas and put up strings of colored lights and bake cookies. We'll do all the things we wanted to do but Daddy wouldn't let us."

Violet reached inside her purse for her wallet. She pulled out the battered paper that told the story of the man and the butterfly. It had a phone number written on it. Walter Frontenac had written it there himself in 1955. It was his number. He was a butcher from a little town north of Bangor who had seen her dance at Vic's Playpen. She left with him that night, after the show was over, and all he did was take her for coffee and then walk her back to her room. He was a very quiet man. Even dull, Violet had thought at first. He had two fingers missing on his left hand, a hazard of his trade. Violet didn't want to see him again but he kept coming in to watch her dance. When she had no other offers, a cup of coffee with Walter Frontenac was better than going back to a cold motel room alone.

They would sit across from each other in the Bluebird Cafe, which stayed open twenty-four hours for truckers, and they would talk quietly to each other. Once, Walter had reached over and squeezed her hand and Violet had noticed the stain beneath his fingernails, dark as blood. The hand with the missing fingers he kept hidden as much as possible, afraid it would offend her.

On her last night at Vic's Playpen, she made plans to go to an after-hours club with a trucker who had driven up from Boston the night before. Dancing, she could see Walter's face in the crowd. The trucker started shouting, "Keep something on for me to take off later, honey!" By the end of the night he was so drunk that he had passed out, head down, at his table. Violet was thankful. He had embarrassed her in front of Walter. But at the back door she found Walter waiting for her.

"Wally, you're as faithful as an old sheepdog," Violet said and linked her arm in his. They went a final time to the Bluebird Cafe and sat among the noises of the night people, the coffee cups rattling on their saucers as yawning waitresses served their customers. The sounds of grill orders being called out, of truck drivers swilling coffee and boys playing the jukebox. It was not a romantic place, but in Walter's eyes Violet sat in candlelight with rare wine. She put her hand under the table and touched his.

"You're a good man, Walter," she told him. "The only good man I know." And he smiled, revealing the beginning of a cavity on his front tooth.

"Call me any time you're ready to give up this traveling life," Walter told her, and she reached into her wallet for something for him to write his phone number on. Walter took the paper, but before he wrote on it, he opened it and read what was written there. Then he folded it and carefully formed each number so that there could be no doubt what they were, no mistaking them in the future. He gave the paper back to Violet over the table in the Bluebird Cafe. "You're a butterfly," he said.

When the bus stopped in Bangor, Violet gathered up her paper and coat, slung her purse over her shoulder. The soldier had chatted with her some on the way down, told her he was sorry to be in the army at a time when there was no war. Now he was asleep in his seat, going on to Portland. Violet smiled when she passed his seat. "He'll have his war to fight when he gets back home," she thought, remembering the straggly haired young wife back at the drugstore, a child in her arms and another growing in her stomach

Several people were getting off in front of her so she waited for the aisle to empty. Getting her suitcases and the unharmed cardboard box, Violet left them in a corner of the bus station and went to look for a pay phone. Digging a handful of change up from the bottom of her purse, she piled nickels and quarters and dimes on the shelf beneath the phone and lifted the receiver.

"I'll be back at exactly 2:15 tomorrow. Maybe we could have a drink or two."

Violet jumped to hear the voice so close, to feel the breath on her neck. She turned. It was the bus driver.

"Please leave me alone," she said to him, and he snorted like a baby bull, as if to say "With pleasure," and went back out to his bus. Some men, with their endless quest for women, amazed her. "If they put that much effort and care into avoiding war, we wouldn't have any," she thought, and gave the operator her mother's number. The old woman answered after two rings, sounding younger in spirit than Violet had ever known her to be. "It must have been living under Daddy's thumb," she thought. She would be home in a few days, she told her mother. She had some things to do first. Shopping. Tying up some loose ends.

"It's all over, Mama," she said and the old woman began to cry.

"Come on home, Bethie," she told her daughter.

Violet hung up the phone just in time to see the bus driver pulling away from the station. He waved to her and she pretended not to see. Digging again in her wallet, she brought out Walter Frontenac's phone number and took a deep breath.

"If he can teach me to clean up my act," Violet said, "I can teach him to clean his fingernails. All eight of them."

Castle for Sale:
The McKinnons Lose
the High Ground

"MacKinnons . . . are of royal descent, being a branch of the great clan Alpin. About the year 1400, the MacKinnons fell into misunderstanding with other clans, who were jealous of their rising influence . . ."

"The McKinnon Coat-of-Arms: quarterly, (1) a boar's head holding the shank-bone of a deer in its mouth, (2) a castle, triple-towered and embattled, (3) ship with oars saltirewise, (4) a hand couped fesswise holding a cross crosslet."

"The Badge is *pinus sylvestris*, a slip of pine tree."

—FROM R.R. McIAN, *The Clans of the Scottish Highlands*

THERE'S NOT MUCH left to say when lives are over. Like a record that's been played and then put away, a man or woman's life is recorded in the grooves left in the living. Some replay it. Others forget to. Some speak well of the dead, using adjectives that once would have choked them. Others remain true to themselves. A Gifford, for instance, never says a praiseful thing about a corpse if he didn't say the same things when the corpse was a living person. Not even if the dead is another Gifford. And that's to be commended.

There's no end to the stories in small towns. Story endings are inherited by the next generations, and just when you tire of one about some man or woman, they have a child who picks up the plot and carries it to new heights. Modernization can always be counted on for new twists. Once plant food was accepted at Lyman's store as a scientific way to produce healthier plants, it could only be expected that folklore would meld with science to provide an enduring myth for the townspeople. And it did. Ginnie Craft was accused of delivering an illegitimate baby and burying it beneath the lilac trees in her Mama's backyard, resulting in the bushiest, lilaciest one in town. Ginnie really miscarried at four

months, was attended by a doctor, and came home from a visit to her Aunt Louisa's in Watertown as a slim girl given a second chance. There's always some truth in folklore. And some truisms in small towns:
Willie O'Brian could stop blood but he couldn't stop drinking.
Sarah Pinkham could hold her breath but not her husband.
Marge McKinnon needed a man like she kneaded bread.
Chester Lee Gifford was as hung as Nathan Hale.
Bert Fogarty skimmed the truth like he skimmed milk.
And a child of Amy Joy's will come home from school one day and ask, "What did Mike McClennan mean when he said we need more homework like Ed Lawler needed more bullets?" And people will be hurt anew, generations of them wounded by one bullet.
But that's how it is in small towns. Even in cities. It's all a matter of deism. Our ancestors came in with their bold dreams and vague visions and, godlike, they laid down examples they themselves couldn't follow. Then they died and went off somewhere. Forgot about us. Took no further part in our functioning. And we've been spitting into the wind ever since. We're limping into the computer age while dragging behind us the rotting rituals of the Middle Ages.
In 1842, during the dispute with Great Britain over the Maine–Canada boundary, a fort was built in Watertown, in case soldiers marched that far north. One man died during the war, of pneumonia. He was not considered a hero for having done this. But neither was he considered a coward. He was locked somewhere in the middle in a kind of humorous limbo that allowed schoolchildren to laugh out loud at his misfortune. Edward Elbert Lawler, on the other hand, a lone soldier in his own kind of boundary war, *was* considered a coward. Just why suicide was deemed less than noble never occurred to anyone in Mattagash. Unless you were one of the romantic heroes who did it for love, or for country, or for honor, you were weakhearted. Why it would be more valiant to pursue one dull, predictable day after the next until death came upon you unawares than to plunge willingly into the black uncertainty never surfaced in their minds. It was gritless. To kill yourself for no reason other than a little depression was an act of cowardice. It was an ignoble way out, an ideology no doubt planted

in the minds of peasants by their kings who envisioned an empty kingdom if suicide became an expedient among the disgruntled, miserable masses. By priests who liked full churches. By pharaohs who needed the living, antlike bodies of slaves to build their tombs. Ed Lawler, by placing a gun to his head and planting a bullet in his brain, had earned himself a place in Mattagash history, more certain but less tasteful than the pneumonic soldier whose battle against the bleak winter of northern Maine was harder to fight than the enemy.

Three deaths in Mattagash in a matter of twenty-four hours were something to buzz about. The elderly could drop like flies and no one would be surprised. No one would get that rush of hot blood flushing through their veins in appreciation of the life still in their own bodies. They would be surprised at the first sounds of the siren but, after the ambulance pulled into the yard of some elderly man or woman and the telephones rang around town and people listened in on party lines, they would be satisfied that the grim reaper had claimed no undue morsels and the women would go back to their ironing boards and wringer washers and children would leave their stands around the telephone to go outside and roll their hula hoops about the backyard.

Marge McKinnon's death came as no surprise to anyone, but Ed's and Chester Lee's measured among those choice occurrences that caused blood to pump through veins that had nearly clogged with boredom. Theirs were the deaths that myths are made of, but there was a general feeling in the town of having been cheated out of a ritual. The Gifford funeral was a social event that only Giffords and their relatives, either legitimate or of the same blood, cared to attend. There was a closed casket at Chester Lee's funeral. It was said in Mattagash that this was because they feared someone from among the mourners would steal the silk pillow out from under Chester's head. It was also said that the pallbearers had to push the casket up to the grave because Bert Gifford had stolen the handles. But the one story that will most likely outlast all others, true or not, was of Chester Lee propped up in the backseat of Bert's old Ford and accompanied by Bert and his brothers, who had been released from the state pen for the occasion, being driven around Mattagash for one last frolicking family get-together. Bert Gifford told that one himself, saying that they stopped at Lyman's store and everyone went in and stole a pack of cigarettes while Lyman was out gassing up the old Ford. Even Chester Lee. Bert said a little thing like rigormortis couldn't keep Chester Lee from a free pack of Lucky Strikes.

Marge and Ed were buried on the same day, at the same time, in the same corner of the Protestant graveyard. It was the first time in their relationship they had gotten along so well for so long a time. For a McKinnon, Marge went back to the earth peaceable. There was no fanfare, no gathering except for the immediate family. Ed's suicide made a normal funeral impossible. Marvin and Junior Ivy had come by early the morning of the funerals to see that the graves were dug properly. A matter of semantics to funeral directors. As if the earth would spit Marge and Ed out like watermelon seeds if the dimensions were a quarter-inch off. The whole quiet affair was so unbefitting to Marge that it fit her exactly: "Never let them think they've got you figured out," she once said. "Keep them wrong all the time."

That morning was a bright sea-blue one, with the Ivys and Sicily and Amy Joy leaning into a strong autumn wind that whipped their clothing about them, as if they were a field of crows waiting for the first sign of a seedling to come from the planting. Sicily stood over Ed's grave on that high hill where the Protestant graveyard lay, and wept painful sounds into the wind that carried down off the hill and echoed along the river like the ancient sounds of bagpipes the McKinnons had played when they marched into battle, long before the clan sought refuge in Ireland. The sounds of a wife mourning a husband dead in battle. Musical chords and notes inherited and dragged down the ages with us, our instruments from the old country broken or lost so that we chant the same laments a cappella, wringing our hands as if in memory of the lyre, as if longing for the smooth, narrow body of the flute. The last of the McKinnons in Mattagash, in blood if not in name, stood on the hillside to mourn their dead. Then they came down from the high ground, that favorite spot of the builders of castles that looks far out on the whale's-road, on the swan's-path for the first glimpse of an enemy coming to take the high ground. Sicily and Amy Joy and the Ivys came down from the Protestant graveyard that overlooked the Mattagash River. They came down empty-handed and went home, went back about the idea of living, to the foolish notion of life, and left the earth freshly piled behind them. Left Ed and Marge alone, to sink down into their bones like the hulls of old ships come aground in the storm. They left the fragile, gossamer dreams of the dead where they belong, up on the high ground, where the wind could sift through them gently, where they could quietly, softly go back to dust.

The leaves will drop from the trees, leaving them bare as bone. The river will rise to cover the rocks along the shore; in early December it will freeze over. Red fires made from sticks and blown-out tires will dot the black night beneath the bridge where skaters have gathered, their cloudy breaths hanging in the air like frozen words, like an Impressionist painting. Until spring comes, the woodsmen will wade in snow up to their chests, cutting the trees and hauling them out of the woods with tractors, if they can afford them, or with work-tired horses that pull them from memory.

When the ice finally leaves the ground, the graveyard will take in the dead: the ill and aging, the young and unlucky. Babies born in January's cold with little stamina. A young woodsman crushed beneath a falling pine. The occasional lone figure who goes off to the river and slips in, or who goes to the barn with a rope and quietly closes the doors.

Summer will bring the tourists who drift down the Mattagash River in red and green canoes and gaze up at the backs of houses that line the river, never seeing Mattagash from the front but seeing only the shabby backside of the town, the occasional out-house, the gutted cars, a chicken pecking here and there. And they'll laugh their sharp city laughter. The one or two who don't laugh have drowned in the fast white rapids a mile below the falls. That's where, as everyone in Mattagash knows, the river laughs at tourists.

Mattagash will go on with its cycles of life. There will be hus-bands lying down in the wrong beds. Wives caught in the wrong arms at the wrong time. There will be hasty weddings. The dying will die and move aside for the living to die, and the patterns of life will continue, as they have since that wet autumn day the first tiny group of settlers scraped their pirogue up onto the banks and stepped out, trembling with cold and expectations and maybe, at least for one of them, needing a spot to pee. A kind of squatter's right. After the deaths that rainy fall of 1959, Mattagash will lie dormant for many uneventful years. And when some excitement happens again, it will, as it always does in a little town, happen in a big way.

The Last Load:
Filling in the Empty Spaces

harvest home 1. The last harvest load brought home.
—WEBSTER

> I bring the harvest home to her,
> I bring the last load home.
> She sits and rocks the night away,
> She rocks at night alone.
> So who will separate the chaff
> So we can eat the grain?
> 'The wind' she said to me at last
> And closed her window pane.
>
> —FICTIONAL OLD FOLKSONG, Mattagash, Maine

MARVIN, JUNIOR, THELMA, and the little Ivys went back to Portland driving a rehabilitated Packard. Pearl would have liked for Marvin to stay on, but business was waiting. "They're dying in other parts of the state too, you know," he told her. Pearl stayed on an extra week to be at Sicily's side, to help get her adjusted to the rough spots, to clear up the loose ends of Marge's estate.

What money Marge had left from the modest inheritance from her father and the sale of her personal belongings would not, it was legally decided, go to the Widows of Missionary Brothers. The president of the organization, it was discovered, was Luther Toot, brother to Harley Toot, a real-life missionary from Bangor, now dead. Frances Toot, Harley's surviving widow and treasurer of the fund, as well as Luther's girlfriend, swore there had been no false representation in the advertisement that Marge had clipped out of one of her many religious magazines. Frances Toot, although she had refused to accompany her husband to China in 1929, was indeed a missionary's widow. Marge's will was declared void. She was not in the presence of her faculties.

"She wasn't even in the same room," said Pearl. She had fin-

234

ished packing and was waiting for Jasper Gardner to give her a ride to Watertown.

"Jasper is charging me three dollars for a ride to Watertown," Pearl laughed. "Remember how I paid his daddy a dollar to take me to Watertown the first time I left? Seems I'm always paying to get out of here."

"They sort of think of themselves as a kind of taxi service," said Sicily. "The whole family does."

Amy Joy hugged her aunt Pearl and then went off into the kitchen in her endless quest for food. The two sisters stood on the front porch of the old homestead looking out at the field across the road.

"They say everything happens in threes," said Sicily.

"Maybe we asked for it," said Pearl. "Coming up from Portland with our suitcases full of black clothes, expecting a funeral. Maybe we brought it all on ourselves."

"I should have waited until Marge died to call you. But the doctor said she wouldn't last the night. It's modern living is what it is. In the old days people didn't hear about someone dying until they were dead. Like we heard about Daddy. And then, well, what can you do? You accept it and go on about your day. But now it's all different. That's the way the whole world is now-adays. Fast-paced. Everybody wants to know everything before it happens and only God should know things like that."

"People just want to be prepared is all," said Pearl. "They don't want the devil to catch them sitting down."

"The river rose a lot from all that rain," said Sicily.

"I can hardly sleep for the sound of it. It sounds like a thundering downpour to me," said Pearl.

Jasper's car pulled slowly into the driveway. Jasper flicked a cigarette butt out into the yard through his side window and it lay smoking near a mud puddle.

"Are you sure you won't come with me, Sissy? You could get a nice little place just down the street. Amy Joy could go to a good school."

"No, Pearl, really. This is home to us. Amy Joy has school here. And our friends and our roots are here. I'm thinking of turning Marge's house into some kind of a shop since you don't want your half. I could cater to tourists. Maybe get the women in town to make quilts and little souvenirs and such. And we could turn a couple of the rooms into a community center for the kids so they'd have a place to go, something to do in the evenings. I don't think any of them would get into any trouble if they just had something to do with their time. I even thought I'd get a little plaque to put on the door, saying something like 'In Memory of Edward Lawler, Principal.' You can get them made at the Western Auto in Watertown. Ed had one made once for old Girdy when she retired from teaching."

"That sounds real nice, Sissy," said Pearl, hugging her. "We're tougher than we thought, you know. It wasn't just Marge all these years who knew how to roll with the punches. We rolled with a few ourselves."

Jasper tooted his horn. "I got to get Myrtle to her doctor's by nine o'clock," he shouted out his window. "And Sarah and Belle to the bus by nine-fifteen."

"Good Lord!" said Pearl to Sicily. "Am I going to have to ride to Watertown with Sarah Pinkham? I'll hear all the gossip I missed in the past twenty years!"

"She and Belle's going down to her sister's in Vermont. Winnie says it's cancer and Sarah's going to take care of her until she dies."

"I can't imagine Sarah Pinkham having that big a heart," said Pearl.

"Winnie says she and Albert ain't really pulling very well. She says she'll fill me in on it once I get back out and about for a cup of coffee. But I hear there's a will involved if Sarah takes care of her."

"Don't say *will* to me," Pearl said and winked. Sicily squeezed her sister's hand, then watched the body that looked so much like her own amble, the way a McKinnon does, down to Jasper's car. Before the car pulled out of the yard, Pearl turned in the backseat and threw Sicily a kiss. When the car disappeared around the turn, Sicily finally went inside Marge's old house, the old McKinnon homestead, to pack up Amy Joy's things so that the two of them could go home. Before going in, she opened the back door. Listening hard, she could hear the rapids, a distant seashell sound, the way it must have sounded over generations to the ears that listened for it, except for a few rocks that would have shifted some in the spring jams, changing the melody a little but keeping the same refrain. But no matter how hard she listened, she couldn't hear Pearl's downpour of rain. So she closed the door and left the problem of the river for nature to work out, left it for God to understand.

Back in her own kitchen Sicily put the teakettle on and stood listening as it came to a slow boil. She poured the water over a tea bag and milk that waited in her cup. Then taking one last look around the kitchen to see that everything was in its proper place, she took her cup of tea, turned out the kitchen light, and walked slowly through her living room where several days earlier the family had gathered to discuss plans for Marge.

The whole house was so quiet around her that the only sounds came from outside, from the old birch behind the house that began its career in growing before the Reverend was even born, its mossy limbs fighting off the wind. From an empty pop bottle that rolled in the wind across the yard and banged into the front steps. From the wild cats that were living in Willie's abandoned barn, holed up in the gray firewood that had been tiered along one wall and forgotten when Willie was killed by lightning and Margaret went alone into the big barn to hang herself. The original ancestors were house cats owned by Willie, but after he passed away they had taken to living off the land, raising their litters in the barn, each generation growing further and further away from human contact, until the image of their ancestors curled sleepily on a braided rug in front of man's fire was no more meaningful than the dim red reflection in each other's eyes as they gazed down from the barn's upper windows at the bonfire by the river where man had come to skate, until the fire finally went out, until man finally went home, and they settled down upon their paws, snoozing, sensing the danger had passed.

"Amy Joy has got to stop throwing her pop bottles down wherever she happens to finish them. We're getting as bad as the Giffords," thought Sicily, then cringed at the comparison she had used. She had promised herself, the day they buried Chester Lee Gifford, to stop using the Gifford name to denote all that was distasteful in the human condition. It was the same way she used the word *Communist* until Ed asked her one day if she had ever met a Communist, and if she hadn't perhaps she should reserve her judgment until she did. Ed's way of correcting her was the same one he used on Amy Joy, by asking the ridiculous and then forcing an answer.

Sicily opened the screen door a crack and heard the cats far off in Willie's barn, at each other's throats again, too many generations born to know they were all related, all still of the same blood and bone. Their numbers never seemed to fail them. Despite the occasional one here or there being picked off by a wild boy with a new rifle in his hands, or the not so rare sight of one flattened in the road by a pulp truck until it was board-stiff and thrown into the river, or the old ones who caught some sickness or simply went off to die of age, the cats in the barn survived even the slow-moving, food-scarce winters, *would* survive, until the day when one of the kittens was caught and brought back to the human hearth, given back its rightful bowl of warm milk.

"They remind me of a den of snakes," Sicily thought and closed the door, wishing the town would do something about them. Sicily turned off the light at the foot of the stairs. Amy Joy was in her downstairs bedroom in pajamas and ready for sleep. Sicily had kissed her good night earlier but she was still up. There was a light beneath her door.

"Mama?" Amy Joy shouted from behind the door. "Are you going up now?"

"I thought I would," said Sicily.

"Good night then."

"Good night, honey. You sleep tight." Sicily stood with her hand on the railing, not able at first to go up the stairs alone. Since Ed's death she had not felt truly alone in the house. Amy Joy's bedroom was just downstairs. And Pearl had been sleeping in the extra room across the hall from Ed and Sicily's room. Sicily had put a cot in there for her, and at night Pearl's snoring had been as comforting as song. Ed used to snore, but Sicily never really heard it. At least it never bothered her. It was like the river you grew up too close to. You were so used to it you'd never know if it quit running. It was because Pearl had been living in Portland so long that the river kept her awake at night. Sicily, on the other hand, had never gone anywhere long enough to miss the river. To miss Mattagash. To miss the people she was always around.

"Watch out the bedbugs don't bite," she told Amy Joy and went on up the stairs alone.

Upstairs, Sicily avoided the bedroom at first, going instead to the bathroom and drawing a full tub of hot, sudsy water. Then she took off her robe and eased herself down into the pleasant, engulfing warmth as goose bumps sprang up on her arms like little pleasure domes.

"That feels so good," she murmured, then felt a twinge or guilt rise up inside her for participating in the act of being alive. Ed was dead. Ed would never feel goose bumps again. That Ed had chosen a cold bleak grave over a hot bubble bath did not occur to her. She felt, as all of Mattagash did, as all the world would, that if Ed could heal the gashing canal into his brain, he would choose life over death. It was, after all, only natural. It was what man's entire quest was about. Keeping alive. Keeping one step ahead of the grim reaper. If suicide was the better alternative, why were so many people still alive and doing well in the world? No, if Ed could undo what he'd done, he would. That's what made his suicide so hard to accept.

"If he could have just gotten through the night," Pearl had said to Sicily. "Tomorrow would have been a new day."

"The sun always shines brightest after the storm," the minister had told her. "If he'd only waited for the sun." No one, not even Sicily, suspected that Ed had gone through many storms and found no sun waiting for him. Had staggered through countless painful nights and found the same old tomorrow descending on him like a bird of prey.

Sicily toweled herself dry. In the mirror she studied her figure. Her breasts drooped. The extra weight around her stomach and thighs that refused to leave after Amy Joy's birth was so familiar a sight to her that she had forgotten the silky feel of the size-nine wedding gown that Marge had zipped her into on her wedding day. The day she married Ed Lawler. The day Ed Lawler married *her*, thinking she was pregnant with his child. Sicily lifted one breast, then let it flop back down on her chest. As young wives, she and Martha Fogarty and Winnie Craft had joked about the bodies that they'd donated to the cause of childbearing. Sicily's, having been used only once, when the one-of-a-kind Amy Joy was brought squalling into existence, had suffered less ravaging than the other two women, Martha with eight children and Winnie with five. Yet Sicily never kept her figure fit. She let twenty extra pounds wrap themselves about her like a blanket, like protection, padding that would deaden the touch of her husband's hands in the night. And that was it, really. That was the secret of fat thighs and bulging stomachs that nearly every woman in Mattagash dragged around like armor. Like umpires at fixed games. Something to replace the obsolete moat around the castle. A modern chastity belt. Most husbands, on most nights, chose sleep to amorous encounters with these queen bees. Some, like Ed, went in search of satisfaction to leaner arms.

"I'd never pass the pencil test now," Sicily said to her reflection. Martha Fogarty used to remind them that if a woman put a pencil beneath her breast and it stayed there she was in trouble. There was too much droop. Like a suspension bridge that has begun to sag. "I could hold as many pencils as Amy Joy's pencil box now." Sicily let the breast flop once more and then moved in closer to look at her face. She was still pretty. Her cheekbones, a feature she'd once been so proud of, were still there. A brush stroke of blush or two could bring them back. And her hair. She'd always hated the red of her hair. She could dye it a different color. But that wouldn't be a good example for Amy Joy, who was pining away for Sensous Ash. But maybe just a dark rinse to take the edge off the redness. That wouldn't hurt. A person should have the right to change the things about themselves that they didn't like, if that person was older than fourteen.

"What am I thinking about prettying myself up for?" Sicily asked her reflection. "Me with a husband not cold in his grave. Oh, God!" She put a hand to her heart. The thought of Ed in a cold casket in the ground was a picture she was just not ready to deal with. She began to whisper the Lord's Prayer to keep her mind off Ed.

There were spaces everywhere in the bathroom, a space between her hair spray on the shelf and the talcum powder. Ed's shaving cream used to sit there. The absence of a man's belongings was so obvious to her that it was like a loud noise. Like one of those puzzles in the *Grit* that asks "What's wrong with this picture?" and you realize that there's a mouse sitting in the fish bowl or that a lamp is hanging upside down from the ceiling. The disappearance of Ed's things was the work of Pearl, who had thoughtfully packed everything into boxes and stored them in the closet of the spare room until Sicily found it possible to sort through the items and dispose of them accordingly. It had seemed like a good idea at the time. But now it all seemed so contrived. The whole house was like a big dollhouse. As if it wasn't the real thing. A *pretend* house. Sicily smiled, thinking of the dollhouse out back that Ed and some of his students had built when Amy Joy was five years old. When Sicily had something that was no longer useful, she'd give it to Amy Joy, who would push it out to the dollhouse in her baby carriage. Out went old lamps, a broken toaster, a chipped dinner plate, empty perfume bottles, a broom whose straw had begun to fray. Maybe Pearl had given Amy Joy all of Ed's things and they were hanging at that very moment in the dollhouse. Waiting for the daddy of the house to get home. "Little Amy Joy setting up house in the backyard," thought Sicily, and remembered how Amy Joy used to tell her that when she got married and had babies she was going to live in her little dollhouse. "And stay close to you, Mama," she'd say, her chubby hands burying themselves in Sicily's dress.

"Sometimes," Sicily thought, "I think what all of us want is our mamas. Men too. We want someone who loves us for who we are and doesn't judge us. Not even God can do that."

Sicily squeezed some toothpaste onto her toothbrush and quickly brushed her teeth. As she put her yellow toothbrush back into the holder, she noticed that Ed's big red brush still hung there, an oversight on Pearl's part. Sicily touched the tip of one finger to the brush, just to see if it was real or if it would evaporate to the touch, the way things in TV commercials did when housewives least expected it. But it was solid. It was, after all, Ed Lawler's old toothbrush, the bristles half their original size from overuse. "His gums used to bleed, he used that brush so hard," Sicily thought. "It seemed like he was always punishing himself for something, making even the little things extra hard on himself."

She rubbed some cold cream into her face and neck, then brushed her hair a few times. She put the hairbrush back on the shelf. Flicking the light out, she crossed the hall to her bedroom. When the bedroom light filled the room, Sicily blinked. It was so big.

And chilly. She rubbed her arms to help the circulation. The extra blanket would have to come out of the closet. She opened the closet door. Pearl had taken Ed's clothing and scattered the hangers holding Sicily's dresses and blouses as best she could across the rod to make up for the empty spaces. Missing Ed, Sicily still had to smile at Pearl's thoroughness. It was more like Marge than Pearl, but in trying to protect her younger sister from unnecessary pain, Pearl had thought of almost everything.

Blankets turned down, Sicily said her prayers, ending with a special plea for God to forgive Ed and take him into his fold. She thought of all the McKinnon ancestors in heaven, including the indomitable Reverend Ralph. "They won't like each other." Sicily thought of the two men in her life meeting for the first time. She prayed that God would intervene and see to it that the McKinnons accepted Ed as one of their own without treating him as an outcast for what he'd done.

"It'd be just like them," she thought and kicked off her slippers. She tossed her housecoat across the end of the bed and slipped beneath the covers. The bedside lamp turned out, the house was now in darkness. A stillness crept up to the sides of the bed. The autumn moon soon found its way about the room and brought a ghostly, bluish lighting to the interior.

Sicily lay back and listened to the night. Near her head the little clock Marge had given her for her birthday a few years back was beating quietly, like a tiny heart in the darkness. Like the heart of the house, bruised but still alive. She closed her eyes, but she was not sleepy. If she thought about it, she really wasn't alone. Now all the families were back from the harvest. She'd seen the last truck go by just that day, the Ryans, loaded down with their personal belongings. All over Mattagash her neighbors were asleep, or soon to be, with mothers and fathers awake and whispering in the dark about the kids' lunch money or a payment due at the bank. Or touching each other with warm bodies tired from the day. It hurt to think about husbands caressing their wives, because hers was not there to do the same. Would probably not touch her if he was there. Had stopped touching her when something in their relationship went terribly wrong. Something no one could make right again. So instead she thought of her neighbors the way children do their dolls, as mamas and daddies who sleep in the big bed in the biggest room after they've put their children to bed. Mama dolls and daddy dolls who exist in a world where there is no sex, or birth, or death. She thought of all Mattagash as a huge dollhouse and her bedroom as just one of its rooms. They were all a large, happy family, and if she listened quietly she could hear the rhythmic breathing up and down the road, the soft, almost inaudible coughs made by children tossing in their sleep, the dogs whining on all the porches, and she felt instantly safe. The bedroom door opened a crack.

"Mama?"

"Amy Joy, are you still awake at this hour?" Sicily asked as the door opened wider.

"I'm scared, Mama."

"You come get in bed with me then," said Sicily and lifted the blanket for Amy Joy to crawl under. She put her arms around her daughter and pulled her close.

"Do you remember when you was little and you'd crawl in between Daddy and me and he'd say, 'Mama, I think there's a bedbug in this bed' and you'd say, 'It's me, Daddy. I'm the bedbug.' Do you remember that, honey?"

"Uh-huh," said Amy Joy. "Mama, next year can I go picking potatoes with Cindy's family and make my own money?"

"We'll see. Next year is a long way off," said Sicily and smoothed Amy Joy's hair back. "What in the world has happened to your hair, Amy Joy? It's stiff as a board!"

"Cindy and me ironed it to straighten out the curls. It's too naturally curly."

"You ironed it? Dear Lord, Amy Joy, one of these days I'll wake up to find you bald. Why can't you learn to accept yourself the way God created you?"

"I just don't like some of the things he did is why."

"Don't say that, honey. It's blasphemy."

"Are we gonna spend Christmas here?"

"What in the world made you bring that up? Christmas is three months off. We'll cross that bridge when we get to it."

"What are you gonna get me this Christmas?"

"I saw your little red rocking chair down in the basement this morning. It was all covered with dust and old books. I'm gonna bring it up, put new padding on the seat, paint it, and put it in your room for one of your old dolls."

"For Christmas? You're gonna give me my old rocking chair

for *Christmas?*" said Amy Joy, prematurely disappointed.

"No. Just for fun. You used to sit in it every single morning when you was little and wait for your breakfast."

"It had Little Bo-Peep on the back."

"You used to put your dolls in that little chair when you was playing nurse and give them strawberries you kept in an aspirin bottle. Those were your little pills."

"I did real stupid stuff when I was a kid," said Amy Joy and snuggled in closer to the warm body of her mother.

"Your little tootsies are like ice!" said Sicily. "Here, put them next to mine and get them warm."

"I didn't wear no socks."

"I can feel that you didn't. You're gonna catch pneumonia. It ain't summer no more, you know. Before you know it there'll be snow on the ground."

The two lay together in the quiet of the Lawler house, lay bonded more by their sex than their kinship. Women alone in the world were pioneers. They learned to stock the woodbox before the heavy snows came. Learned to use the gun that would keep the coyote at the outskirts of the red firelight. Learned to balance checkbooks and change tires. Learned to sprawl alone in a bed made for two. Learned to utilize the empty spaces around the house where a man would have put his things.

"I'll help you shovel this winter," said Amy Joy, as if reading Sicily's thoughts, which were of how Ed had always done the shoveling, complainingly maybe, but reliably.

"That'll be a big help," she said. She held Amy Joy even tighter. They were the last of a long line in Mattagash. When Amy Joy married and left, she would be alone. She had always envisioned growing old as a settling in. The way an old house settles down on its foundation each spring, shaking the cold from its bones, a little tired maybe, but pleased that it had passed another winter and was still there. A kind of smugness, perhaps. She had always thought there would be summer evenings, long ones, shelling peas on Marge's front porch, while Marge rocked in the swing like the pendulum on an old clock. Thought there would always be Ed to eat breakfast with in the morning. Someone to turn and say, "I think the swallows have started south." Someone to rub against in the night, like a bobbing boat rubbing against the pier.

Had thought they would spend their old age together, as if it were something they *could* spend, like money. Something they had saved all their lives to squander in an instant. It was as if she were now forced to be the person she would have become if she hadn't married Ed. If she hadn't married anyone. Except that she was older and responsible for a child. Sicily smiled at the thought of Amy Joy in her life. She had been, after all, given to her by God to bless her old age. Amy Joy could keep the spark burning, could keep the indispensable fire aflame. Amy Joy would be her warm blanket on cold nights. Amy Joy would give her grandchildren to help fill in the empty spaces. She would never again see Marge point to the mountain across the river and say, "Look how them white birches stand out among them red and orange leaves. This is the prettiest autumn ever." But she might turn some evening, after cleaning wild strawberries, might wipe her hands on her apron and turn to Amy Joy and say, "We ought to press some leaves and cover them with plastic so they'll keep. Just to save them a while longer. Like your Aunt Marge used to do. I swear they're prettier this year than they've ever been." Or she could watch the happy faces of her grandchildren as she opened a box of Breeze detergent and said, "The free dish towel *is* red and white. Which one of you guessed red and white?" That's what she would do. She would simply rewrite the scenario of her old age. She'd prepare herself the way kings do for battle. Sweep the cobwebs off the castle. Dig a new moat.

"Mama, do you think Aunt Marge got a room in heaven like she wanted?" Amy Joy asked.

"I'm sure she did," said Sicily, thinking that Marge was probably redecorating that room this very minute to suit her own taste.

There was no more talk from Amy Joy for several minutes and Sicily assumed that the little girl was asleep. But then Amy Joy asked softly, "And Daddy too. Has he got a room?"

"Daddy too," said Sicily and squeezed her daughter's fat hand. Moonlight came in the window and fell across the bed. Amy Joy lifted one foot as if to make it move. Like kicking at a dog to go someplace else and lie down. In Willie's old barn two cats snarled at each other, then went off into the woods. The first signs of frost lay on the hill and the fields, caught up in the moonlight. The land was shifting, heaving, settling down so that it could carry the tons of snow that would come. An occasional car passed on the road and went its way into the heart of town.

"That's Brian Hughes's old car," said Amy Joy. "Listen to it. It ain't got a muffler."

"Out drinking in Watertown at this hour," said Sicily and lifted her head to look at the clock. It was twelve-thirty.

"Amy Joy, we'll never get up in the morning. It's going for one o'clock."

"Then let's just sleep all day if we want to."

"Can you imagine such a thing! Sleeping all day? What would people say?" Sicily laughed. It felt good to laugh. The muscles in her stomach were sore from the tension of the past days and laughing stretched them out, loosened them up.

"I should have brought my sheets in off the line," said Sicily. "There's gonna be a frost and that's not good on cotton."

"I don't care what people say about me," said Amy Joy, and picked at a hangnail with her teeth.

"That's because you're so young. When you get older you care. You have to face your neighbors every single day."

"I ain't gonna get old here in Mattagash, so I won't never care."

"Where are you going to grow old?"

"I'm saving my money," said Amy Joy. "I'm gonna pick potatoes and save all my birthday and Christmas money, and from now on I just want money for Christmas. And when I get enough I'm taking the Greyhound out of Watertown, just like Aunt Pearl did."

"You might end up over a funeral home in Portland, Amy Joy." Sicily was teasing.

"I ain't stopping in no Portland, Maine. I'm going straight to Hollywood, California. I don't care if I have a job when I get there or not."

"If you're going on a Greyhound bus from Watertown, Maine, to Hollywood, California, you won't need a job. You'll be able to draw Social Security by the time you get there," said Sicily and tickled Amy Joy, who squirmed in giggles.

"In Hollywood they let you dye your hair," said Amy Joy, who had settled down for the night and felt the heaviness of sleep coming to her eyelids. The last of the harvest moon climbed higher into the night sky that covered the town. The river that had brought the McKinnon brothers to its headwaters curled silently like a long, black tongue, flicked at the bushes along the shore, gossiped near the rocks that lay at the edge. Like a child whose bedtime story has finished, the whole town was ready for sleep, the last car home from Watertown, the last light turned off, the last clock wound and set. And the pulse of the town beat evenly, slowly, restfully. Like an old insect queen, the town rested, her workers, her soldiers and her fighters, her dreamers and her lovers, all little pulses beating inside her.

"When you live in Hollywood, you can go by their rules, but while you're under my roof, Amy Joy, you'll live by mine. Is that understood?" asked Sicily and pulled the extra blanket up about them.

Half asleep, Amy Joy turned on her side, her back to her mother. "I guess." she said, and as the moon floated higher, the old queen slept.

Printed in the United States
28273LVS00002B/1-39